Winter Winds

of Wyoming

Also by Caroline Fyffe

Prairie Hearts Series

Where the Wind Blows
Before the Larkspur Blooms
West Winds of Wyoming
Under a Falling Star
Whispers on the Wind
Where Wind Meets Wave
Winter Winds of Wyoming

Colorado Hearts Series

Heart of Eden
True Hearts Desire
Heart of Mine
*An American Duchess

McCutcheon Family Series

Montana Dawn
Texas Twilight
Mail-Order Brides of the West: Evie
Mail-Order Brides of the West: Heather
Moon Over Montana
Mail-Order Brides of the West: Kathryn
Montana Snowfall

Texas Lonesome
Montana Courage
Montana Promise

Stand Alone Western Historical

Sourdough Creek

Stand Alone Contemporary Women's Fiction

Three And A Half Minutes

Winter Winds of Wyoming

A Prairie Hearts Novel
Book Seven

Caroline
Fyffe

Chapter One

Logan Meadows, Wyoming Territory, December 1883

"For a man who's just cheated a life of slavery, and most likely death, I'm a sorry example of cheer and goodwill." A cloud of frosty air engulfed Dalton Babcock's face. "Ebenezer Scrooge has more Christmas spirit than me."

Christmas is only two and a half weeks away.

The small apartment above the Logan Meadows sheriff's office felt cramped. Dalton stared a hole through the sheet of paper laid out on the rickety desk where he sat. One side of the sheet was labeled CLIENTS and on the other, CASES. The paper was otherwise blank. His plan to open a detective agency hadn't thrived.

Before being shanghaied by Hugh Hexum's men, he'd been gainfully employed as a security guard for a construction site in San Francisco. To supplement his income, he'd helped a private investigator who rented the apartment next to his. Dalton enjoyed searching for clues, putting together pieces of a crime puzzle, and solving mysteries. But that occurred in San Francisco—a city vastly populated compared to Logan Meadows. In the coastal community, jealous spouses paid dearly to have their husband or wife followed, suspicious they kept someone else on the side. Employees embezzled from employers. Expensive jewelry disappeared from

duly locked safes. Logan Meadows, on the other hand, had barely
evolved from frontier days.

Annoyed, Dalton slapped the pencil he held onto the desk with
a *thwack*. Ignoring the sharp teeth of hunger gnawing his belly, he
stood and stalked to the window. Below, near the hitching post across
the street, Gabe Garrison strummed Christmas carols on his guitar
with Seth Cotton accompanying on the fiddle. Happy townsfolk
stopped to listen. Not lingering too long in the cold, they stayed a
few minutes and then hurried away. So many new faces to meet and
old friends to remember.

Dalton shivered in his wool-lined coat that did little against the
bitter cold. He shoved both hands into his armpits, glaring at the jolly
scene transpiring on the street. As impossible as the fact seemed here
in Wyoming, the small apartment above the jail didn't have a
woodstove. The upstairs living space had been an afterthought,
converted from a storage room long after the building was
constructed. Because of that, the stovepipe from below had been
routed along the exterior wall. When Dalton could afford to, he'd
install a woodstove of his own. Until then, he'd best throw his pride
to the wind and join Albert and Thom downstairs before he turned
into a block of ice. He'd huddle next to their heat and thaw his bones.
"I'm not a polar bear," he muttered wryly, still rooted to the spot. His
belly, empty since the meager meal he'd consumed several hours
earlier, grumbled another protest.

Outside, snow began to fall. Across the street, the pitched roofs
of Harrell's Haberdashery, Lettie's Bakery, Ling's Laundry House,
and Doctor Thorn's medical office slowly turned white. Here and
there, wreaths of varying sizes, decorated with red and green bows,
hung above windowsills and on doors. A twenty-foot-tall Douglas fir
had been erected yesterday in the middle of the street between the
haberdashery and the saloon. Tomorrow evening, the town would
gather to add the decorations. Dalton spotted Nate Preston and
Markus Donovan playing in the loft of the livery, trying to catch

snowflakes in their hands as they hung from the upper door by one arm.

Feeling grumpy and in need of some Christmas cheer, Dalton wrestled up the window to a blast of frigid air.

"Good King Wenceslas looked out, on the feast of Stephen. When the snow lay round about, deep and crisp and even..."

The rich voices deepened the ache in Dalton's chest. Almost six weeks had passed since he'd stepped off the train to a welcoming crowd at the Logan Meadows depot. He'd been delivered from purgatory by Jake Costner and his sisters, Adaline and Courtney. In all reality, if Jake hadn't shown up in Newport when he had and then acted on his good instincts that the ragged prisoner with the caramel-colored eyes being held in the trainyard resembled his friend, Dalton would now be in Alaska, slaving in Hexum's gold mine. Or perhaps he'd be dead. In the drug-induced state he'd suffered, Dalton had been in no condition to save himself, even though he'd wanted to. God had sent deliverance in the name of Jake Costner.

Then, after only a few days in Logan Meadows and to his utter dismay, Dalton learned his life savings had been absconded from the bank in San Francisco. The dishonest bank owner gambled away every cent entrusted. The man had been tried, convicted, and now served a life sentence, but his incarceration meant little to Dalton. If not for the generous ten dollars Albert loaned him upon arrival, he'd be hard-pressed to eat.

Dalton shoved an icy hand into his pants pocket and fingered the money.

I need work. Real work. And soon!

Below, wrapped in a stylish, dark-burgundy winter coat with a fur-trimmed hood, Tabitha Wade walked beside Hunter Wade, her husband and part owner in the Bright Nugget saloon, a gloved hand tucked into the crook of his arm. At this time of day, the two were most likely headed to the Silky Hen for their noon meal. Marigold

Canterbury, Tabitha's mother, walked alongside, her flitting gaze taking in the sights.

Dalton had heard the story of how the older woman and Tabitha fended off a killer bounty hunter, saving the Lings' young daughter, Lan. A lot transpired in Logan Meadows in the months he'd been away.

When he scanned the opposite direction, Dalton sucked in a breath, his heart thumping against his ribs. Susanna Robinson Preston approached with a wicker basket swinging on her arm. Some six months ago, he fancied himself in love with Susanna. Thought they might even make a life together. But she'd chosen Albert. Watching her, he pressed a hand on the sill, his throat tightening. Could he really live in the same town with her? See her every day?

Tabitha and Susanna halted directly below Dalton's window. Hunter stepped inside Albert's office.

As much as he enjoyed seeing Susanna's and Tabitha's smiles and hearing their laughter, their jovial moods made him feel worse and his plight all the more clear. He couldn't remain in Logan Meadows on charity. As a man, he had to earn his way. Albert, kind fellow that he was, provided this apartment for free. Well, not exactly free, but a rent of one dollar a month was practically nothing. If a paying case didn't present itself soon, he'd consider other options— one being returning to his hometown of Breckenridge, where his parents lived. Or go back to San Francisco. But starting over again would take some money—funds he didn't have.

About to turn away from the window and head downstairs, he halted.

A buckboard came up the street, leaving tracks in the thin layer of new fallen snow. The wagon pulled up directly across the street. Maximus and Clementine, Win's shaggy winter-coated buffalo, gazed at the arrivals from behind their corral fence.

Jake, Daisy, and... *Adaline.*

Since arriving in Logan Meadows, a day hadn't passed when Adaline hadn't searched him out in his office, the mercantile, or the Silky Hen Café to ask some question a local could easily have answered. She made him feel special. Memories of how she'd nursed him when he'd been so sick in Newport—first, the stormy night in the abandoned pig shed and then, high in Freddy Bennet's treehouse—warmed his heart. Their conversations and the sound of her voice awakened something deep inside. He wasn't sure what the stirrings meant, but he was too cold to think about the reasons just now.

"I'm past due for coffee and a warmup downstairs by the woodstove." Albert issued an open invitation along with the one-dollar rent. "I won't consider the hospitality as charity just yet. Hopefully, I've already hit the bottom of my barrel, but one just never knows about fate."

Chapter Two

"Come in, Dalton," Albert called as Dalton stepped through the door. "Pull up a chair. You just missed Hunter."

As expected, Susanna and Albert sat side by side at his desk, eating from the basket Dalton previously saw draped over Susanna's arm. At the sight of her, the heaviness of his heart returned. Her dark-blue woolen dress fit like a glove. A row of bright white buttons began at her neckline, marched down her chest, and disappeared below the desk. Dalton's face warmed and he cut his gaze to her wavy black hair pulled back in a bun at the nape of her neck, not a strand out of place. His memory hadn't done her justice.

The sheriff held a golden-brown chicken leg—fried to perfection—and a wide smile split his face. A second untouched plate, Dalton assumed for Nate, sat on Albert's desk as well.

Not only beautiful, but she works at the restaurant! Who could ask for more?

Albert used the drumstick to point toward the iron stove in the back of the room. "A fresh pot of coffee is on the stove brewed not five minutes ago. Help yourself!"

Dalton steeled his senses against the aroma of the fried chicken, being careful to keep his gaze trained far away from their plates. He'd be humiliated if either knew how hungry he was. Especially after how he and Albert competed for Susanna's hand only a few months back. Losing her stung. But no one could have won her away from Albert—at least, that's what Dalton told his injured pride. He recalled with bemusement how they'd gone to fists under Shady Creek bridge, right in front of Violet Hollyhock. The granny took them both to task for acting like schoolboys. Dalton sported a black eye for his efforts and Albert a bruised face. With such demeaning history, he'd rather keep his lack of funds to himself. A man could only take so much.

"Thanks, Albert." He kept any hint of shiver out of his voice. "I don't mind if I do. Much obliged." He dipped his chin and smiled. "Good day, *Suzie*."

Albert chuckled and lifted a shoulder.

Dalton wouldn't get his goat today.

"Good day to you, Dalton," she replied.

Her green eyes sparkled, totally unaware of the playful jab between the men.

Reaching out with a napkin, she wiped a spot of something from Albert's chin.

Albert lifted a brow and smiled.

Marriage agrees with her plenty. And Albert, too. Dalton headed to the back of the room, conceding to Albert's non-verbal teasing, the cold of the day, and the burning of his empty stomach. As he poured, warmth seeped through the folded cloth from the metal handle. The heavy pot felt mighty good. Finished, he took a deep gulp and ignored the scalding heat, after which he set his ceramic cup on the small stand next to the stove. He held his hands out, standing as close as he could without looking silly.

"You surviving upstairs?" Susanna asked.

He glanced over his shoulder to find her staring.

"Before we married, Albert used to complain about the cold all the time. You need to install a woodstove."

Albert straightened. "Complain? I was just making conversation."

"Sure, sure," Dalton responded. "Living in the icy wonderland isn't that bad. Especially since I can come down here to warm up." Inching closer to the heat, he reached for his cup and took another long draw. Coffee never tasted so good.

Albert cleared his throat. "I have something I'd like to ask you, Dalton."

"Oh?" He turned in their direction and warmed his backside. Feeling almost human again, he smiled. "Go on. I'm all ears."

Albert set the cleaned drumstick bone onto his plate and wiped his hands on a napkin. "I have several projects in mind to build Nate for Christmas. Along with some other tasks for my wife." He glanced at Susanna and smiled. "But with my job, I never find the time. The days keep passing."

"By the way"—Dalton glanced at the untouched lunch plate and lifted his brows—"I saw Nate not long ago. If you're looking for him, he and Markus are in Win's loft. At least, they were right before I came down."

Susanna went to the window and looked out.

"You were saying, Albert?"

"Since you're looking for work, I believe I'd like to take some time off. But only because I know the town will be in good hands. I know and trust you—"

Hope welled in Dalton's chest. "You want me to fill in?"

Albert rose and met him in the middle of the room, the two standing eye to eye. "Only for a short time. Most likely, you won't have much to do and you can still continue to cultivate your own clientele. I'm not one to take time off, but in light of the son I never knew I had having so recently come into my life, I think time's arrived that I do. I'd also like to take Susanna and Nate on a short trip. You know, before the real snow falls. Just over to New Meringue for a few days."

Susanna whirled from the window. By the look on her face, the trip was a surprise to her as well, and one she wholeheartedly approved. She'd never looked at Dalton with such an expression.

Albert winked and nodded. "We'll only be away a handful of days, but I'd keep you on, making the rounds, until after the New Year."

"A-Albert?" Susanna stammered.

"What? Is wanting to spend some uninterrupted time with my new wife and son so unbelievable?" He closed the distance to Susanna and clasped her hands. "Sound good, sweetheart? Would you like to take a trip? And then have me around the house all day long—at least, for a time?" He gazed at Susanna's wide eyes. "Susanna? Say something."

"That sounds like a dream come true."

"Well then, the decision is up to Dalton. If he wants the job." His brows tented when he looked at Dalton. "You'd take my shifts here as deputy. You and Thom would be working together."

Dalton didn't know what to say. Did Albert know how desperate he was? Had he talked in his sleep somehow? Could this offer be Albert's way of giving him charity?

"And that's not all," Albert hurried on after dropping Susanna's hands. "I know only too well how cold the apartment upstairs can get. When I couldn't stand the cold a moment longer, I'd bring one of the cots out of a jail cell and sleep in the office next to the stove. Feel free as well, if you want to. Actually, I offer that solution anyway, even if you don't want the job."

Not want the job? Dalton needed this job more than ever. He looked away. Had this plan been concocted just to help him out?

Albert's smile faded. "An entire month. Twenty-five dollars. I'm sorry I can't offer you a full-time position like I'd mentioned before. Money is tight in the winter. Later in the year, I'd have no problem getting approval from the town council. I hope you…"

Dalton held up a hand. He had one more question, but voicing it in front of Susanna would be difficult. "You don't have to say another word. I want the job. But I'm trying to decide if you're just offering me work—to help me out," he forced out through a dry throat.

"Believe me when I say I have no ulterior motive beyond pleasing my family." He glanced at Susanna with a small smile. "On top of that, I don't think I've *ever* stepped away from my responsibility here in Logan Meadows. I think I've earned some time off."

Susanna turned from Albert to Dalton. "Thank you, Dalton," she gushed. "I'm ever so grateful. I can't imagine time with Albert when he's not sheriffing—or thinking about his duties. This trip is going to be a real family holiday."

"Consider the case closed," Dalton blurted, before Albert changed his mind. "Of course, I'll take the job!"

"Can you be ready to go by tomorrow?" Albert asked Susanna. "I don't see why we should wait. Nate's out of school, and I'm itching to get away."

The door banged open and Nate ran inside, soaked through from the snow. His nose, cheeks, and lips were ruby red. "Sorry, Ma! I forgot about eating." When he saw the plate of chicken, coleslaw, and two golden-brown biscuits, his eyes bulged. "That mine?"

Susanna smiled once at Dalton as she picked up Nate's plate. "Yes. But you're eating back here by the stove, young man. Your face is as red as an apple, and you're wet. Remove your damp coat and hat before you catch your death."

"Do we have ourselves a deal?" Albert asked.

Dalton grasped his hand. "You *bet* we do. Thank you! I won't let you down."

Albert went to his desk, pulled out a badge, and tossed the pointed silver symbol to Dalton.

The cold metal star sent a thrill of excitement as well as relief for the necessities the job represented.

"I wouldn't've hired you if I thought you would. The people in Logan Meadows mean the world to me. You're capable, and I trust you. Now get down to the Silky Hen. I saw you eyeing Nate's plate of food. Tell Hannah you want a double portion. You can afford a good meal since you're now gainfully employed. From this moment on, you're on the clock, and I'm off. How's that sound?"

Dalton barked out a laugh. "Darn good. Thank you."

"Get!"

"I'm gettin', I'm gettin'."

"Please tell Hannah I'm heading back momentarily." Susanna leaned over and kissed the top of Nate's head. His clothes were still in a wet pile in front of the stove. "Eat every bite, Nate. Supper's not for some time. You know how hungry you get in-between meals, especially when the weather's cold."

"I will, Ma!" His words were garbled around a mouthful.

Filled with wonder, and more than a few warm sentiments for Albert, Dalton strode down the boardwalk feeling like a new man. *Deputy Sheriff of Logan Meadows*. Imagine that! Ten minutes ago, he'd been bemoaning his future. For at least one month, he didn't have anything to worry about—not even the cold.

Passing the Bright Nugget, he opened the door and called out a cheerful greeting to Kendall behind the bar. At the bank, he tapped the window, eliciting a smile from Frank Lloyd. At the mercantile, an amber glow inside showed Maude in discussion with Beth Fairington.

When the younger woman looked up, she smiled and nodded.

He tipped his hat and kept walking. He wouldn't let Albert, or the citizens of Logan Meadows, down. December had the town at a standstill. And in a little over two weeks, Christmas would be here. He planned to sit back and enjoy the ride.

Chapter Three

Courtney Costner carefully wrapped a forgotten strand of snowy-white popcorn around the Douglas pine Chase Logan, her new-found brother Jake, and the other ranch hands of the Broken Horn ranch had delivered earlier in the day. The men set the short, full tree in the main room of the ranch house close to the front window. Then they'd all spent a joyous hour helping Jessie Logan, Chase's wife; their three-and-a-half-year-old son, Shane; and eight-year-old daughter, Sarah, decorate until the Christmas tree was the prettiest Courtney had ever seen.

At the moment, in the kitchen, Jessie and Sarah were making cookies and Shane was down for his nap. The others said their goodbyes an hour ago.

Her life had taken a definite turn for the better since moving to Logan Meadows. She couldn't be more thankful. Alone in the quiet room, Courtney listened to Sarah's high-pitched voice drilling her mama with Christmasy-type questions.

"When will the cookies be finished?"

"Can I have one before dinner?"

"What do you think Santa will bring me this year?"

"What do you want to bake next?"

At the murmur of Jessie's soft responses, Courtney straightened, her heart pinching. Blinking back tears, she gazed up at the homespun angel perched at the top of the sweet-smelling pine. Her life could have been so different...

How foolish. I could have been with child. But fate spared me and gave me a fresh start in a new town. Fifteen and unmarried is no way to begin. I have so much to be thankful for this Christmas, one being my wonderful brother who so gallantly saved me from myself.

Only three weeks prior, eating and sleeping were difficult. Her monthly was late. So much so, she'd believed herself in the family way. Fear and shame kept her from telling Adaline. Back in Newport, Adaline insisted Courtney be careful. Not meet Wil alone. But Courtney believed romance a game. She'd lied, skipped school, and promised Adaline nothing unseemly transpired between her and her all-too-old beau.

Jake knew about the possibility of a child. To her horror, he'd caught her and Wil together on the couch back in Newport before they'd come to Logan Meadows.

Thankfully, on the day of Jake and Daisy's wedding, her monthly arrived. No baby had been conceived. That day, she'd promised God she'd be a perfect lady. Never again act so foolishly. She'd treat others the way she wanted to be treated. She'd think before she spoke. She'd keep a check on her temper and tame her mischievous tongue. She'd not look for confrontations, like she'd done the past year, but look for ways to help.

And, to tell the truth, being good was much easier than she'd expected. She kept busy helping Jessie around the ranch house and sometimes Jake in the barn. She awoke early, ready to do chores, and fell asleep tired. She never let her mind stray back to Wil—and their past.

Her lips wobbled. The fact her actions had plagued her dying father was penance enough. How could she have acted so thoughtlessly?

"Courtney," Jessie called softly from the kitchen. "You still out there?"

Pulled from her thoughts, Courtney hurried to the doorway. "Yes, I'm here."

Jessie wiped her hands on her apron. "Wonderful. The room was so quiet I thought you might have gone upstairs. I need to run over to the bunkhouse to see if Tater Joe has any baking soda I can borrow. I've used the last of mine, and Sarah and I still have some baking to do. Do you mind watching her? I'll only be gone a moment."

Jessie and Sarah made a pretty picture standing at the kitchen counter. Jessie's slim figure looked lovely in anything she wore. Today, a cheerful red-and-gold Christmas apron covered her soft blue skirt and long-sleeved, cream shirtwaist.

Sarah kneeled on a chair so she could reach the rolled-out sugar dough. With firm little hands, she pressed a cookie cutter in the shape of a star. Her waist-length, nut-brown hair, pulled into a messy ponytail and tied with a pink ribbon, swished to one side. So intent in her work, the child didn't even look up.

Aromas of cinnamon and apple cider scented the air. "Of course, I will. But better, let me run to the bunkhouse so you don't interrupt your important work. I've nothing to do since finishing the tree. The fresh air will do me good."

Jessie tipped her head. "You sure? Wyoming is much colder than what you're used to in Oregon."

"I'd love to get out in the snow for a little while. I was contemplating a walk myself."

She'd loved Jessie from the moment the woman had taken her into her home with open arms, making both her and Adaline feel a part of the family. Courtney would do anything to keep her past secret.

"In that case, I'll let you." Jessie laughed playfully as she gestured to the full rack of coats hanging by the kitchen door. "Take one of Chase's, and my scarf and boots. Your clothes aren't suited for a Wyoming winter—yet." She winked.

Again, the sensation of unconditional love.

Hurrying over, she lifted a heavy, wool-lined coat and struggled into the garment. Wyoming inhabitants needed such protection to live in the harsh elements. She must have made a face because both Jessie and Sarah softly laughed bringing a smile of her own. Next, she wrapped a green plaid scarf around her neck and tucked the ends next to her shirtwaist and buttoned the coat. Unlacing her shoes and removing them, she stepped into Jessie's tall boots. Breathing heavily, she straightened. "I feel like a snowman and can hardly move. I'm not sure I can walk."

"You say that now, but you'll be thankful the moment you step out the door. Now, don't stay out long. The snow might look pretty, but the temperature is dropping. Don't be fooled."

"What about Jake and Daisy? Will they be all right on their way to town?"

Jessie's sifter created a flour snowstorm in her large mixing bowl. "Your brother has lived in Wyoming for most of his life, and Daisy, pretty much, too. If the snow begins in earnest, they'll most likely stay in town or with Mrs. Hollyhock. Jake mentioned he'd like Daisy and his mother to get better acquainted. So don't worry. Chase doesn't expect more than a light dusting today. The heavy snowfall usually happens a good month after Christmas."

"I guess I have a lot to learn."

"That you do, young lady." She smiled warmly.

"When I'm finished, we can take a walk in the snow," Sarah called. "I'll show you where a fox has a den in the rocks."

"You'll do no such thing, Sarah." Jessie turned to her daughter with a shaking finger. "You've just gotten over a runny nose. I'll not have you take sick before Christmas. You're staying inside."

Sarah made a face.

Opening the door, Courtney gasped at the blast of prickly cold that stung her face. She hunched her shoulders and started toward the bunkhouse, lifting her skirt to keep the light dusting of snow from wetting her hem.

On the other side of the fence, horses bucked playfully and raced off.

She allowed her worries to ease away. Mr. and Mrs. Logan were kind and caring. She'd been given a second chance, and she'd not throw away such a precious gift. Nobody would discover her past.

Jake promised her to keep what he knew to himself.

The sounds of a guitar floated across the yard from the bunkhouse, a sweet melody that made her smile. She'd met the ranch hands several times, but they'd hardly said more than a few words to each other. Did they have other homes somewhere, or mothers and families they were missing at Christmas?

She thought of Gabe Garrison, the Logans' adopted son, who spent time in the ranch house as well as the bunkhouse and had a talent to make her laugh. The same age as Adaline, he had a sweetheart named Julia who worked on a ranch on the other side of town.

Tyler Weston, Jake's good friend, seemed shy. He had a nice chuckle when kidded by Jake or Gabe. She couldn't help but compare his clear, honest-looking eyes to Wil's, whose had always seemed bottomless. Tyler wasn't a man she'd call handsome, but his strong jaw and dimple were very attractive—or would be someday, to some woman.

At the bunkhouse, she stepped around the hitching rail, onto the porch, and up to the door. Suddenly, she wished she hadn't been so quick to offer her services. Would anyone see through her pretense? Would they discover her shame? She glanced back at the ranch house, wondering if Jessie watched through the window. Without any other option, she lifted her cold fist and knocked.

Chapter Four

Dalton stepped inside the Silky Hen to a bustling café. The clingy air felt fine and smelled delicious.

Hannah Donovan, hands filled with three heaping plates of corned beef hash, flashed him a warm smile. "Good to see you, Dalton. Take any table you like. Even the dirty one by the window, if you'd like. Mother will be out directly to clear the dishes."

Being gainfully employed sure changed his mood. A little money coming in made all the difference in the world. "Thanks, Hannah." Feeling more at home with a job under his belt, he fingered the badge resting in his pocket. "Susanna asked me to tell you she's on her way back momentarily."

"Thank heavens. The tables filled the second she walked out the door—and haven't quit since. I'm not complaining, mind you. Take a seat, and I'll be right back."

Jake, Daisy, and Adaline were at a table in the back of the room in deep conversation and hadn't noticed he'd entered. He didn't want to intrude on the family any more than he already had since Newport. Several tables were occupied, with plenty of noise to go around. Dr. Thorn dined with Reverend Wilbrand. Across the room, Nell and Charlie, and Charlie's cute-as-a-button, blind daughter, Maddie, were eating with Seth and Ivy, who had recently wed. Seemed Logan Meadows was having a matrimony explosion of late. Seth and Ivy rarely came to town, but Seth must have a soft spot for his fiddle and Christmas carols. This was his third day straight.

Adaline turned in her chair, as did Jake and Daisy.

Had they recognized his voice?

"Dalton!" Jake waved a hand. "Come join us."

Adaline beamed and pulled out the chair next to her.

"Don't mind if I do." He crossed the room, feeling a bit self-conscious under Adaline's scrutiny. He wasn't ready to divulge the information about his new position quite yet, in case Albert changed his mind.

Susanna breezed through the front door, crossed the room, and disappeared into the kitchen. She reappeared one moment later, divested of her coat and wearing a white apron and approached their table. "My, my, every time I leave, hungry patrons come out of the woodwork and stampede the place. Only two tables were occupied when I left, and now look at the place. Maybe I should leave more often." Her face brightened. "And I might, for a short holiday."

Daisy, who also worked at the restaurant on different days, perked up. "I was just about to go for my apron and take some orders. Now, what's this about you going away? When? For how long?"

Susanna's eyes beamed. "Possibly tomorrow, if Hannah will let me off. Since Albert has hired an additional deputy, he wants to take me and Nate on a short trip over to New Meringue. See some sights. Enjoy the town's Christmas decorations. Eat in a restaurant where I don't work." She laughed. "Just a few nights away in a hotel sounds like a dream come true." She winked at Dalton. "I'm off to get you a cup of coffee."

"New deputy?" Jake barked after she'd walked away. "I had no idea Albert was looking. I wonder who."

Dalton cleared his throat. The decision to wait or to tell had been taken from him. Withdrawing the badge from his pocket, he opened his hand. "You're looking at him, Jake. I'm the new deputy."

All three friends stared in stunned silence.

"It's not *that* much of a surprise, is it?" he said, a bit defensively. "I've ridden guard for Wells Fargo and the First Bank of Denver. And the position is only temporary. So Albert can take this trip and then do a few tasks around the house he's been putting off. Unfortunately, I'm just filling in for a month."

Adaline pressed her hands, one atop the other, onto her chest, her eyes bright. "That's wonderful news, Dalton. You're perfect for the job. Who knows where this might lead. I'm happy for you!"

Dalton felt a silly grin. Although they'd only met in Newport when she and Jake had busted him out of the prison camp, she was his most ardent fan, and as much as he didn't have a right to, he enjoyed her admiration. But here, in front of everyone else, her warm gaze felt a bit awkward. "Thank you, Adaline. I hope you're right."

If possible, her face became even brighter. "I've heard all the stories. How you bravely used dynamite to blow the roof off the reinforced train car to rescue your fellow guard. How you thwarted a band of outlaws singlehandedly by pretending to be one of them. That's the stuff of dime novels." She sighed deeply, making her feelings quite obvious. "Has anyone documented your achievements? Written a small story? I can't think of anyone so brave. And you saved Susanna's and Albert's life! Just ask anyone around town. You're the local hero here in Logan Meadows, and I can see why."

Unease slid through his bones. Adaline was *seventeen* years old, he reminded himself. Barely a woman. Still, his heart felt a strong pull in her direction. "Anyone would do the same."

"I think not, *Dalton*," she teased. "You're *much* too humble."

Jake chuckled as his brows tented. A crease from his hat marked his damp hair all the way around his head. "*Easy*, Adaline, you best settle down. But you know, Dalton, she's right. Everyone thinks very highly of you. Maybe Adaline can write about you herself. The written word is her first love. I rarely find her without pen and paper."

Adaline's face turned ruby red.

Jake had changed, all for the better, since learning he had a last name and meeting his father. But maybe marriage did that for a fella, too. Only a little over three weeks ago, he and Daisy had said their 'I do's. They were still newlyweds and the toast of the town.

"But more than that," Jake went on. "If Albert didn't have complete faith in you, he'd never have suggested such a thing. I think congratulations are in order!"

Everyone nodded.

Daisy, usually quiet, straightened and smiled. "The Christmas competition will be so much fun this year with my two new sisters-in-law. And the town council has raised the prize to ten whole dollars!"

Dalton whistled. "That's a lot of money. I've heard rumblings about some upcoming competition but don't really know all that much."

Daisy and Jake exchanged a warm look. "Our community cares about those in need," Daisy went on, a shy gleam in her eyes. "And I used to be one of the recipients—but not again. After the gathering tomorrow evening to decorate the Christmas tree, the rest of the businesses will unveil their window displays."

"Unveil?" Dalton asked.

"The displays have been planned and constructed but hidden until the unveiling," Daisy replied. "Tonight, everyone will work through the wee hours but will keep them covered. Logan Meadows looks magical all dressed up for the holiday."

Dalton nodded, intrigued and thankful he'd be here for such a special time—without wondering where his next meal was coming from.

"So tomorrow commences a friendly competition for the best display," Jake said. "The winner is announced Christmas Eve at the Christmas party. This year's celebration will be held in the new community hall. In years past, the church, Winston's Feed and Seed, and the mercantile have all hosted."

Daisy smiled at Jake and rubbed his arm. "Everyone who can afford to brings a gift or two, as well as foodstuffs, and everyone shares—so families who are struggling will still have a nice Christmas. After the party, Reverend Wilbrand has a candlelight church service for all who are interested."

Impressed, Dalton widened his eyes. "Who won last year?"

"Nana's Place, the restaurant on the other side of town," Jake replied.

Susanna appeared with a coffeepot and extra cup. "Sorry for the delay. A new pot just finished perking." She refilled everyone's cups and gave Dalton his first. Finished, she fished a small pad from her pocket and pencil from behind her ear. After taking the group's order, she hurried away.

"Who judges?" Dalton asked after gulping down half the cup. The hot coffee thawed his still-cold insides. God's simplest pleasures were the best. "Same person every year?"

Jake shook his head. "Nope. New judge. Tomorrow, after the tree is decorated, names will be thrown out and a vote taken with a show of hands."

"And the Silky Hen provides hot cider for anyone interested," Daisy added.

Susanna appeared with a basket of bread and a crock of butter. "I'll be a mite sorry to miss tomorrow's festivities, but not so sorry I'd give up time away with Albert and Nate."

Delighted for Susanna's newfound happiness, Dalton just smiled. He was content with having a job—*a real job*—for a whole month. He'd concentrate on watching the town. Deputy Sheriff in Logan Meadows at Christmastime was a fine windfall. He chanced a glimpse at Adaline to find her quietly watching him.

When their gazes touched, she smiled shyly and looked down at her cup.

Worried, he looked at his own coffee cup. When he'd been in Newport with Jake and his sisters, he'd heard rumblings about Wil Lemon. Jake and Adaline hated the man. Jake wasn't saying outright, but Lemon had hurt Courtney. Broke her heart before they came to Logan Meadows. And Wil, being much older, should have known better. He had been twenty-four or so, she barely fifteen and—according to Jake—too young for *any* relationship.

Well, Dalton was twenty-five, making him almost eight years older than Adaline, and in almost the exact same boat with Wil. Certainly, Jake wouldn't approve of anything between Dalton and Adaline, either. Jake had made himself perfectly clear. Men didn't go after girls! Not now, not ever.

Dalton had heard his friend—*and rescuer.* And he couldn't agree more. Jake wouldn't welcome a courtship between Dalton and his little sister. That's exactly why a romance between them would never happen. He had Logan Meadows to focus on, anyway. Nothing more. He'd worry about the rest of his future *later*—after the holidays.

Chapter Five

Later that night, in her bedroom at the Red Rooster Inn, Adaline sat before her mirror brushing her hair. She recalled the day in bits and pieces. Decorating the Christmas tree with her sister and brother at the Logans' ranch, the wagon ride into town, and then running into Dalton at the Silky Hen.

She stilled her hand mid-stroke as a flurry of butterflies tickled her tummy.

Did Dalton think she was pretty? No one had ever said she was beautiful except her father and Hugh Hexum, the disgusting banker in Newport. At seventeen, many women had already had several suitors or, perhaps, were even married. Adaline had been too focused on her studies, writing, and poetry to ever really like a boy. Dalton had opened her world. Colors seemed brighter, scents more attractive, and a world of fantasies kept her mind abuzz. She could sit and think about him for hours.

The sensual thoughts inspired by Dalton warmed her face. Dusty rose spread across her high-set cheekbones and traveled to the swell of her breasts, barely visible at the neckline of the borrowed, empire-waist nightgown where her robe fell open. The lace trim moved as she slowly breathed. The flushed hue of her face accented the vivid blue of her eyes—more round than almond and trimmed with dark lashes. Next, she considered her brows, finely shaped, if not a bit thick, and a few shades darker than her honey-blond hair. She lifted one, practicing a seductive come-hither expression—and then giggled, thinking she looked more like a pet hamster they'd had when they were young than a vixen impressing her *amore*.

A frustrated huff escaped her lips.

Why doesn't Dalton see me? He thinks I'm a girl, nothing more. Jake's little sister to pester him.

Feeling discouraged, she stood and crossed her tiny room to the small bed where her journal entry remained half finished. She stared at the page and her shoulders drooped. *What's to become of me? Where's my life going? How should I prepare for my future? I'm adrift in a sea of uncertainty.*

Back in Newport, before her father had taken ill, she'd been on track, knew she wanted a job where her love of expression could be explored. Her best subject in school had been English. Her teacher had encouraged her to write, write, and write some more—saying practice made perfect. Alas, none of the short pieces she'd submitted to the local newspaper had been published. Still, she hadn't allowed the rejections to deter her resolve, but now here in Logan Meadows…

A soft knock on the door brought Adaline out of her troubled thoughts.

Darkness had fallen, and she'd thought most occupants of the Red Rooster had gone to bed long ago. "Yes?"

"You still awake, honey-pie?"

Violet.

Adaline hurried to the door in her wool socks—also borrowed. "I sure am." She opened the door. "I thought you were asleep."

A white porcelain candle holder with the nub of a candle wobbled in Violet's hand.

Adaline reached out and took the stub of light before an impending drip had a chance to burn Violet's hand. Stepping aside, she made room for the old woman to enter. For eighty-seven, the innkeeper moved around extremely well.

"Was kneelin' at my bedside, saying my prayers, when you popped into my head."

"I did?" She placed the candle holder on her nightstand. Closing her journal, she set the book aside and patted the quilt in invitation. "Why, I wonder?" She gave a smile, appreciating the fact someone other than her family looked out for her. "I was just brushing my hair before bed." *And bemoaning my future.* She lifted a shoulder where several tresses cascaded over to her bodice.

Violet, now settled on the bed, resembled a small, stuffed doll in her calico dress and warm shawl. She hadn't even dressed yet to retire.

"Don't rightly know, dearie. Ya seemed awful quiet at supper, I guess. More so than normal. Did somethin' happen today? Are *you* worrin' 'bout anythin'?"

Worried about anything? My life's mission? Being a canoe without a paddle, maybe? If not that, perhaps someone? The man who's stolen my heart but thinks I'm a child? Nothing more. "No, Violet," she whispered in case Marlene, Jake's mother, and Beth Fairington, had already gone to bed. Marlene had been a saloon girl for most of her life and lived in the room next to hers. Beth Fairington, right across the hall, had the ears of an elephant. Adaline didn't want to bother her. She'd been chewed up one side and down the other by Beth more than once for making too much noise and disturbing her sleep. Keeping quiet was far more enjoyable. "I guess I'm just tired. Well, maybe a little homesick, too."

The wrinkles on Violet's face softened. "I've been expectin' such. When ya first moved in, there was lots ta do ta get comfortable. Settle in. Now, all the work's done, and the dark winter nights have descended."

Violet stroked the back of Adaline's hand, the leathery palm much softer than Adaline expected. And warm. She thought of her father, so recently passed away. Without warning, wetness welled, and a fat tear slipped out and ran down her cheek.

Violet's forehead crinkled. "Being young's more difficult than flyin' to the moon. I'd never wish ta go back, even iffin I could. Jist want ya to know, I'm mighty glad ya moved into the Red Rooster. Ya brought laughter and joy. Me, Marlene, and Beth can get plenty morose at times, and yer jist the medicine we needed. I hope ya like living here. If not, and ya want to go back to the Logans, feel free. I'd never want ta stand in the way of yer happiness. Thought being closer ta town would make meeting friends easier. Where Courtney has a need of a mother and father, she has that in Chase and Jessie."

Adaline wiped away another tear. Violet felt like the grandmother Adaline and Courtney never had. "Thank you. I love living here. I feel very independent and grown-up, even though I know you're looking out for me. Thank you for letting me take a room."

Violet patted her hand. "No need fir thanks. How're ya settlin' in at the haberdashery? Mr. and Mrs. Harrell treatin' ya well?"

"Being a part of the store, even if only for the few weeks before Christmas, is a joy. Mrs. Harrell has been very kind. And I *am* meeting new friends."

"Well, ladies. I thought I heard some chatter in here." Marlene gazed through the half-open door, her dark-blue robe wrapped tightly around her body.

Being she was her brother's mother, Adaline had taken to her right off.

"If this isn't a private party, may I join you?"

Violet's eyebrow tipped. "Marlene, can't ya see the little miss and me are havin' a heart ta heart? Now's ain't the time—"

"Now's *not* the time," Marlene corrected. Ignoring Violet, she crossed the room and sat on Adaline's other side. "You were quiet at supper, Adaline. Did something happen?"

Violet huffed. "We've already gone over that, Nosy Nelly."

"I'm just stating what I saw—don't get cranky, Violet. Orneriness doesn't become you."

"Watch yer sassy mouth."

Marlene chuckled.

Adaline gazed back and forth between the women, flattered by their motherly attention. They had a long history—one Adaline didn't completely know. Jake was close-mouthed whenever the topic of his mother came into the conversation—and she hoped someday he'd open up. Seemed the two were working through years of hurt. Beth Fairington was only all too happy to whisper everything she knew about Marlene and Jake, going all the way back to Valley Springs, Wyoming. Marlene's lies about Jake's father—*Adaline's father, too*—the verbal abuse, anything Beth felt like sharing. Adaline was taken by surprise by the gossip the first time, but after that, she'd been ready. The next time Beth tried to natter, Adaline cut her off and told her never to speak about her brother again. Or his mother. Life was too short to dwell on past hurts. Present day survival was difficult enough.

Marlene lifted her brows. "I think I know what's bothering our little miss. And I can help."

Intrigued, Adaline sat straighter. If Dalton didn't see her as a woman, someone else would come along and steal his heart away before she even had a chance to tell him how she felt. Ever since the stormy night in the pig shed at Yaquina Head lighthouse, Adaline was besotted. But to him, she was nothing.

"What on earth?" Violet went to stand.

Marlene gently nudged her back to the bed. "Give me a moment to explain, old woman, and you might come to see I know more than you think I do." She narrowed her eyes. "Adaline's in love."

Adaline dropped her jaw. She gripped a handful of quilt, shocked her secret had been discovered.

"Am I correct?"

Violet looked as if a burst of wind had just knocked her best hat into the mud.

Adaline almost laughed. She would have, except Marlene's astuteness was shocking.

"You don't have to say a word," Marlene went on. "I can see by your reaction I'm right. I've spent practically my whole life around men and women and what transpires between the sexes."

Violet flapped her arms and a squawking sound emitted from her lips.

Marlene shushed her with a look. "Quiet, Violet, or I just might think you've turned into one of your hens. Adaline?"

She'd better be careful. If not, the whole town would know how she felt and she'd be a laughingstock. But worse, she'd embarrass Dalton and then he'd avoid her like a spoiled egg. How she wanted to confide in someone, though. The words were tumbling around inside, just begging to squeeze out.

Marlene shook her head. "You don't have to say, but don't wait too long to act on your feelings, dear girl. Regret has much less of a sting if you try your best, not just sit back and hope. Now, if you *are* pining, as I believe you are, I have a few words of advice to hurry along the process."

What on earth is she suggesting?

Marlene softly laughed. "I'm just saying a little sigh goes a long way."

She gaped at Marlene.

As did Violet.

The years seemed to melt away from Marlene's face.

"Watch and learn." Marlene smiled and slowly lowered her lashes. A lingering sigh, rising in timbre right at the end, emitted from her lips. "To add impact, dip your chin and gaze up through your lashes at the same time. Like this." Marlene dropped her face, then slowly raised her lashes, one eyebrow lifting. "Let your fingers brush, linger, like the kiss of a butterfly. Don't be pushy. One thing a man hates is a bossy ol' mare. If you follow my instructions, you'll have your fella's full and complete attention, I assure you. No man can resist, if the two of you are meant to be."

Heat inflamed Adaline's cheeks. She couldn't think of one reply because the image of her brushing Dalton's fingers still occupied her full consciousness. Could she possibly do any of those things?

"Well, I'll be, Marlene. I think ya hit the spike on the crown. I'd never a'knowed our little missy was sufferin' from a heartache."

A scanty sneeze brought the three around to the door where Beth stood.

Had the woman deliberately walked quietly, to eavesdrop?

Every warm, fuzzy feeling inside evaporated. What had she heard? Everything? If yes, at least Dalton's name hadn't been mentioned. Beth couldn't know the identity of the man she was pining for—she could only guess. From here on out, Adaline would need to be very careful. Beth would go straight to Dalton and tell him everything, just to spite her. When she'd moved in, Adaline had tried to befriend Beth, but that woman didn't want friends. Adaline actually felt sorry for her, but not enough to let her in on her secret.

"What's going on in here?" Beth asked, her narrowed gaze skipping from face to face.

"Never you mind." Marlene reached over to pat Adaline's hand before she stood. "I think that's enough for one night. Come on, Violet, let me walk you to your room and help you into your nightdress. I'll put a few more logs on the fire as well, so we all don't turn into blocks of ice before morning."

Adaline kissed Violet's cheek and stood and did the same with Marlene. She smiled at Beth, who turned to go. Adaline didn't want to have enemies. Especially now that she felt a bit of hope where Dalton was concerned. The Christmas tree decorating party couldn't come fast enough. Tomorrow was a new day. One where she was determined to show Dalton she wasn't just some silly, young girl.

Chapter Six

Main Street Logan Meadows teemed with enthusiastic citizens all waiting for the Christmas tree decorating celebration to commence. Excitement sizzled in the air with laughter, friendly smiles, and hugs, a community brought together with a common goal. Dalton actually felt an eager joy he hadn't experienced in months. Like something good was about to happen. Like he was a part of a mission larger than day-to-day life. Like the three meals he'd enjoyed today were building him back to his former strength.

Across the street, a crowd of customers milled in and out of the haberdashery while Gabe and Seth serenaded anyone who stopped to listen, their harmony moving Dalton as the melodious sound hadn't the day before. Standing by himself, Dalton nodded politely to people he knew and smiled, his heart thawing to the season. What a difference a day made.

The location of the tree was different each year, he'd been told, allowing the businesses of Logan Meadows an equal opportunity for foot traffic. The door of the Silky Hen was also packed with families, bundled in woolen caps and mittens, and large, bulky coats. They ventured inside for free hot apple cider, only to reappear a few minutes later with a steaming cup clutched tightly between their hands. Trays, outside the front door, held the used dishes. This would be a Christmas to remember.

Earlier in the day, he and Thom Donovan, the good-natured, Irish-born permanent deputy who was married to the owner of the Silky Hen, had said their goodbyes to Albert, Susanna, and Nate seated in a wagon from the livery. New Meringue wasn't far. They would be there by now.

Dalton smiled and looked around, still feeling fortunate to have landed this prime position, if only for a month. Logan Meadows was in capable hands.

"Babcock!"

Speak of the devil. Dalton watched Thom striding his way.

"Looks like every single citizen of Logan Meadows has come out to celebrate," Thom stated shaking his head. "Don't think I've ever seen the place this crowded. And look how tall the tree is. Reaching the top will take some doing."

"Sure will," Dalton replied. "I wouldn't want to be the man on the ladder. Reminds me a little of the last Christmas I spent back home."

"In Breckenridge?"

Dalton nodded. "That's right. You've got a good memory, Deputy."

"That's my job, Deputy," Thom kidded back.

Before Dalton had been shanghaied, he'd earned a generous wage to escort a million dollars from Denver to San Francisco. Thankfully, he'd sent home a good portion of that pay to help his parents in Colorado. If not, even those funds would have been lost.

Another family, with a handful of children, headed into the Silky Hen.

"Hannah was up most of the night preparing for the onslaught." Thom waved a hand toward the sign proclaiming free hot spiced cider.

"Where do you get apples this time of the year?"

Thom swayed back on his heels. "Guess you don't know my wife very well. She plans all year for this event by drying several crates. She loves tradition. Nothing on this earth could stop her."

"That's a good woman you have, Thom."

"Don't I know. Funny, some couples are just meant to be. Even when she was just a girl, she had her eye on me. And, if truth be known, I enjoyed every second of the chase. If she hadn't given me a chance when I came back to Logan Meadows after my prison sentence, I might have moved on." He swept his arm wide, taking in the festivities. "She took on the whole town, supporting me when others turned their back on the ex-jailbird."

Dalton shook his head. "Difficult to believe anyone thought you a rustler. Or distrusted you."

"Distrusted me?" He chuckled and then his smile faded, and his eyes took on a faraway look. "They *hated* me, with Roberta, my dear mother-in-law, leading the charge. She would have done anything to keep us apart."

"Your *adoring* mother-in-law?" Dalton shook his head in disbelief. "But she's your most ardent fan."

"*Now*, she is. Back then, she didn't want me within a mile of Hannah. I wasn't good enough for her daughter. Thing was, Hannah just wouldn't stay away from me, thank God. Our love simmered for years waiting to blossom. I have so many mixed feelings about those times." He turned and looked Dalton in the eyes. "Depends on my mood when I go back and revisit them. You know, I was in a coma for months, but Roberta was the one who cared for me because Hannah had to run the restaurant. She had Markus to think of. Had to keep a roof over his head and food on the table. I shudder sometimes, thinking I could have been comatose for years." He rubbed a hand over his mouth. "Frightening."

"Quite amazing. I hadn't heard the details before." Dalton gave a soft whistle. "Life's funny. You with your coma, me being shanghaied and drugged, then Jake coming to my rescue."

Thom smiled. "Let's not forget about Adaline Costner—Jake's pretty little sister. I hear she had a large part in your liberation and escape."

As if on cue, from across the street Jay Merryweather called out to Dalton, waved, then crossed the road with a hurried step. His rolled-up trousers and too-large coat attested to the fact his clothes were borrowed as well. He adjusted his mangled glasses each time they were about to fall. "Dalton! I've heard the good news." Jay peered through the empty space where one of the lenses used to be. "Congratulations! Deputy Sheriff. I must say, I'm not surprised."

The small dandy thrust out his hand to Dalton, and they shook. "Thanks, Jay. Good luck has kissed my face."

"Not good luck at all," Thom stated firmly. "Albert's been thinking about taking a trip to New Meringue for months with Susanna and Nate. Now, with you here to fill in, he could. And I've never seen Nate so excited about anything—even froggin' on a hot day under the bridge. They'll have a job keeping him in the wagon."

"Well, thank you for your vote of confidence, Thom." Dalton enjoyed the chilly night air. Just something he liked about winter evenings. "I must say, awakening in the sheriff's office this morning was a welcome change. Much warmer than upstairs." He gave Jay an inquisitive look. "How did you hear so quickly?"

"Beth Fairington came in yesterday and spread the news to anyone who would listen." His eyes narrowed. "Do the two of you have a history?"

Heat sliced through Dalton. "What? No! Don't know what you're talking about."

Thom laughed.

"What exactly did she say?" Dalton glanced around as if the woman would appear from out of the night at any moment.

Jay lifted one shoulder. "She musta said your name fifty times if not once." He looked between the tall men. "Her face turned rosy, and she giggled. Said the two of you had been friends for quite some time. That's all."

Dalton harrumphed. "No longer than anyone else here in Logan Meadows—except for Susanna. Hmm, I wonder how she found out about my position to begin with?"

"Susanna, Hannah, Markus, Roberta." Thom ticked off his fingers. "Any number of ways."

Jay's lips pursed. "She's not so bad, Dalton."

He'd not touch that statement with a ten-foot pole. Time to change the subject. "Where're the decorations for the tree?"

"Winthrop stores the adornments and beautifications in the livery," Thom responded. "He'll be here momentarily with a wagonful."

Smiling, happy folks had been arriving continually throughout the hour. The road was jammed. Maneuvering a wagon would be difficult.

Dalton stomped the cold out of his feet and beat his bare fists against his arms. "So, what exactly is this Christmas contest? I've heard a little here and there, but I'm still fuzzy on the details."

Jay's face lit up. "I've been hearing about the contest since I've been working in Harrell's. They're going all out to win. They're—"

Thom held up a hand. "Shush, Merryweather! The displays are supposed to be secret. You're committing the first sin of the holiday season contest, and Mr. and Mrs. Harrell would be none too pleased to find out their new employee has been running off his mouth." Thom twisted his fingers in front of his lips, mimicking a key and lock.

Jay slapped a hand over his mouth. "You're absolutely correct. I almost forgot. I will say the larger shops have grand displays where the small ones only might paint on a slogan or greeting. Mrs. Harrell will be showcasing a new line of tiny glass ornaments she imported from somewhere back East. Maude will be green with envy. I haven't seen anything near as nice in her mercantile."

"You don't say," Dalton muttered, much more comfortable with this topic than he'd been with the one about Miss Fairington. He kept an eye out now but didn't see the woman anywhere. Last April, he'd reprimanded the store clerk for being unkind to Susanna. Had he been too hard? The exchange hadn't entered his mind once since that day. Thinking back almost made him blanch.

"Your comments were meant to inflict pain more than anything else. It would do you well to mind your own business and tend to your own heart. Perhaps you'd have more friends."

"Haven't you heard, Mr. Babcock? I don't have a heart, just a hard chunk of granite in my chest."

"People can change, if they want to."

Thom nodded at some women. "Jay's right, and then we celebrate Christmas Eve in the new community center."

Dalton kept one ear on what Thom was saying as he watched Adaline, Courtney, Jessie, and Sarah making their way through the crowd. Adaline looked especially pretty. Behind her were Violet and Marlene. Jake and Daisy walked arm in arm, and Tyler Weston strolled alongside, tipping his hat at all the young ladies. He couldn't help but notice Adaline again and how her face beamed. Her eyes were brighter, prettier than the stars above. Whenever she...

Alarmed, he jerked his thoughts, only to land his gaze on the Italian singer Hunter Wade had brought in to stir up business at the Bright Nugget. She stood in another small circle with Hunter and Tabitha Wade; Brenna and Gregory Hutton, the schoolteacher; and a few other people he didn't know.

Thom nudged him with an elbow. "Lots of pretty young ladies out here tonight, Dalton. Anyone in particular catch your eye? More than one match has been made in the Christmas season."

He was afraid one had, but he had to steer clear of her at all costs. Jake's little sister was not meant for him.

Chapter Seven

This year was Tyler Weston's first Christmas in Logan Meadows. The people and all the excitement in the street had him walking tall. Living in a tiny farmhouse in South Dakota, his family of seven had always been too poor, too strapped, and too tired to have anything more than a Christmas supper consisting of a skinny chicken, musty old potatoes with gravy, and a handful of corncobs left over from summer, with more kernels missing than were present. With no tree, no toys, no sugar for a maple syrup walnut pie, still they'd had plenty of love to go around. His mother and father had made sure of that. After the dishes were washed by the three older children, they'd gather around the fireplace and his father would read the Christmas story from his mother's well-worn Bible. His sister and brothers would sit quietly, enjoying the sound of their father's deep voice, and the look of love on their mother's face. They hadn't had a lot, but they had the better portion, for sure.

Funny, he'd never felt deprived as a child, even when he and his siblings returned to school to hear about all the finery and festivities other families experienced. Logan Meadows was doing Christmas right, and he hadn't had to pay a penny. The hot apple cider was nothing to shake a stick at. He was enjoying the drink immensely.

"Look." Daisy gazed at the tall tree. "Goes all the way up to the sky. And still a few snowflakes falling. Oh, how I'm hoping for a white Christmas."

"It's a mighty fine sight." Jake rubbed her gloved hand, protected in the crook of his elbow. "And be careful what you wish for. Your desire just might come true—in spades." Chuckling, he tweaked her red nose. "But for you, I hope for a white Christmas as well. But just not too much."

"That's some tree, all right," Tyler agreed. "Almost broke my back getting it set." He smiled and nodded. Daisy's nose might be red, but the chill was nipping his ears with sharp teeth, making him wish he still had the old wool hat his mother had knitted when he was six years old. His Stetson didn't do much for his ears—but he wasn't complaining. He'd found a warm bed in the Broken Horn's bunkhouse, the best outfit he'd ever had the privilege to work for. And, truth be told, the ranch felt more like a family than a job. There he'd met Jake and Gabe. He was a lucky man.

Two young women passed by close, smiling up at him before walking off. One batted her eyes.

Daisy giggled. "They're noting you, Tyler," she said. "You better watch out. I think you have some admirers."

He smiled and ignored her comment. "I don't mind the backache. I've never put up a Christmas tree for a town before." *Or for a family.* "Anchoring the fir was tricky. But I liked the challenge. Makes me feel useful. With all the men helping, the task wasn't bad at all."

He drifted his attention over to Jake's sisters, standing in another group. Courtney had stopped by the bunkhouse yesterday for some baking soda from Tater Joe. Tyler had marveled at the blueness of her eyes when he'd opened the door. She was shy and held back, just like he did most times, making him feel like they shared a kindred spirit. He'd like to get to know her better.

Daisy took a sip from her cup. "Is the tree secure? Can the wind knock it over?"

Jake shook his head. "No chance. Chase and Hunter buried the anchors deep, and Tyler and I made sure the two ropes were just as strong. Only possible with a hurricane, and Logan Meadows has never had one of those."

Halfway down the block, the light in Ling's Laundry house burned in the window. Ever since he'd given Mrs. Ling such an unintentional scare by peering in her window uninvited from the alley all those months ago, Tyler held a special affinity for the family. Whenever the ranch had laundry to drop off or pick up, he volunteered for the chore. Just something he felt compelled to do. He wondered how Mrs. Ling was tonight, with all the commotion on the street and the coming baby. She was due anytime. "I'll be right back. I'm going to say howdy to the Lings."

"Say hello to Lan for me, if you see her," Daisy said. "Tell her I'm bringing over some cookies tomorrow."

"Will do," Tyler called over his shoulder as he walked away. He tried the front door, but the lock was already turned. He went to the front window and looked inside, making sure he wore a nice, friendly smile.

When Mr. Ling passed with a stack of clean, folded towels in his arms, he glanced up and smiled, too. Setting the laundry on the counter, he hurried over. He unlocked and opened the door. "Mr. Tyler. He gave a slight nod in greeting. "You need something for the ranch?"

"Nope, nothin' like that," Tyler replied, realizing that's the impression he'd given showing up so late. "I just wanted to say hello. Daisy sends a greeting as well and said to tell Lan she's baked cookies and plans to bring some by tomorrow."

Tap Ling smiled. "Very kind. Thank you."

"Seeing Marlene at the festivities tonight made me think of Mrs. Ling. I thought I'd come see how she's feeling. Any baby yet?" He asked the question but knew if Mrs. Ling was in labor all the women would be abuzz with excitement, and he would have heard.

"She and Lan already home. Resting. She past her time. We think baby come tomorrow. Or next day."

"That soon?"

Tap nodded and then chuckled. "Do not worry, Mr. Tyler. Babe will arrive safely."

I hope so. Even with four siblings that lived, Mother still lost three little ones. Birthing isn't an easy task.

Tyler nodded and turned, converging with the street of people reverberating with anticipation.

Jake waved him over. Seeing Adaline and Courtney had joined the group lightened Tyler's step. He arrived just as Winthrop crossed the bridge, his buckboard overflowing with finery for the tall pine. Would this Christmas be different from years past? He'd been watching out for his siblings so long, he'd never given his future, or his happiness, much thought. He chanced another glance at Courtney and felt his face heat. Perhaps times were changing. He'd just have to wait and see.

Chapter Eight

When a rattle of harness leather and iron sounded on Shady Creek bridge, Dalton looked up to see Win, wearing a tattered red Santa hat, carefully making his way across the bridge. The excited horses tossed their heads and more or less pranced in their harnesses. They weren't used to the chaotic throng or the tall obstacle anchored in the street. "We better get to work." Dalton was anxious to act in an official capacity as deputy. "No one is getting hurt tonight under our watch."

He and Thom strode forward, leaving short Jay Merryweather where he stood.

Dalton put out his arms and backed up several paces, making room for the wagon. "Give Win space, please. That's a heavy wagon coming your way. No one wants to get injured before Christmas."

Thom did the same on the other side of the road, and people fell back, clearing the way for the buckboard.

When the wagon drew close enough, Dalton grasped the headstall of one of the jittery horses and maneuvered the wagon close to the Christmas tree.

Thom kept away excited children. "Win, I see you remembered the ladder!" he called, gesturing to the wooden legs sticking out the back of the wagon.

"Think this is my first year?" he called back, and everyone laughed. "I loaded the wagon yesterday and checked my list twice—just like good ol' Saint Nick. Everything's here."

With the wagon in place, Thom lowered the tail gate of the buckboard with a bang.

Men and women alike stepped forward.

Win climbed into the wagon bed and handed out the crates of ornaments and doodads. "Start at the bottom on the other side with these, while we decorate the top on this side—" He wrestled the ladder from the bed of the buckboard, positioning it in the wagon. "When we're through, we'll swap sides. Won't take long to get this tree looking like Christmas. Let's go, people! Someone jump up here and support this ladder."

The voices quieted as young and old, short and tall, grumpy and sweet all pitched in. Gabe and Seth provided the music, and the town started to look enchanted. Red bows and small white candles were attached to the branches. Some held quilted ornaments: stars, angels, and trees. A few more expensive ornaments were made of glass and even some oranges poked through with cloves. Other ornaments were wooden and looked ancient. Dalton wondered about the founding fathers of Logan Meadows. Who were they? Where had they migrated from? Had this tradition been carrying on for years?

"Good evening, Deputy."

Dalton didn't need to turn around to recognize the lilting quality of Adaline's voice. He realized he was anxious to see her. This had been the first day she hadn't sought him out—and he'd missed her friendship. Eagerly, he turned. She was bundled to ward off the chill, with a scarf wound around her neck and then up and over her hair. He noticed a slight change in her eyes. He couldn't put his finger on what, but a difference existed. "Good evening, Adaline," he replied jauntily.

She held a red ornament made of wood.

"I believe this is the first day you weren't in town," he said. "You must be very busy." *Is she batting her eyes?*

"Today's my day off at the haberdashery, so I stayed at the Red Rooster helping Violet with some chores."

She dipped her chin and looked up at him through her thick lashes, a move quite surprising for her. When he took a tiny step back, he saw a small crinkle appear between her brows but quickly went away.

On the ladder in the wagon, Win placed the star at the top of the tree, and snow began to fall in earnest.

Children laughed and clapped their hands.

Across the crowd, Dalton found Beth watching him and Adaline. Feeling uncomfortable, he glanced back at Adaline's expectant face. "I best get helping."

The tree was swarmed with helpers. The wagon was moved several times and the tree took shape. Not a branch was left unadorned.

Finished, the ladder was laid back in the bed of the wagon. Win pulled off his hat, waving the red-and-white fabric. "It's time to choose this year's judge for the Christmas competition! Let's hear your nominations. Holler 'em out. Don't be shy."

Dalton glanced around. A prosperous older-looking woman, if he were to judge by the quality of her expensive coat and hat, raised her hand.

Win pointed to her. "Yes, Mrs. Brinkley?"

"I nominate my best friend of the last twenty-five years— Roberta Brown. She's resided in Logan Meadows far longer than most and is considered a matriarch. She's headed the quilting circle several times and co-chaired the Founder's Day picnic for four years, at least. I can't think of a more qualified person."

Dalton didn't know about all that. Roberta had been accommodating whenever he'd stepped into the café for a bite to eat, but she did have a fondness for gossip—about anyone and mostly those less fortunate than herself. Would she be fair-minded with her opinionated judgments?

Hannah's mother preened at Mrs. Brinkley's long-winded compliment and smiled warmly.

"Noted," Win called. "Who else? Come on, folks, don't be shy. Someone has to give Roberta a run for her money."

Brenna Hutton, the nice young woman married to the schoolteacher, raised a hand.

Dalton met her and her children the last time he'd been in Logan Meadows, as she and her brood strolled by the bank where he'd been guarding the million dollars. He recalled her kind smile and the way she'd made him feel welcome.

"I nominate Hannah Donovan," she said.

Hannah slapped a hand over her mouth while a ripple of laughter went around the gathering.

"Hannah always has the pulse of the people and is in the know of just about everything." She gave a long pause. "Although, I do hate to pit daughter against mother. But I've been planning on bringing her name forward for months."

"You've forgotten the rules, Mrs. Hutton." Win's words came out in puffs of frosty air. "Only people who won't have a stake in the race are eligible. Hannah usually outdoes herself at the café. She's won several times, if my mind serves me correctly."

Hannah beamed. "That's true, Win. Thom and myself, as well as my staff, have a fun idea planned for this year, so I must decline. But thank you, Brenna, for thinking of me. In turn, I'd like to nominate Brenna. You don't have a business with a window, although you're an incredible seamstress."

Brenna gasped at the same time Roberta did.

A chuckle slipped out. Seemed Hannah's mother didn't appreciate having her own daughter give her competition.

Roberta sputtered. "But her husband decorates the school and competes, with the help of the children. She'd easily feel swayed by all the young faces, the hopes and dreams."

"My wife is fair-minded, Roberta." Gregory laid his arm over Brenna's shoulders. "She'll judge the school as equally as the rest. Finding someone totally impartial is impossible in such a small town. I think Hannah's idea is a fine one."

Roberta's smile faded.

Dalton was sure Brenna was much more beloved than Roberta who, with her meddling ways, could be irksome. He liked the idea of Brenna Hutton judging. This night was shaping up just fine.

Win pounded his gloved hands together. "I wholeheartedly agree. And me, wearing the Santa hat, I get the last say. Brenna Hutton is now on the list. Now, how about someone to represent the men of the town? We need to give the ladies some opposition."

Mumbling and laughter rippled about.

"Men have judged the last two years," someone called out.

"That's true," Win replied. "That don't count 'em out now. There ain't no rules saying such. But if propriety means that much to you, throw out another woman. I don't care."

"I nominate Dalton Babcock," a female voice spoke up.

Dalton whipped his head around to see Beth Fairington standing at the far perimeter toward the livery. The heavy layers of coat swamped her thin form.

She kept her gaze trained far away from his. "Not long ago, Dalton saved our town from a horrible tragedy with the Stone Gang—risking his own life to save others. His bravery and wit are well noted. Since he's not lived here long, he can be unbiased, unlike the two women who have already been nominated." She glanced at Brenna and then at Roberta. "And lastly, he's very worldly and wise. He's from Breckenridge, Colorado, and has lived in San Francisco. Not many can claim the same. Not a better person lives in this town."

Shock ricocheted through Dalton's chest. He felt as if he were staring down the Stone Gang again, and this time without his gun. People turned to look at him, their faces bright with expectancy.

Seems I'm somewhat of a celebrity here in Logan Meadows.

He slid his gaze from a laughing Jake over to Beth. Standing straight and tall, she smiled prettily, if one could call her expression that, and gave a slight nod, acknowledging his attention. A light of something he'd never seen before was in her eyes. Playfulness? Admiration? He wasn't sure. Why had she nominated him? After he'd clipped her wings last April over speaking so nastily to Susanna, one would think he'd be the last person she'd admire. He dipped his chin respectfully. Along with Albert giving him a chance at deputy, her vouch for his character had singlehandedly raised his station among the people of Logan Meadows.

"That's a dandy idea," Win called from the back of the wagon. "And with the temperature dropping faster than a stone in Shady Creek, I'd say we have three commendable candidates. Anyone else wanting to get in on the action better speak now. If not, I'm calling a vote. I don't know about the rest of you, but I'd like to get back to my fire." He thumped his shoulders and then blew several deep breaths into his gloved hands.

The air was bitterly cold. Almost too cold to snow, Dalton supposed. His thoughts turned to Susanna, Albert, and little Nate, hoping they'd reached New Meringue without incident and were now tucked into a cozy hotel room, enjoying their holiday.

"Good. I thought not," Win yelled.

A tittering laughter floated through the group, but no one spoke up.

"All right then, this year's judging candidates are, in the order they were nominated, Roberta Brown, Brenna Hutton, and our new, temporary deputy, Dalton Babcock."

Brenna smiled broadly at him, but Roberta wore a sour scowl. Seemed she felt threatened the vote wasn't going her way.

"Let me see a show of hands for Roberta."

Only Roberta and Mrs. Brinkley raised their hands.

Win made a show of pointing to each as if counting, all the while his lips wobbled at their edges. "One, two. All righty. Now, let's see a show of hands for our own Brenna Hutton, who keeps us bachelors' clothes finely mended."

When Dalton, Hannah, and Gregory were the only ones to raise their hands, Dalton began to sweat. He'd thought for sure the teacher's wife would win. Why on earth would the town vote for him?

Laughter went around the group.

Win cleared his throat. "One, two, three."

Conspicuous as if he had dried egg all over his face, Dalton kept his gaze on Win. *Seems I've been had.*

"Three votes. That beats Roberta. Time to move on and get this fierce competition decided."

At the controlled laughter in Win's voice, heat flamed Dalton's face. He swallowed hard, and his gaze dropped on Adaline who, along with everyone else, was staring straight at him. He'd never been the center of attention before. Not like he was now.

"All those in favor of Dalton Babcock, raise your hands!"

In a whoosh, all the hands went up.

"Dalton wins in a landslide. Sorry, ladies, the men have won fair and square three years in a row. There's always next time." Win waved his hat once more, with the Christmas tree decorated in red bows with a smattering of handmade or store-bought ornaments behind.

A moment of magical wonder—for the religious season upon Logan Meadows, for the recent events in his life which had brought him to this point, and for the fact that almost every single person in the town had welcomed him in as one of their own—filled Dalton's chest.

Quiet descended.

They were waiting for him to say something. Feeling humble, and even a little nervous, he straightened his shoulders. "Thank you, folks. I appreciate your vote of confidence. I'll do my best with your competition. Not only that, I'll do my best to fill in for Albert while he's away. I'm truly grateful for the chance and trust you put in me today." He swallowed, glancing around the faces. Adaline and her group smiled warmly, but when he looked to the edge of the crowd, Beth was nowhere to be seen.

Chapter Nine

One hour later, after the crowd admiring the Christmas displays on Main Street had dwindled, Dalton remained at his spot leaning against a post outside the sheriff's office. He was chilled to the bone and anticipated his warm fire within.

A few cheerful revelers mingled up and down the boardwalk, talking and drinking hot apple cider.

Amazingly enough, Gabe and Seth still played softly in the background, refusing to quit until the last of the townsfolk had gone. Dalton gave the musicians credit for their stamina.

Tired, he ambled back into the sheriff's office, feeling amazed and satisfied. All the heartfelt congratulations bestowed upon him still rang in his head. He glanced at Ivan, Thom's old, wolf-like dog, gray around his muzzle, eyes, and ears, stretched out before the stove. The animal adopted the jail as his territory and remained there most days, where he stayed warm and made sure all was well with the law. "Seems you're the only sensible one in town, boy," Dalton said, feeding the stove. "I'd be curled up right here too, if I could." Dusting his hands, he stood.

Violet Hollyhock pushed open the door. "May I come in, Deputy?"

"Of course! Warm yourself by the stove."

The old woman shuffled into the room, bundled from chin to toe.

The quiltmaker looked like an overstuffed coverlet herself. "Shouldn't you be on your way home?" he asked politely.

"Come ta give ya my congratulations, Deputy, if that's all right." She clenched her chattering teeth. "I think ya'll make a fine judge indeed. Not like last year, when Dr. Thorn chose Nana's Place. Mrs. Manning jist about made my face turn blue with all her gloatin'." Violet continued into the room, moving closer to the heat. "Jist warmin' these old bones before I set off. Don't know how many more Christmases they got to last through."

He chuckled and placed a chair next to the stove. "I'll bet you outlive most people in Logan Meadows. You're spry and strong. Now, sit and get warm."

"Actually, there *is* something else I want to discuss, Deputy."

He placed a chair across from hers and sat. "I'm curious—with *me* deputy or *any* deputy?"

After she peeled off her gloves, she held her trembling hands out to the black iron stove. "Deputy Babcock and none other. Twern't you the one who used ta be a detective in a big city?"

He kept the smile off his face. Her teeth rattled together like a handful of dice. He hoped she didn't expire right here in the sheriff's office. "Yes, San Francisco. One and the same. Let's hear what you have to say. The sooner you speak, the sooner you can get home to your warm bed. Did you walk all the way from the Red Rooster? Do you have a ride?"

"Quit yer yappin', young pup! If I'm still breathin', then I'm still able ta get around without hilp. I'm in need of yer services, if yer willin' ta take on an ol' granny."

"Services?"

"For a private detective! Didn't ya come to Logan Meadows to open a detective business? Work with Albert solving crimes when they arise?"

A private-eye case for Violet? A rush of excitement filled his chest.

"Well? Ya lookin' fer work or ain't ya? Yer only deputy for a month, I hear."

"Yes, that's true. And I am looking for work." With her short fuse, he better get down to business. "What's transpired? Has someone stolen one of your quilts? Made off with one of your chickens?"

"Ain't that. Though, I'd be plenty annoyed iffin either happened. As ya know, Logan Meadows has a secret do-gooder. Well, he or she has struck again—at my place. Yesterday, I'd set out two dozen apples in preparation for baking. I put out pie plates, flour, lard, eggs, and the fixin's. I went to feed my fire in the living room so it'd not go out while I worked. My fireside chair looked inviting. I sat, just for a moment, mind ya … and fell asleep. When I awoke two hours later, I found two large apple pies all done up and ready to be slipped into the oven. Whoever came right into my kitchen through the back door while I snored by the hearth, peeled the fruit, and made the crust without me hearin'." She wagged her head back and forth. "I still don't understand how."

He did. At eighty-seven, her hearing wasn't what it used to be.

"Besides my mysterious pies, I heard the sheriff's lanterns were all polished clean last week—and nobody took no credit. Before that, someone tied a pretty ribbon around the neck of Winthrop Preston's barn cat, and Buckskin Jack, the piano player for the Bright Nugget saloon, found a napkin full of oatmeal cookies in his coat pocket two days afore that, which he gobbled down with no manners at all. Gregory Hutton said he went to check on the empty schoolhouse and found a whole box of pencils had been sharpened so well he'd never seen the like. I say the do-gooder's workin' overtime."

"Well, this *is* December, Violet. Perhaps all these occurrences have to do with the season. I think Christmas has everyone feeling like Santa Claus—as well as a do-gooder. When I was in town guarding the bank, I was the recipient of a good deed myself. I found a cloth full of cookies, just like Buckskin Jack. And boy, they were tasty."

She huffed and rolled her eyes. "'Course Christmas has everything to do with it! Christmas is the time for givin', and doin', and carin', and forgivin'."

Okay... "Getting back to your case..." Dalton rubbed a hand over his mouth. "At the time of the mysterious culinary intrusion, was your door locked? Darkness falls early these days."

Violet snapped straight. "Ya makin' fun?"

"Absolutely not." In actuality, thinking about something besides his plight felt nice.

"The day I hav'ta lock my doors is the day they can put me in the ground."

"So, no. Your doors were unlocked. What about Beth Fairington? Could she be responsible for peeling your apples and making the crusts? Perhaps your pies were not the result of the do-gooder but someone else who was hungry."

"Let's not forget the pie innards!" Violet squawked. "They's what take the time."

He patiently nodded as Violet rubbed a shaky hand over her damp bun. He needed to get her home to her warm inn and preferably into bed. Her shivering was getting worse, not better.

"Beth? Why, she ain't never lifted one finger she didn't have ta. Twern't her—hungry or not. Besides, she was workin' at the mercantile when the deed was done."

"And Jake's mother? Marlene? She lives at the Red Rooster, correct? Was she home at the time?"

"Twernt' her, neither. She was in town at the Lings, washing clothes, I suppose. Jist me and my chickens. We were alone."

"And Adaline? Baking a surprise pie sounds like something she would do." Dalton ignored the warm feeling he got whenever he said her name. Instead, Jake's angry tirade about the older Wil Lemon and his sister Courtney echoed through his head.

Violet narrowed her eyes "Your mind wandering, Deputy?"

He straightened. It was as if she had read his thoughts.

"That's better. That little gal's been a blessing since she's come and taken the room across from Beth, but no, not Adaline, either. She was at the Logans' yesterday, visiting Courtney. I'm completely hornswoggled on who's responsible. I've always been intrigued by the do-gooder. Thought by now I'd have figured out the mystery. I'm runnin' out of time, Deputy, and I want ta know!"

With her advanced age, her days *were* numbered. But everyone's days were numbered. She'd been lucky to have lived so long. "Why? Why is knowing so important? A nice gesture was done. Shouldn't you be grateful instead of curious? Pretty obvious they want to remain nameless, since they've stayed hidden throughout the years. Do you really want to spoil their fun?"

Violet's eyes narrowed again. "I ain't never seen no proprietor so set on turning away business." With a frown, she tugged her coat snuggly around her throat and struggled to stand.

"Wait!" He placed a calming hand on her arm. "I'm sorry. I didn't mean to ruffle your feathers."

She pointed a gnarly finger in his face. "Just so happens, young man, I want ta know so I can say thankee, and return a favor or two. I'm always hearin' this and that about the do-gooder. I want ta know so I can reciprocate. Seems I'm often the recipient of his or her generosity. Time ta turn the tables."

"In that case, I'll take the job."

She tented a brow. "I got ta say upfront," she went on. "I don't have cash ta pay with. I do have pies, suppers, herbal remedies, and the like." Her grin lit up the room. "You havin' any trouble with yer bowels? Happens to a lot of folks around this time of year."

He pushed back in the chair and held up both palms, warding off her last statement. "My bowels work just fine, thank you very much."

"I have just the thing that'll fix ya up good as new right quick. Don't be shy."

"No, no. But I will take you up on your offer." Visions of roasted beef and gravy danced through his mind, so real he felt lightheaded. "Bachelors can't get enough *good* home cookin', in my estimation. You can pay me with a meal, and I'll see what I might dig up. But I only agree if you give me your solemn word to keep what we find to yourself. The do-gooder wants to remain anonymous. Agreed?"

"Ya have my word, Deputy Babcock. Ya can take my oath to the bank. When will ya be out ta the Red Rooster ta look for clues? Ya better come quick. Don't want the case to go cold…"

"No, absolutely not. I wouldn't want that. I'll stop out as soon as I can. Maybe tomorrow. Now, up with you." Dalton took her hands and helped her to her feet. "I'm going to the livery for Win's buggy and take you home. I won't take no for an answer."

How fast his circumstances had reversed. A grumbling sourpuss yesterday; the celebrated contest judge, as well as deputy, today. Life couldn't get much better. At the coat rack, he layered on more outer clothing as Violet waited. He'd be delighted to help her, if he could. As silly as the task sounded, discovering the identity of the do-gooder wouldn't be easy. But he was up to the challenge. Not much else would transpire from now until Christmas.

Chapter Ten

"Last night you asked me to stop by, Violet," Dalton said, explaining his appearance at the Red Rooster the very next day. The wind swept across the porch of the old guesthouse, sending a chill up Dalton's back. He hunched his shoulders against the December cold and glanced into the room where Marlene and Adaline both watched him from their seats next to the fire. He hadn't realized the two might be home.

Violet's brows drew together. "I did? I don't recall saying nothin' like that, Deputy. Ya sure you're not makin' up a tall tale?"

Surely, Violet's request was meant to be a secret. Feeling silly, Dalton leaned forward and lowered his voice, "Yes, I'm sure. So I can hunt for clues regarding the do-gooder and your apple pies. Remember, somebody completed your baking the other day when you were napping?"

A quick smile pulled taut the sagging skin around Violet's mouth. "That's right, now I recall. Thank ya for ticklin' my memory," she whispered. "And it's right kind of me to want to thank the caring heart, iffin saying so ain't bad manners." She cast a secretive glance at the others. "Marlene and Adaline are home for their noon meal. We'll have ta be careful. I don't want them ta know." She opened the door wider. "Come right on in, Deputy. I have stew warming on the stove. I'll dish ya up a bowl along with the others."

A smiling Adaline had stood and come closer.

Mrs. Hollyhock walked off to the kitchen.

As he recalled from his last visit to Logan Meadows months ago, the varnished wooden logs of the inn were separated by a thick layer of white chink and covered by colorful quilts all stitched together lovingly by Violet herself. The window glass was washed sparkly clean, and not a speck of dust or mud marred the floorboards. Noticing a few pairs of boots sitting by the front door, he toed off his own, not wanting to be the one to tramp in slush. After yesterday's snow, the ground outside was awfully wet.

The room was cozy. Lanterns flickered on the mantel, an end table, and golden light glowed into the room from the kitchen. Outside, the day was dreary, but inside, the atmosphere couldn't be nicer with the fire crackling and Adaline looking at him the way she was.

"Adaline, Mrs.—er, Marlene," he quickly corrected, removing his hat. He'd almost forgotten and called Jake's mother Mrs. Costner, but that wasn't her last name. He wondered if she had one she went by.

"Dalton, what a nice surprise." Adaline moved even closer. She dipped her chin, and then looked up at him through her lashes, which fluttered several times.

The flirtatious move, most unlike her, reminded him of last night. "Something in your eye, Adaline? If you'd like, I can take a look."

She pulled back and touched her face, her high-set cheeks suddenly ablaze with color.

Marlene bolted from her seat. "That's kind of you, Deputy. She was complaining about the discomfort right before you arrived, but with Violet's age and my poor eyesight, we haven't been able to help her one little bit. Go on, Adaline, don't be shy. Let Dalton examine your eye." She took Adaline by the arm and towed her closer to the window. "Come here, Deputy, you can't do anything to help from there."

"It's just dust, Marlene. I'm fine." Adaline struggled to pull away.

With the peculiar way she'd been acting and the attraction he'd been feeling, he'd just as soon not take a look, but Marlene's militant stance brooked no refusal. He swallowed nervously. "Which one?"

"The right eye," Marlene exclaimed.

At the exact same time, Adaline said, "The left." She slowly blinked a couple times and then touched the outside corner of her left eye. "This one. But whatever was there is now gone."

"He'll be the judge of that." Marlene rested her fisted hands on her hips. "Now, just stay still."

"B-but…"

"All right, Adaline," he said. "You rose to the occasion when I needed help in Newport. I was sick, and you stayed with me, unmindful of putting yourself in danger. Only right I return a favor."

He turned her head so the light gave him a good view. Up close, her blue eyes were striking. He took his time to make sure nothing was *really* there, which he wholeheartedly doubted. The slight scent of cinnamon and vanilla made him wonder if she'd eaten cinnamon toast for breakfast. Unbidden, he scanned his gaze to her velvety soft–looking lips. In all honesty, those lips had appeared in his dreams several times since the stormy night at the Oregon coast lighthouse.

With the moment stretching, Adaline smiled and inched away. "See, nothing there. But thank you for offering." Now a good number of feet back, she relaxed and smiled. "Congratulations on being voted judge for the Christmas competition. The citizens of Logan Meadows like you."

A sense of pride filled his chest. "I guess they do. I appreciate that fact and also the job Albert trusted me with. One month at a time,

I say. For a few days in Newport, I thought I'd never see anyone in this town ever again. Guess I was wrong."

"Guess you were," Adaline softly replied, the craziness of a moment ago now gone.

"And I have you to thank for that."

"Jake was the mastermind, I only followed orders."

"You were brave, considering all you'd already lost." He meant those words. He couldn't think of another woman as courageous as Adaline Costner. A familiar stirring in his chest made him tear his gaze from hers. Hadn't he just gone through this hell with Susanna and lost? Only fools rushed in where angels fear to tread, or some such thing he'd heard somewhere. Seemed love took experience, and he didn't have any know-how at all.

Beth Fairington picked that moment to come through the door. When she saw him standing with Adaline, she pulled up short and began working the buttons on her calf-length wool coat. Her nose was as red as a cherry from the brisk walk from town.

Wanting to avoid her, Dalton had purposely chosen this time to visit Violet. He'd noticed her yesterday eating her noon meal in the mercantile. Guess she didn't have set hours. Why had she spoken up for him last evening, throwing his name into the competition? Dipping his chin politely, he glanced for help to the kitchen. "Violet," he called.

She poked her head around the door. "Supper's almost on the table! Hold yer pants on."

Beth hung her coat on a peg next to his hat.

"That's the thing. I won't be staying to eat. Just remembered a chore back in town. I'll stop by later today, if I can."

"Nothing doin', Deputy," Violet said in her scratchy voice from the other room. "Come on in and get comfortable. Eatin' don't take long." A moment later, she appeared and grasped his arm, tugging him into the kitchen and the table. "You jist got here. Besides, I promised ya a few meals to have a look around, and we'll begin with this here banquet today, and be grateful to the Lord for small blessin's. Beef stew, warm soda biscuits straight from the oven, and freshly churned sweet butter. No more backtalk."

Capitulating, he pulled out a chair for Adaline, then Marlene, and then Beth. Three open places were set on the table. Was another boarder at the inn? Seeing Violet gesture for him to sit, he did and got comfortable.

Violet withdrew several coffee cups from a cupboard and set them on the table.

"Why, Violet?" Beth asked. "What's our *fine* deputy doing in return for these promised meals? I can't imagine." She tapped her chin with a long, thin finger and smiled.

Dalton didn't like the way Beth's tone changed when she'd said the word 'fine.'

"Are you selling the inn?"

"Never you mind," Violet replied as she set a crock of whipped butter on the table between the large bowl of stew and a plate filled with golden-brown biscuits. "Yer curiosity will cook yer goose someday. Iffin I'd wanted my plans known all over town, I'd'a told ya yesterday. But I don't, and I ain't."

"No need to bite off my head, grouchy granny," Beth replied on a laugh. "My question was fair. I live here too and have a right to know." She took a biscuit from the plate and passed them along. "I wonder, wonder, wonder what's in the air?"

Violet finally took her seat. "Would you please do the honors of dishing our bowls, Deputy? And Beth, best keep yer nose out of other people's affairs 'fore it gits bit off. If ya think I'm grouchy now, just keep pesterin'. That's all I have ta say on the matter."

Feeling uneasy with the quibbling, Dalton dished a portion of the thick, rich-smelling stew, causing his mouth to water. He passed the bowl to Adaline, who passed it around to Marlene. With everyone served except the vacant setting at the end of the table, he lifted a hand and gestured. "Are we expecting another visitor, Violet? Should I dish his serving now, or wait until whoever it is shows up?"

Beth cleared her throat. "You'll be waiting till the cows come home if you do, Deputy Babcock. Violet sets a place for her long-lost son every single meal in the hopes today will be the day he comes home. Isn't that right, Violet?" She sent Mrs. Hollyhock a knowing look. "But Tommy *won't* be back, not now, not ever. I don't know why she's so stubborn. I think her pappy must have been a mule."

Adaline's and Marlene's loud intakes of breath made Dalton blink.

"Beth! That's enough," Marlene snapped, her eyes blazing. "Have some respect."

Violet's face blanched. Her mouth flattened, and she dropped her gaze to her bowl. But then, color slowly seeped back into her cheeks, and she began to shake. Her scowling lips wobbled. "How *dare* ya be so mean-spirited to me! I took ya in when ya had nowhere else ta go! I fed ya and put up with yer sassy mouth for years—in Valley Springs and now here! If my dear Tommy run off back then after the two of ya were betrothed, he had good reason. And by God, I'm glad he did. Better I never see him again than for him to be yoked to the likes of you! Wherever he is, and whatever he's doing, his life is better because of his good sense. Now, get yer backside off *my* chair and go pack yer belongin's. When ya walk out the door of *my* house, ya won't never be back. Ya hear me?" she shouted. "Ya've seen the last of the Red Rooster Inn—and Violet Hollyhock. I'm not takin' any more lip. The Good Lord forgives me today and probably wonders what took me so long to come ta my senses, ta see the light, ta grow a backbone, to throw you out!" She slammed her curled fist onto the tabletop, making all the dishes rattle. "My Tommy will walk through my door before you do, Beth so-cranky-people-run-at-the-sight-of-ya Fairington! I make that pledge on my grave!"

Dalton, a large bite of stew still in his mouth, glanced at Adaline, who stared at her bowl so intently one would think the contents had begun to moo.

Marlene's angry expression had turned to concern for Violet.

Beth blinked rapidly and her nostrils flared. Was she gearing up for a fight or startled speechless? He couldn't tell.

Silence descended on the group.

"Well? What are ya waitin' for?" Violet jabbed her crooked finger at the door several times. "Ya think I'm gonna change my mind and apologize? Or for me ta go pack for ya, like always? Go on, git, ya snake…" Violet's voice began to wobble on her last sentence.

Without another word, Beth set her napkin beside her place and scooted back her chair, her chin high and tilted. A moment later, she'd disappeared down the hallway.

Dalton swallowed the stew stuck in his throat and wiped his mouth with his napkin. He hadn't known the little grandmother type had such fire inside. Hopefully, she wouldn't have a spell after such a display. Perhaps he should have intervened, saving Violet from the outburst that possessed her. And then again, perhaps such a dressing down was a long time overdue.

Chapter Eleven

Adaline didn't know where to look. The bite of bread she'd taken right before Beth and Violet's outburst wedged in her throat like an old shoe. The altercation brought to mind the frightful arguments her father and younger sister used to have over the scoundrel Wil Lemon, before their father had passed away. Glancing up, she reached out and covered Violet's hand with her own.

"I never stop hopin'," Violet whispered. "Someday, Tommy's gonna come home." A tear leaked from her eye, slid slowly down her crinkled cheek, and plopped onto the tablecloth beside their hands.

Mirroring the mood inside, the wind stirred the tall pines above the inn, creating a mournful wail beneath the eaves. A mixture of rain and snow splattered against the windowpanes.

"He will," Adaline whispered, hoping her words were true. With her advanced age, not much time remained for Violet's dream. She was a rock in the community. She'd done so much for so many others, and their lives were so much better because of her. Was seeing her son before she died asking too much?

Marlene wiped her own tears.

Dalton was silent.

Sounds of Beth's packing came down the hall.

Adaline would like to go give her a piece of her mind but didn't want to make matters worse. Best just to let the situation die down and then speak with Beth later. Where would she go? As soon as Adaline came to town, she'd been warned by Susanna, in a nice way, to be careful of what she said around Beth. Beth could twist a story in three hundred and sixty-five ways, one for each day of the year, if she felt the need. Most in Logan Meadows knew her temperament well and steered clear as much as possible. Even if the townsfolk put up with her at the mercantile, most wouldn't want her living in their home. Maybe Beth would actually leave town.

"How old was your boy when he left?" Dalton asked.

His face softened, and clearly he was moved by the situation. The concern in his voice touched her.

Marlene's head jerked up. "She doesn't want to talk about him right now! Can't you see she's hurt? Speaking about Tommy will only make matters worse." She sniffed loudly. "I can take her sharp jabs but can't abide her tears."

Violet withdrew her hanky from the pocket of her thick calico dress and loudly blew her nose. "Ain't so, Marlene. Been so long since I spoke of Tommy, sometimes I think he's a figment of my imagination. Everyone is fearful of hurtin' my heart, so they steer clear of the subject. Only Jessie asks about him now and then. Always brings me a small bouquet of spring flowers on his birthday. He'd left before Jessie come ta Valley Springs, so they never met, but she understands that the not rememberin' him hurts worse than pretendin' he never was." She glanced at Marlene. "Ya remember him, don't you, Marlene? I didn't conjure him out of nothin', did I?"

Marlene sat back, drawing in a deep breath. "I remember Tommy. He was handsome and older than me by quite a bit. The fact he'd become betrothed to Miss Fairington seemed outlandishly strange because of the huge age difference. I didn't know him well, mind you, not in a business sort of way." She blushed. "When he was in the saloon drinkin' he was always respectful—even to a saloon girl. He never got out of line, not like some men do."

Adaline studied Violet, trying to imagine what her son might look like. Would he be slight like his mother? What shaped nose? What color hair? Adaline had no idea if Violet had been a blonde, brunette, or redhead as a young woman, because all she saw now was gray. She'd known Marlene had been a saloon girl but putting the fact into perspective now was eye-opening. It actually painted a picture of the woman that she could see in her mind's eye.

Violet sat straighter. "Not drinking too much, I hope."

"Not much at all. Just smoothing down rough edges after work." Marlene wiped a tear as she gazed at Violet. "Had a distinct voice, one you could pick out anywhere—and a great, deep belly laugh that rumbled around the room. His shaggy brown hair often fell into his face. And he was kind to Jake, even though my son was just a tot. I should have been a better mother to Jake, like you were to your boy, Violet. Tommy was a good man."

"He's *still* a good man," Violet said forcefully. "Jist in some other place than here—and maybe not as young as he once was, but still *my* boy. Might be I even have a grandbabe or two." She sniffed and again blew her nose. "If so, I hope I get ta meet 'em someday…"

A tapping sound made everyone at the table look toward the window. Snow fell slowly in large white flakes.

Beth appeared in the hallway, a carpetbag held in one hand and a box with a string handle in the other. She set the load on the floor and reached for her coat and scarf.

As bitter and unpleasant as Beth had been to her since she'd moved into the Red Rooster, Adaline couldn't stop a rush of compassion. The woman had lost her last friend in Violet, but Adaline wouldn't fault Violet in the least for kicking her out.

"I can't carry everything at the moment, Violet, so I left a few of my belongings behind." She wound a scarf about her head and neck and then pulled on her gloves. "I'll return and—"

"I'll send 'em ta the mercantile!"

Dalton looked at his bowl of stew and quickly scooped in several large bites of meat and potatoes. He swallowed and stood. "The snow's starting in earnest out there, Miss Fairington. I'll help you carry your bags to town." He glanced at Adaline and then Violet. "Thank you for the meal, Violet. Everything was tasty. I'll be back when time permits."

Violet nodded but kept her gaze trained on him and not Beth waiting at the door.

Seeing Dalton don his heavy coat, do up his buttons, and reached for his hat, Adaline felt a loss.

Finished, he picked up Beth's bag and string-handled box, transferring them to one hand. When he opened the door, a burst of wind and snow swirled inside, crossed the living room, and swept both Dalton's and Beth's napkins to the floor in an icy gust of air.

As she watched him pull the door closed, Adaline shivered. She was no closer to Dalton seeing her as a grown woman than she'd been before. And poor Violet, as stern as she acted, when Christmas rolled around, she'd be hurting over the broken relationship, as contentious as the friendship had been. If Christmas miracles were true, she needed one as much as her old friend.

Chapter Twelve

Early the next morning, Courtney rode into town with Chase Logan and Tyler Weston, the buckboard wheels squeaking on the snow-covered earth. They'd just turned onto Main Street and would arrive at the mercantile in minutes. Yesterday, Tabitha Wade, owner of Storybook Lodge, had invited her to stop by at her earliest convenience. When Jessie asked if Courtney would do an errand, Courtney decided to combine the two tasks. Doing something to earn her board and keep was important. She didn't want to be a burden.

Jake and Adaline were adamant she return to school when classes resumed after the Christmas break. Mr. Hutton had issued a personal invitation. Thing was, because of her past, she was no longer a child—and hadn't felt young for months. If the townsfolk ever discovered her past, they might stamp a large H, for harlot, on her forehead. But that would never happen. Jake was the only one who knew, and he'd promised never to say a thing. Her secret was safe in Logan Meadows.

Now, nestled between Tyler and Chase and enjoying the rhythmic rocking of the wagon, she let her gaze wander over the town. She spotted Jake's mother making her way down the boardwalk toward the laundry house. Everyone knew Marlene's past. Some folks treated her with disdain, but not everyone. Courtney liked her.

Tyler drew back on the lines and the two horses, shaggy in their long winter coats, lumbered to a halt in front of the mercantile. The scene in the large window captured Courtney's attention.

A Christmas tree stood center stage, adorned with all sorts of clever gift ideas from inside the mercantile, each bedecked with a pretty ribbon or small colored wrapping that sent one's imagination to play. A dainty china teacup hung from one sturdy branch of the Christmas tree. A can opener, potato peeler, hair ribbons of all colors, delicate hankies, some knitted socks, and a crocheted bib much too pretty to use all hung like ornaments over the branches. Maude Miller was a clever woman. Any fella, stumped with what to give his wife or sweetheart, would have an easy go after studying the tree. A shiny blue pocketknife caught her eye, and she instantly thought of Wil, who had a penchant for anything sharp.

Wil is my past! Jake would love a knife just as much as Wil. When I'm finished with my errands, I'll take time to go inside and examine the festive tree more closely.

Glancing up, she found Maude and Beth watching her through the glass. The proprietor wore a wide-eyed look of anticipation, most likely wondering what Courtney thought of the display. Fabric as white as snow mounded beneath the bottom branches, and on top of that, several wrapped packages nestled together, giving the appearance Saint Nick had already arrived. Courtney smiled and nodded to the tree, and a wide smile appeared on the proprietor's wrinkled face. "How long will you be?" she asked, huddled between the large men.

Chase glanced behind to the tarp-wrapped side of beef in the back of the wagon. Other boxes and crates were there, too. "An hour, at most. Won't take long to drop this by the butcher shop, visit the bank, and deliver a few donated garments for the poor to Reverend Wilbrand." He smiled at Courtney. "When Jessie gets cleaning the closets, no telling what she'll toss out. But, if you have a need, we can stay longer. First though, I'll go inside to see if there's any mail.

I'm in no particular rush, and I'm sure Tyler would enjoy some free time in town. Better we drop you at the bookstore."

She liked Mr. Logan's deep voice and kind eyes. He was so fatherly and yet, with Jessie, he seemed a young man. She often turned away, embarrassed at their frequent show of affection. "No, sir. I'm inspecting the window displays on my way there but thank you. After I visit Mrs. Wade at the bookstore and see what mysterious thing she wants to tell me, I'm taking these few garments Sarah's outgrown to Brenna's house for altering like Jessie asked. They're intended for Maddie." She glanced down to the small bundle in her lap. "I'll be back here by eleven, if not sooner. I won't be late."

Chase had already climbed down and helped her to the street. "No worries if you are, young lady. Town's small enough for us to find you wherever you are."

Young lady? As she clutched the cloth bag of garments to the front of her coat, she cringed inside. "Thank you again."

Tyler sat quietly on the wagon seat but gave a nod as she hurried away.

Courtney silently hoped Mr. Hutton wouldn't be home when she stopped by. He had a one-track mind about education and a possible new student. Yesterday, in the middle of the street, even though they were there to decorate the Christmas tree, he'd good-naturedly quizzed her about her studies in Newport, what time frame in history she'd already studied, and what books she'd read for pleasure. If Brenna hadn't rescued her, they might have stood there all night. If he was home today, he was sure to start another conversation. He was nice enough and meant well, like Father had, but she hoped any talk of school could be avoided. Her mind was made up. She wasn't going back.

Mr. Lloyd, looking as dapper as he always did but especially so on this chilly December morning, stood in the doorway of his bank, smoking a cigar. She walked forward, stopping beside him.

He nodded and smiled. "Good morning, Miss Costner," he offered in a frosty breath.

She got the distinct impression he was waiting for people to walk by so he could personally show them his Christmas display. "Good morning, Mr. Lloyd." She smiled and obliged him by gazing through the large bank window. "My, your display is quite fascinating!"

On the other side of the glass, a rectangular table had been pushed close and held an adorable winter village that looked exactly like Logan Meadows. Each small building was a replica of those on Main Street. She gasped and looked up at him in surprise. "Did you make these yourself? They're astonishing. And see, here's the bank!" She couldn't stop a laugh of pleasure. The small buildings were carefully painted and placed strategically in the very position of each property.

"Why, yes I did," he replied. "A little hobby of mine."

Mr. Lloyd's tone was filled with pride and pleasure. Wonder filled her. A grown man—and a businessman like Mr. Lloyd—carefully making, carving, and gluing. Bringing the miniature town to life with tiny details. "How long did this take you? I can't even imagine."

"Most of two years. I've been planning for some time, sketching the buildings to get the correct dimensions and such—that is, after all my bookkeeping was done. I guess I'm more than a little proud of the finished product."

"As you should be! They look so real. I expect to see myself right here on the street looking in the bank window." She pointed through the glass. "And see! There's the bridge and livery." Her voice raised a notch with each word. "And Maximus and Clementine! You've thought of everything. Storybook Lodge is so cute!" She hugged her bag of hand-me-downs to her chest. "I'm sure you'll win first prize in the contest. I'd bet you could sell these for a large sum, Mr. Lloyd." She was shocked with herself for having such a long conversation with a new acquaintance. "Did you ever think of that?"

He laughed, his eyes squishing up from the movement of his cheeks. "I don't have that kind of time on my hands, Miss Costner, but thank you. One miniature town is enough for me."

Courtney bid him goodbye and continued past the Bright Nugget, not daring to look inside.

Winthrop Preston stood on the bridge, a shovel in his hands, chatting with Dr. Thorn. Nell Axelrose approached in a buggy with Julia Taylor, the young lady Gabe Garrison was sweet on. Maddie sat between the two women, her face pink from the cold. Both Julia and Nell waved.

Courtney waved back. Seemed Logan Meadows was abuzz with the Christmas spirit. Although everyone had taken her in like family, Courtney felt more alone than ever. The secret she held inside kept her at a distance, always fearful someone would see the truth in her eyes. Oh, how she wished she could turn back the hands of time.

Chapter Thirteen

At ten o'clock exactly, and to the splashing sound of Shady Creek, Courtney opened the door to Mrs. Wade's bookshop and stepped inside, the slight jingle of bells above making her smile. A cozy warmth chased away the chill of outside.

Storybook Lodge was decorated beautifully. Evergreen boughs accented with red berries twisted down the bannister, bringing inside the fresh scents of outdoors. A chain of bright-colored paper circles, cut in strips and glued together, swagged around the shop, making the whole place feel like one large Christmas tree. On a bookshelf in the lending library, a two-foot-tall replica of Saint Nick guarded the area, complete with pipe, bushy white beard, suspenders, and tall black boots. More holly branches placed about made the shop cheery, and some cinnamon must also be warming on the stove. Either that or perhaps Tabitha was baking. That, mixed with the warm, homey aroma of thousands of book pages lovingly worn thin by constant use, made everything smell heavenly. Above Tabitha's desk dangled a clump of mistletoe tied together with a red ribbon. A small tag hung low enough for everyone to read. Written in red ink: HUNTER WADE ONLY.

Courtney smiled.

A door upstairs closed. A moment later, Tabitha descended the staircase, light as a feather on the breeze. She was as pretty as usual in a dark-blue, long-sleeved dress. A lacy shawl draped her shoulders. Everyone had heard the story of how she and her new husband had been exact opposites when they'd met—him a saloon-owning trail boss, and her a proper lady and lover of books. The match was strange. And yet, the newlyweds were inseparable, just like Jake and Daisy.

"Good morning, Courtney. I've been anticipating your arrival." She stopped halfway down. "I've just put out my sign and unlocked my doors. I'll run back upstairs for the items I want to show you. I'll only be one second."

What was this appointment about? Had Tabitha and Adaline arranged something without her knowledge? Or was this about more charity? She couldn't take anymore…

Tabitha reappeared at the top of the stairs with a small crate in her arms.

Surprised, Courtney rushed up to help her. "That looks heavy. Let me take one end."

"Thank you, this is bulky more than heavy. I appreciate your help." They clunked their way down without falling and set the container on the floor. Tabitha knelt and reached for the lid.

"What's inside?" Courtney asked as she knelt down beside her.

"Some things I've collected for you and Adaline, all graciously donated from the women around town." Tabitha lifted a dress from the top of the stack so Courtney could see. "It's no secret you and your sister had to flee your home with just the clothes on your back. I know you're expecting more of your belongings to arrive at some point. These few items will hold you over until they do. The women of Logan Meadows were delighted. Helping is in our nature."

Mrs. Wade had kept a bright smile on her face, but Courtney knew as well as anyone, this was her way of softening the charity being offered. Until now, she'd had a few garments from Jessie and Daisy, but she and Adaline did have very little.

Tabitha continued lifting apparel: several dresses, some blouses, a plethora of undergarments that would be very welcome. The shopkeeper smiled and pressed her lips flat. Several knitted shawls and two coats were included.

So plentiful, indeed! These garments would certainly make their lives easier. How generous of the women in town. "I-I can't accept these," she mumbled into the quiet shop. She thought of her father taking charity from Hugh Hexum.

Mrs. Wade stood.

Courtney followed suit.

Tabitha reached forward and took her hands, giving them a little shake. "Of course, you can. We'd do the same for any newcomer to town. If the tables were turned, you'd help as well. One good deed deserves another, I always like to say. Aren't you giving me the opportunity to stock your father's books in my shop once they arrive? Now, let's go upstairs where you can try some of these and see what fits. The rest you take for Adaline. Anything you can't use, you can bring back."

Her smile was so warm, Courtney didn't have the heart to say no but was still hesitant.

Tabitha lifted a wool dress with a wide, blue-and-green plaid design. Row upon row of layers draped this way and that. The seams were sloppy, some even looked as if they were coming loose. She wrinkled her nose. "I knew this wouldn't work. Much too matronly for either of you and I said as much, but Mrs. Brinkley insisted. I'll save the gorgeous garment," she winked at Courtney, "for someone else, if the need arises."

Relieved, Courtney nodded. She'd not want to wear such an eyesore to her own funeral. She fingered the fabric of another.

Tabitha made a cooing sound in her throat. "I believe Hannah put that in—she has an exceptional eye for fashion and always looks so nice. This will look lovely on you."

Courtney couldn't take her gaze off the cobalt-blue winter dress. The high neckline and tapered sleeves were trimmed in a cream-colored lace, and a long sash at the waist would make a nice, large bow. The thick material looked warm. She wanted the fetching garment instantly.

Tabitha lifted the dress. "This color makes your blue eyes sparkle. You *must* try it on. And this tangerine one as well." In a rustle of fabric, Tabitha lifted another dress from the trunk. "You'll look adorable. I hardly think alterations will be needed."

After trying on the two dresses and taking another two for Adaline, Courtney was filled with hope. Her appreciation for what the ladies had done was immeasurable. In an unprecedented move for her, she reached forward and hugged Tabitha. "Thank you so much, Mrs. Wade. These are wonderful—and needed. Will you please thank the others for me?"

"I will. But truly, no thanks are necessary. We're all so pleased to have such *fine upstanding* young ladies to add to our circles. What a joy to hear about life in Newport, the ocean, and more. I'm from New York, but most women who live in Logan Meadows have never seen a lighthouse or smelled salty sea air. We all will be thanking *you* for moving to town. You and your sister have brought much-needed excitement—and at Christmas time, too."

Fine upstanding was the only thing Courtney heard. If Mrs. Wade only knew the truth…

The bells sounded when Tabitha's husband stepped into the shop. When he saw the dresses overflowing the sides of the crate, Hunter Wade pulled up. "Ladies?"

Tabitha rushed over, pulled him down, and kissed his cheek.

A lopsided grin appeared. "Are we stocking women's clothing, dear wife? I hadn't heard. But the idea has merit." He nodded politely at Courtney. "Miss Costner."

Tabitha laughed, still clutching him by the arm. "No, no, you silly goose. The ladies of Logan Meadows have offered a few necessities to Courtney and Adaline until their belongings arrive from Newport. A woman can only go so long in one dress."

Courtney held her smile, not having anything to add to the conversation.

He chuckled and then briefly glanced toward the kitchen area. "I see."

"Oh my gosh, Hunter—I'm sorry. You're hungry and expecting to eat. Involved with this project, I totally—"

"We have different eating schedules," he said to Courtney. "I arise much earlier than my wife and have a bite to eat before I leave, or I rustle up something at the saloon with Kendall. So around nine or ten, when I know she'll be eating, my stomach just naturally starts to grumble." He squeezed Tabitha's shoulders, drawing an affectionate gaze. "But don't worry about fixing anything now. I saw your mother a moment ago, and she invited me over to Hannah's to taste the stew she made last night."

Courtney resisted the urge to rub her forehead. So many people. So many connections, this way and that. "The Italian singer lives there as well, with Hannah, I mean?"

"That's exactly right," Tabitha said. "It was kind of Hannah and Thom to welcome not only Marigold, my mother, into their home, but also the beautiful Miss Dichelle Bastianelli, until she leaves for New York in the spring." She glanced up at Hunter. "She and Hunter are old friends from Soda Springs."

The bells above the door jingled again. Dalton stepped inside, holding a box large enough to contain a pair of men's boots. "Mornin'," he said with a smile.

Courtney could see why Adaline had soft feelings for Dalton, even if her sister had never said as much. Courtney could read her sister like a book. And this book was getting quite interesting. She appreciated Dalton's special attention now, making her feel like she belonged. She didn't know him as well as Adaline did, but she thought him nice enough. Whenever he was around, he brought an ache to her heart since he'd been in Newport at the time of her father's passing.

"I believe this belongs to you, Tabitha." Dalton set the package on her desk and then glanced up at the mistletoe, a half-smile peeping out.

"Read the sign," Hunter warned.

Tabitha stepped up to the desk, gazing at the brown paper wrapping. "Oh? What's this?"

"I wouldn't know. I was searching the back of Maude's storeroom for a case of overdue cartridges she said had arrived some time back and stumbled upon this box addressed to you."

She cut her gaze to her husband and blinked several times. "Lost by mistake?"

"Could be. Sometimes articles get misplaced." Dalton smiled amicably. "Have you been waiting on some order? Maude was just as surprised as you seem now. She sends her regrets."

As Tabitha examined the return postmark, her head tipped, then she sucked in a deep breath. "Of course! My Christmas cards from Boston! A clever printer brought the price down enough to make mass production possible." She ripped the brown paper off the box and lifted the lid. "Christmas cards had just come into fashion a few years before I planned to leave New York for my new adventure in Logan Meadows. But only the very rich could indulge. Look." She held up a card depicting a pretty red flower and reading, WISHING YOU A MERRY CHRISTMAS AND HAPPY NEW YEAR in swirling script print.

Courtney watched with interest. "I've never heard of Christmas cards."

"Yes, like calling cards, only a bit larger. They have Christmas scenes and greetings. My mother brought a newspaper with her from home, and I saw an advertisement. Right away, I began dreaming of having some of my own to sell." She took Hunter's hand into her own. "Hunter sold my best china teacup to customers when I first

opened! He was watching the shop, and two ladies came in from
New Meringue looking for a gift for a sick friend." A fond look
passed between husband and wife. "When my shock wore off,
Hunter suggested I add a few novelty items to my inventory. I took
his words to heart." She gestured around the room to a rack of dainty
handkerchiefs, a few china cups, and unique stationery. "Since the
weather has turned cold, I've canceled my weekly readings until
spring and needed something unique to bring in prospective buyers.
Thank goodness, the Christmas cards have finally arrived. Any later
and I'd have to wait until next year. Honestly, I'd forgotten all about
them with Jake's return and then his and Daisy's wedding. Maude
will be absolutely green with envy." She glanced at Hunter and
narrowed her eyes. "That is, if she doesn't already know..."

"Just get that thought out of your head right now, Tabby. I'm sure
your package was misplaced by accident. Maude wouldn't purposely
lose it. That's bad business. And besides, how would anyone know
what was inside without opening the box?"

"*I* knew."

"That's because you were the one who placed the order from
Boston."

Tabitha straightened, her lips pulling down. "Maybe not Maude,
but Beth Fairington might. She's disliked me since I came to town."

Courtney watched in tense silence.

Hunter shook his head. "Don't look for trouble."

"You're right, I guess. Still, Maude's been talking for months
now how she's ordering in some delicate glass ornaments. Perhaps
Beth was looking out for her boss's interest, thinking shoppers can
only afford one such luxury. She's probably right."

Hunter took her hand. "It's Christmas. A time of joy and peace.
The operative word—peace."

Courtney let go the breath she'd been holding.

Dalton caught her eye and gave an almost imperceptible nod.

A smile creeped back onto Tabitha's face. "You're right. I won't think the worst when the best is right in front of my face. Christmas is a time of love and charity. I won't let an overactive imagination ruin my holiday." Tabitha examined the small, three-inch by three-inch card, and held it out again to Courtney. "So beautiful. Just like a tiny work of art. Each will cost between ten to thirty cents, depending on their size. Some are larger than others." Tabitha began placing the cards on her desk so all could see.

"Tabitha, I'm surprised you're not in the window display competition," Dalton said. "I'd think you'd be the first to sign up."

A wistful expression crossed her face. "I'd been looking forward to the competition for months, and then that horrible man ruined the back door of my new shop when he broke in to kidnap Lan Ling. I've never been so terrified. And since he met his demise upstairs—I just didn't have the heart. Next year, though—when the memories have faded. This year, I have my new greeting cards to have fun with. See if they sell."

Courtney, feeling conspicuous, drew slowly toward the door. "I have another errand to do before I meet Mr. Logan for a ride back to the ranch." She didn't want to be late and keep him waiting. "Thank you so much for your kindness, Mrs. Wade. Adaline and I are very grateful."

"My pleasure, Courtney. Can you manage with the garments? Or will you need help?"

Dalton stepped forward. "Where're you meeting Chase? I can deliver this trunk anyplace you like."

"The mercantile?"

"Perfect. You go on then, and I'll take care of this," Dalton stated. "I'm headed that way, anyway."

Courtney sighed. Her passing days in Logan Meadows flowed seamlessly. So filled with good feelings and love. Would they always be? Where was her life going? A niggle of unease slid through her, making her wonder at the reason. She needed to forgive herself.

Once she did that, every other aspect of her life would fall into place. And this was the season for new beginnings. The timing couldn't be more perfect.

Chapter Fourteen

Gratitude lifting the weight from her shoulders, Courtney stepped back out into the cold with the bag holding the hand-me-down dresses and other items for Maddie in her arms.

Hooooot hoooot hoot!

Pain gripped her chest. The train whistle always brought a melancholy ache. The sound reminded her all too much of their flight from Newport. Her break from Wil. Her and her siblings' new life without their father.

A tempest of feelings descended on Courtney, none of which was pleasant. Regret, anxiety, hopelessness … *shame*. Thoughts of Wil always brought the same. So much for forgiving herself of her past mistakes.

Across the street, a group of children stood at the fence talking to Maximus and Clementine, the two bison living at the livery. Penny Lane, a couple years younger than herself, watched over her younger sister and brother. Prichard, the boy Brenna Lane Hutton had taken in years ago, was there, too. Markus Donovan, Hannah's little boy, straddled the top rail of the corral, one leg dangling inside. Maddie Axelrose clutched Penny's hand, her face rosy pink from the cold. Penny looked up and waved Courtney over.

Penny was tall. She had pretty hair the color of chocolate frosting. A warm memory squeezed Courtney's heart. Mrs. Torry, their housekeeper back in Newport, had always described people in terms of cakes, cookies, and pastries—a remedy sure to make Courtney smile. *Strawberry-cream skin. A face as yummy as a sugar cookie. Green unripe-apple-pie eyes. Ruddy like a fruitcake.* Heat lodged in Courtney's throat. *How I miss her!*

All the chatter stopped as Courtney crossed the road.

The boys stood shy and silent.

Jane, Penny's little sister and younger by a year, beamed a smile. "Wasn't the tree decorating party fun?" A thick coat wrapped her snugly, and like the others, she wore a wool hat and wool gloves. She looked off at the Christmas tree not far away. "It's the loveliest tree ever."

Everyone followed her gaze, as did Courtney. The tree didn't catch her eye but Tyler Weston did, leaning on the hitching rail in front of the haberdashery. He was too far away to see his expression, but he regarded them with interest.

"You say the same thing every year, Jane," Stevie blurted. "Looks exactly like last year's tree and the year before. I don't see nothin' different."

Penny and Courtney exchanged a knowing look.

Sitting on the fence, Markus looked at the package in Courtney's arms. "What's in there?" The boy was so intent on her answer that when Maximus ambled forward and sniffed at his knee, Markus let out a shriek and almost toppled into the corral.

Prichard laughed loudly and slapped his leg.

"Be careful, Markus!" Penny admonished.

Maddie yelped and grasped at Penny's side burying her face in her skirt. "What happened?"

"Markus almost fell in the buffalo pen from atop the fence." Courtney bit the inside of her cheek to keep from laughing. The boy's face had gone stark white.

"No one's allowed in the corral with Maximus and Clementine," Maddie added. "It's a rule."

Penny rubbed the girl's back. "Yes, well, Markus almost fell inside."

"Maximus is nice enough. I'm not afraid of him. But look!" Markus, now recovered from his scare, pointed. "Strangers coming this way. I seen 'em get off the train, but thought they were just stretching their legs while the train took on water."

The group turned.

Glancing in that direction, Courtney blinked and looked again. Three men walked their way. An older man, and man with a crutch, and ... *Wil!*

Her past love was as tall and broad as ever. His shoulders were thrown back with confidence. She didn't recognize the long, dark coat he wore. Had he seen her standing with the children? She didn't think so, but he would within a minute or two if she didn't get away. She needed to get out of sight before her chance was gone.

A thousand sensations tumbled through her mind. Lying in his arms, kissing his lips, and more... *Why are you here, Wil? Did you come for me?* What would bring Wil to Logan Meadows, if not her? He'd attacked Jake and must know Jake hadn't forgotten. None of this made any sense at all.

Frightened to face him alone, she stilled her trembling hands and held out the bag of clothes to Penny. "I suddenly have a horrible headache. Can you please give these items to your mother? They're Sarah's hand-me-downs to be altered for Maddie. I'm going to the wagon so I can go home and rest."

Penny reached out to take her arm, her eyebrows furrowed. "You're as white as a sheet, Courtney. Come to my house to lie down. It's much closer than the ranch. I can brew you some willow bark tea. The boys can tell Mr. Logan."

She couldn't see Wil now. Couldn't speak with him. Her feelings were all mixed up. She needed time. Suddenly, what they'd done together felt so much more intimate—and shameful. Heat flamed her face and she knew her cheeks must be dark red.

The group of men were much closer. In a few minutes, they'd reach the bridge. Her chance to leave would be gone. "No, but thank you. I really must go." Without another word, she picked up her skirt and darted across the street and out of sight.

Chapter Fifteen

Courtney's sudden flight across the road caught Tyler's attention. He'd been ruminating about his family back in the Dakotas and how they were getting by. If they had anything planned for Christmas, and if food was on the table. Being the oldest, he'd been sent to find gainful employment elsewhere so he could send money home, which he was glad to do.

He'd been gazing at Courtney and a group of the town's children when she bolted from the group as if her petticoat had just caught fire. Had something happened? Did one of the boys say something to upset her? Hurt her feelings? She liked to act tough, but Courtney Costner was soft inside and took every comment anyone said quite personally. He'd noticed her sensitivity straight away when they'd met and because so, he was always careful with his words. Since her arrival, the two hadn't shared much time together, but when they had, Tyler had been drawn to her deep sadness. The shadows behind her eyes. She was hurting. He wouldn't believe anything different.

Alarmed, he glanced down to the mercantile, hoping to see her emerge from the alleyway and go inside. With no sight of her, he focused his attention back on the strangers who'd disembarked the train. Closer now and almost to the bridge, they crossed the picnic grounds slowly. One of the men looked as if he was hurt or sick. Tyler couldn't tell from this distance.

Penny and the other children Courtney had been speaking with broke up and went their separate ways.

What had gotten into Courtney? He rubbed his chin, searching the street. Even stranger than her suddenly dashing away was she hadn't hurried down the street to the ranch buckboard as if she were ready to get home, but she'd disappeared into the alley between the bookshop and Albert's office.

Should I seek her out? Make sure everything's all right? Or will she think I've lost my marbles and laugh in my face? How much do I know about her? About as much as I know about how a camera makes an image appear like magic. Do young ladies make a habit of skirting out of sight just for fun?

Since he didn't want to cause Jake's youngest sister more undue stress after the recent passing of her father if he didn't have to, he'd let the matter alone. Best stick to his own business. She'd been mysterious when she came to the bunkhouse in search of baking soda, staying only a moment, not really engaging with anyone other than Gabe. She kept her gaze anchored to inanimate objects—the lantern, a pair of leather chaps hanging on a nail, the antler rack full of old hats—as if she were a mouse among wolves, and if she didn't look at anyone, no one would look at her.

He couldn't deny Courtney Costner was a looker. Fit and strong in a different way than a more ladylike Adaline. He'd bet she could ride and rope with the best of men, which he knew was a silly figment of his imagination since she'd grown up in a coastal town doing citified things, going to school, and socializing. No strong breeze would blow *her* away. He liked that. Still, her expression of vulnerability had caught him and hadn't let go since their first meeting.

He pushed away and started for the mercantile and the ranch wagon, passing the festive Christmas tree, feeling anything but cheery. He was halfway across the street when the three men who'd arrived on the train caught him, their boots crunching on the frozen earth.

"Stranger," the man closest to him said.

A toothpick hung from the man's bottom lip, and his arrogant, gray-black eyes sent a silent warning. If Tyler had to bet, this fella wasn't afraid of killing. Not frightened but wary, Tyler kept a pleasant expression on his face. Something told him to be on guard. He gazed back, waiting for the men to state their business.

"Would you happen to know where I can find Jake Costner?"

The request was said friendly-like, but the infinitesimal narrowing of the man's eyes told Tyler his first impression was correct. On top of everything else, Tyler didn't like the gun he packed on his hip. Could be a gunfighter.

"Sure don't, *stranger*." He glanced at the other two men who'd stopped when the question was asked. The man in the middle, who he'd first thought was old and feeble, was really a younger man; maybe twenty but he was leaning heavily on the older man who, by the resemblance, must be his father. He was painfully thin and his skin was white, almost albino. Unnerved, Tyler glanced back to the gunfighter, feeling like trouble had just walked into town. The gunfighter was fit, with wide shoulders and death lurking behind his eyes. He pushed up his hat.

"You know him, though?" the gunslinger asked. "Jake Costner."

Tyler stemmed his irritation at being spoken down to. "Everyone knows Jake."

The older man smiled. "Good, good. That's wonderful news after our tedious train ride. Can you please point us in his direction?"

"I could, but I don't know who *you* are and *why* you're lookin'. Here in Logan Meadows, we watch out for our own."

The smile of the amiable-looking older gentleman widened. "That's good to know. And I can see just how Mr. Costner came to be the man he is. I can assure you, we mean Jake no harm. As a matter of fact, just the opposite—but I don't want to ruin the surprise by saying anything more. We'll check into the hotel down the street, and perhaps you can put out the word we'd like to speak with him." He looked past the mercantile where Chase's wagon was parked in front of the El Dorado Hotel, and then shifted the younger man's arm more firmly around his shoulders.

That was a decent request. If he told Jake where they were, then Jake could make the decision on whether or not he wanted to seek them out. Besides, he'd said they brought him good tidings. Was this something more about the father he'd so recently found? "How long will you be there?"

"Until we speak with Jake," the man replied, his eyes bright with a secret.

Tension from the gunfighter rolled his way. He was none too pleased they couldn't speak with Jake right away.

Flicking the toothpick from his lips, he nodded. "Let's get Allen in a room and settled. I'm sure the cold is getting to him."

"Don't worry about me, Wil. You haven't felt true cold until you've lived through an Alaskan winter. Cold like *that* bites all the way down to the bone and is impossible to shake. Makes no difference how many layers of clothes you wear."

Wil? Was this the same Wil Lemon from Newport that Jake had a run-in with? Had the man followed his sister here?

The gunfighter's wolf-like gaze brightened. Had he caught movement down the street? Was Courtney finally coming out of hiding and going to the buckboard? Not wanting him to know Tyler was keeping an eye on him, he didn't turn to follow his line of sight.

"Tell Jake we're looking for him. Want to talk," Wil said. "We're not leaving until we do."

"Suit yourself," Tyler drawled, lazy-like. "Makes no never mind to me. I'll relay your message as soon as I can, but I have no idea when that might be." He watched the three go, the constant wind pushing at his back on this chilly, misty morning.

The older man helped the younger and the gunfighter walked along without a care, taking in every corner of the town.

Dalton appeared at Tyler's side, having come from the sheriff's office. "Who was that?"

"One was called Wil and the lame one Allen. And they're looking for Jake. Came in on today's train."

Dalton took a closer look.

"They're checking into the hotel. Staying until Jake looks 'em up. Asked me to pass the word. One of 'em mentioned Alaska."

Dalton's expression darkened. "Think I'll mosey down there myself and see what I can find out."

Tyler nodded and watched him go. At the moment, he was more concerned about Courtney and her startling reaction. The young woman seemed to already have enough ghosts of her own. He hated to see more arrive on the train.

Chapter Sixteen

With the supplies loaded and Chase finished with his business in town, Tyler helped Courtney into the wagon, taking note of her chalk-white complexion. She hadn't said more than three words since she'd appeared as if by magic by the side of the buckboard only a moment ago. She'd been hiding out, he was sure. Something to do with the newcomers.

Beth Fairington fussed with a ribbon on the Christmas tree in the mercantile window, all the while watching them on and off from beneath her lashes. Word around town was Violet had kicked her out of the Red Rooster, and the woman was now homeless. Maude had taken her in for the time being, letting her have a tiny room beside the mercantile's storeroom. He'd heard the rumor from Mr. Harrell, who'd heard the news from Penny, who'd been told by Maude herself when the girl had gone in to purchase a bag of flour.

"All right, let's get home." Chase finished tying off the rope he'd used to secure the rocking chair, a secret Christmas present for Violet, close to the front seat. "I know Jessie's waiting for some of these baking supplies we picked up. And Tater Joe, too." He glanced at Courtney, already in the middle of the seat. "Your day go okay, Courtney? You're pretty quiet."

She smiled and nodded.

But Tyler could tell she was mulling over something important in her head.

"Yes, very well, thank you. Mrs. Wade has collected a few garments from the ladies in town to help Adaline and me until our personal belongings arrive from Newport." She turned and pointed toward a crate in the back. "Deputy Babcock carried the trunk to the wagon."

Chase chuckled and gave Tyler a look. "That was my next question, although I thought the crate belonged to you, Tyler." He climbed up and got comfortable.

Tyler followed suit.

"Then let's get moving."

Tyler wouldn't argue with that. He clucked loudly, and the horses started off. Only twenty minutes or so had passed since the strangers had arrived. He wondered if Dalton uncovered their reason for wanting Jake. He chanced a side glance to Courtney, speculating where her brother was today.

As the wagon rumbled across the icy bridge, Winthrop, outside the livery, glanced up and waved. The buffalo snorted and ambled around their pen.

Tyler waved back, but the other two were quiet on the seat, each lost to their own thoughts. Slapping the lines, he urged the team onward. Soon, they'd pass the Huttons' house, as well as the sheriff's vacant one across the street, and continue onward to the Broken Horn. The well-worn wagon path weaved through the familiar countryside which was bedecked in browns and grays with the steel-blue sky as a backdrop. Tyler wouldn't mind when spring arrived, with the different shades of greens making the earth feel new.

Beside him, Courtney felt small. Why did he worry about her so much? He didn't like to see anyone cowed, and that was a fact. Were his feelings anything more? Her fright today made him think something was off-kilter, but she wasn't saying.

Hoof beats sounded up ahead.

A second later, Jake appeared around the bend on the way to town, and he reined up.

Tyler stopped the wagon.

"Well, I'll be," Chase said with a smile. "Three going home and one going to town. Daisy at work?"

Not much was happening at the ranch, and most men were just doing odd jobs—chores left from the fall or running errands.

Jake's saddle leather creaked as he shifted weight. "Sure is. Thought I'd go harass her a little. Jessie asked me to bring back an apple pie for your supper, if the restaurant has any to spare."

Chase chuckled. "There's a reason I love that woman."

Tyler rested his boot on the brake when the horses, anxious to get home, fidgeted in their harness. "You have some visitors in town looking for you. Arrived on today's train."

A strangled sound came from Courtney. She braced a hand on the front board and almost stood.

Jake sat forward, his brows drawn down. He frowned. "That's an oddity. I wonder… Court, something wrong?"

She shook her head.

"Who? Where're they from?"

"Don't know, but they told me to pass the word there're staying in the hotel to give you some good news. Two of 'em look like father and son."

"Don't go, Jake!" Courtney blurted. "Please!"

Chase turned to her in his seat. "What's this about, Courtney? Do you know something we don't?"

Tyler heard the deep intake of her breath. He looked back to Jake. "Your sister was frightened when they arrived. I saw her reaction." He pressed harder on the brake and tied the long reins on the handle. "I'm going with you. I didn't like the feel I got from the fella named Wil. He never said, but I believe he's Wil Lemon, the man you told me about from Newport."

Jake's eyes narrowed as he gazed at Courtney. "Has Wil followed you to Logan Meadows? Did he send word he was coming?"

Ahh, the plot thickens. This fella Jake mentioned meant something to Courtney, more than anyone was saying. Everything was beginning to make sense.

She shook her head. "Wil's in town, but I didn't know. I promise. I'd have told you. I didn't invite him here, Jake. I have no idea what he wants."

"Okay, okay, I believe you." He looked off in the direction of town.

Tyler climbed off the seat and stood beside the buckboard, wishing he had his gun. Jake did. That was good.

Courtney turned to Chase. "Mr. Logan, please don't let Jake face Wil alone. Wil's a killer. He hates my brother more than anyone else in the world."

"Just relax, Court," Jake replied. "Nothing's gonna happen. And Tyler, you're not walking all the way back to town. I'm not looking for trouble. But I'm not hiding, either. I'm not scared of Wil Lemon. He's a punk and nothing more."

"You're wrong," Courtney gasped. "He won't bat an eye at shooting you for getting the best of him in Newport."

"Settle down. Think about what you're saying. He won't kill me in cold blood with the whole town watching. This must have something to do with Father or his death. I've got to go." Jake's expression brooked no argument. "If you'll feel better, I'll take Thom or Dalton."

Tyler climbed onto the wagon seat and gathered the reins. What Jake said made a whole lot of sense.

"Jake's right," Chase added. "This character won't be stupid and get himself hanged. But he might try something when you're not looking. We'll spread the word to keep watch for anything suspicious." He glanced at Courtney's frightened face. "That help?"

She nodded. "I guess—since there's nothing more I can do."

Tyler hoped she meant what she said. Men's work was best left to them. She wouldn't try anything on her own, would she?

Jake straightened in his saddle. "Glad that's settled. And Court, if you run into Wil or if he comes lookin', you're *not* to speak with him. Do I make myself clear?"

A long, meaningful look vibrated between brother and sister.

Jake raised a brow. "Courtney?"

"Yes. I wouldn't think of it."

Tyler heard her words but her set expression said different. Courtney Costner may be frightened to death at the moment, but she was the type to take matters into her own hands to protect the ones she loved. The question was, just how far would she go?

Chapter Seventeen

In deep thought, Jake took the hotel stairs two at a time. To keep the peace, and to keep Courtney off his back, he'd checked in at the sheriff's office to see if either Thom or Dalton was there, but the place had been empty. From there, he went to the Silky Hen and spoke briefly with Daisy but hadn't mentioned the visitors in the hotel. Until he knew what they were about, he'd keep that news quiet.

Was he foolish to speak with Wil? He didn't have anything more to say to the horse's backside, except stay away from Courtney. Was he here to take revenge for Jake spiriting Courtney out of Newport and away from him? Was this some sort of elaborate trap, bringing in two other men with the name of Ford, as he'd been told? Jake didn't think so, but he wouldn't put anything past the snake. The fastest way to get Wil out of town was to deal with him head-on and end this, once and for all.

Stopping at door number five, he squared his shoulders and rapped several times in quick succession. The door opened to the older man he'd heard about. A younger fella, stretched out on the bed, gave a wobbly smile. Wil Lemon was nowhere to be seen. Jake took a deep breath. "I was told Wil Lemon is lookin' for me."

"You must be Jake Costner."

Anger rattled up and down Jake's spine. Would a gunfighter be lying about when his target arrived? Jake seriously doubted that. "I am."

The man's face split into a wide grin. "I thought as much but didn't want to jump the gun as I did with Deputy Babcock who came to call a little while ago."

Poor choice of words.

The older gentleman glanced over his shoulder to the younger man, anticipation shining in his eyes. Tyler had told Jake he thought they were father and son. The older was tall and thick-shouldered with graying hair. His face was lined with great suffering, if Jake had to guess. The younger, reclining on the bed, was no more than a scarecrow and looked weak and bent. His skin was sallow, and he suffered dark circles under his eyes. The son looked weathered beyond his years, and Jake wondered what the heck was wrong with him. Did he have some sort of sickness?

The man before him waved Jake inside. "Please, come inside, Mr. Costner."

"Where's Wil Lemon?" Jake asked before stepping inside the room.

The man's brows drew down at his curt tone. "Went out after we arrived and haven't seen him since. But his job is finished. He offered to escort us here to Logan Meadows and help with my son, who, as you can see, is incapacitated at the moment. I'm Kenneth Ford, and that's my son, Allen."

The affection in Mr. Ford's voice confused Jake. Who were these men, and what in the world did they want with him? The sooner he found out, the better.

"I'm a weight around my father's neck." Allen exchanged another look with his father. "Still, now that we're reunited, I never want to be anywhere else."

"And you never will be," Mr. Ford said. "I mean to help you each and every day of your life." He turned back to Jake. "You have a nice town. Logan Meadows has welcomed us kindly. Wyoming's a mite cold, but other than that…"

"The weather usually is in December."

"You're correct. And I guess I better get down to business before I run you off with small talk."

What in the world was going on? Jake didn't have a clue.

"You see, Mr. Costner—*Jake*," he said, a kind smile pulling his lips, "I hope you don't mind if I call you that. You saved my son's life. My *only* son. Allen was an unfortunate victim of the infamous banker, Hugh Hexum. He was shanghaied and taken to Alaska seven months before your friend Deputy Babcock suffered the same fate. If Allen had remained even a few weeks longer in the harsh environment, he'd be dead." Kenneth walked over and laid a hand on his son's shoulder. "I'm indebted to you for bringing him back from the dead. His mother and I have suffered terribly since his abduction. We exhausted every avenue to find him, to no avail. And now, because of your bravery, he's been brought back into our lives."

Everything made sense. Warmth crept into Jake's face. Allen was one of the others, the unfortunate workers he'd heard Hexum and Lee Strangely speak about in Newport's sheriff's office. He'd thought briefly of the men kept in the Alaskan mine, knowing since the truth had been revealed, the wrong would be put to right, and the men would someday return to their homes and families. But his upcoming wedding to Daisy, worrying over Courtney, and the return to Logan Meadows had kept him from dwelling on the matter for long. Wonder swished through him again at seeing Allen on the bed. "I'm glad you were released, Mr. Ford."

"Please, you must call me Allen."

Jake dipped his chin. "How many men were rescued? We didn't have time to stick around and find out." He gave a mirthless laugh, thinking how easily his plan could have gone wrong, landing him and Dalton aboard the *Tigress* bound for Alaska.

"I suppose you didn't, young man, but your sheriff took care of that with his telegrams."

"There were about forty," Allen replied. "The number changed as men died off and others arrived. I don't like to think how many men perished, and I went free."

Mr. Ford took out his kerchief and wiped the moisture from his eyes. "I can't thank you enough for your bravery, Jake, and for doing what was right instead of closing your eyes, as most men would. We've come to Logan Meadows to reward you for your heroic and noble efforts."

Jake blinked and straightened. He hadn't expected to hear those words. After he showed up and Lemon hadn't been around, he'd relaxed and was just getting to know these men. He shook his head. "I could never take money for doing what's right."

Ford glanced at his son, and his gaze softened. "We insist! And so does my wife. I've learned a lot about you since our arrival. You're well liked, and people were happy to talk once they knew my intention. You're a newlywed. Any newly married couple can use a little extra money. I also know you're a proud man and will most certainly refuse, so I've taken the liberty of putting the money in the bank under your name. The funds will sit there, earning interest until you decide what to do. Consider the one thousand dollars a wedding gift. The deed is already done. As soon as Allen is strong enough to travel, we'll depart for San Francisco."

Shocked speechless, Jake just stared. Was this some kind of trick? Maybe Wil thought this distraction would allow him time to whisk Courtney away. The frightening thought made Jake double his intention of keeping her on a short line until Wil was gone and the coast was clear. He'd decide about the reward later.

Chapter Eighteen

As soon as the chores were finished the next morning, Courtney, feeling uneasy since seeing Wil in town yesterday, sought out Jessie to ask if she could go back into town and do some Christmas shopping. December twenty-fifth was only thirteen days away. She'd told Jessie she intended to make something small for Adaline and her new sister-in-law, Daisy, and needed to purchase some fabric. But only if Jessie didn't need her to watch the children. Jessie had given her permission and arranged for Tyler to drive her into town.

Now, bundled against the cold, she sat next to him once more in the wagon, feeling like the biggest fibber alive. She needed to speak with Wil, and to do so, she had to get to town. What were Wil's intentions? Was he out to kill Jake? Or maybe he meant to exact revenge on her by telling everyone about their sordid past. Could she appeal to the decency supposedly inside every human and hope he'd let bygones be bygones? How she loathed the thought of bringing shame to her family. Beneath the thick blanket, Courtney twisted her gloved hands together to the point of pain.

The wagon rolled along. A hush encased the stark winter landscape, everything different from Newport. After the weeks of living here, she knew the road well. Wouldn't be but a few minutes and they'd reach Logan Meadows and cross the bridge. Tyler had been relatively silent the whole ride out, probably contemplating her outburst yesterday about Wil and Jake. What must he think of her? Her heart trembled. She hadn't been in town long, but she'd made some nice friends, women and girls, all who treated her with kindness and respect. And even more because she was Jake's sister and resided out at the Logans' ranch. Her life could change any second. She sighed, and a puff of white crystals danced before her face.

Beside her, Tyler glanced down. "Why so quiet?"

Me, quiet? He hadn't said more than two words since they'd left the ranch. He'd be shocked to his boots if he knew the extent of her relationship with Wil. "Just thinking about the bonnets I'd like to sew as Christmas presents. One for Adaline and one for Daisy. If I begin tonight, I think I'll have time."

"You been sewing all your life?" he asked, relaxed on the wagon seat. "You seem like a clever kind of girl." He gave her a winsome grin.

She knew she was being stubborn, but his compliment rankled. All she'd ever done was be contrary. And now, because of her, Wil would ruin Jake and Daisy's life here in Logan Meadows. He was a loaded gun, so to speak, ready to go off at the slightest provocation. Walking on eggshells would be a welcome reprieve other than figuring him out.

"Why would you say such a thing?" she replied irritably. "You hardly know me. I'm not clever at all."

After momentarily glancing her way, he shrugged. "Don't know about that. Perhaps the fact you got a ride into town when we weren't planning on coming in today has me thinking. That's pretty clever." He tipped his hat with his thumb.

Light flooded under the brim of his Stetson, allowing her to get a good look at the mischief dancing in his earnest brown eyes. He had a straight nose, strong jawline, and chiseled lips that, at the moment, quivered with mirth. Brown hair curled ever-so-gently around his nape. She cut her gaze back to the scenery.

"Still don't believe me? How about when you got Shane to stop chasing leaves in the ranch yard and go back inside—all without a fuss—by pretending to see a bear cub hiding behind the kitchen door?"

She couldn't stop a small smile. Staying one step ahead of the little cowboy took work. When he wanted to throw a fuss, he could only be stopped by Mr. Logan.

"What did you tell the scamp when he found out no critter was inside?"

"Mama bear must have called him home for supper." The memory of Shane's big eyes brought a flush of pleasure. He was so cute.

Tyler pointed. "Holy smokes! A smile."

Embarrassed, she ducked her head.

"No, don't do that. You have a pretty smile. You should smile more often. Let your light shine for all to see."

She chanced a look at him and was rewarded with a wink. A fluttery feeling squeezed her chest, and she felt her lips pull up.

"I could get used to seeing that."

She made a face and started to speak, but the piercing cry of a hawk cut her off.

Tyler chuckled. "See? Your creator agrees with me."

Amazed, she just stared.

"He's speaking to you, Courtney. Like a sunset when the sky is awash with fiery colors, a wispy-soft morning as the fog tickles the earth in swirls of white, or the sight of twin fawns watching you in wonder, having never before seen a human face. You're not alone, even when no one is with you."

Feeling confused, she clutched her hands more tightly. "You say the strangest things."

He just lifted one shoulder and encouraged the horses onward.

"What will you do while I'm in town?" she asked to change the subject so the rapid beat of her heart could subside. "Or will you return to the ranch?"

"Not sure. Jessie mentioned her laundry might be done early. I'll check, since I'll be right there. And I need to see if the beef's running low at the Silky Hen. Little errands like that." He rubbed a hand along the side of his face. "Gives me things to do. People to visit. I'll stop at the saloon and see what the talk is around town. Can't come to Logan Meadows without doing that."

If only she had simple chores to do instead of trying to find Wil and discover what he was about. Maybe she'd be granted her most ardent wish and he'd already be gone. *Never to return.* "I wonder if Mrs. Ling has had her baby."

"There you go again," he chortled. "More smiles. They're gettin' easier all the time. You look like a different girl when your lips tip up and a little light shines in your eyes." He tweaked her cold nose. "I like it! If Mrs. Ling has delivered, I'm sure to find out, and I'll let you know. If you want, we can stop in so you can say hello."

Tyler had a way about him. He brought out the best in people. *Even me.* He'd surprised her when he'd tweaked her nose, but the action had made her smile even more. Maybe, coming from a large family, he knew how to handle younger siblings. In the six weeks she'd known him, this conversation was the most they'd ever talked. The easy banter felt nice, giving her a chance to forget her past mistakes and forgive herself for a few fleeting moments.

The rumbling wagon wheels crunched on the frozen earth as Tyler guided the buckboard with ease around potholes and crevasses. Overhead, wispy gray clouds made the day feel all the more oppressive. What would she say when she found Wil? How would he react?

The wagon approached the onset of town where the corner with Winston's Feed was on one side and the bridge over Shady Creek on the other. "You can let me off here, and I'll walk to the mercantile, since the feed store is right there." She pointed over the bridge. "My destination is on the opposite side of town than yours."

"One of my stops is here and the others by the mercantile. Ling's and the Silky Hen?" "But—"

The buckboard rattled across the bridge. "I'll take you."

She bit her bottom lip. Wil seeing her with Tyler might spark his anger. She didn't like telling untruths, but until her old beau was out of town, she feared that was exactly what she'd be doing fairly often. "Actually, I feel the need to stretch my legs. Can you please stop?"

"Just hold your horses, we've almost arrived."

Courtney ignored the irritation that surfaced at Tyler's response. He was trying to be nice, courteous. She needed to remember that. The Christmas tree was a beautiful sight, as were the decorated shops and homes. Wreaths and pine boughs were displayed everywhere. Logan Meadows would be a nice place to live out her life. The hominess wrapped around her like a thick wool coat, making her feel treasured. And too, the amused looks from Tyler were conjuring up warm feelings she'd sworn herself against after the trouble she'd landed in with Wil. This was her new life. If she got through the situation and came out on the other side intact, she'd not be tempted again to ever love another man. She'd been granted a second chance. Not every woman was so lucky.

Suddenly, the short hairs on the back of her neck prickled. A man she didn't know stood outside the Silky Hen, watching their approach. She touched Tyler's arm. "Who's that staring at us?"

Tyler pulled back on one long line, turning the wagon around back in the direction they'd come, and stopped in front of the mercantile on the street's opposite side. He set the brake with his boot. "Dwight Hoskins. Cousin to Hannah Donovan's first husband. Couple years ago, or thereabouts, he was wooing Hannah before she married Thom. Trouble finds him faster than a fool with money. And he has the manners of a flea. He actually almost hanged your brother for *not* rustling cattle."

"Jake told us about that!" She shuddered at the vision of Tyler's words.

Tyler gave a small chuckle. "Don't fear. Thom and the sheriff showed up to intervene. If you want more details, ask Jake. I wasn't in town back then, but I've been here long enough to know Dwight—and *not* like him. In a small town like this, everybody knows everything about everyone. Gossip flies faster than a murder of crows." He wiggled his eyebrows. "Don't let nothin' private get out if you don't want every last individual whispering behind their hands."

What a field day they'd have with me. "Why doesn't Mr. Hoskins stop staring? Makes me uncomfortable."

Tyler gave Dwight a dismissive flip of a hand. "Makes me more than that!"

Dwight frowned, turned away, and started down the street.

"Stay clear of him. Like I said, he's nothin' but trouble."

She glanced away from Tyler's strong profile as he hopped down and circled the wagon to assist her to the street. So far, Wil was nowhere to be seen. Her heart constricted at the meeting she was sure would come. He hadn't traveled all this way to help the Fords. Not in this life. He'd come for her, and that was what had her spooked to high heaven. Bolstering her courage, Courtney stepped back and watched Tyler climb back into the wagon and drive away.

Chapter Nineteen

As Courtney entered the mercantile, she spotted Wil from the corner of her eye as he stepped from the alley beside the bank. Her breath caught. She slipped back out, not wanting to engage either Maude or Beth. If possible, she didn't want anyone to see what she was about.

Wil gazed at the bank's Christmas display.

Had he seen her and Tyler only a moment before? Knowing what she had to do, she took a deep breath, raised her chin, and strode unwaveringly toward the man who'd taken her innocence. He turned but didn't look surprised. A cunning smile appeared on his face, leaving no doubt he'd seen her arrive. Funny, she'd used to think his smile so handsome. A long coat she didn't recognize almost touched the ground. Buttoned against the cold, she couldn't tell if he wore his gun.

"Courtney, I've been waitin' on you." He put out a hand.

She halted far enough away to make touching her impossible.

His gaze narrowed. "How've you been?"

Hurt and anger pushed up her throat. Outguessing Wil was like predicting which way spooked cattle would run. She'd never figured him out, so why should she now? The sound of hollow hoof beats marked Tyler's wagon crossing back over the bridge, taking the calm she'd felt before. "How did you know I'd come? Maybe I don't want to see you."

"You always come. All I do is crook my little finger."

Heat scalded her cheeks.

"You're easy to read, Court. Don't take a crystal ball to know what you're thinkin'. Feelin'." He leered as he looked her up and down. "I can read you same as always, darlin'."

"Don't call me darling. I'm *not* your darling—and never will be again. If you thought of me as your darling before, you wouldn't have treated me the way you did. I was only a girl. I didn't know better." At the lie she flushed with shame. She *had* known but hadn't cared. She'd wanted to be wild to get back at the life that had hurt her. Destiny took her mother at an early age and was taking her father, too—leaving her and Adaline orphans. But she should be allowed to start her life over now and do better than she had. "I should have listened to my father about you. My sister as well. I should have stayed far, far away."

His eyes glittered and he chuckled. "But you didn't, did you? I was irresistible."

"You're a swine!"

"Ohhh, the princess has a bee in her bonnet, does she?" He stepped closer. "I love when you get mad; when you fight—you're never more beautiful..."

Frightened, she inched back, keeping him out of reach. Fear swelled in her throat. Wil didn't negotiate. And fighting fire with fire didn't work. He'd do and say what he pleased, not caring a whit what the revelation did to her reputation. One word from him and she'd be ruined. She needed to keep her wits about her. Not get caught in his web again. Combating this way would do no good. She needed to placate him. Appeal to his sense of fairness. Did he have a sense of fairness? She wholly doubted. The task felt totally impossible. If she didn't face him now in private, he'd track her down and not care who heard what he had to say.

Acutely aware of the townsfolk, she inched forward. She wished for someplace private they could talk. "Please, Wil," she begged, forcing a pleasant smile on her face. The expression felt weird and gruesome, so she looked away to gather her courage. "Please choose your words carefully. I'm just a girl. I need to live here, but I won't be able to if…"

Wil Lemon here in Logan Meadows was a disaster. Yes, he'd ruin her reputation and laugh all the while. She had no doubt. Even after he'd claimed to love her. And that he'd die for her. What she'd done with him would bring shame to Jake and suspicion on Adaline's character, even though her older sister was as pure as the driven snow. Hot moisture pricked the back of her eyes, but she'd not show him her weakness. She'd fight him with every last breath she had.

"I know exactly what I'm saying, darlin'. What the truth getting out would mean for you and your high-brow sister. Your brother and his new wife—the reformed soiled dove. My, my, this town does have some history. I've done my homework. Ask Daisy to give you some tips when you start serving whiskey and entertaining men in the saloon." His gaze turned hostile. "That is, if you don't do exactly as I say. Your sister never even gave me a chance. I wasn't good enough for you from the start, no sir. Not three ways from Sunday. Her heart'll break in two to learn her sweet little sister isn't quite so sweet." He barked out a laugh. "Don't worry, love, I like you well enough. And I'm anxious for you to fall back into my arms."

He stood there, boldly intimidating. Clearly enjoying the power he held over her. He knew how to cut deeply, and he wasn't holding back. She had to be very careful. Watch her every word from here on out. If she lost her temper, her world would never be the same. "You're right," she whispered. "I did have a change of heart." She glanced around to see if anyone was watching. If this meeting got back to Jake, he'd be furious. Had the two met? Talked? She didn't know if Jake would tell her. "Still, can't we be friends, Wil? Be nice to each other? For old time's sake? We once loved each other. Remember?"

He wasn't wearing a hat, and a gust of cold wind stirred a thick strand of dark hair into his eyes.

Her heart shuddered, and her fingers tingled to push the silky softness back into place. Once, they'd been lovers. She'd thought she wanted to spend her life with him. The memory conjured up a sweetness she thought long ago forgotten. He'd been her first love … her only love. As if they'd been spoken yesterday his whispered words came flooding back. She needed to be strong—for her family's sake. Forcing her gaze to the window, she studied the quaint little town Mr. Lloyd created in the bank, wishing she could command herself there, a place with no more trouble and no more tears.

"I remember. And I still love you. All you have to do is be nice."

Nice? She'd never be nice to him again, not in the way he wanted. Talking about their past made her mouth feel like cotton. She needed to steer the conversation to something else. "Have you seen Jake?"

"Not yet, but I'm looking forward to our reunion. I owe him something, and I mean to pay him back. I'm letting him get used to my being here, before we have our little talk."

Did Wil know about Jake's reward? Surely, he had to, if he'd traveled all the way from Newport with the Fords.

"I don't want to talk about Jake at the moment. Or the weather or anything else." He glanced at her midsection, letting his gaze linger. When his eyes met hers, the hunger was apparent. "I want to talk about you, Court. And whether you're carrying my child. A man has a right to know if he's gonna be a pa. You don't look any different."

"Wil!" She rushed forward, frantic with fear he'd speak so openly. Surely, he was enjoying her predicament. He couldn't care less about her. She'd better formulate a plan—and fast. "Please, if you've ever cared a whit about me, about my reputation, I beg you not to speak like that." From under her lashes, she glanced through the large bank window. A man stood at the counter with his back to her, speaking with the teller, a tall, thin young man who'd smiled at her a time or two since she'd arrived in Logan Meadows. He made eye contact with her now and then went back to his work. "Please," she hissed through clenched teeth. "Please, Wil, please don't say anything else. I beg of you."

He glanced around, his shoulders shrugged, and palms turned up. "There's that word again—*beg*. I kind of like the image. The picture I conjure up in my mind."

"Why did you come to Logan Meadows?"

"I just told you. I want to know if you're expecting."

"I'm not."

"In that case, I want to marry you."

Her throat clenched. *When pigs fly. You want to use me again. Be in control.* "You don't. You want to get back at my family. Hurt them through me." *Or get your hands on Jake's reward.*

Wil's eyes narrowed. "You and me had a good thing going. I want that again. Soon."

"Then you'll wait forever, Wil, because we're finished for good. Please, go back to Newport and leave me alone. There's nothing for you here. Dragging this out can only make the situation worse." She was cold. Frosty air bit at her face, and she shivered uncontrollably.

Wil shifted his weight from one foot to the other. "I can see you're set."

"I am. I won't change my mind. If you stay, you'll only find trouble. You'll end up in jail. Or worse. You have a life back on the coast."

He studied her a long time. "Fine. But you owe me for running off and embarrassing me in front of my friends. You made me a laughingstock, getting the better of me the way you did. Pay me a hundred dollars, and I'll go away forever."

A hundred dollars! "I don't have any money, Wil. You know that."

"Your brother does."

"I can't make a withdrawal. The reward is in Jake's name."

His eyes hardened. "Then *steal* some money. I don't care what you have to do. The ranch you're living at is top-notch. I did my due diligence. The Logans are rich. I'm sure you'll think of something." His smile broadened. "I'll give you a week, and if by then you don't come through, I'll spill my guts all over town. Tell everyone what kind of a girl you *really* are."

The air whooshed out of her lungs in one huge breath. She glanced past Wil's shoulder, beyond the Shady Creek bridge, and up to the feed store. Movement caught her eye. Tyler was still up that way, but he could return at any moment. "And if I do, you promise you'll go—for good?"

"You have my word."

His word? What was his word good for? Only ruining her life.

Chapter Twenty

With the four o'clock hour quickly approaching, Dalton leaned just inside the doorway of the Bright Nugget sipping a cup of lukewarm coffee as he watched Hunter traverse the room with a tray of dirty whiskey glasses stacked precariously lopsided. Greasy, bean-and-gravy smeared plates littered the bar top. The buzz of conversation competed with piano music.

Dalton contemplated his duty as judge with growing apprehension. He'd studied the display windows and what each and every business had to offer. The larger businesses—such as the El Dorado Hotel, the mercantile, the First National Bank, the Silky Hen, and the haberdashery—had gone to an enormous amount of work, and to his unstudied eye in the way of fashion and design, they all sort of looked the same.

Now, the smaller establishments were a different matter altogether. Dalton found those quite unique. The school's was simply a drawing of shepherds guarding their flock and placed in a window.

Lettie's Bakery, where he tasted her wares each time he went in, displayed a grouping of sketches she'd put together in a collage depicting the manger scene when Jesus was born. They were placed on a tabletop next to the window. One had to be careful on entering so a gust of wind didn't scatter them to the floor.

In the telegraph office, Abner Wesserman had created a Christmas elf from corn stalks and several lumps of coal. The Santa's helper lookalike sat leisurely on a stool labeled in red as the North Pole, gazing upon the world outside. Abner was a wealth of town information, and Dalton learned something interesting each and every day, a fact a newly hired deputy found very useful.

Now, on a different scale, Kendall Martin and Hunter Wade at the Bright Nugget had used their newly constructed performance stage as the focal point. Positioning a large chair in the center, one of the working girls dressed up as Mrs. Claus and sang, danced, or let the men sit on her knee and tell her what they wanted for Christmas—all for a price, of course. Proud as peacocks, the two saloon partners boasted the only live display—and one which earned a profit as well.

Dalton had walked the quarter mile to the train depot to see if Mr. Hatfield had gone to the trouble of setting up a display. He wasn't disappointed. In the center of the room, a train circled a knee-high Christmas tree. The track went through bridges and up and down several hills. Parked alongside was a miniature of a depot. The handsome black engine was done in great detail. With a tiny push, the brightly painted train cars—which included a coal car, two boxcars, one livestock car, a tanker, and a caboose—glided around the track, bringing the display to life. A person not taking delight in such a presentation would certainly be labeled a scrooge.

Earlier in the day, on his way to the haberdashery to visit Merryweather, Dalton watched a conversation taking place across the street in front of the bank between Courtney and the newcomer, Wil Lemon. At her look of agitation, he'd wanted to step in, but thought better of the intrusion. Later he'd seen him hanging out in the alley between the laundry and the telegraph office looking mighty bored. Now why would a newcomer have time to kill?

Lemon! That man gives me a sour stomach.

Roaring laughter came from the back of the saloon where Wil Lemon, Dwight Hoskins, and three other men were deep at cards. They'd been playing since morning, after the man's conversation with Courtney.

"Pssssst."

Dalton turned.

Adaline stood behind him just outside the doorway, bundled from head to toe.

Her blue eyes smiled a welcome. He hadn't seen her since last Wednesday, when the altercation at the Red Rooster had occurred. His unruly heart skipped a beat or two. Had she missed him? She sure had a way of brightening his day.

"Adaline." He set his coffee cup on a nearby table and stepped out onto the boardwalk and away from the door. "This is a pleasant surprise. Is there something I can do for you? Is there something you need?"

Her smile faded. "No, not really. Was just wondering if you'd learned anything more about Wil and when he might leave town. My sister won't rest easy until he's gone. I've barely seen her. She stays close to the ranch."

Not entirely. He'd not upset Adaline and tell her about the conversation between Wil and her sister this morning. No laws had been broken. "I've been watching him."

Adaline wrinkled her nose. "Any word from Sheriff Preston and Susanna? When will they return?"

"I received a message by courier. They're having such a good time they're staying on a while longer, since the town's quiet and we don't have any major happenings—except for Wil. I encouraged them to stay as long as they liked."

Her eyes sparkled and a small smile appeared on her lips. "And the longer Sheriff Preston stays away, the longer you have a paying job? Could work security have anything to do with your enthusiasm?"

"I never doubted you for a clever girl, Adaline. If Albert wants to stay away a year, then I'll be the first one to embolden him to do so. I won't deny I'm enjoying being deputy more than I can say."

She laughed. "Dalton, you're such a schemer."

He wiggled his eyebrows making her eyes dance even more.

"But on a serious matter, poor Violet hasn't been the same since she kicked Beth out. She stays in her room almost all day, and when she appears, she looks so sad. So beaten. I wish I could do something to cheer her up." Adaline looked down the street toward the mercantile. "Do you think Beth might apologize? I think hearing she's sorry for her cruel remarks would be a start, and maybe enough to do the trick."

"I have no idea about Beth."

A blush crept up Adaline's face. "Have you seen her in the store or about town? Where's she staying? I haven't heard."

He rubbed a hand over his jaw, realizing he'd forgotten to shave. By now, his normally thick whiskers must look plenty unkempt—or maybe dashing, by the way she was smiling at him. He'd delayed the wet, cold chore until the sheriff's office warmed—and then promptly failed to recall. "Maude came down with Albert's mail and told me Beth's staying in the small room in the back of the mercantile." He shrugged. "Hey, I heard about Jake's good fortune. The reward will set him up. I'm glad for him and Daisy."

"They're in shock. Mr. Ford wouldn't take no for an answer." Her gaze roamed his face. "How's the judging going? Have you been around to view the businesses to consider each one? I'd love to judge. I'd take a notebook and jot down my reactions to each. Makes recalling easier."

A wagon rolled by, followed by several riders. The town was alive.

"I have. But deciding between them might not be as easy as you think. Each display is so different, carefully constructed with so much thought, devotion, and hard work. I hate to dash anyone's hopes. Especially at Christmas."

"Dalton, everyone goes into the competition knowing the rules. Only one winner can be declared. Don't be so hard on yourself."

A gust of wind pushed her long skirt up against his legs, and he blushed. He shouldn't keep her so long in the cold. Huddled into her coat, she awaited his reply, her smile never dimming.

"Easy for you to say. Can I mention here, Frank, out of the blue, invited me to supper?"

She tented one brow. "So? He's just being nice to the new deputy."

"Maude left a basket of cookies on my desk. Her note only mentioned me and not Thom, although the three dozen could have fed half an army. I was embarrassed when he came in."

Her other brow joined the first.

"Mr. Hatfield offered me free train fare—if I was inclined to take a trip, and..." He pulled a pair of leather gloves from his back pocket and shook them at her. "Mrs. Harrell, at the haberdashery, said these were last year's style and wanted me to have them for free. Last year's style? Who cares about that? They're gloves! I tried to pay, but she became insulted. They're all bribing me, Adaline, so I'll proclaim their display this year's winner. Such tactics won't work. I can't be bought." He hitched his head back at the saloon. "Hunter and Kendall have said everything they stock is on the house. No brand is too good for Deputy Dalton. I've only ever taken coffee..."

Adaline had the audacity to laugh. Her eyes, sparkling with merriment, made him smile and his indignation evaporated into thin air. Her little red nose almost looked painful as she shivered like a leaf in the wind. "You find this funny?"

"I do. Nobody in this town thinks you can be bought, Dalton. There's not a more upstanding man around. The bank in Denver trusted you with a million dollars! That's a testament in itself. Just have fun with the competition. Choose the display that means something to *you*. One that touches your heart."

That was good advice. Her virtuous opinion warmed him from the inside out. She gazed at him in wonder. A progression of emotions crossed her eyes. He jerked his gaze and then realized someone inside the saloon had just hollered, and then a melee of voices erupted. He turned in time to see Wil Lemon and Dwight Hoskins tumble out the door and crash into the hitching rail, busting the length in two.

Horses galloped off.

The two men landed in the snowy mud with a thud.

Dwight scrambled to his feet just as Wil threw another punch. Both men were bleeding from the nose and other parts of their battered faces.

"Cheat!" Dwight shouted. "That last hand was mine!"

The two rolled this way and that, their fists flying, the sound of flesh striking flesh ringing the air. The men somersaulted together beneath two horses tied at the other hitching rail. One gelding pulled back, snapped his reins, and bucked all the way down the street. The other danced, his eye rolled in fear, trying to avoid the fighting men under his hooves. An excited cry from the children admiring the Christmas tree brought their mothers from the haberdashery at a run.

Hunter stepped out of the saloon to watch the show. Kendall followed, a whiskey bottle still clenched in his hand. Seemed as long as the Bright Nugget was safe, they had no problem letting the men fight.

Dalton stepped forward. "One more second and I'm gonna smack your heads together like quarry balls that need cracking!" he shouted.

Neither paid a lick of attention to his command which embarrassed him in front of Adaline. They continued to bash each other's brains while rolling through a fresh pile of horse manure.

Dalton grabbed Dwight by the back of his shirt, hauled him up, and punched him in the face.

Hoskins reeled several times on one boot heel, looking like an ugly ballerina, and landed facedown.

Adaline shouted a warning.

Dalton turned to find Wil advancing. Dalton pulled his gun, stopping Wil in his tracks. "Let's go, hothead," Dalton barked. "Time in a cell will cool you off. You and Hoskins need to learn a little respect for the law."

Hunter stepped into the street and pulled Dwight to his feet.

"Show's over, folks," Dalton called to the gawkers, feeling like he'd finally cut his teeth on the new job. "Go back inside and get warm. Nothin' more's gonna happen out here today."

Taking a second, he glanced around to find Adaline watching from the boardwalk, her hands gripped on the boardwalk railing. He felt taller noticing the semblance of pride shining in her eyes. She exhaled and a winning smile appeared on her sweet lips. She was an exceptional woman, he admitted for the umpteenth time. Smart, funny, beautiful. She'd make some man a remarkable wife someday. Too bad that man wouldn't be him.

Chapter Twenty-One

Later that day, Adaline, well-bundled against the cold, had just finished her two-hour shift at the haberdashery and walked brusquely toward the Red Rooster, thoughts of the warm fireplace swirling in her head. The street was deserted. Darkness had fallen, and the air was crisp. Delicate layers of ice covered any standing water in the road. Warm, golden light in the windows looked inviting.

A cup of hot cocoa sounded so good.

She contemplated crossing the street. Was Dalton still at the sheriff's office with Wil and Dwight? She'd like to stop in but feared he'd feel obliged to walk her home if she did. Instead, she pulled her coat more firmly around her shoulders and continued onward. The walk home didn't frighten her at all.

Movement caught her eye. Mr. Ling hurried her way. She thought the laundry man looked distressed but couldn't tell for sure in the darkness. As he approached, his eyes opened wide.

"Miss Costner!" The name practically tumbled from his mouth in a puff of frosty air. "Please, help. Baby coming."

Help? Mrs. Ling? What can I do? "I'll be happy to fetch Dr. Thorn for you, Mr. Ling. His office is right there." She glanced back. She'd just passed the small wooden building, but his window had been dark. Was the doctor out on a call?

"Bao wants no doctor."

The Lings were very private people. She understood how Mrs. Ling, Bao, might not want a man attending her. Most likely, she'd want a woman to assist with the birth. Adaline glanced at the buildings. Susanna came to mind, but she was in New Meringue. There was Hannah, but Adaline had heard she'd gone home early this evening, feeling poorly. Maude might be available, but Beth, who now lived at the mercantile, would surely want to come along. Putting up with her off-handed comments would be torture. Mrs. Harrell might be available, but she was squeamish about everything. Just the other day, a large spider on the Christmas tree display caused her to trip backward and fall to the floor with a thump.

Mr. Ling touched her arm. "Please, you help?"

Him touching her was unprecedented. "Yes, if I can, Mr. Ling. But I've never even seen a birth before. I won't know what to do."

"You can get Mrs. Hollyhock? She know Bao. She is a friend."

Of course! I should have thought of Violet first thing. "Right away." *I hope she'll come. I haven't heard more than two words out of her since the argument with Beth.*

Golden light spilled from the sheriff's office window like a beacon of hope. "Better yet, I'll send Dalton for Mrs. Hollyhock. He'll be much faster, and I'll come to your home to wait for Violet to arrive. I'll run to the sheriff's office right now."

Relief flashed across Mr. Ling's face. He gave a slight nod, turned on his heel, and was gone.

Adaline lifted her dress, dashed across the road, past the saloon, and clamored into the sheriff's office. At her noisy entrance, Ivan, stretched out before the wood-burning stove, lifted his head and blinked several times.

Behind the desk, Dalton bolted to his feet. "Adaline? What's wrong?"

"I need you to go to the Red Rooster and fetch Violet. Mrs. Ling is having her baby!"

Wil and Dwight watched from their separate cells along the wall.

"Mrs. Ling is having her baby," she repeated when he just looked at her. "I'll sit with her until Violet arrives. Can you go?"

Dalton strode to the rack for his hat and coat. "What about Dr. Thorn?" He shouldered into the thick, sheepskin-lined garment. "Wouldn't he be better? He's right here in town."

"She doesn't want him—since he's a man and she's very shy. She and Violet are friends."

"*Those* kind of people don't need help birthing," Wil called in the pause of conversation. He still looked half-drunk, and his face was dirt-stained and bruised. "They're like rabbits, multiplying every time you look away."

Dalton shot him a warning glance. "Shut your mouth!"

Wil laughed and rubbed a hand over his face. "Didn't mean no disrespect. How are *you*, Adaline? We haven't spoken since I arrived."

How she hated the vile man. Her stomach tightened just being in the same room. Once Courtney took up with him, she'd become secretive and combative. She'd shut out Adaline. "Don't talk to me. And leave Courtney alone!"

Scowling, Dalton strode to the jail bars. "You just earned yourself another day behind bars. Dwight'll be out in the morning— but you won't." He returned to her side and pushed on his Stetson, an angry scowl marking his face.

"Still on your pedestal, Adaline?" Wil said, barely above a whisper.

Dalton jabbed a finger toward the jail cells. "Keep talking and you'll spend Christmas here with me." He made a sweeping look around the room. "Thom will be here shortly, so don't get any wild ideas."

Dwight shook his head in compliance.

But Wil just stared back with a black, soulless gaze.

Dalton ushered Adaline onto the boardwalk.

"Please be careful around Wil. He's not like most men. He'd just as soon kill a man as walk away. He frightens me."

A crooked smile appeared on Dalton's lips. "Worried about me, Miss Costner? No need. I've faced much more dangerous men than Wil Lemon. He's nothing but a gnat under my thumb."

"A wily, malevolent, dangerous gnat, Dalton." She straightened her shoulders and nodded. "You do as I say."

"Yes, ma'am. Now, I'm off. I'll be back with Violet as quick as I can. I'll get the buggy from the livery. Hitching up won't take any time at all, and I'll get Violet back here quickly."

Adaline gripped his arm, suddenly very thankful she wasn't alone in this undertaking. "Thank you, Dalton. Violet is extremely fond of you. If anyone can get her to come, it's you. She's in a dark place. I feel so badly for her."

He nodded.

Then he surprised Adaline by reaching out to touch her cheek. The gesture was quick and seemed to startle him as well.

"Put away your worries. Violet will be at my side when I arrive. Now, run back to the laundry house and try to calm poor Mr. Ling. Those two are like peas in a pod. One without the other is unthinkable."

She gasped. "I'm not thinking anything like..."

He took her shoulders. "Neither am I. Just go, and I'll bring Violet as fast as I can."

"Thank you." She liked his warm gaze roaming her face. Would he ever think her more than a girl? She wished she could just tell him what was in her heart.

"All you had to do was ask, Adaline. No thanks necessary. Go on now." He gave a slight nudge. "You need to get back to the Lings'. By now, I'm sure Mr. Ling thinks you're not coming."

Chapter Twenty-Two

Violet had been inside the Lings' home a handful of times. She remembered the sparsely furnished room, the braided rug, and the scent of scorched linen that must cling to their clothes traveling from one building to another. Against one wall, a bright-red chest with ancient gold- leaf etchings caught her eye. A wooden stool with a curved, varnished black seat. At the back of the room stood a table, stove, and some cupboards.

Mr. Ling greeted her when she entered.

Lan, curled in one of the two cloth chairs, jumped up, ran to Violet, and threw her arms around her waist.

"Don't ya worry, little one. Yer mama'll be jist fine." Violet reached into her box and drew out a small bag of oatmeal cookies. "These are jist for you, child. Soon, ya'll have a babe to hold—so be patient." She wasn't a midwife, although she had been called on a few times to see an expectant mother through.

Lan leaned back and smiled into Violet's face. "Thank you. I like your cookies." Distracted, she took one and nibbled the edges.

Violet glanced over her shoulder at Dalton, who'd remained by the door when he'd entered. His hat dangled in his fingertips, and his brow crinkled in a concerned frown. "Ya best stay here, Deputy, whiles I go check on our mama." *Sure is quiet. I'm used to women screamin' and hollerin'. The silence jitters my nerves.*

Inside the bedroom, Bao was covered with a bedsheet. Her normally smooth brow was sweaty and creased. A loose bun kept her long, dark hair out of her face. Swallowed up in the bed, she looked like a girl. Her eyes were closed.

"Thank goodness, you're here," Adaline whispered, taking the box of remedies and setting them on the dresser at the back of the room. "Everything has been very calm so far. She hardly makes a sound, even with a contraction. I have no idea if anything is wrong."

"Wrong? Nothin's wrong. Pain starts, and the baby pops out. Couldn't be easier."

Adaline smiled. "That's good to hear." She turned for the door.

Violet caught her elbow. "I'm gonna need yer hilp, missy."

"M-Me?" Adaline sputtered. "But I've never— I thought…"

"You a fainter?"

Adaline shrugged. "I don't know. I've never delivered a baby before."

Violet narrowed her eyes. "Guess we'll jist hafta hope fer the best." She went to the bedside and smoothed the blanket over the woman's round belly, the hump resembling the award-winning melons Violet used to cultivate back in Valley Springs when she had her mercantile. Bao had grown over the last two weeks, and she was a small woman. The combination might spell trouble. A shiver crawled over Violet's skin. Childbirth was a dangerous process. A matter of life and death.

"Violet?"

Adaline touched her arm, making her jump.

"Is everything all right?"

She shook off the ghoulishness and gave a small smile. "Sure, sure, I'm jist assessin' the patient. Always good ta sit back and observe before jumping in with my eyes closed." *And taking time ta pray to our maker for deliverance for Mama and child.* She glanced around the small room, barely large enough for the bed, a nightstand,

and chest of drawers. "Stuffy in here. Can ya crack the window? We want the air ta be sweet. Good for the babe's little lungs."

"Should you do something? Examine her?" Adaline whispered.

The words tickled Violet's left ear. *Everyone expects me ta work miracles. Well, I ain't God.*

She turned to her small brown bottles. "I am, child, jist as soon as she awakens with another pain. I'll examine her then, and not a second before. Best she git as much sleep now as she can—preserve her strength, so to speak. No tellin' how long this birthin'll take. Sometimes days. A woman needs fortitude. Now, while we're waiting, and yer're willin', take these raspberry leaves and make a pot of very strong tea. The brew will help prepare her woman's muscles and slow bleedin', iffin any occurs. Hilps ta expel the afterbirth too—when the time comes."

Adaline stared at the shriveled black leaves Violet shook from the jar and into her palm. Unconsciously her brow furrowed.

"Ya gonna second-guess every step I make, girl? Because if so, I don't need that kind of hilp."

"Oh, no, I'm sorry. These just look so—*black.*"

"They're dried from summertime. Ya'd be black and stiff too, iffin I'd stored ya away in a brown jar with no light. They might be ugly, but they'll work jist the same. Now, light a fire under yer feet or I'll have ta call for Mr. Ling."

"Yes, ma'am!"

With that, Adaline left her alone with the sound of Bao's quiet breathing and her haunting memories from years long past. Violet had come to peace with them, because that was the only thing she could do. The past couldn't be changed. She'd done everything in her power to deliver those babes without heartbreak. But some things just aren't meant to be—and no one knows why except God.

Bao slept on, undisturbed, the blanket rising and falling with each breath.

Feeling lightheaded, Violet lowered herself into the chair. Most births were easy, uneventful deliveries—just long and painful. Sweet, pink, bright-eyed young'uns were the prize. Their skin soft and rosy. Their eyes as clear as a mountain stream in the springtime. She'd keep those memories in mind and chase away the dark ones. Nothing untoward would happen tonight.

Chapter Twenty-Three

In the kitchen alcove of the small Ling home, Dalton rested a hip against the wooden counter in deep thought. The bedroom was eerily quiet.

Tap Ling sat at the table, staring into a cup of tea he'd yet to taste.

Lan still rested in the chair by the door.

The bedroom door opened, and Adaline stepped out.

Her face was oyster-shell white and she held something in her hand. She was frightened. And why wouldn't she be? He was nervous as well.

Mr. Ling looked up.

"How's she doing?" Dalton knew from experience birthing a baby wasn't quick or easy. Strange how he kept getting thrown into similar situations over his lifetime. Once, when he was a delivery boy for the mercantile in Breckenridge, he'd taken a package a short way out of town and was greeted at the door by a red-faced, frantic woman, nearly scaring him to death. She begged him to run to town for help.

Then, back when he worked as shotgun messenger for Wells Fargo, a woman passenger went into labor. They'd stopped, and everyone exited the conveyance so she could give birth inside. With no shade in sight, the scorching sun beat down on the compassionless travelers, all men, who were none too happy being waylaid for hours in outlaw-ridden country. Thankfully, another woman was aboard. Dalton sat atop the stage, rifle in hand, baking in the mid-day sun, and kept watch. As long and as hot as those hours were, they didn't compare to the horrible sounds coming from inside. Each time the woman screamed, the horses trembled in their harnesses. Every person, including himself, feared she'd bring outlaws down on their heads. When the travelers demanded she be left behind to wait for another stage, Dalton held them off with a few well-placed bullets between their boots. No one would be kicked off *his* stage without due cause. Especially a defenseless woman and tiny babe. He'd been mighty proud to learn she'd named her son Dalton Braveheart McCann.

"No baby yet," Adaline responded to his question. "Violet's waiting until after the next contraction to examine her." She looked down at the crumpled black leaves she held in her hand. "I'm to make tea. Violet puts a lot of stock in her herbal medicines. She says raspberry tea will help."

Dalton lifted the kettle, finding a good amount of water inside. "This water is already hot." He gestured to Mr. Ling's cup then went to the cupboard. All the cups were tiny. They wouldn't hold enough to help a flea. "I'll run over to the Silky Hen for a coffee mug." He fed the woodstove with two additional logs and was gone.

The cool air bathed Dalton's moist skin like a welcomed splash into a cool lake. His nerves were strung tight. The town was quiet. Lanterns glittered behind drawn curtains. By now, Thom had been to the sheriff's office and wondered where he was. Dwight might have offered an explanation, but Wil certainly wouldn't. For the last three days, this was the time of the evening Dalton had pulled his chair close to the stove and read his detective manual until he felt sleepy— which was usually after one page. He'd much rather read a newspaper—too bad Logan Meadows didn't have one.

A few months ago, the Chinese uprising in Rock Springs was all anyone spoke about. Had tensions died down with the migrant workers and the whites? Had more Chinese been murdered?

As soon as he delivered the cup to Adaline, he'd take five minutes to return to the sheriff's office and let Thom know about Mrs. Ling and that he was remaining with Adaline for as long as he was needed. Entering the Silky Hen, he went straight to the kitchen, purposely ignoring the few diners so he wouldn't be sucked into a conversation. He didn't have a moment to lose. "I need to borrow this." He surprised Roberta when he plucked a clean mug from the shelf.

On his return trip, the older gentleman who'd arrived with Wil Lemon from Newport waved his arm from a table by the window and called him over.

Just what I don't need. All he could think about was Adaline's frightened face. "Mr. Ford." Dalton felt pressed for time.

"Deputy. I just wanted to say hello. We'll be leaving as soon as Allen feels up to another journey. My wife is anxious to have him back in San Francisco."

Dalton glanced around. "Where is your son?"

"Up in the room. He didn't feel strong enough to sit through supper. I'm taking him a tray when I've finished."

Impatience burned inside Dalton.

"I've had plenty of time to think. If Jake hadn't seen you, his friend, in the camp and risked life and limb, as well as his sister's, for you, I'd have never learned what had happened to Allen. You're just as responsible for Allen's good fortune as Jake."

Dalton held up his hand. In no way, shape, or form would he take any credit belonging to Jake and Adaline. "No, Mr. Ford, I'm not responsible, and I don't want any glory or thanks. Jake and Adaline were the heroes, not me." He glanced at the door, the cup in hand. "I'm off. Need to let Dr. Thorn know Mrs. Ling is giving birth."

The man straightened. "Oh! I'm sorry for the delay," he said quickly. "Then I must hurry. First, my wife and I don't have fluid funds available to give you a reward, as we gave what we could to Jake—but I really want to thank you in some way. You'll always have a job with me if you return to San Francisco. The foreman in my furniture company is retiring next year. Until then, you could learn the business and what's required to keep the place running well. You'll have a good salary and stability. We're indebted to you for the rest of your life. Or, if you like, I can refer you to some of my friends who own other types of businesses. I don't mean to boast, but I'm well liked, and my word carries weight. I have many, many connections. We can find you something to suit your interests. You'll be a wealthy man."

Stunned, Dalton just stared. "Thank you, Mr. Ford! I'll keep your generous offer in mind," he finally got out. He wouldn't take a reward, but a good-paying job was something else entirely.

"I'll leave my address with the hotel. If you decide to take me up on the offer, just send a post."

Dalton nodded and turned toward the door.

"Wait!" Mr. Ford called to his back.

Dalton glanced over his shoulder.

"I can save you a trip to Dr. Thorn's. He came to see Allen earlier today and began to feel unwell. He had a fever of his own and has retired. He's concerned about the rest of the town. Roberta told me her daughter went home early today as well. The doctor thinks the courier from New Meringue brought the illness. He's staying with the doctor."

Dalton suddenly recalled the message he'd gotten about Albert and Susanna staying a few days longer. He hoped they weren't in danger. Or little Nate, either. "I see. Thank you for letting me know."

As the door closed, Dalton heard Mr. Ford call, "Keep my offer in mind, Mr. Babcock. The door is always open. We need good, honest, and brave men like yourself to build up our growing city. If nothing else, we must stay in touch and…"

Once Mr. Ford got talking, he could go on for minutes without taking a breath. Dalton meant no disrespect, and he was certainly humbled and amazed by the offer. But all that could wait. He glanced at the blue-speckled porcelain mug in his hand, wondering how things were progressing, if at all, across the street.

Hurrying down the alley, Dalton stopped and stared at the quiet house.

No doctor tonight!

The front door opened.

"Dalton? Is that you? I thought I saw movement out here," Adaline whispered from the doorway. "Did you get a mug? The tea is ready."

He sucked in a breath of cold December air. "I sure did, Adaline." He strode forward with a smile. *I got the mug and a whole lot more bad news. No doctor. Influenza. But I won't share my revelations unless absolutely necessary. No one here needs to know no help will come tonight.*

Chapter Twenty-Four

Feeling bolstered now since Dalton had returned from across the street, Adaline headed for the quiet bedroom with a hot, strongly brewed mug of raspberry tea.

Finished with his errand, Dalton took on the task of entertaining Lan, distracting her with stories from his past.

Just the sound of his deep, confident tone brought relief, as well as longing. She'd done her best to catch his gaze and smile knowingly, as if they shared a wonderful secret, as Marlene had instructed. But he never seemed to pick up on her subtle hints. Marlene was the closest person she had to a mother. But she'd also been a saloon girl. Was she unintentionally leading her astray? Most of Marlene's words felt motherly, except for the seduction and get-him-to-want-you part. Adaline was conflicted.

Opening and closing the door quietly, she found Violet slumped in the chair, the same place she'd been when Adaline left the room. She looked old and weary. Dusky circles swagged beneath each eye. The long, gray hair Violet took such pride in was haphazardly knotted on top of her head, resembling a bramble bush. At some point, while Adaline had been out of the room, she'd donned a full-length, snowy-white apron, free of any crease, crinkle, or crumple. The garment covered her mulberry flannel dress almost to her shoes.

Bao panted. A light sheen of perspiration covered her face. The small woman gave a wobbly nod.

Adaline forced a smile and brought the tea close with unsteady hands. "This is for you, Mrs. Ling. Violet's tea made from raspberry leaves. It should help."

Grimacing, Bao wedged herself onto her elbow and cupped the mug with a trembling hand as Adaline kept a firm grip herself. Mrs. Ling blew on the surface for a few moments and then took several tiny sips. "Thank you." She sighed deeply. "How is Lan? Frightened?"

Adaline shook her head. "Not too much. Mr. Babcock is regaling her with stories from his past—but nothing too scary."

"Regaling?"

"He's a fabulous storyteller and is quite entertaining. He adds dramatic facial expressions and funny sounds. But she's tired. I'm sure she'll be asleep soon."

Bao's nod was so small the movement was almost imperceptible.

"And Mr. Ling? He is sensitive man." Her eyes smiled. "Worried when labor start. I am concern more for him than Lan."

"He's fine." *Men. What did they have to worry about?*

Using the chair arms, Violet pushed herself to her feet.

"So?" Adaline studied her old friend. "I haven't heard a peep from in here. Any contractions? And did you get a chance to examine her?"

"Yesiree," Mrs. Hollyhock finally said and winked at Bao.

Relief washed through Adaline. For a moment, she'd been fearful Violet had lost her wits. Now, she seemed back to her normal self.

"Checked a few minutes back. Everything looks dandy. This little lady is strong and productive—and quiet. I won't go into the details and shock ya, ya bein' a young girl still. Best I can figure, she's more than halfway there. Shouldn't be too much longer."

By the way Violet gnawed her lower lip, Adaline wasn't reassured all that much. Well, they always had Dr. Thorn if Mrs. Ling needed medical assistance Violet couldn't provide. And he was only two doors down. Adaline helped Mrs. Ling take more tea and then busied herself smoothing the sheet on the side of the bed. She snuck another look at her old friend. Was she feeling all right? Violet did know what she was doing, didn't she?

After a slow hour of intensifying contractions, she was sent out for more tea. She felt like a sleepwalker, stoking the fire and adding water to the kettle.

Dalton appeared at her side out of nowhere. A dark shadow stubbled his face beneath his concerned gaze.

Surprised, Adaline glanced around. "I'd thought you'd left an hour ago."

"I did. To tell Thom where I was in case he needed me. You walked right by me."

"What did Thom say about Wil and Dwight being locked up?"

"He wasn't there. He'd left a note. He's staying home to nurse Hannah, who isn't feeling well. The men don't need watching."

She nodded. "Yes, I heard about Hannah earlier today. I hope she recovers quickly. Where's Mr. Ling? Did he go out, too?"

"He's in with Lan. He put her to bed some time back, but she came out several times, asking for this or for that, worried about her mama."

"Who isn't worried? I know Bao is young and everything will be fine, but I'd just feel better if Dr. Thorn was here. Violet seems so distracted. And even unsure at times. It scares me."

Dalton gently took Adaline's shoulders and turned her toward him. "Women have been having babies since the dawn of time. And most of the time, on their own. Don't go looking for trouble, Adaline. Things'll work out."

She nodded but didn't reply. He was being kind again, brotherly. Why couldn't she just tell him how she felt? Why must she play silly, flirtatious games? Was she wasting her time? Getting her hopes up for nothing? She wished she could just be honest.

His brow tilted. "It's been quiet, I have to ask. Is anything at all happening in there? I haven't heard one scream or cry."

See? She was thinking of Dalton again, and Dalton was considering the situation at hand. Any chance of a romance with him was no use. "She's having contractions and labor is moving along, but she stays quiet. Violet says she thinks we're more than halfway there."

She could barely breathe at the tenderness blatant in Dalton's gaze. Did he still think of her as just Jake's little sister? Or had his thoughts gone other places, grown and blossomed into something else entirely, like her own?

"It's you who's valiant, Adaline. First breaking me out of a dangerous prison camp and now assisting in a birthing for the first time. I respect your fearlessness."

Her heart dropped like a stone. Respect? That's all she'd get from Dalton Babcock—respect and broken dreams.

Chapter Twenty-Five

Feeling trapped, Courtney paced the length of her bedroom for the fiftieth time, her mind numb with fear. The pretty quilted bed and the cheerful curtains brought her no peace. What in the name of heaven would she do about Wil? His ultimatum rang loudly in her head over and over. *One hundred dollars!* Acquiring that sum of money would be impossible. He hadn't been fooling. Was there any way out of this mess besides running away? When she'd discovered she wasn't with child, she'd been so relieved. She'd made a hundred promises to God on how she'd live her life from that instant forward. She'd be grateful for every single day. She'd never take another moment for granted. But now this! Wil had followed her. Once, she'd dreamed of being in his arms for love, now she contemplated going there again just so he'd return to Newport and leave her alone.

A soft tapping on her door made her turn. "Yes?"

"It's me, Jessie. I saw the light under your door."

Courtney had retired soon after the supper dishes were washed and put away, claiming a slight headache. Darkness had fallen and the house had grown still. She'd thought the children were already abed, and Chase and Jessie were quietly reading in the large room by a crackling fire.

Taking a calming breath, she went to the door. A moment of panic seized her when she realized she hadn't even changed into her nightgown and robe. She opened the door.

Jessie's eyes widened and then she smiled. "How're you feeling? Any better?"

She nodded. "I am, thank you." She remembered the sheet of paper on the desk listing the pros and cons of running away. "I was just, well…"

Uninvited, Jessie came into the room and softly closed the door. "If something is bothering you, Courtney, you needn't be frightened. You're safe here. And you're welcome for as long as you like. If you tell me, I might be able to help."

A moment of weakness descended. How nice sharing the burden of Wil's ultimatum would feel. If only she could pour out her troubles to Jessie. "I'm just tired," she replied weakly, hating herself for nurturing the ability to think up falsehoods in the blink of the eye. In that regard, she was becoming more like Wil every day. Perhaps the two of them *were* the same. He always said so. "Before long, school will start. I was almost finished in Newport, and I don't want to go back. I don't see the need to get my grade school certificate." Irritation at Adaline and Jake for insisting she complete her studies curled in her stomach. Why did they maintain her need of an education? She felt so different from other children. She was a woman now.

Jessie's face softened, and the worry lines on her forehead and around her eyes eased away. "Is that all? I thought something serious had happened. You barely touched your supper and hardly said a word. You need to slow your pace a little and quiet your mind. You've lost your father recently and moved to a new town. Do nothing more than sit in front of a nice fire with a cup of cocoa." Jessie glanced around the room.

Courtney feared she'd see her list on the desk and go to investigate.

"School will be fun. I was raised in an orphanage and never had much schooling. I wish I'd had a better opportunity. If you don't take the time now, you might regret your decision. As you grow older, other responsibilities take all your time." She gave a knowing look. "A husband and family."

Heat scalded Courtney's face. She knew Jessie had her best interest at heart, but her mentioning a family to her, after what she'd done, felt odd. No decent man would want to marry her now. Not if he knew her past. "You read and write so well."

"Thank the heavens we were taught our letters and the barest of numbers. Most of what I know now came from the reading I've done. I'd hate to live in a world without books. When I open the cover to a new story, a magic carpet appears to take me to some faraway land or different time."

"I already read and write well. And I'm good at math."

"All true. But Mr. Hutton's class covers history, geography, and how our nation is run. The laws. The Constitution. There's so much more to school than reading and doing sums. You only need one term to finish. Think long and hard before you decide not to go back. As you get older, you'll learn time seems to speed up. The months you have left probably look like an eternity to you now, but to me, I hardly lift my head from the pillow and soon the day is past and it's time to go to bed again." Jessie ran a hand down Courtney's arm. "Take the little time and graduate. You'll be glad you did."

Courtney listened carefully, all the while thinking she wished her only problem was whether or not to return to school. Even though she didn't fancy the idea, if the problem of Wil was removed, she'd happily sit through days of lessons without complaint. "I know you're right," she heard herself saying. "My father felt the same way. I've decided to go, Jessie. I don't want to let my family down."

"I'm so happy to hear that! Sarah would be very disappointed if you didn't. She's looking forward to sitting with you. Tonight, she said you're her big sister and wants to be just like you when she grows up." Jessie laughed softly. "She doesn't realize you're just a girl, too."

I am grown up, Jessie. And if you knew to what extent, you'd not want Sarah around me. Or any of the children of Logan Meadows.

"I won't keep you up any longer," Jessie went on. "Go to bed and get some rest. You have your whole life ahead of you—and whether or not to finish your schooling is just the beginning of all the decisions you'll have. Your future will look much brighter in the morning. My own mother, before she left me at the orphanage, used to remind me all the time: when the dark of night has your mind circling around itself, just think up something that makes you happy, something that makes you smile. In the sunshine of the new day, you'll feel better." Jessie smiled and quietly closed the door.

The click of the lock stabbed like a lance to Courtney's heart. If only Jessie's words were true. A bright, sunny day without Wil to threaten her. Facts were facts. She needed to come up with one hundred dollars or pack her bag and run off with him. Those were her options. How horrified Jessie would be when she learned the truth.

Chapter Twenty-Six

Bao's intensified panting signaled another contraction was imminent. Hours had crawled by painfully slow. Adaline didn't know how the slight woman kept on. Was something wrong?

With a length of leather between her teeth, Bao clamped down, her eyes squeezed tight. She moaned and writhed back and forth on the damp bedsheet darkened with sweat and blood.

Violet reached forward and gently swabbed the sweat from Bao's forehead.

"Should you check her again, Violet?" Adaline asked, exhausted and beyond frightened. The baby should have already come.

"Ain't no use. Ya'll know when she has ta push. I hope it's soon. This baby is taking his sweet time for being a second delivery. Not much can be done until the head crowns. Then jist put out yer arms and hope for steady hands ta catch the slippery little cub."

Bao gasped and then reached out a hand. "I must push."

Violet winked at Adaline. "Now I'll give her a little checksie. See what this youn'un has in mind." She went to the side of the bed, lifted the sheet, and leaned in close. A few seconds later, she lowered the drape and turned to her medicines on the dresser at the back of the room.

Adaline couldn't miss the tremble in her hands. She rushed to Violet's side and wispered, "What's wrong? What's happening?"

"That obstinate babe wants ta be born butt first. Must be a boy! Only other time I delivered a breech was a boy."

"Breech?" she whispered to Violet. "You can deliver a breech, can't you? Violet, you look frightened. Please tell me Mrs. Ling and her baby aren't in danger!"

Violet glanced up at the ceiling with a scowl. "Ya think this is some kinda joke ta play on ol' Mrs. Hollyhock, Lord?" she hissed out. "I'm not appreciatin' yer humor a'tall!"

Adaline grasped Violet's arm, fear clogging her throat. "What should we do?" she asked in a panicked voice.

Bao was bearing down.

Perhaps she wasn't supposed to just yet?

"Too many years have passed. I need hilp. I might have forgotten some things, but I do remember the noggin should come a'fore anything else. This way, the baby can get stuck. Doesn't take long for 'em *both* ta perish. Send your deputy for Doc Thorn while I try ta hold things off. Tell him ta hurry! I have ta put pride aside in this case. He knows more than I do."

With each word, the crinkly skin of Violet's throat wriggled reminding Adaline of a snake. "What about Bao's wishes? Mr. Ling said she didn't want the doctor."

"Got no choice! We have ta do what's best." She cast a secretive glance over her bony shoulder to the bed. "Look at her. She don't care if the whole saloon came through right about now—drunks and all. Our aim is ta get the young'un into this world alive."

Relief cascaded through Adaline. She'd be so thankful when the doctor took over. She turned and smiled briefly at Bao. "I'll be right back, Mrs. Ling. You're not to worry."

Bao was too busy moaning to respond.

Adaline scooted out the door and ran straight into Dalton's chest. He must have been listening through the door. His waiting arms closed around her. He held her for a few long seconds, allowing her to exhale the choking fear trapped in her lungs. He caressed her back, causing her to sink more fully into his embrace. His warm breath brushed her ear.

"What's wrong, Adaline? Has something happened?"

His soothing voice was all she wanted to think about. She was transported back instantly to the stormy night at the lighthouse. Where they'd talked and been so close. He'd asked her about her family and she'd shared the painful fact her father had died. She'd lost her heart to him then, although she hadn't realized until later. She drew back, gazing into his penetrating caramel-gold eyes, so unlike any other she'd ever seen. She glanced past him to see Mr. Ling at the table, his forehead resting on his forearm. "Yes," she whispered, trying to keep the alarm out of her tone. "The baby is breech. Violet is rattled and wants Dr. Thorn. She's asked you to fetch him as fast as you can. Their lives are at stake."

Dalton cast his gaze at the floor.

"Dalton?"

He slowly found her face.

"You're scaring me. What's wrong?"

"Dr. Thorn is sick. Several cases of influenza have erupted in Logan Meadows. He's one of them. Mr. Ford told me when I went to get the coffee mug. The doctor won't be any help."

She gasped quietly. "Maybe Violet's been depending on him all along, knowing he was so close, waiting in the wings. I don't know what she'll do. She looks so old, Dalton, and confused, muttering to herself, and keeps going to her box of herbs as if she'll find some answers there. What should we do?" She felt her panic rising.

Dalton steadied her, his expression resolute. "This is what we're doing—first, stay calm. Second, make a plan. Third, act accordingly. Mr. Ford might be wrong about the doctor. You know how gossip gets around. I'll go find out for myself. And if Thorn can't come, he can give some instruction."

"I won't tell Violet yet. I don't want her to panic."

"Good thinking." Dalton pulled her close one more time.

She thought she felt him kiss her head. Why? For luck, or something more? Time in life was fleeting. All too apparent, with poor Mrs. Ling facing more than the birth of her second child. Death could be near. And what about Violet, in her late eighties? No one lived forever. *Not one second of precious life should be wasted on insecurities and doubts. If I'm sincere in my feelings, I should tell Dalton. He can't read my mind. Maybe Violet and Marlene are from the old school, where one hides feelings and intentions. I don't want to be like that. Do I?* She clutched his arm as he turned to go.

He turned back.

"Dalton, I have something I'd like to tell you."

"Yes?" His gaze searched hers.

"I..." She faltered and began again, "I *love* you. Love you with all my heart. I have since the first night we met. You mean everything to me. My heart stumbles when you walk into a room. You're my last thought before I fall asleep and the first when I awaken. No man can ever mean anything to me, for you have captured my heart for all time."

His gaze widened. He blinked several times.

Her heart sank. She'd ruined any chance she had with him. What had she been thinking, to blurt out her heart? Especially at a moment like this. Feeling as if she was going to be sick, she held out a placating hand. "Please, you needn't respond. I just wanted you to know..."

To her utter disappointment, he took her at her word and didn't respond, just bolted out the door without even taking a moment to slip on his coat. A burning chunk of coal smoldered in her gut. Well, she'd gone and botched things now. Thinking she knew better, she'd done the exact opposite of what Marlene instructed. Feeling like the biggest fool on the face of the earth, she turned and reached for the bedroom doorknob.

Chapter Twenty-Seven

Unable to sleep, Tyler leveled himself up on his elbow and glanced around the pitch-black bunkhouse, listening to somebody snoring in the dark. The sound wasn't loud and seesawing like an old man would make, but a long snuffling and short sniff, enough to rouse Tyler and keep him awake. Chase and Jessie had been talking about expanding the building in the spring, so all the men could have their own small rooms. He'd be sure to remind them.

Falling back to sleep wasn't in the cards tonight, so he sat up and pulled on his denims, socks, and boots, making as little noise as possible. Crossing the room to the coatrack, he wrapped a warm woolen scarf around his neck and shouldered into his coat.

Outside, the crisp night air bit at his face. The moon was bright and not a snow cloud was in sight. With his palms resting on the porch railing, he took a minute to let the cobwebs clear from his mind. Inside the ranch house, a small glimmer of light winked several times, drawing his attention.

Interesting, because in an offhand comment one day, Jake had mentioned Courtney's bedroom had a side view of the bunkhouse, and she'd once waved a scarf out the window for fun. That small fact had played over and over in his mind, and especially so since he and Courtney had recently taken a few buckboard rides to town. He liked her, finding himself thinking about her every so often. Like now…

The question was, why was a lantern glowing in Courtney's room now? Was she sick? Or frightened of the dark? Had she been awakened by a dream? When the light blinked off, he straightened. Another window glimmered, as if she'd taken the lantern and was moving down the hall. His curiosity piqued, he stepped off the porch and walked closer to the house, being careful where he placed his feet. He'd not want to explain to Chase what he was doing creeping around the man's home in the wee hours of morning. No one took kindly to that behavior.

The light had disappeared. Had he imagined the whole event? Maybe she'd gone downstairs to the kitchen for water and, for fear of falling, had taken her lamp.

More likely, she'd blown out the flame and gone to bed.

Carefully making his way around the end of the house, past the shed where Chase stored his firewood and then an outside well, he pulled up. Courtney stood in the living room, looking like an angel in the golden light of the lamp. She wore a long robe and her hair was free around her shoulders. She stared into the glass case Tyler knew well. The same place Chase and Jessie kept their most precious mementoes.

The first time he'd been invited to dinner with the family, Jessie had shown him every item, taking them out and telling a story about each. An empty perfume bottle she'd received on their first Christmas sat on the top shelf. A sterling silver frame which held the first portrait they'd procured. Four twenty-dollar gold eagle coins, a portion of the first profitable sale Chase had made selling off his two-year-old stock, put in the cabinet as a reminder of the hard work of building the ranch. The value of those stood out next to a single rumpled bootie Jessie said was more precious than all the money in the world. She'd knitted the piece and its mate for Sarah when the child was just a baby, and they'd both lived in a New Mexico orphanage. Her eyes had brimmed with tears in the telling, and Sarah came close to hear, too, wrapping her small arms around her mama. A few other items were present Tyler couldn't exactly remember.

Courtney stood before the case, alone in the darkness.

What on earth is she doing? Surely, Jessie's done the same with her, sharing everything. Is Courtney after one certain item?

Is she sleepwalking?

When he saw her bend, set the lamp on the floor, and slowly reach forward, Tyler sucked in a breath.

With both hands, she worked the handle.

He suddenly wished he hadn't been so curious. Hadn't followed her around to the back of the house. He willed her to stop. Anything done under the cover of darkness boded ill.

As far as he could tell, Courtney hadn't moved. Should he tap on the window? Interrupt a weak moment? Stop her from making a mistake she'd no doubt later regret? He'd been taught at a very young age honesty meant everything. No clear conscience, no good night's sleep.

Whatever she'd taken fit in the palm of her hand. He waited, praying, wishing the next thing he'd see was her returning the article to the glass shelf.

She closed the case and lifted the lamp from the floor. A moment later, the light was gone.

In a panic, Tyler retraced his steps to the bunkhouse, not wanting to look back at the ranch house. Not wanting to see what he knew he'd see next. And right on target, her bedroom window glowed once again. He heaved a deep sigh. What now? What was he supposed to do with this information? He worked for Chase and Jessie and was loyal to a fault. But he cared for Courtney, too. What if she was just infatuated? Planned to return whatever she took in the morning, before anyone noticed? He didn't want to get her into more trouble than she already had hanging around her neck.

Chapter Twenty-Eight

"A fine kettle of fish," Violet grumbled as she closed the door to a sorry-faced Dalton. How dare Dr. Thorn get sick! Everything rested on her antique shoulders. "Adaline, quit lookin' like yer facing a hungry grizzly bear, twisting yer hands in front of yer skirt. We have things ta do!"

Panting hysterically, Bao stared at them with wild, red eyes. Sweat ran down her temples. Her face squished into a frown, and she bore down.

There wasn't a thing left to do but get to work. Taking a steadying breath, Violet flipped the sheet coving Bao over the woman's knees and looked closer. The smooth skin of the baby's buttocks was visible. "Well, little lady, yer boy is comin' out backwards—iffin I want him to or not. But we ain't gonna let his unique position bother us none. Scooch right down here," she commanded, not questioning Dr. Thorn's advice relayed by Dalton. She'd never heard of a delivery like this, but for once, she didn't feel the urge to dispute the wisdom. Taking Bao's arm, she and Adaline eased the mother-to-be to the end of the bed.

Bao's face was frozen in fear at this new position. "You do this before?" she gasped in between pants and grunts. "Baby comes wrong?"

"Nope, I sure haven't. This here's something new for both of us, but that's the way we're doing it," Violet replied with confidence she didn't feel. "I know ya want to push something terrible, Bao, but this youngster needs ta come slow, like pouring honey in December. Pant and don't push. Can ya do that?"

Seeing Bao nod, Violet was instantly transported back to the birth of her only child. The labor had been long and painful, but in the end, the midwife laid a perfectly formed little boy in her waiting arms. *My Tommy. Will I ever see you again?*

Adaline shook her arm. "Violet?"

"Stop pestering me! Can't ya see I'm busy?" She looked at Bao, whose cheeks resembled a squirrel's filled with nuts. "That's good panting, girl. Take some rest between breaths."

Almost instantly, Bao cried out again and bore down.

"Easy, now. Easy, now. Good, the butt end is out." The doctor's instructions flashed in her mind like bats out at sundown. "Now, the rest of ya can keep still!" Violet was barely aware of anything around her except the sight of the baby's hind end. Not Adaline or even Bao as the mother cried out in pain. "No pushes, not till I say so. I need ta get these legs out. No pushes a'tall." *Lord Almighty, hilp me now.* "Bite the leather if ya have ta push, nothing more."

Going slowly, Violet carefully hooked one scrawny leg with a finger and gently brought out the appendage resembling a chicken wing.

Behind her, Adaline sucked in a sharp breath.

"Don't ya faint on me, Adaline! I'm gonna need you." Expecting to hear a thump, Violet didn't take her eyes off the job at hand. "Keep holding back till I have this other bony limb, Bao. Puff, puff, puff. Like a train chuggin' up a hill." Feeling a little dizzy herself, Violet repeated the process.

When she saw the babe was indeed a boy, she straightened, feeling a tiny stab of jubilation at being right. "Jist as I predicted. No girl would ever come out butt first." She glanced up at Bao to make sure the mama had heard, but she was in the middle of the contraction, alternating biting the leather and puffing like a fish out of water. The months of Bao's pregnancy came flooding back. From dawn to dusk the woman worked herself to exhaustion without complaint.

"Shoulders are delivered. Hand me the towel." This was part she'd been dreading. Thorn had instructed her to wrap the baby so it didn't get cold and gasp while still in the womb. Any such act would be very bad. Then, to let the baby hang for a couple moments without support. Following direction, she slowly let the baby go.

If Adaline's gonna faint, now would be the time. I jist might faint myself.

"One, two…" Violet gently took hold once more. "Little pushes now, Mama. Time's come fir this young'un to be born." A wave of dizziness hit Violet, and she swayed to the side.

"Violet!" Adaline cried.

Bao was too busy breathing, gasping, and clenching the sheet to have heard Adaline's distressed cry.

The next instant, the tiny baby boy, as still and blue as death, laid in her hands. Remembering this part well, she grasped his heels, held him up, and swatted his bottom, bringing a howl of outrage. "That's what ya get for scarin' ten years off my life. I don't have that many left." A swift punch of pride gripped her, making stars dance before her eyes. She might be old, but she wasn't dead yet.

"Bao?" Mr. Ling called through the door in a shaky voice. "Bao?"

"Leave us be!" Violet snapped. "Things still need doin'. Cleanin', cord cuttin', and deliverin' the afterbirth, unless ya'd like to attend to her yerself."

Silence was her answer.

"Didn't think so. Ya'll be the first ta know when she's ready for visitors."

Thirty minutes later, with Bao back on her plumped pillows, Violet placed the cleaned and wrapped infant in Bao's waiting arms. "Ye've a fine, hungry son," she said, unable to keep a ring of pride from her voice. Perhaps she wasn't as old as she thought. "He looks as if he has no idea what jist happened," she said on a chuckle. "I couldn't agree more."

Chapter Twenty-Nine

Slumped at the bunkhouse table, Tyler rubbed his gritty eyes, having slept very little after last night's revelation about Courtney. The room was quiet. Everyone besides the cook was gone. His back and neck ached. A dull throbbing thumped his temples, worn out from the troubling thoughts dogging his heels all night. The vision of Courtney taking what he believed to be the gold eagle coins from Chase and Jessie's keepsake cabinet had left a burning hole in his chest. She wasn't *that* kind of a girl, was she? No matter how much she pushed people away, he wouldn't believe Courtney a thief.

Lifting his cup, he gulped down several mouthfuls of the strong brew Tater Joe, the bunkhouse cook, had set before him, doubting even the strength could chase away the cobwebs in his brain. He'd not like to tell Chase what he'd seen, but he did work for the man. Chase and Jessie had treated him well, enabling Tyler to care for his father and siblings back home. At every turn, the big-hearted couple treated him like family.

Since coming to the Broken Horn, he'd settled in Logan Meadows and made an effort to make friends. He liked living here. He owed the Logans his loyalty. Besides all that, eighty dollars, even without the sentimental value, was a hell of a lot of money! Why did she need money like that? Was she planning to run away? The gold eagles' absence wouldn't go unnoticed for long.

Tater Joe cocked his head as he leveled his gaze on Tyler from his spot in front of the enormous, cast-iron, almost-too-large-for-the-room stove. "What's got you down in the mouth, boy? You were fine when you hit the sack last night. Coffee too strong? My biscuits weighing heavy in your gut? What? Don't hold back on me."

Tater Joe's standard overalls were protected by a none-too-white apron; a raggedy leather jacket, stained black at the elbows and cuffs; and an old red bandanna folded into a narrow strip and tied around his head to keep his stringy gray hair out of his face. Looking at the fifty-year-old man could curb anyone's appetite—until you got to know him.

Belying the way he looked, Tater Joe was well-educated and quite articulate—having completed his eighth grade year. When he wasn't cooking and straightening the bunkhouse to a livable condition, he was reading philosophy. Books with three-inch-long words which made Tyler break out into a sweat. Tyler wondered how the man had come to cook for a bunch of hungry cowboys at the Broken Horn ranch. He never complained, even when the men did about his fare, and he never spoke of his past.

Tyler shook his head and gave a half-smile. "Nothin', really, Tater Joe. Just one of those nights. Tossed and turned. Didn't get much sleep." He looked down into his cup. He best not give Tater even an inkling or the man wouldn't quit until he'd heard the whole story—and Tyler wasn't ready to spill his guts quite yet. Not until he had a chance to speak with Courtney. Tyler had watched the cook fish information out of Gabe and Jake before. When he was on a mission, he stopped at nothing.

With strong movements, the cook scraped at the bottom of the iron skillet with his wooden spatula. "If you say so. I heard the door creak last night and got up to take a look. Make sure no grizzly hadn't snuck inside. You were outside looking at the moon. Or, at least, that's how you appeared. Was something else going on?"

Damnation! Tyler straightened. Had the cook seen more? Surely, he'd not keep anything back from Chase if he had. Not a robbery like that. If Tyler didn't speak up, the facts might appear as if he'd been in cahoots with Courtney. They'd spent some time together. Or maybe the blame might fall on him alone.

Tater set his spatula on the counter and wiped his hands on his apron. "Not rattling your cage, Ty. You look like you've painted yourself into a corner. I'm friend, not foe. Talking notions through sometimes helps. As my mama used to say, two brains are better than one." He pointed to his head and then at Tyler. "You agree?"

The tone meant look out. He wasn't through with Tyler just yet. Once the cook had an idea in his head, he was like a hungry badger— and hung on for dear life. He'd put on his ciphering hat and couldn't wait to dig in. "Sure, I do. My pa says the same all day long. Just, I don't have anything bothering me. Not a sin to have a restless night. Nothin' to be troubled over."

Tater Joe tented one brow. "If you say so."

The ranch hands were Tater Joe's family. Being older, sometimes he came down a bit heavy-handed with his concern. But most times he was good-hearted. Tyler wished he'd back off.

The door opened and Chase, of all people, strode inside, his jaw covered in the whiskers he'd yet to shave. Blowing breath into his reddened hands, he smiled. A leather jacket, but much longer than Tater Joe's, complemented his large frame and almost touched the floor. His boots, already wet stained, proved he'd been out to the corrals. He wedged off his hat and skillfully ringed a hook on the hat rack, making the headpiece twirl several times before slowing to a halt.

"Mornin', Tyler. You're just the man I wanted to see." He glanced about, then leaned to the side to see into the long room which held all the single beds. "Gabe already out and about?"

"Sure is. Went out early." Tyler had finally fallen asleep around four, only a half an hour before Gabe rolled out of bed. Soon after, the rooster had begun to crow and sleeping was impossible. The scent of bacon drifted around, followed by coffee. This was a day he'd operate on little sleep and fall into bed the minute the December light faded over the hills. Nothing would wake him then.

Chase shrugged and straddled the bench. "Fine. I'll speak with him later." He glanced over to Tater Joe at the stove. "Any coffee left?"

"I'll pour you a cup."

"Thanks. The coffee out here has more of a kick than what Jessie brews. I can use that today."

Within moments, Chase had wrapped his hands around the large porcelain cup. "Tyler, I got to thinking this morning. I never got back to you on your request for a few weeks off—so you could go home and see your family. I have no objections. The ranch is buttoned up until spring. You're welcome to go and return around March or April. You'll always have a job at the Broken Horn."

Tyler glanced up, his thoughts elsewhere.

"You still thinkin' about goin' home for Christmas?" Chase asked. He took a large slurp of his coffee, his eyes twinkling.

Chase was in a jolly mood. With all the happenings in town of late, Tyler had forgotten about his request to go home for a short while. He missed his younger sisters and brothers. Being the oldest, he was protective, liking to know what was happening in their lives. In short, he loved them—just like Jake loved his two sisters he'd just gotten to know a short time ago. Going home at Christmas would be nice—would've been nice. Now he wasn't so sure. "Uhhh, yeah. Still thinkin'..."

"Just thinking? Well, you're free to go. I hope you'll return in the spring, though. I don't want to lose you. You're a darn good hand. And who knows how long Jake's gonna want to stay on? He's married and fixing up the place on Shady Creek. The Broken Horn won't run itself."

Tyler sipped his coffee thoughtfully, feeling Tater Joe's hot stare on his back. The cook was hoping to prove himself right with the answer he'd give Chase. Tyler should tell Chase about Courtney immediately—but he didn't have the heart. Could be she'd changed her mind last night, after Tyler had gone inside the bunkhouse, and returned the coins. That *was* possible. He owed her at least a chance to set things straight before saying anything. After which, if she refused, he'd go to Jake first and then Chase. Even though he'd circled around to his conclusion, this plan stuck in his craw—being he never told a lie or broke any laws—he followed the rule book. Honesty was everything. "I'd like to go, but not until next month. Too close to Christmas now."

Chase's face fell. "I'm sorry! I know how much you wanted to spend time with your family." He rubbed a hand over his whiskers.

Tyler couldn't let Chase believe his late response to his request was the reason. Especially after the lecture he'd just given himself about honesty. "Naw, better this way, Chase. Even if you'd told me four or five days ago, I'd come to the same decision." He thought of Courtney and her taking the coins from the cabinet. But then the image in his mind changed, and he was holding her in his arms. Staring into her eyes. Heat warmed his face, and he glanced away. Courtney might be in trouble. Now was not the time to leave the Broken Horn, not while she was making life-changing, stupid choices. "Goin' would've been nice, but now, with Christmas only twelve days away, I have a hankering to spend Christmas here in Logan Meadows. The place is beginning to feel like home. The trip back to the Dakotas will happen when it's supposed to."

Chase nodded and took a drink from his mug. His gaze slid over to the cooking area. "You want to give me some suggestions so you don't end up with a doll for Christmas, Tater Joe? Sarah is set on giving *her* Tater Joe a present. I've heard ribbons, dolls, and even a kitten being discussed. Jessie's trying but not getting far. Help us out here, will you? Jessie and I are at our wits' ends."

The cook's face brightened. "She sure makes the sun shine on a rainy day. Don't know why she's taken such a liking to an ol' crustacean like me, but I'm not complaining. Her voice is like a flock of sparrows and twice as squirrelly."

Chase laughed. "Could be your sourdough flapjacks, if you were to ask. But I'm not. She likes you. Any ideas on a gift?"

Tyler sipped his coffee, thankful the conversation had drifted elsewhere. Surely, Chase couldn't have discovered the disappearance of his coins. He'd never be this happy. And what of Tater? Did he know and was testing Tyler to see what he would do?

Tater plucked at his dirty apron and examined a few stains. "I could sure use another one of these, so I don't have to wash so often. I can't stay clean for long."

Didn't look like the garment had ever been washed.

Chase brightened. "That's a darn good idea. And easy enough for Jessie to sew up before Christmas. She told me not to leave the bunkhouse without some ideas straight from your mouth. She and Courtney left early this morning for town. Got word Mrs. Ling gave birth and are taking the family a meal." He shook his head. "Those women keep this town running smoothly, I can tell you that. Now I just need to figure out what to give my *wife* for Christmas. She says not to give her anything, but that's no fun—and I know from years of experience, she really doesn't mean it. Come Christmas morning, she's as excited as the children, maybe even more. I need to make her see how much she's changed my life. Before I met Jessie, I was a tumblin' tumbleweed."

Chase's voice had grown softer with each word until he was mumbling. He smiled into his coffee cup, lost to good memories. He looked up and nodded. "It's true, fellas. She turned my life around. Made each day worth living."

The door banged open, and Gabe entered, his face wrapped in a wool scarf, his long chestnut hair whisking back and forth on his broad shoulders. He held up a large, caramel-colored rabbit, the white tips of the thick winter pelt glistening. He was making a rabbit muff for Julia's birthday at the end of January. His plans were about all they heard about when the bunkhouse settled down for bed. Smitten, Gabe planned to ask for her hand on Christmas Eve.

"Rabbit stew for supper, anyone?" he asked, his joyful voice hampered by the scarf. "With this last pelt, I can make a matching set of earmuffs." He unwound the scarf from his face, exposing a wide smile full of straight, white teeth.

The men exchanged pleased glances, unaware a crime had been committed the night before. Had Courtney taken the stolen money into town? Was she buying Christmas gifts, or something for herself she'd seen and couldn't resist? He'd best get moving and find out. Someone needed to save her from herself before she dug in any deeper.

Chapter Thirty

"**W**e were so pleased to hear about the baby." Jessie reached forward and carefully moved aside the soft blanket to reveal the baby's face. "We came as soon as we got the news." She made an adoring sound in her throat. "He's so sweet. Look at all his hair. Has he been awake much? I know how sleepy a newborn can be. Or loud and fussy. Which is your son?"

Courtney took in the scene in Mrs. Ling's bedroom. Jessie stood at the side of the bed, admiring the baby cradled in her arms. Lan was tucked contentedly to her mother's side, and Mr. Ling had vacated to the front room as soon as Courtney and Jessie had arrived. Sarah and a surprisingly quiet Shane stood with Jessie, being very well-behaved. Adaline looked exhausted and stood beside Courtney. Mrs. Hollyhock snored softly in a chair in the back of the room. According to Adaline, Dalton had stayed the entire night and only left the hour before. The room was warm and cozy and smelled like spiced orange and cinnamon.

"He is both, Mrs. Logan," Lan spoke for the first time with a wide smile. "He lets us know when his tummy is empty. He can howl louder than a pack of coyotes."

Jessie laughed. "I remember those days." She glanced down at Shane, who was still taking in the scene with awe.

"I'm amazed, Adaline," Courtney said quietly to her sister, alarmingly aware of the gold eagle coins wrapped in her handkerchief and tucked away in her skirt pocket. The whole ride into town, seated in the jiggling wagon, she'd been frightened as well as miserable. Beside her, Jessie hadn't an inkling to what had transpired in the night. What would happen when somebody discovered the coins gone? She was easily the only suspect. "You helped deliver a baby!" When Adaline looked her way, she smiled. "I'm so proud of you. Were you frightened?" She hadn't seen Adaline for several days. She missed her sister and wished they lived together as they'd done back home in Newport before their father passed away.

"Frightened? I was terrified." Adaline responded. "But when Mr. Ling begged me to come to his house, what could I say? If I'd turned him down, I'd never forgive myself. Violet did everything, really; I was just here as a second set of hands. Which does come in handy in a situation like this." She gave a soft sigh while staring at the mother and new babe. "But seeing a birthing was exhilarating, too. The beauty still leaves me numb."

Courtney studied her sister's profile while Adaline watched the conversation between Jessie and Mrs. Ling. How she wished she could fling herself into her sister's arms and pour out her heart. She'd made so many mistakes in her life and, with the stolen coins in her pocket, was about to make more. She could never tell Adaline everything. Her heart would be broken. "Well, by all those smiles, you did a fine job. You should be proud. I don't think I could have done the same."

Adaline turned to her, her eyes bright with surprise. "Of course, you would. I know you, Court. You're the strong one between us. You always were and always will be."

Why did Adaline always think the best of her? Shame strangled her throat. If Adaline only knew how wrong she was. Courtney wished she could share her burden but knew she never would. To get the truth off her chest would be such a blessing—if only doing so didn't mean risking her sister's love.

The sound of the front door opening and closing made them both look to the open bedroom door.

"I just heard the news." Daisy breezed into the room, a small lavender blanket draped over one arm. She hurried to the bedside beside Jessie. Leaning close, she gazed at mother and child. "How adorable. What's his name?"

"Ying," Bao said softly. "Means intelligent. Clever." Her loving regard never left the child's face.

Courtney blinked several times but didn't smile. *Ying Ling?*

"A perfect name for a perfect little prince," Daisy replied without missing a beat and placed the unwrapped gift on the bed beside Lan. "Congratulations. I'm so happy he's finally arrived. Jake brought me the news and I had him bring me directly to town. How do you feel, Bao?"

A small smile appeared on Bao's lips. "As light as air."

"I'll bet." Daisy looked between Jessie and then back at Adaline and Courtney. "And you, my dear sister-in-law, helped deliver this little rascal. How wonderful is that?" She giggled and glanced again at the sleeping child.

"She might feel light, but she had a difficult time poppin' him out." Violet had awakened and stood just behind Courtney and Adaline, watching the women coo over the baby. "She's not gettin' out of bed until the doc is feelin' better and has a chance to examine my work."

Bao shook her head. "I have work. Will be up tomorrow. Must keep up. Feed family."

"You'll do no such thing." Jessie looked between the four other women in the room. "You're not to worry about work for one second. We'll help out in the laundry house until you can come back. When I work, Courtney can look after Sarah and Shane, and vice versa. We'll make a schedule." Everyone nodded.

"She's absolutely right, Bao," Daisy added. "I'll be here when I'm not at the restaurant. And I'm sure both my sisters-in-law can help, too."

Adaline went to stand by Daisy's side.

Courtney followed her over.

"She's right, Mrs. Ling," Adaline agreed. "I'll be happy to take some shifts when I'm not at the haberdashery. I'm only working part-time. We'll all help Mr. Ling keep up with business, so you don't get behind." She glanced at Courtney.

"You can count on me as well, Mrs. Ling. As long as someone shows me what to do."

"Marlene can do that," Daisy said. "Jake's mother has been working for the Lings for some time and knows all the ins and outs. There won't be a problem with instruction."

"No, no." Bao held out a hand. "Mr. Ling not want charity. He won't like."

"He will *this* time—unless he wants to deal with me," Violet commanded. "I won't hear another word of protest." She grasped the chair back and straightened. "And thankee to all you good-hearted, God-fearing women. Humbles my soul to be among ya," she said, gazing first to Jessie, then Daisy, Courtney, and Adaline. "I appreciate everyone jumping in ta help without being asked. This little lady needs ta rest and heal."

"I have nothing to do at the moment, so I'll stay with Bao," Daisy said. "Violet, you and Adaline need to go home and get some sleep. And I'm sure Jessie and Courtney have errands."

A shouted string of curse words from outside interrupted the conversation, making all in the room look around. The children started for the door.

Jessie caught their shoulders. "You stay right here."

"We'll take a look." Adaline gestured for Courtney to follow.

The living room was vacant, Mr. Ling having gone over to the laundry house. They hurried down the alley. On the other end of the street, in front of the sheriff's office, Dalton stood with Dwight Hoskins, having a conversation. They didn't look angry with each other. "I wonder what's going on," she said, watching the two men.

More shouting sounded from inside the jail.

Adaline took a breath and twisted her lips. "I should have known he was behind such language. That's Wil cursing from inside his cell. He and Dwight were locked up for fighting. When I went to fetch Dalton yesterday for help with Mrs. Ling, Wil besmirched the nice Ling family. Dalton threatened to keep him jailed a day longer because of it. And true to his word, Dwight's going free, and Wil is remaining. You stay clear of him when he gets out, Courtney. He'll be angry."

A million thoughts flashed through Courtney's mind. How could she speak with Wil locked up in the sheriff's office? She felt the slight bulge of the money in her pocket. Heat behind her eyes prickled and fear made her heartbeat quicken. She wished she could run back to the ranch and replace the coins to their rightful place.

But she wouldn't. Paying off Wil was the only way. The only way to get rid of him forever. Why wouldn't he let bygones be bygones?

"Wil has the filthiest mouth I've ever heard," Adaline said, her mouth twisting. "I'll be relieved when he's gone." She glanced over at Courtney.

Courtney didn't miss her sister's disgusted tone but kept her face expressionless.

"Court, are you all right? You look pale."

"I'm fine. And I feel the same as you. The sooner he's gone, the better. I'm sorry he's giving Dalton so much trouble. I feel responsible."

Adaline whirled to face her. "Don't you dare say that! You're not responsible for anything he does. Nothing, do you hear me? You did your best to be rid of him when you left Newport. He followed you, not the other way around. Dalton will make sure he doesn't bother you. Just stay clear of him, at all costs. Do you hear me?"

Courtney nodded, knowing the moment she left Adaline's side this morning, searching him out would be the first thing she did. If she could. See if he'd take eighty dollars instead of one hundred and clear out as soon as he was released. If he wouldn't, she really didn't know what she would do. If he persisted in his threat to ruin her life, he'd also ruin Adaline's. And Jake and Daisy's. Courtney couldn't let him do that.

"Come on." Adaline took her arm. "Let's go tell the others the shouts were nothing to worry about. We have plans to make, with working in the laundry and the approach of Christmas. I like living in Logan Meadows now, Courtney. Actually, more than that. I've already come to love the town. So many good people looking out for us. After years without our mother, the kindness feels nice. We're lucky how our lives have changed for the better. Are you adjusting to living here?"

Courtney couldn't do anything else but nod. Her life was in a shambles, without any hope in sight. She sighed and smiled. Turning to follow Adaline up the alley, she spotted Tyler riding slowly up the street. His gaze stationed on her. They'd spent some time together, and she couldn't deny to herself she'd enjoyed his company and conversation. By the time he reached her side, Adaline had already disappeared down the lane.

"Miss Courtney." He touched the brim of his brown Stetson.

He appeared larger than life, gazing down at her from the saddle. Bundled in a thick coat and leather gloves, he was quite handsome. Something was different about the way he was looking at her.

"I heard Mrs. Ling had her baby last night," he said after a moment. "How're they doing?"

Courtney swallowed and glanced at his horse's hooves, thankful for the question breaking the connection when their gazes caught. "Very well. A boy. Healthy and hungry. *Ying* Ling. Ying means intelligent and clever." She rubbed her hands up and down her coat sleeves. She'd run out without her gloves and was more than a little cold. When he didn't ride on, she felt conspicuous. Did he want something?

"What brings you to town so early?" asked Tyler. "Weren't you here yesterday? And yet, if I recall correctly, you went home empty-handed…"

His probing gaze roused her anger. What game was he playing? "You know I was, being I hitched a ride with you. Question is, what brings *you* into town so early on this chilly morning? Did you forget some supplies?" She reached out and stroked Dakota's velvety-soft muzzle. She liked horses—most especially this one. She'd had a chance to get to know the gelding at the ranch. An appaloosa, or so Tyler had told her. The dark bay had a snowy white blanket over his hips and hind legs, sprinkled with different-sized dark spots. His unique markings reminded her of a springtime robin's egg. She loved the gelding's kind eyes. Horses didn't judge people. They didn't expect you to be perfect, either. They couldn't care less about your past mistakes. "Well, Mr. Weston?" She smiled to soften her words. His eyes narrowed, but not in a mean way. A curious way, like he was working a thought over in his mind.

"Nope, didn't forget any supplies. Just not much doing at the ranch. I'm here on a personal reason. I actually came in to speak with you."

Me? He wants to talk with me? Why? Does he know I stole the money from the Logans? Her pocket felt especially heavy. "I can't imagine why. You could have waited until I returned. Is the subject matter so important?"

He lifted one shoulder. "Not sure. Well, I hope not. You want to go to the café and get a cup of coffee? You're shivering from the cold. I don't want you to get sick because of me."

Fear of the unknown, more than the cold temperature, was making her tremble.

"Courtney?" Adaline called from the Lings'. "What are you doing?"

She turned and saw Adaline at the end of the narrow alley, gripping the lapels of her coat with one hand and the other stuffed in her pocket. Her brows were drawn into a frown.

"Be right there, Adaline." Relieved she had an excuse, she waved to her sister and then turned back to Tyler, all smiles. "I'm sorry. I can't now. We're making a schedule to help Mr. Ling at the laundry so Mrs. Ling needn't return to work so soon."

He nodded. "We can talk in an hour. I'll go stable Dakota at the livery and meet you at the restaurant. Take all the time you need. I'll keep busy till then."

His determined gaze made her stomach twist tighter.

"Will that work?" he asked. "I'd rather speak with you here in town than out at the Broken Horn."

Another bolt of fear. *He knows! He knows!* Without any other way to avoid him, she nodded.

He gave a quick smile and touched the brim of his hat. "Thank you, Miss Courtney. I'll see you at the Silky Hen." He reined Dakota and the horse moved off with ease.

What had she gotten herself into today? She was sinking deeper and deeper into quicksand. She had nowhere to turn. The only thing she could do was speak with Wil and make him understand. Get him to agree to leave town without saying anything about her. Would he comply? That wish was as likely to happen as her turning back into the innocent she'd been before they'd met.

Chapter Thirty-One

Dalton sat at Albert's desk, thumbing his way through a *Farmer's Almanac* and thinking of everything except the book in front of his face. Finally closing the volume, he gazed at the cattle and hogs sketched on the front cover. A dull ache pushed painfully between his shoulder blades, and his gritty eyes stung from lack of sleep. Resting his forehead on the palm of his hand, with his elbow braced on the desk keeping everything up, he strained to remember each and every word Adaline had said. He'd been tired. Maybe he'd misunderstood? Or read something more into the meaning of her words? He wasn't sure, but for some reason, he wanted to recall every last syllable.

Adaline was little more than a *girl*! Seventeen, just three months ago. Eight years separated their ages. If she were somewhat older, say twenty, the eight years would be nothing. But barely seventeen? What were her dreams? Aspirations? He had no idea. She was as smart as a whip and should go to college. With the proper education, she'd go places. Places larger than Logan Meadows. She didn't need a jobless husband with no future hanging around her neck. He'd saddle her with a houseful of young'uns and then, in ten years, after her dreams were squashed and she was exhausted from working day in and day out just to get by, she'd regret her mistake. He couldn't live with that. She was mixed up. They'd shared some dangerous days back in Newport when Hexum's men wanted them dead. And then a stressful experience last night.

Jake would have a fit! He hated Wil Lemon for going after his young sister. How would he and Adaline be any different?

Do those facts explain my feelings, too? Am I only infatuated? Adaline is the first woman to touch my heart since Susanna. Granted, Susanna wasn't long ago. Still. I think of Adaline day and night. I may even love her.

Damnation! He was in a pickle.

At the moment, Adaline was probably rocking darling little Ying to allow Mrs. Ling a few moments of sleep. He, on the other hand, had released Dwight Hoskins and told him to beat it back to New Meringue and not to come back until he found some respect for the law. Dwight had been contrite and bore the dressing down in silence. The night in jail had cooled him considerably.

Feeling the short hair on the back of his neck prickle, Dalton glanced up without moving his head.

Wil Lemon glared from the cell across the room.

Probably still furious to be behind bars. If Wil thought he'd forget the disrespectful outburst yesterday about the Lings in front of Adaline, he was plumb crazy. Keeping him one more day, where Dalton knew his whereabouts, felt right.

With a bang of the door, Maude burst into the sheriff's office amid a flurry of snowflakes. Earlier this morning, a bank of dark clouds had crept across the darkened sunrise and shortly thereafter a few snowflakes had begun to fall, pushed around by blustery gusts of wind. The beloved ornaments on the tall town Christmas tree bounced and waved, clinking together dangerously. Snow drifts had begun to build against the buildings. A thin layer accumulated on the boardwalks, leaving tracks whenever anyone walked by. Snowflakes skittered across the office floor all the way to the small rug where Ivan slept.

The dog lifted his head to see who'd entered but didn't get up.

Maude pushed the door closed with her back and smiled. She was bundled in a thick coat, with gloves and scarf. Black boots poked out beneath the hem of her garments.

She gripped a basket to her chest, much like the one she'd left the other day along with a note inviting him to visit her store. More goodies for him, he presumed.

"Why, Deputy Babcock, I'm so happy to catch you here. I stopped by yesterday evening, but you were out." She glanced at Wil Lemon, slumped in his cell.

"You've found me now, Maude. What can I do for you? Cup of coffee, maybe?" He really didn't want to make small talk—especially with Maude; maybe with Thom or Albert, if they were here, but anything to keep him from dwelling on what Adaline had gone and said was welcome.

"I just wanted to bring these by." She held out the basket. "Fresh from my oven. I'd never want you to go hungry—you being our law for now. I need to fatten you back up to your previous weight when you were in Logan Meadows before, with the train of money."

Must she remind him every time they talked? He missed his weight as much as she did, and yes, he felt different, less effective. But in cold weather like this, when his body was using fuel to stay warm, bulking up took work.

"You look almost like a scarecrow."

A deep chuckle came from the cell that Dalton ignored.

She brought the basket to his desk and snatched off the red-and-white-checked napkin with a flourish.

He stared down at a variety of cookies and bars. "Thank you, Maude, but there's no need." He stood, went to the back of the room, and retrieved her other basket, now empty of the chewy cookies he'd consumed with pleasure. "Here you go. And you best take these others as well when you go—even though I know your heart is in the right place, we wouldn't want anyone to think you're buttering me up."

Her mouth dropped open at the same time she raised a hand to the neckline of her coat. "Butter you up? What on earth do you mean? I'd *never* do a thing like that."

He quirked one eyebrow. "No?"

She shook her head. "What would be my aim?" She set her chin in a stubborn line.

He reached around to his back, where the dull ache he had earlier was now a full-blown pain, and pressed a thumb between his shoulder blades. "Mr. Hatfield offered me free train fare," he said. "Frank, a hot supper. Hunter and Kendall, drinks on the house anytime I want." He smiled, softening his words. "Need I say more?"

She gasped. "What! Those scoundrels! They're bribing your affections. They should be…" She snapped her mouth closed and glanced at the snowflakes pattering against the window, a dark hue creeping up her wrinkled skin. "You don't think that of me, do you, Deputy? I'm bribing you so I'll win the Christmas display contest?"

She looked as if she were facing a walk to the woodshed. He almost smiled. "No, I'm not accusing you of anything, Maude, but you can see how this might look to others, can't you? Two baskets in a few short days?" Lifting the sweets off the desk, he handed the basket back. "I'm sure you can find someone else who might like fresh cookies."

"I would."

They both looked at the jail cell.

Wil stood at the door with both hands wrapped around the bars. A moment of pity tried to grasp Dalton but didn't quite.

Maude glanced at him. "Can I, Deputy?"

He shook his head. "No. This fella needs to learn some respect." *Not only for the law but other people.* The nasty comment about the Lings still had him fiery hot.

"Suit yourself." Her lip turned up. "That man and Jake were furious with each other last night. If not for the bars, I think Jake might have taken his head off right here in the jailhouse."

Shocked, Dalton cut his gaze back to Maude's face. She was waiting for him to ask more. "What's this about?"

She turned her back to the cell and cupped her mouth. "I'm not exactly sure, Deputy. But I stopped by last night with a plate of biscuits and gravy—" She held up a preemptive hand. "Mr. Lemon and Jake were shouting insults—one right after the other, and each more disturbing than the last. They hadn't heard me enter. I thought I heard Courtney's name and then Jake lunged at the bars and said if Mr. Lemon weren't locked up, he'd kill him with his bare hands. Dwight was all eyes and ears as well, but he kept his mouth shut. You know how he's always looking for something to use against a person. Anyway, when Jake turned and saw me, he stormed out without a word of explanation. Bad blood is simmering between the two. And if I had to guess, Courtney is the cause."

Dalton remembered the animosity between the two in Newport. Jake had disliked the man being so much older than his sister but didn't say too much of anything else. *Like he'd be with me and Adaline. I can't fault him for that.* He'd been close-mouthed about the situation and seemed relieved when he delivered his sisters safely away on the train without any trouble. And now Lemon had showed up here unannounced, causing more strife. Dalton would be extra alert until Lemon left town.

Maude waited for his reaction.

"Why don't you take this nice basket of cookies over to the Lings? I think they'd appreciate them. Did you know Mrs. Ling delivered last night?"

"Yes, I've heard! And you were there. Explains the dark circles under your eyes. You should get a little rest."

"Thank you for your concern."

"Thank *you* for the suggestion. I hope you'll stop by the mercantile again soon to see what we've added to the display."

With a hand on her back he ushered her to the door. "I will, Maude. I appreciate your thoughtfulness with the cookies. Under any other circumstances, I'd be more than happy to accept." She'd taken time from her day to do something nice for him—and he did appreciate the effort. As a matter of fact, he'd enjoyed the first basket very much.

Her eyebrow spiked. "I understand, Deputy. You will not play favorites."

A wide smile stretched across his face. "No, I won't."

Her speaking about the mercantile reminded him about Beth. He held nothing against her, except the disrespectful way she spoke to Mrs. Hollyhock and others. She had nominated him for the judging position. He lowered his voice. "How's Miss Fairington? I hear she's living in the back of your store."

"Ahh, Beth… Yes, she is. And she's as impertinent as ever—maybe even more since she was tossed out of the Red Rooster. I can understand Violet; I really can. But my heart does go out to Beth as well. She's her own worst enemy. Whenever anyone warms up to her, it's not long before she cuts them to the quick. No one is safe, not even me." Maude's wrinkled brow furrowed. "That poor woman can't find an ounce of joy in anything. Not sure how long she'll stay in town, since her one and only friend has thrown her out on the street. Sometimes I hear her muttering about teaching everyone a lesson by leaving Logan Meadows for good. Honestly, I have no idea where she'd go. I believe Violet has been her only friend for years. Like a mother to her." She shook her head and sighed. "We'll just have to wait and see what happens."

Dalton opened the door and watched Maude plod away toward the laundry house in the ever-deepening snow, a route which took her past the bank.

Frank came out as she passed.

Words were shared.

After a few moments with his head bowed in her direction, he straightened and glanced back at Dalton, watching from the sheriff's office. A none-too-happy expression marred his normally pleasant face.

Damnation. Dalton's words had been for Maude alone, and he'd thought she knew better than to say anything. Didn't anyone keep anything to themselves these days? He had no doubt Maude would search out each person he'd mentioned and tell them what he'd said, creating ill will right before Christmastime.

Frank turned on his heel and disappeared inside the bank.

Mumbling to himself, Dalton returned to the warmth of the office. If Wil weren't here, he'd lie down on his cot by the stove and take a nap. He wasn't making friends in Logan Meadows by being the judge of the Christmas competition—the exact opposite. Somebody should have warned him of the politics and pitfalls. Life would be so much simpler if he was just deputy. Thom hadn't come in this morning. Dalton figured he was still home nursing Hannah. He hoped she and Dr. Thorn made a swift recovery and no one else in the town fell sick. Christmas was only a few days away, and the last thing they needed was an epidemic on their hands.

"I'm hungry," Wil called. "I could use some more coffee, too. Make yourself useful and brew another pot. I might as well enjoy my time off in this wonderful establishment."

The man had already eaten a plate of ham and eggs from the Silky Hen and consumed three cups of coffee. In contrast, hunger gnawed at Dalton's belly.

"What are you waiting for, Deputy?" A smirk twisted his mouth. "I need a smoke, too. That's the least you can do for detaining me for no reason."

Dalton went to the hat rack for his Stetson and coat.

"Have them throw in a piece of walnut pie."

"I'm not going for you. You'll eat when you get fed and not a moment before. I'm getting *my* breakfast, so settle back on your cot and get comfortable. You won't get anything more before noon." Dalton stepped into the slush, sucking in a cold breath. The town appeared quiet, but he'd learned the hard way appearances could be deceiving. The snow had stopped. As a few rays of sunlight fought through the clouds, silver-and-gold-colored trinkets glimmered on the Christmas tree. All seemed well on the surface. So why then did Logan Meadows feel like a powder keg?

Chapter Thirty-Two

Courtney hovered near the window inside Harrell's Haberdashery, covertly watching the sheriff's office across the street. Her stomach pinched with fear. She wasn't sure what was worrying her the most, speaking again with Wil or meeting Tyler at the Silky Hen? She swallowed, her dry throat painful, and glanced at the sky. Clouds were gathering.

At the Lings', she'd claimed she needed something at the mercantile she couldn't divulge, being Christmas was right around the corner. She'd left Adaline with the others as they'd penciled out a tentative work schedule so Mrs. Ling needn't worry about getting back to work anytime soon. As long as each woman had a little extra time on their hands, they were happy to help.

As was Courtney. If she could get this mess with Wil squared away, she'd donate all her free time to the Lings when she wasn't watching the children for Jessie. A penance for her past indiscretions with Wil. She'd embrace each hour spent washing, ironing, and folding as a gift. One she was grateful for. If only Wil would take the money and directly leave town. She'd still have the crime of stealing to work through, but she would save every cent she could and somehow repay the Logans, even if doing so took her whole life.

"Is there something I can help you find, Courtney?" Mrs. Harrell asked from behind.

She'd been so deep in thought, Courtney hadn't heard the woman's approach and jumped at the sound of her voice. She raised a hand to her throat as if the shop owner could read her thoughts. "Uh, no, Mrs. Harrell. I'm just looking at all your fine things." She glanced toward the nearest shelf of knickknacks and forced a smile. "They're beautiful. Deciding is almost impossible."

"But you're not shopping. I've watched you stare out the window for a good ten minutes. Is something troubling you, sweetheart? You can tell me."

Everyone knew their past, how they were parentless, and her living at the Logans'. "I'm, I'm—thinking about what to give Adaline. I don't have but a few coins to spend." The Logans' eighty dollars pulled weightily on her pocket, belying her words. The sooner she concluded this business and Wil left town, the better.

A smile appeared on Mrs. Harrell's face. "Well, you should have said something sooner. I know exactly what Adaline would love for Christmas that almost anyone could afford. Follow me, and I'll show you a pretty scarf she's been admiring for days. I can sell you the accessory at cost since it's for an employee." She gave a bright smile.

Courtney didn't want to leave her spot at the window. She'd skirted by the sheriff's office before coming here, noticing Dalton in the back of the room, shaking the coffeepot. Since then, she'd been at this spot, praying he'd step out before too long and give her an opportunity to sneak inside without being seen. She only needed a few seconds to dart in, convince Wil to leave with the gold eagle coins, and be gone forever. Only five minutes.

Following Mrs. Harrell would ruin her plan. This might be her only chance. She grasped the woman's arm, pulling her to a stop. "I'm sorry. I just remembered something I must do. I'll come back later to see the scarf. Thank you, though."

The woman's face fell. "But what if someone buys it first? Adaline will be disappointed…"

Courtney was halfway out the door. "I'm sorry."

Across the street, Dalton stepped outside, turned left, and continued on his way wherever he was headed without seeing her. She let go a deep breath and pretended to admire the Christmas tree while the distance between them grew. Besides him, the street was practically empty. Without a moment to spare, she looked both ways, dashed across, and checked the boardwalk one more time. Casting her luck to the wind, she grasped the cold door handle.

The cloudy day outside made the room shadowy. One lantern flickered on the desk and one in the back of the room. She couldn't see into the dark cells without moving closer. Her heart pounded against her ribs. The rushing in her ears drowned out every other sound. She held her breath and took one step farther into the room.

"Took you long enough, Court." He inched closer to the cell door. "No fun spending time in jail—*alone*."

She stayed several arm lengths from the bars, the coins burning a hole in her heart. His silly grin was out of character. He looked old and tired; a couple days' worth of dark stubble covered his jaw. The way his gaze roamed up and down her body made her feel dirty. She wanted to run out the door and never return. That was a luxury she didn't have. If she didn't use these few minutes prudently, all might be lost. She took another deep breath. "I need to talk with you. *Really* talk. No more avoiding the issue."

"I'm listenin'."

"I have part of the money you demanded."

"Demanded is such a harsh word."

She steeled her nerves. "Eighty dollars. That's all I can get." She'd not give over the money yet—not until she had his word. "You promise to take the money and leave? I can't get another cent."

He just stared.

Did he want her to beg? She would, if she had to. "*Please*, Wil. I'm sorry for running out on you. Please forgive me." She hated to let him off the hook for using her. She knew well enough he'd not think himself culpable at all. But she didn't care. She'd shoulder every ounce of guilt if he'd leave Logan Meadows and never return. "What do you say?"

"I say nope. You owe me one hundred dollars, Court. And I'd say you're getting off cheap for all the pain and anguish you caused. I aim to collect. You got the money with you now, don't you? I can tell by the look in your eyes."

A noise in the back of the room made her start.

Several moments later, the sheriff's dog moseyed out from behind the woodstove, his toenails clicking on the wooden floorboards. He stopped halfway across the room.

"Just the mutt. Now, let me see the money in your pocket," Wil demanded.

The amusement lacing his tone moments before was replaced with annoyance. A shiver inched up her spine. "I'd never carry around money like that. It's hidden in town. A place easy for you to retrieve. Forget about us, Wil. Let go of your hatred for Jake. No one will suspect a thing." She gave a wobbly smile. "Better this way."

He grasped a bar and pushed his face closer. "Better? Better for who? If I agree, you'll still owe me twenty dollars. How about you meet me tomorrow evening for one last hurrah? Then I'll call us even. Eighty dollars and you for the night."

How hateful! Her throat tightened to the point of pain. She glanced at the dog, still watching, as she thought of a way to escape. What would happen if she came clean? How would her past affect her family? She wished she knew. "That'll never, ever happen!"

"You might feel differently tomorrow when people start whispering when you walk by. Crossing the street so you don't taint their children." He paused and smiled. "When I get out of here, I'll be staying at the hotel. Come around back and wait on the old staircase. I'll find you, Courtney, and collect on what you owe, after which I'll disappear from your life. If you don't come, come morning people will see you in a whole new light. I promise you that. Won't be pretty or even my fault. You done what you done by your own free will. I never forced nothin'." He grinned from ear to ear. "This whole mess is on your shoulders, sweetheart. When you want to hate me, just remember that."

She inched away, heat scalding the back of her eyes. He was right. She was at fault. Unable to stand one more second with him, she turned and ran out the door, being careful to keep one arm down on her pocket to keep the coins from jangling.

Chapter Thirty-Three

The mood in the Silky Hen was festive. Talk and laughter reverberated about the room. The café was bursting with customers. But Tyler only stared at his half-full coffee cup, brooding. He didn't want to have this conversation with Courtney. She'd suspected something this morning when he'd said he wanted to speak with her. Her eyes darkened, and she'd looked away. If he had to guess, he'd been perfectly correct with what he'd thought he'd seen the night before.

He cast a sidelong glance at Gabe and Julia, who'd arrived a few minutes ago. They held hands across the table as they smiled and spoke softly. Hunter and Tabitha were just finishing their meal. Before their food had arrived, she'd almost talked Tyler's ear off for a good ten minutes about her new Christmas cards before he was rescued by her husband. Tyler liked the bookshop owner, she was pretty and nice, but at the moment, he had important things to worry about.

Had Courtney forgotten the invitation? Or maybe she remembered but had no intention of showing up. The longer he sat sipping his coffee, the larger the urge grew to help her before she found herself in more trouble than what she might already be in. A warm, intense feeling shoved inside his chest. Something about Jake's little sister got to him.

Dalton ate alone at a table across the room. He and Frank had exchanged a frosty hello when the deputy had entered, making Tyler wonder. Dalton had stopped by Tyler's table as well, mentioned he was still holding Wil Lemon, and then took the solitary table when Tyler failed to invite him to sit. He couldn't. The conversation he had in mind would be for Courtney's ears alone. He halfheartedly hoped some of these diners would clear out for more privacy before she arrived. Either way, he'd make sure no one overheard their discussion.

Seth Cotton let out a barking laugh, reminding Tyler of a mule at feeding time.

The rancher sat with Ivy, his wife; his sister, Nell; and her husband, Charlie Axelrose. Maddie, Charlie's daughter, sat between him and Nell, listening to the grown-ups' conversation.

In the mix of talk, Tyler picked up plans for Christmas, what they'd cook, Christmas cookie recipes, and the like. Sounded like they were bringing some of the choice wine which had been discovered in the cellar of the Cotton Ranch to the Christmas celebration.

When Tyler had come to town and was hired on at the Broken Horn, he'd met a slew of folks. The town was tightly knit. He'd never seen the like. Where he was from, people were neighborly, but this was different. What affected one of them seemed to affect them all. And he'd been welcomed into the fold. He liked the comfortable feel about Logan Meadows. That was one of the reasons he wanted to make this place his home.

My decision doesn't have anything to do with Courtney Costner, he told himself. The way the sound of her voice pulled at every fiber of his being was just a coincidence. Seeing a tremble in his hand when he lifted his cup was the last straw. A breath of cold air would clear his head. He stood and started for the door.

"Are you leaving, Tyler?" Roberta asked as she set a plate of food on Frank Lloyd's table. "I was just about to refill your cup, but I won't if you're done."

"No, ma'am. Just stepping out for a moment in need of fresh air." He smiled and shrugged. "I'm still waiting on Courtney, but she's taking a bit longer than expected. Can you keep my table?"

"Of course. That's no problem at all." She came closer and whispered, "I can't handle many more customers on my own, so doing so will be a favor. Daisy is set to arrive any time."

"Then I'm happy to help. I'll be back in two."

"Take all the time you need. No one will steal your table."

Boyish laughter rang out. Tyler turned in time to see Markus, Stevie, as well as Prichard, dart past him and out the front door, almost knocking over a chair and pulling down coats from the overfilled coatrack. The door slammed shut behind them.

Roberta scowled and shook her head. "If I could catch those three, they'd learn a lesson they'd not soon forget, but there isn't a chance of that. They're like wild coyotes drunk on juneberries when out on Christmas vacation. Boys!"

Forcing a smile, Tyler proceeded to the door until Charlie waved him over. "Tyler, can you relay a message to Chase for me?"

Tyler nodded. "Sure. Going to the ranch as soon as I finish here."

"Good. I'm bringing over the yearling stud colt later today. Just want to be sure you're ready for him. He can be a handful, most times. I wouldn't want him to get into any trouble already at his new home."

"You bet. His stall is ready and waiting—and has been for days. Chase and Jessie are excited about getting him."

"Yeah, I'm glad he went to the Broken Horn as well. I'm anxious to see how he matures."

"We both are!" Nell interjected, her coffee cup raised to her lips. "Charlie likes to take all the credit around our ranch. I rope him in now and then and remind him I'm still a part of the operation." She laughed, a life full of love shining in her eyes. "He's old-fashioned. Thinks a woman's place is in front of the stove, not riding unbroken broomtails."

"I think no such thing!" Charlie scolded. "Stop making up stories."

Maddie's wide grin reminded Tyler of his little sisters. "Then we'll watch for you both." Tyler remembered the story he'd been told of how they'd rounded up a herd of wild horses to save Nell and Seth's ranch. Tyler nodded and stepped outside, anxious about the conversation to come. The frosty air stung his face and cleared out the fog permeating his mind.

Two guests from the El Dorado Hotel, unfamiliar faces to him, were out on the boardwalk early this morning, gazing around the town. Logan Meadows was experiencing more and more tourists from the East, and this couple looked as if they belonged in New York. They smiled when their gazes connected, and he could see their curiosity. He was a riddle. A cowboy who'd tamed the West. He'd heard talk how ranch hands were considered little more than a youth in understanding but brawny in build, strong of arm. Strange, indeed. He'd trust Chase Logan with money matters a hundred times more than an Easterner. Because one worked outside in the sunshine and rain didn't make them any less clever than a man who sat behind a desk. He turned.

Courtney darted out of the sheriff's office, ran past the saloon, and then stumbled to a halt at the bank. She grasped a post. With closed eyes, she glanced up at the sky.

Was she praying? He squelched a sudden urge to run to her and wrap her protectively in his arms. All that bothered him from the night before vanished, and all he cared about was Courtney—her safety, her feelings, her heart.

Why was she in the sheriff's office? Looking for Dalton or Thom? Dalton's mention of Wil being locked up resurfaced. Did he have something to do with what Courtney had done? What other explanation was more plausible? Was he holding something over her head? Since Lemon had arrived, she'd changed. A thousand possibilities, and none that he liked, rifled through his head. Anger sprang up. If Lemon had hurt her in some way, if he'd compromised her, Tyler'd beat the stuffing out of him before he sent him down the river on a waterlogged tree.

Courtney lifted her chin and started his way, not seeing him between boardwalk posts, water troughs, and the few townsfolk milling around on this chilly morning. She'd arrive in only moments. Should he say he'd seen where she'd been or wait and see if she volunteered the information? He didn't want to be devious, but she hadn't been forthcoming so far, and he'd guess with the matters of Chase Logan's money she'd be no different. He had to save her from her fear—and whatever else was pushing her into thievery. The mystery around Courtney Costner just kept growing deeper by the day.

Chapter Thirty-Four

Moving along the boardwalk with resolve, Courtney took several deep, mind-clearing breaths, trying to shake the bad feelings rolling around inside. When she met Tyler, she couldn't appear nervous or shaken. He'd seemed so different today. A man with a mission, if nothing else. Breathing in and out several more times did little to calm her racing heart.

What had possessed Wil? He had changed so much. The look in his eyes, almost like he was at the finish line and about to win a great prize, had shattered her resolve to appeal to his conscience, get him to understand what this town meant to her, and why keeping quiet was so important. Her insides shrank with disgust and regret. How had she ever been attracted to him? Just the memory of his eyes, shining with victory as he issued his impossible ultimatum, made her want to retch. That's the person she'd given her innocence to. A stranger, and not just that, a wicked stranger to boot.

She had to face the truth. Even if she gave him the Logans' eighty dollars, and somehow found twenty more, he'd never give up. He'd keep blackmailing her until she could no longer pay, and then he'd tell her secret anyway. She had to do the right thing now. Return the money. She'd felt sick ever since drawing them out, the room silent with her conviction. Somehow, she'd return the four gold eagles to their rightful spot tonight.

But along with that, she'd need to confess to Jessie as well. Courtney felt dirty and sneaky. Could she ever right all her wrongs? She didn't know Reverend Wilbrand well enough to feel comfortable with the preacher, and she didn't want Jake to know she'd made another stupid mistake. Would she ever stop being so impulsive and foolish? Oh, how she wished her father hadn't passed away.

Almost to the Silky Hen, she slowed, dreading the confrontation ahead. And then she saw him. Tyler! Out front, waiting for her. How long had he been there? Had he seen her come from Albert's office? He smiled when their gazes connected, but the expression didn't reach his eyes. If she had to guess, the answer was yes, he'd seen her and wasn't pleased.

"There you are, Courtney. I wondered if you'd show up. I thought you might have gone back to the ranch."

He was acting strange—*again*. She wished she knew what he knew. "I didn't forget. I've just been busy. I hope you haven't waited long."

"Not really. I just stepped out for a bit of cool air. Busy in there. Stuffy, too."

Nodding, she reached for the doorknob.

He leaned around her and pulled open the door.

His long arm and large chest cocooned around her, bringing a sense of calm. He made her feel small and protected. As he was quite tall, she had to angle her head to glance up to see what he was about. He tipped his head courteously and smiled as she passed through into the busy room.

Roberta darted by, her face red and brow shiny.

He escorted her to a table already set with two cups, one half full. "Here we are." He pulled out her chair.

He's very polite! She'd never really noticed such manners before. He'd always been kind, but today the mood between them seemed strained. Once Courtney was seated, Roberta came by with the coffeepot and filled her cup and topped off Tyler's.

"Would you like something to eat?" Roberta asked.

"No, thank you," Courtney answered. Why had Tyler invited her? She lifted the small pitcher of cream, the white porcelain cool in her fingers, and added a portion to her cup. Then she stirred in a teaspoon of sugar, something she loved.

He waited for her to finish.

She felt his gaze on her face. Did this meeting have something to do with Adaline? Or Wil? "What did you want to talk about, Tyler?" she asked, suddenly feeling a bit put out. He had no right to question her or stick his nose in her business. What was he up to?

The small smile faded from his face. "I couldn't sleep last night and went out for some air. The time was late, well past midnight."

Oh my stars! He knows! Her stomach clenched painfully and her breathing quickened. "And you're telling me this, because…?" She made sure her voice didn't quaver and give her away. She'd already made the decision to return the coins, no matter what, but she hated Tyler might know what she'd done in the first place.

He glanced around before speaking. "Courtney, if you're in some sort of trouble, maybe I can help. Tell me what you're tangled in. I can't do anything if you're not honest with me. Your good word is everything. Trusting me is your best option."

She glanced down at her cup, fretting over her best course of action. Doubt no longer remained. He knew something, but she just didn't know what. Had Jake told him everything? The two friends were as close as brothers, but Jake had promised he'd take the knowledge of her past indiscretions to his grave. To not even tell Daisy. She couldn't imagine her big brother going back on his word.

She looked up at Tyler through her lashes. No, it was bad enough what she'd done, she didn't need to draw him into her shame—no matter he offered help. "I really don't know what you mean, Tyler. Me, in trouble? That's nonsense. People always think that because I prefer my own company to others. I'm a loner. Always have been;

always will be. Nothing is going on." Would her words kill his overcurious mind? Probably not.

His lips flattened, and besides being put out with his overbearing behavior, she was astounded how attractive he was when he was irritated. Sitting directly across, she took a good, long, fascinated look, considering each of his manly features. In doing so she wasn't being rude or forward, after all, they were having an important discussion—she was *required* to stare. His healthy tanned complexion, apparently sun-kissed by many hours in the saddle, was smooth with only a hint of beard this morning. His shoulders, wide. He toyed with his spoon with long, tapered fingers. Clean fingernails. Thick brows fell low over earnest eyes the color of the coffee in her cup, lightly splashed with cream—and were so piercing at the moment they seemed determined to delve deep into her most secret thoughts. A handsome nose led down to finely formed lips…

"Courtney! Pay attention! Your mind is wandering! This is serious business we're discussing."

Snapping her gaze back to his annoyed expression, she frowned. Paying attention was a good idea. Her future was at stake.

"As I stated before, last night was dark. With the lamp you carried, I was able to see inside the ranch house, even though I wasn't close to the building. I didn't go looking or try to peep in. But I saw you in your room and then you went downstairs."

She gasped and recoiled in her chair. Her anxiety over what he might know exploded into red-hot anger.

Frank glanced over.

Dalton's fork stopped halfway to his mouth.

She was drawing attention, the last thing she needed.

Roberta appeared. "Is everything all right, Courtney? Did you spill your coffee and burn yourself?" She looked around on her person but didn't find anything. "Shall I bring a rag?" Next, she bent over and glanced at the floor and under the table.

Mortified she'd been so transparent, Courtney shook her head. "Oh no, Mrs. Brown, but thank you for asking. I'm fine, really. Just being clumsy and frightened myself."

Roberta's mouth opened and closed a few times, but she didn't say anything else, just shrugged and started for the kitchen.

She waited for Roberta to be out of hearing range. "You watched me through the window?" she hissed, struggling to keep her outrage in check so she didn't make another scene. "Followed me from window to window? Noted my progress through the house! You should be *ashamed* of yourself, Tyler Weston! If Chase Logan knew what you've done, he'd fire you on the spot. Do you watch Jessie, too? How about little Sarah?" Hoping for the upper hand, she flung the last part, although quietly, and knowing it wasn't true about someone as upstanding as Tyler. What exactly did he know? Maybe he was just confessing he'd watched her and didn't see the thievery.

"Of course not. And I didn't start out watching *you,* either. Went out for some night air and there you were in the window."

She tipped her brow, mind racing. How should she handle this? She needed to know a little more before she committed. "Did you enjoy the show?"

He stretched out a hand.

She didn't reciprocate. She had no idea where this was leading. Did she really want to know?

"You're frightened, Courtney." Tyler leaned toward her. "The coins probably haven't been missed. There's still time to undo your poor decision. I won't say anything if you promise to return the coins where they belong. They're special to Chase and Jessie. A memento of starting the ranch. Do you know what a memento is?"

Shame bubbled up around her like sticky quicksand. Now she knew where she teetered—on a precipice with a bottomless pit from where there was no return. He not only thought her a thief but a dummy. Humiliation swirled within, and she fought the heat pooling behind her eyes. How far she'd fallen. If he only knew, he could add the word harlot to her other names. Repairing what she'd become was impossible. She might as well run away tonight. Nothing made a difference anymore.

"Courtney," he whispered with urgency. "*Talk* to me. Let me *help*. I saw you come from the sheriff's office just now. You were upset. Does Wil Lemon have anything to do with the trouble you're in? Is he threatening you in some way?"

Adaline came through the door with Daisy and Mrs. Hollyhock. They looked as if they'd been washed in cold water and hung out to dry. Adaline carried Mrs. Hollyhock's revered box of medical supplies.

Daisy hurried into the kitchen.

Adaline saw her, smiled, and started over.

Thank heavens! Relief crashed through Courtney. She'd never been so happy to see her big sister.

When relief washed over Courtney's face, frustration sizzled inside Tyler. With her reluctance to speak about the crime she'd committed, *he* was the one in a tight spot. He should tell Chase. Or he could be labeled as a Peeping Tom. But regarding Courtney, he knew he wouldn't—not now. Or at least, not yet. Not while time still existed to get her to undo what she'd done before anyone was the wiser.

Adaline, with Mrs. Hollyhock holding her arm, approached their table.

Courtney's sister looked pleased to find them together.

"So, this is where you went after the mercantile." Adaline gave her sister a secretive smile. "I wondered. I'm walking with Violet to the Red Rooster and—"

"I don't need no *nursemaid*," Violet interrupted, none too gently. "I'm as steady on my feet as ever. And I can make the walk alone, iffin I want."

"That's entirely true." Adaline nodded. "But I'm exhausted and need a nap as badly as you do." She glanced at their old friend. "Would you deny me that? Just because you don't want to be seen walking with me?"

"Ya know it ain't that, girlie," Violet said, a bit softer this time.

Adaline touched Courtney's shoulder. "Daisy penciled you in to work at the laundry this afternoon about one o'clock. Jessie said she'd watch the children."

Courtney dipped her chin. "Whatever works for everyone else is fine with me."

She was all smiles now that her sister had rescued her, Tyler noted. He had to find a way to get through and talk some sense into her.

"One o'clock is enough time to go home and do a few tasks and then come back," Courtney added. She slid her gaze to him but didn't smile. "Marlene'll be there to show me the ropes, right?"

"She will. I think you'll be ironing. The work's not hard, just tedious."

Violet nodded. "That's what Marlene's said since the day she started. Mindless work gives ya time to solve the mysteries of life."

"Anything you worked out is perfectly fine with me," Courtney said. "I won't complain a bit."

Of course she wouldn't complain, Tyler thought, smoldering inside. The schedule gave her an easy way to avoid him. He'd be on the ranch, and she'd be in town.

"Good then," Courtney said. "It's all settled. Did Jessie leave for the ranch without me?"

"Not at all. She's waiting with the children in the buggy while I round you up. She thought you'd want to go home and change. Then she'll arrange a way for you to get back. They're right outside."

Courtney stood and ran her hands down her skirt. "Goodbye, Tyler. Thank you for the cup of coffee."

They needed to resolve the situation. He stood, too. "I'll walk you to the buggy."

Courtney's eyes flashed dangerously, but she kept a smile on her lips. "No need. The buggy's across the street. I'm sure you have things to do."

They locked eyes.

"I don't."

"Fine," Adaline finally said, shrugging. "Violet and I are grabbing a quick bite to eat and then we're off."

Courtney had already started for the door.

He'd have to hurry to catch her before she reached the buggy. And then he'd only have half a second to say what needed saying. He placed payment beside his plate. "Take our table." With that, he was out the door. "Courtney, wait!"

She was just stepping into the road.

Jessie sat in the driver's seat of the buggy with the two little ones beside her.

Would Courtney stop?

Courtney turned. "I know you're only trying to help, Tyler, but I wish you wouldn't. You can't do anything. I'd appreciate you minding your own business."

What in the devil did she mean? Was she so far gone she had no choices at all? He stifled the urge to grasp her by the arms and give her a good shake. "No doubt. But I beg to differ. Something can *always* be done." He disliked the defeated look on her face. "The question is, are you brave enough to try? Nothing of value is ever easy—and especially not when your *reputation* hangs in the balance."

She blanched.

He wished he could take back his words and say them a bit more softly, but he had to get through, and this was the only way he knew how.

"What do you know?" she whispered, and then glanced over her shoulder at Jessie, a red stain creeping up her neck. "Jake *promised* not to tell a soul. I'll not forgive him until the day I die."

A stone dropped in Tyler's belly. His suspicions were true! Wil Lemon had compromised Courtney and now blackmailed her with the threat of exposure. He'd kill the black-hearted piece of beetle dung with his bare hands—and enjoy every second! Did Jake know what was going on? He wholeheartedly doubted. Jake wouldn't stand for such evil shenanigans with his youngest sister. "Jake hasn't said a word. I put two and two together and figured things on my own."

Courtney's gaze searched his for several long seconds as the meaning of his words sank in. Then her face crumbled. "Fine, so now you know. Go and get away from me, a fallen woman, before I taint such a good, upstanding man as yourself. You're always talking about your father and all his honesty lessons. The importance of a good reputation and responsibility for one's actions. I'd hate to see his expression if he was faced with the likes of me." She flung one arm wide. "Get out of my sight. I know you want to."

She turned and bolted for the buggy on the other side of the road just as he opened his mouth to reply. A surprised-looking Jessie and the children, already seated inside, watched as Courtney lifted her skirt and scrambled onto the bench beside them. A moment later, they were off.

Chapter Thirty-Five

"Let me fix you something to eat, Violet. Scramble some eggs or make some mush to fortify your old bones. The bags under your eyes resemble cornsacks."

Violet glared up at Marlene from her chair by the Red Rooster's warm hearth. "And ya don't look like no princess yerself, ya ol' she-goat. I jist ate at the café."

Marlene gasped and whirled to glance at Adaline, who'd just returned with another throw to place over Violet's legs.

During the walk home, she'd begun to tremble uncontrollably, more than what the weather had caused. Adaline was worried.

"See what I put up with? I was just being nice. She's reverted back to her not-so-charming self. Reminds me of my arrival in Logan Meadows. I can't abide her sassy tongue, especially when I'm being nice. I never told you, Adaline, but she threatened to change me into a salamander and fling me under the stagecoach horses."

"And you were stupid enough to think I was capable, too," Violet said on a cough, and then cackled. "Thought I was a witch with powers to hex ya. Yer face screwed up tight, and ya got all sweaty. I sure had some good laughs at yer'en expense. The saloon girl–mother looking for her son. Ha!" Violet shook her head. "That's a crock of sour milk."

Adaline wondered at Violet's nasty attack. Usually cranky but loveable, Violet wasn't typically downright mean to the people she loved. Or even the ones she didn't love, as in the case of Beth Fairington. She'd given Beth miles and miles of chances, overlooking her harsh words, rolling eyes, and lazy ways. Everyone wondered how she put up with her for so long. And now, this attack on Marlene was uncalled for. No matter how the two women's association had started, no one doubted Violet now loved Jake's mother. The two had been living together for months. The water under the bridge had long since cleared away the hurt and hard feelings to a beautiful friendship. At least, that was what Adaline had thought. Why was Violet treating Marlene this way now?

Adaline placed a calming hand on Marlene's arm in time to feel Jake's mother bristle. Being careful not to incur Violet's wrath, she arranged the throw over her bony knees.

"Don't mollycoddle her, Adaline," Violet snapped. "Marlene's had a full night's sleep and still acts like a long-nosed busybody— reminds me all too much of Beth..." She jerked her gaze to the crackling flames in the hearth as her eyes filled with tears.

Adaline went down on one knee and took Violet's hand. No matter how the old woman acted or what she said, she missed Beth and felt poorly about the blowup. Angry words never did anyone any good and were sure to cause the opposite. Alarming heat radiated up through Adaline's fingers.

"Violet, you're boiling hot." Adaline placed the back of her hand on Violet's forehead. "Burning." She gently took a hold of her thin upper arms and drew her to her feet. "Come on, you're going to bed this instant. I won't take no for an answer."

Marlene bustled forward, all the animosity stamped on her face only moments before, vanished.

Violet tried to pull back. "Leave me be. Can't an ol' worn out biddy sit in peace?"

"No!" Marlene snapped. "You can't. You're going to bed this instant, just like Adaline said."

Adaline exchanged a glance with Marlene. Had Jake's mother heard people in town were sick with influenza, and Dr. Thorn and Hannah Donovan were both down with the illness? Those two were both strong and healthy—and young! What would happen to Violet?

Violet struggled a moment, and then calmly complied like an orphan lamb. Why hadn't Adaline noticed sooner? The poor thing. She should have been in bed last night, not staying up all hours delivering a baby determined to come out feet first.

In Violet's bedroom, Marlene steadied her while Adaline rushed forward and drew back the quilt and sheets. They assisted her to a sitting position, and Adaline worked the buttons on the front of her dress.

Violet tried to slap her hands away but after one try, was too weak.

In only moments, the dress was gently lifted over her head and then the three petticoats she wore for warmth were the next items to go. Adaline left her wool socks and then assisted Marlene to lower her flannel nightdress over her shoulders.

"Don't be shocked when ya see I don't wear no corset no more," she mumbled to no one in particular, her face flushed and eyes glazed. "No need, once yer my age, none a'tall. Just leave me be, girls. I'm so sleepy."

"I'll go for Dr. Thorn," Marlene whispered when they were done.

Violet lay quietly with the sheet pulled up to her chin, more than enough warmth with her temperature, even in the cold December weather.

Adaline smoothed the quilt folded on the end of the bed. "Haven't you heard? Dr. Thorn is sick. And Hannah, too. That's why we delivered Mrs. Ling's child and not the doctor. Jessie and the children were exposed. Daisy came by to see Bao, as well. And what about Bao and the baby?" *And Dalton. And the whole of the café. Why did we stop to eat? We should have come directly home.* She glanced at Marlene, searching her face. "I'm frightened."

Marlene's solemn expression never wavered. "We have no time to be frightened. How're you feeling, Adaline? You've been with Violet the longest." She reached over and touched Adaline's forehead. "Do you have any stomach pains or a headache?"

The trace of Marlene's cool fingers felt good. "I'm absolutely fine." She glanced at Violet on the bed. She hadn't moved since they'd laid her back and put the sheet over her. "We have a dear friend who needs us." She went to the water pitcher for a wet washcloth to wipe Violet's face.

"I'll make some chicken broth straight away," Marlene mumbled. "This poor little hen needs some nutrition and love. That's something I can do right now. As well as heat water for willow bark tea. Do you know anything about her herbal remedies? I must confess, whenever Violet starts going on and on, I head for my room. Now I wish I'd listened. I believe she might have something called purple cornflower for fever, but I couldn't identify it from others."

"I'm sorry to say I don't know, either. But I'll look through and see if anything is labeled. I did overhear Jessie speaking well about sassafras root tea for such. We need to get word to Dr. Thorn to see what he can tell us and also alert Jessie. She's Violet's oldest and dearest friend... as well as Beth Fairington."

They exchanged a long glance. Violet and Beth hadn't spoken since Violet had thrown her out of the Red Rooster.

"What do you think? Should I tell her as well?" she whispered close to Marlene's ear. "Violet might be sicker than we know. God forbid, the worst happens and she dies without a chance to make amends."

"You're right. I know Violet, and that wouldn't sit well with her. She always says she wants to be shiny and bright when she meets her maker. Tomorrow'll be four days, and Violet hasn't been her old self since the fight. I thought the whole thing would have blown over by now."

Violet tried to struggle to an elbow but sagged back onto her mattress. "I'm going home today, gals. Up ta Jesus and my heavenly reward. Don't cry over my grave too long. I'll be singing and dancing with my Savior." She gazed around and then her smile faded. "Where am I, anyway? I don't recognize this room."

Adaline knelt beside the bed and gently took Violet's fragile hand, frightened at the heat.

"You're not going home just yet. You're still on earth in your room at the Red Rooster, where you'll be tomorrow and the months to come. You're stuck with us for a while longer, no angels or fluffy white clouds yet."

A sheen of perspiration shone on Violet's forehead.

"I have a say in this," Violet sputtered. "I'm goin' home in time for Christmas! Stop hangin' onta me. We all go sooner or later. I'm so tired I can't lift another foot." She reached over and patted Adaline's arm. "But remember ta feed my chickens when I'm gone. In this weather, those critters can't go without scratch for long."

"You're not dying, Violet, so just be quiet," Marlene groused. "You're scaring Adaline. She doesn't know you as well as I do. You're tougher than a bucket of horseshoes. Stop soaking this opportunity for every ounce of sympathy."

Adaline needed to get word to Dr. Thorn and Jessie, but her feet felt like they'd been nailed to the floor. Violet didn't look on death's door quite yet, but with influenza, one never knew which breath would be the last. How in the world would scrawny little Violet get through a bout of December influenza? They could lose her in the blink of an eye.

Chapter Thirty-Six

With a stabbing side ache after her run into town, Adaline took a moment on the mercantile's boardwalk to catch her breath. The brisk, snow-scented air refreshed her heated skin and moist forehead. They'd needed a few items for nursing Violet, and she'd volunteered to fetch them while Marlene sat by her side.

Adaline gulped air and let her heart settle, reading over the list she'd hastily scratched out. Quinine powder for fever. Baking soda and soda crackers to settle Violet's stomach, more tea, and flour for baking—they were completely out, and Violet would need something substantial when she felt better—God forbid the Lord took her before then.

The Red Rooster was just far enough out of town to make going in and out several times a day more inconvenient than a pleasure—especially in this weather. When she finished here, she'd speak with Dr. Thorn through his window, as Dalton had done, to see what else they should do for Violet. Right now, she did nothing more than sleep with a cold cloth on her brow.

To her left, the lunchtime crowd moved in and out of the Silky Hen. To her right and down the street, the Christmas tree stood tall against the slate-gray sky—promising snow.

Gabe was there, plucking a quiet Christmas carol on his guitar.

The lilting sound pricked Adaline's heart. She blinked away the sudden tears. Until now, she hadn't had a moment to recall the words she'd said to Dalton last night. Would he ever speak to her again? What had she been thinking? Had she expected him to fall to one knee and proclaim his love? Pull her into his embrace and kiss her wildly? Except being the best of friends, they'd never before discussed or shared anything about their feelings or relationship. And now she'd gone and wrecked that.

Down the street, Dalton exited the sheriff's office, crossed to the tall tree, and began a conversation with Gabe. Townsfolk moved around town, talking, laughing. Wagons passed in the street. All she saw was Dalton.

The door to the store opened, and Beth stepped out. "Adaline, why're you standing out here in the cold?"

Surprised, Adaline jerked her gaze from Dalton but not fast enough. The look in Beth's eyes said she'd seen who Adaline was admiring. She wore a dress Adaline knew well from living together for the past weeks. A warm wool shawl wrapped her shoulders, partially covering her work apron. A lacy choker ringed her neck and was pinned with a cameo. She looked the same to Adaline, but an unusual expression shimmered in her eyes.

"I figured the mystery man was Dalton," she whispered coyly.

"Dalton?" Adaline questioned. "I don't know what you mean."

"Of course, you do. The man you're smitten with. The one you're trying to seduce with Marlene's advice. You needn't pretend with me."

"Seduce! I'd never!" Her stomach clenched. But she had—or at least tried to flirt, which had gone nowhere. Dalton wasn't interested.

Beth sighed and batted her eyes. "If you say so." Her smile returned. "And that's good news, because I'd never want to see you hurt. Dalton's heart is unavailable. Anyone who falls for him can only be a friend—nothing more."

What? Was the woman insane? Adaline's curiosity sprang to life, overruling her good sense. "What do you mean? He's not married."

Beth's hand flew to her choker where she fingered the pin. "Married! Who said anything about being married? I guess you're too new to town to have heard he's in love with Susanna. Everyone knows. She broke his heart not that long ago. I'm sure, with such a fresh wound, he's still mooning over his loss. Why do you think Albert whisked his wife out of town at Christmastime like he did? Perhaps he didn't want Dalton between them their first year as man and wife. Or maybe not. I don't know."

Adaline gazed back at Dalton. "Susanna Preston?" The name was barely a whisper.

"Susanna Robinson, then. She and Dalton grew up together in Breckenridge, Colorado. He's loved her for most his life. Albert feared he'd lose her to Dalton. So did Winthrop, Albert's brother. Ask him, if you don't believe me. I'm sure he'll tell you the whole story. The scuttlebutt circulated around town for months. Some say the train crash, bringing Dalton to town to reunite them, was his destiny."

Adaline stared at Beth, the words she'd just spoken clanging around her heart.

Susanna Robinson Preston...destiny...in love...

"Better yet, ask Violet. She caught the two men in a fistfight under Shady Creek bridge, going at each other like schoolboys. You should have seen their faces when they got finished with each other."

Dalton and Albert? She felt weak in the knees.

The door opened again, and Maude stuck out her head. "What in tarnation are you two jabbering about out there? Get in here before you catch your death!" She held the door wide.

In a fog of heartbreak, Adaline proceeded inside having heard quite enough. There was her explanation. Dalton wouldn't love her. *Couldn't* love her. He was already in love—with someone else.

Chapter Thirty-Seven

Creeping along in her stockinged feet, Courtney crossed the large living room of the ranch house and peered into the kitchen to make sure she was alone. Shane had gone to bed early and Sarah soon after.

Several hours ago, a rider had appeared from town with a message from her sister alerting them Mrs. Hollyhock was ill. She had a fever and was in bed. Adaline felt she was very sick and bade Jessie to come at once.

Instantly, Jessie had packed a small bag and Chase had driven her over.

Concern for Mrs. Hollyhock rocked Courtney. If something happened to the old matriarch, Logan Meadows, as well as her brother, Jake, would be devastated. The old woman had practically raised her brother when Marlene, his natural mother, was a saloon girl and had little time for a young son. Courtney liked Mrs. Hollyhock, too. The elderly grandmother-type had been nothing but kind to her, and even sweet, when she was cranky to most. Courtney had felt special to her, and she saw the same feelings in Adaline's gaze. She hoped these would not be her last days on earth.

Adaline had no idea, but her message had provided the perfect moment for Courtney to undo her bad deed. She'd been in the bedroom with Sarah, working up her courage. For some reason, this circumstance felt much scarier than when she'd taken the money in the first place. She didn't want to get caught. Putting what she'd stolen back did exonerate her, didn't it? She'd not spent any. And they were the same coins—*the keepsake coins*—that she'd taken only the night before. All she'd done was carry them around for a day. Thankfully, she'd been strong and not given Wil the money. How she'd handle him in the future, she didn't know. But she wouldn't try buying him off again.

After a shallow breath, Courtney glanced at the stairs one more time to make sure all was still quiet and crossed the room. The closer she came to the display case, the harder her heart pounded. Almost painful now, the blood swished in her ears, resembling the crashing waves of Newport.

Reaching with a shaky hand, she twisted the fragile knob. With the other hand she braced the glass case and carefully opened the door. Taking the coins from her pocket, she laid them one at a time noting the soft click. With a heart full of thanks, she slowly turned to find Chase watching her from the kitchen doorway.

"Courtney?" His gaze went from her face to the cabinet behind her. "Can I help you with something?"

Did he know and was testing her? Or could she say she was just looking? Bile stung the back of her throat. She was tired of all the deception hovering around her. She wanted to be her old self: honest, chipper, alive. She was no good.

"Courtney. You're white. Sit down. I'd prefer you don't pass out. You might be coming down with something as well."

She shook her head. "I'm not sick, Mr. Logan." Her tiny voice came out shaky.

He tipped his head. "That's good news. Something else you want to say?"

He was assessing her and the cabinet again. Was he searching for something missing? The cowboys around here seemed well-versed at looking deep into the soul, as she'd experienced with Tyler earlier today. Mr. Logan was tall and broad. He seemed to fill the doorway. Windblown, shaggy hair rimmed his face, and a shadow of a beard covered his jaw. His perceptive, piercing eyes grasped her gaze and didn't let go. Her life was blowing up all around her. She needed to come clean.

"Courtney?"

"Yes, sir, there is." She dropped her gaze to the rug.

He walked into the living room on his stockinged feet and lowered himself into a chair. He gestured her to the sofa.

She did his bidding. "I—I…" she began again. "I took something from your display case last night and am returning it."

He nodded slowly. "What did you take?"

"Your gold eagle coins."

For several long moments he studied the floor. "Do you need money, Courtney? I'm happy to give you some if you're in need."

His tone was sincere, holding no condemnation, as she'd expected. No anger. She didn't know what to think. "I—" she began, shamed all the way to her soul. She'd love to share the heavy burden about Wil and his threats she carried on her shoulders but doing so with Chase Logan didn't feel right. She shook her head. "I couldn't sleep last night and came downstairs to admire the keepsakes Jessie showed me in the cabinet on the day I first arrived. I took the coins. After I did, I regretted my mistake. Jake and Adaline will be shocked when they hear what I've done." She looked across the room to the dark window and thought of Tyler. "And then, maybe they won't be shocked. They know I look for trouble around every corner."

"That assessment doesn't sound like you, Courtney."

"If you knew me better, you'd think different."

For some reason she couldn't fathom, he smiled. She'd seen that look before, when Sarah was chattering about her day, the snow flower she'd found in the horse pasture, or a flock of birds that followed her down a path. He was a good man. Patient and kind. And intelligent, too.

"Tell you what." The words were soft, said under his breath. "How about we keep this between you and me? Since you returned the coins, no harm was done. You might not believe this, but I was young and impulsive once, too." He chuckled and ran a hand over his hair. "I was a drifter. Never wanted to settle down. I've made my share of mistakes. And unlike you, I didn't put them to right. They tickle my conscience from time to time, but one can't look back too often, or he'll miss what's in front. I've come to terms with who I was back then. And who I am now, thanks to Jessie and my family."

He stretched back in the chair getting comfortable. "I remember once when I wasn't much older than you, I'd been on the trail for days. When a man is powerful hungry, he'll do foolish things. I caught a whiff of a delicious smell. Following my nose, I came upon a small ranch house, tied my horse at the hitching post, and knocked on the door. No one was home. Taking liberties I had no right to take, I circled the small place. The window in back was open. On the ledge was a fresh-baked cherry pie. I knew right from wrong. Taking the pie was stealing. But I couldn't stop myself. I rode off with the whole pie, dish and all. Years later, I was in the area, and my conscience began kickin' up a storm. An old couple owned the ranch. I confessed. They were kind, and happy to have company; they invited me to supper. I stayed several days, doing chores and fixing things a man his age couldn't do any longer."

"You put your wrong to right."

"Yes, but not immediately. You're the only one I've shared that story with." His face turned pink. Sitting forward, Chase gave a nod. "Your indiscretion is just between us."

Courtney took a deep, purgative breath and a coil of tension eased away. Mr. Logan hadn't condemned her as she'd expected. He'd actually admitted to a small indiscretion, which illustrated he wasn't as perfect as people thought. She'd do better from this day forward. She'd fight her battles without fibbing or going against the values she'd been taught as a child. Somehow she'd be victorious against Wil, but with honesty and truth. Then, whatever the outcome, she'd have no more regrets.

Chapter Thirty-Eight

Two days had passed since Adaline had gone into town for the soda crackers and quinine powder. The Red Rooster was crammed with people. Buggies and wagons littered the front yard, as well as the sides and back. A somber mood permeated the air. A number of townsfolk had begun to stop by just after the noontime meal to check on Violet and, in some respects, say their last goodbyes. Word had gotten around town she'd taken a turn for the worse overnight. She slid in and out of delirium and was fading fast and might not last the day. Her friends viewed her from the hallway to say their last goodbyes to their greatly loved matriarch.

The situation was as if everyone had gathered for a wake before Violet had actually passed away. Winthrop was there, Reverend Wilbrand, Hunter and Tabitha, Albert and Susanna. Maude had already been there and was gone, as well as Chase and most of the bunkhouse of the Broken Horn. Frank Lloyd, Kendall Martin, Buckskin Jack, Seth and Ivy Cotton, and his sister, Nell, and her husband, Charlie, stood around the room.

"I'm so thankful we returned when we did," Susanna said, her eyes red from crying. "If I hadn't had a chance to say goodbye to Violet, I'd never have forgiven myself." Her gaze lovingly touched each colorful quilt, the doilies over the arms of each chair, the table bouquet of winter pinecones and golden leaves, arranged in the center of the table. "Even at eighty-seven, Violet made sure everything was just so."

Albert nodded and placed a strong, comforting arm around her back. Hunter and Tabitha stood in the circle with them quietly discussing the situation. "Logan Meadows will be a different place..."

Adaline remained in the kitchen, watching and listening from the alcove. Her job was to make sure the coffeepot was full and hot water was on to boil. Her heart ached for Violet. She'd touched them all in different ways. Adaline struggled to keep her gaze far from Susanna or have the things she'd learned about her and Dalton color the way she felt about her. Susanna had been nothing but kind and accommodating since Adaline and her family had come to town. She liked Susanna very much. She'd not let her feelings for Dalton ever change that.

A soft hand on Adaline's shoulder made her turn.

"Jake's absolutely devastated about Violet," Daisy whispered. "I think he expected her to live forever. Of course, we all know death is inevitable, but no one wants to lose our dear, sweet Violet—even at her advanced age. On top of this heartbreak, Jake hasn't been himself since Wil Lemon came to town and has been acting like a crazy man. He hates Wil." She slowly shook her head. "I'm frightened he might do something foolish. And now this, with Violet, so close to Christmas. Her passing is too sad to consider."

Adaline didn't like hearing this about Jake, as well as feeling something was drastically wrong with Courtney. Her little sister wouldn't open up. Was something more than just Wil coming to town bothering her? The next time they were together, she would ask her straight out and force her to tell. If nothing else, sharing the burden would lighten her conscience. Siblings were closer than any other people in the world. Courtney would have no choice but to open up.

The kettle whistled.

She gave Daisy a tremulous smile and removed the kettle from the heat.

"Has Dalton been by?" Daisy whispered.

Adaline swallowed and shook her head. "No, not yet." *And only I know why.*

The door opened.

Jake came through, looking windblown, unshaven, and disheveled. Adaline didn't miss her brother's red-rimmed eyes.

He passed by everyone without a word and joined her and Daisy in the kitchen, pulling his wife into an embrace. "You smell good, darlin'," he mumbled into Daisy's hair.

"And you smell like a damp, shaggy wolf, Jake." She hugged him tighter. "But I love you all the same. Where've you been?"

"At the depot seeing the Fords off. They'd like to be home before Christmas, if possible. There's another problem I have—the reward money."

Daisy patted his arm. "When the time is right, you'll think of the perfect answer. In the meantime, Hannah and the doctor are recovering, as well as the messenger from New Meringue. No one else has taken ill. Christmas will be sad this year because of Violet but filled with love, too..."

"And every Christmas from now on," he finished for her, stepping away to scrub a hand over his face. "Violet was the one who made Christmas special when I was knee-high to a grasshopper. Always knitting or sewing me something. She made sure I had some sort of toy a boy would like come Christmas morning—a slingshot, a kite, and when I was older, a pocketknife. She'd sing Christmas hymns, cook a goose, and bake several pies. She took me to Christmas service and told me to pay attention to what the preacher had to say—telling us to live a good life, don't take from others, or be kind." He heaved a deep sigh. "Has she woken up?" He glanced at Adaline. "Any news?"

Adaline shook her head. "Yesterday, while she was still able, she dictated a short list of wishes she wanted for her funeral. You to read "Psalm 23," "For the Beauty of the Earth," a hymn of praise sung by Dichelle, and for Reverend Wilbrand to not expound for more than five minutes. She doesn't want a long-winded preacher to set her mourners to daydreaming and lose sight of her day. She wants a plot on the edge of the cemetery with a view of Shady Creek."

Adaline dashed away a tear. Seemed crying was all she did lately. Other than that, Violet hadn't said a thing about her belongings, the cozy inn she'd purchased when she'd moved to Logan Meadows, or her long-lost son she laid out a dinner setting for every night. If she hadn't looked so weak and near death, Adaline might have giggled and kidded her, as the common theme of her life was always dying. She'd been proclaiming the event for years. And now, here she was at death's door, and nothing felt silly anymore. Violet was going home, and she was more than anxious to get there.

"What about today?" Jake asked.

Daisy caressed Jake's arm. "She's been sleeping since you left. We can't even rouse her to eat a few spoonfuls of bone broth or take water. Breaks my heart."

"She's killing herself!" Jake barked out angrily. "What gives her the right? She's been slowing down over the years, but she can still live a good life. People love her. Visit all the time."

The bedroom door down the hall opened and closed, and a moment later, Marlene joined them in the kitchen. She eyed the townsfolk still visiting in the front room. "Has Beth arrived?" She craned her neck as she looked around the room. "That woman better show up soon, if she knows what's good for her."

"She hasn't." Adaline noticed the strain on Marlene's face. She poured hot water into several cups for the waiting visitors and refilled the kettle, placing it back on the stove. "If she didn't come two days ago, then I doubt she'll come now. She's had plenty of time if she were so inclined. If she didn't want to walk, she could have hitched a ride with any of these visitors."

Susanna and Albert waved their goodbyes and left, passing Gabe and Julia, hand in hand as they entered, followed by baldheaded Abner Wassermann, the telegraph operator, and Mr. Hatfield, the depot operator. Gabe's face was lined with sorrow as he clung to Julia's hand. They melded into the group, speaking softly, their gaze darting to the hallway where they knew Violet waited out the last hours of her life. Gabe nodded to Jake but didn't come their way.

"Well, Beth'll have only herself to blame when she has to live with her selfish decision," Marlene said. "After all the times Violet put up with her lazy, self-centered, self-seeking ways and held her tongue, you'd think Beth would forgive her the one time she didn't. But then, we all know Beth Fairington, don't we?"

Adaline nodded, knowing a deep despair at the bottom of her soul. She'd hoped beyond hope Dalton would come out, too. But he hadn't. She'd scared him off for good with her declaration of love.

Chapter Thirty-Nine

Three days passed since Wil had been released from jail, and nothing had happened. Each day, Courtney went into town expecting the worst, only to be surprised when everyone still called out hellos, men still opened the door when she entered a building, and none of the women looked at her any differently. During these days, she'd worked long hours at the Lings' or watched after Sarah and Shane, since Jessie was staying with Violet. Mrs. Hollyhock's condition remained the same. She was weak and never left her bed. Most things she said didn't make any sense.

Upending a cloth bag of dirty garments, Courtney dumped the soiled laundry onto the scarred wooden floorboards, and sorted colors from the whites. Amazingly, she and the others had caught up with the backlog of washing lining the side wall just last week, including linen from the several eateries in town and soiled farmers' clothes. Also, finer garments from shop owners and more genteel customers that needed extra care. Dresses, skirts, and blouses, to name a few. Amazing how many people decided the small price they paid the Lings was worth the hours saved from tackling the chore themselves. With all the women helping, the laundry house now looked as neat as a pin.

Straightening, she pressed a palm to her aching back. Laundry work was exhausting. Knowing the business inside and out now, she'd not want to be stuck here for the rest of her life. The thought of going back to school didn't sound quite as bad as it had three days ago.

Across the room, Mr. Ling toiled away, head down, over the squeaking ironing board.

Marlene was off delivering a stack of linen to the El Dorado Hotel.

When a gust of cold wind whistled through the building's back door, Courtney turned and stared. She swallowed down her fear when Lan scurried by. Courtney always expected to see Wil, a mocking grin on his face. She didn't know when or where he'd show up—just that he would. He was drawing out the tension to break her. Making her wonder when, and to whom, he'd first share his story, ripping her reputation to shreds. The day was coming, and she couldn't do a thing to stop him. But where was he now? As well as the last two days? She didn't dare ask anyone. And especially not Jake.

As soon as she finished, she planned to go to the Red Rooster and see Adaline. She'd had precious little time to spend with her of late and felt a need now more than ever. She'd also like to see Violet.

She'd only seen Tyler in passing at the ranch. He'd stayed away, something smoldering in the back of his eyes. Didn't take a genius to know what was bothering him. Fine with her. She didn't need him meddling in her business any more than she needed anyone else. Mr. Upstanding could just kiss her boots if—

"Miss Costner. Miss Costner."

She glanced up.

Mr. Ling looked her way. "You have a visitor. Ask if you come to counter."

In the confines of her tiny room at the back of Maude's mercantile, Beth Fairington examined her reflection in the tiny cracked mirror on the wall. She supposed she'd have to visit Violet today. She'd waited when she'd first heard the news in hopes Violet would recover and grow stronger, so she'd be spared the humbling experience of returning to the Red Rooster and seeing the woman face-to-face, but Marlene had made it clear that was exactly what she would have to do—and apologize to boot. If not, consequences would result. Would Violet laugh and have someone toss her out once more? She blinked several times, hating her reflection that grew older year after year.

No surprise why no man looks my way. Why would he? Common face, common eyes, and a nose resembling a fence plank—long, straight, and goes on forever. If only my nose looked more like Jessie's. Or elegant like Tabitha's? And look at this hair. My graying mop reminds me of a pile of straw.

Defeated, heat pricked the back of her eyes. She chewed her lips, past the point of pain, but nothing seemed to help. They remained thin and white—just like they were now. The most unkissable mouth in Logan Meadows. Ha! Who was she kidding? The most unkissable mouth in Wyoming Territory. Probably the whole United States. She wasn't a spinster by mistake. Overcome, her heart sank all the way to the floor. Violet was to blame for everything! If she hadn't raised such an impulsive, hard-hearted son, then Beth would be a wife with children of her own.

Tommy Hollyhock. The bane of her life.

The memory of her betrothed brought a quick surge of pain. When the wedding was only a month away, he'd run off—taking her heart forever. She'd thought they were in love. That he'd come to his senses and return, but he hadn't. Before his betrayal, she was a much different person: young, happy, optimistic. She might have badgered a little, but he hadn't seemed to mind. And it was Tommy's treachery that was to blame for her taking up with that horrible gambler who'd stolen her innocence and left her to the two-legged wolves in Montana Territory.

Sagging down to the narrow cot she called a bed, she pushed at her eyes to keep the tears inside. She was totally alone. Nothing would get any better, either. She'd live out her life in solitude, grow older each year until she was as wrinkled as Violet, and eventually die and be buried on the hill.

She tipped her head, catching a sound coming from the store. There again, she recognized the deep voice asking a question. *Dalton Babcock.*

She hated to admit how much his admiration meant to her. She realized he only felt sorry for her. Thought of her as the ugly spinster with the razor-sharp tongue, like everybody else in town. But the day he'd walked her from the Red Rooster to the mercantile, she'd pretended he'd done so out of concern and a deep well of feelings lingering in his heart. She pretended he was sweet on her, and not because he was the fill-in deputy and his obligation was to look out for women and children. He was protecting her. He was…

Burying her face in her hands, she let the tears fall. Silently, but no less painful.

"How is she?" Adaline asked, quietly entering Violet's bedroom. Jessie sat at the bedside where she'd been for hours, switching between swabbing the old woman's face and reading aloud from the Bible. She looked exhausted.

"The same," Jessie whispered. "I wish her fever would break. She'd rest easier. Maybe gain back her strength." She glanced over her shoulder at Adaline, deep worry lines on her forehead. "She's been hallucinating. Seeing people that aren't here. Her deceased husband, lost son, and Virgil, the cousin she left behind in Valley Springs. Maybe this is what happens to people preparing to die."

"Jessie, you need to rest or you'll get sick as well. Let me take over for a spell, and you go lie down. Please think of yourself."

A knock sounded on the heavy front door.

Since Marlene was at the laundry house and almost everyone in town had visited yesterday, Adaline couldn't imagine who might be calling now. She hurried to the door before whoever was there had a chance to knock again and possibly disturb Violet.

At the sight of Dalton, heat flooded her face, and everything she'd said, all her words of love, came rushing back. She'd tried to forget, but a moment didn't go by that she wasn't playing the humiliating scene over and over in her mind. She'd ruined their dearly cherished friendship. Of course, Dalton didn't love *her*. He loved *Susanna*... and always would.

Chapter Forty

Dalton clutched his hat in his hands, feeling like a wet-nosed kid. He tried to ignore Adaline's pretty eyes as they searched his face. She was still hurting, he could easily see. He never wanted to hurt her, but he had no other option. She needed someone steady, someone with a good-paying job. *Someone younger.* Not him. Jake's angry words were always in his head.

"I've come to check on Violet," he said, the cold wind biting at his back. "She's all I've thought about since she took sick." *Liar! Words of love have been rolling around in my head since they passed your lips.* The moment stretched out. He wasn't sure if she'd let him inside. He glanced past her to the quiet room. "May I come in?"

She stepped back. "I'm sorry. Of course, you can. Keep in mind, you might get sick."

He entered, aware of their close proximity. The five days since he'd been so bold as to hold her in his embrace felt like yesterday. His lips tingled at the thought of his kiss to her forehead. Her three little words, spoken aloud, had the power to change the course of history. "I haven't yet, and we both were with her at the Lings'—I think I'll be fine." He looked her over. "You're fine, aren't you? Not feeling sick or anything?"

Adaline nodded but wouldn't meet his gaze. "I'm fine. It's Violet I'm worried about. Her fever is coming down but lingers. Jessie's been with her since she took ill, staying in one of the extra rooms. She knows more about Violet's home remedies than anyone else. Violet looked after Jessie for years when they both lived back in Valley Springs. They're like family."

Dalton nodded, discerning her pensive mood. "I'm glad you have help nursing her." *I wanted to come sooner, to make sure of that, but thought better.*

Adaline glanced nervously around the room. "I'll make you a cup of tea to warm you. Your face looks a little blue." She turned to go but stopped as he removed his coat and hat and hung them on the coatrack. "I hope you won't let the things I said the other night come between us. I was tired and"—she swallowed—"silly. Overwhelmed with the situation."

"'Course, you were. Who wouldn't be with what you were going through? I'd like that—the tea, I mean. And I'm glad you were brave enough to clear the air between us. I agree. I don't think either of us will ever forget the night Ying Ling was born. At least, I won't." He tried to chuckle, but the sound was flat. "I don't think I've made up for my sleep yet." Feeling awkward for going on and on, he cleared his throat. "Anyway, I don't want to lose your friendship either, Adaline, especially over a silly comment." He forced a smile as her gaze searched his face and then glanced down the hall. "Do you think I might look in on Violet?" He didn't like this skittishness between them.

"Of course. Jessie won't mind. The Red Rooster was filled with well-wishers yesterday, but today has been quiet. You go, and I'll put the kettle on the stove."

She smiled prettily, almost breaking Dalton's heart.

"When you're finished, your tea will be brewed. Violet's room is the last door on the right."

Dalton proceeded down the darkened hallway and tapped softly. Jessie opened the door. "Dalton."

"Mind if I come in?"

"Not at all. Violet would be touched if she knew you were here. Maybe your presence will rouse her. I keep hoping something will spark her spirit into recovery. She's been in and out of her mind, talking about people and events from her past." She tilted up her chin. "I'm just not ready to lose her yet. Not ready at all…"

He gazed down at Violet, her bony shoulders, knees, and toes made small peaks in the light bed covering.

Jessie reached down and felt her forehead. "Thank God, she's cool. She wakes up now and then but doesn't really know where she is." She looked up into Dalton's face. "I'm scared. I'm sure she's over the worst of whatever she had, but this behavior is something totally different. She keeps saying she's old and tired and wants to die. I don't think she's far from eternity now."

Violet mumbled and opened her eyes.

Jessie reached for the glass of water on the bedside table. "I'm glad you're awake. Time you had some water." She lifted Violet's head and shoulders.

She turned her head away. "Don't ya listen, girl? I don't want nothin'. Jist let me go. Let me die… Yer only prolonging my misery. I'm supposed to die a'fore Christmas, and that's what I intend ta do."

Jessie replaced the untouched water on the nightstand and took a step back. "That's all she ever says," she whispered. "She's killing herself by rejecting food and water. In her condition, she won't last long." She looked down at Violet. "Why are you supposed to die before Christmas, Violet?" she asked softly. "Please explain."

Violet turned back, since the threat of having to take water was gone. "Don't ya know nothin'? One was born, so one needs ta die. I'm the oldest in this here town, and I'm worn out. I've got nothin' ta live for. I'm tired, cranky, and old as sin. I look forward to my eternal rest, Jessie girl." Her tone softened, and she slowly reached for Jessie's hand. "Don't be angry with me fir that."

"Willing yourself away is not a kind way to treat all the people who love you. Think of Jake and me, Sarah, Marlene. The whole town."

The last word came out on a half-choked, pain-filled sob. Dalton had never seen Mrs. Logan when she wasn't calm, collected, and in control. Even during the train crash at Three Pines Turn, she'd remained unruffled, corralled the children, and kept them safe so their parents could help the injured passengers. Not knowing how to comfort her, Dalton said the first thing entering his mind. "A while back," he whispered, "Violet asked me to discover the identity of the do-gooder. I haven't made much progress. I'd like to fulfill her wish before…" Jessie turned and stared at him with such an expression of surprise he wondered if she was the person he was looking for.

"What did you just say?"

"Violet came to me the night of the Christmas tree celebration. She hired me to do some digging. Try to find out who's responsible for all the anonymous good deeds."

Jessie tipped her head. "But why? The do-gooder clearly doesn't want to be identified."

"That's exactly what I told her, at first. But she's adamant. Nothing I said would change her mind. She wants to thank the person before she dies. I hope I can make her wish a reality."

Jessie turned to gaze at her dear friend once more. "Well, knowing Violet, that makes perfect sense. Having any luck?" She lifted an inquisitive brow.

"That's the problem. I have no way of finding any clues unless I catch the person in the act—and after all this time, I don't think that'll happen. Or I can just ask him or her straight out. Jessie, are you the do-gooder?"

A flash of amusement crossed her face. "Me?" She laughed quietly. "Sorry, Dalton, I'm not the do-gooder. Although, I wish I could say I was."

He studied her face in the shadowy room wondering if he could believe her.

"I promise, I'm not."

By hooky. Judging her first reaction, he'd thought he might have hit the jackpot his very first try. He rocked back on his heels, considering the best way of spreading the word of what he wanted. With Violet being sick, time was of the essence. "I'm disappointed. I thought you just might be her. Can you discreetly ask around?" He glanced at Violet again. "I don't know how much time I've left to fulfill Violet's wish."

The door creaked and a stream of light illuminated the darkened room.

He turned.

"Tea is ready," Adaline whispered from the doorway. "And I'm steeping you a cup as well, Jessie. I'll bring it directly."

"Thank you," Jessie replied, and then touched Dalton's arm. "It's kind what you're doing for Violet. I'll do what I can to help."

That was all he could ask. Someway, somehow, he needed to fulfill Violet's request.

Chapter Forty-One

A few minutes before noon, and after a frigid walk out to the Red Rooster, Beth, half-frozen, stared at the door in front of her face. The wind had picked up again, and snow and sleet whipped around, making each step deplorable. She should have waited one more day. Violet wasn't going to die. The woman was too stubborn to die. Beth shivered, tugging her worn, out-of-date coat firmly around her shoulders. Her nose stung, and all ten fingers, although she wore gloves, prickled painfully. Why was she being a pushover? She no more wanted to see Violet again than jump naked into a freezing river. In all likelihood, the moment the old woman laid eyes on her, she'd throw her out a second time.

I must have lost my mind!

Marlene had been quite clear: come see Violet at once, before seeing her is no longer an option. Still, Beth hadn't gone. The embarrassing tongue-lashing Beth had endured the first time in front of Dalton, Marlene, and Adaline was bad enough. What if Violet took up where she'd left off? Or worse, wanted to talk through every last trespass Violet imagined Beth had committed over the years? Clear the air, so to speak. And if Marlene was home, Beth would be forced to sit quietly and take each insult Violet dished out—with no chance at rebuttal.

As if in reply to her agitated thoughts, the wind suddenly howled with a vengeance, bringing a smattering of sound on the porch roof.

An unsettling feeling gripped her insides, like something was about to happen. Something important—something unusual and unexpected.

The wind blasted again sending an icy chill of snow down her back. Frozen with indecision, she wanted to curse. Over a matter of minutes, the storm had intensified. She should have waited until tomorrow for this mission of mercy or come earlier in the day. If a storm rolled in now, departing the inn might not be possible. Thinking better, she almost smiled. Maybe being snowed in wouldn't be all that bad. She'd welcome a few nights in her old bed. The mattress was much more comfortable than the cot at the mercantile.

Raising her hand to knock, she stopped midair. A vision of a sick Violet, swallowed up by her mattress, came to mind. What if the woman had something extremely contagious? Beth didn't want to catch what Violet had and die herself. She wasn't getting any younger. A winter month didn't go by without her getting a sniffle. She needed to be careful.

With her mind firmly made up, Beth turned on her heel and started back for Logan Meadows. Marlene could soak her head in a bucket of vinegar for all she cared. Beth might be hardhearted, but at least she was alive. Violet should have considered the possibilities before kicking her out. The season of forgiveness wasn't making Beth do anything she didn't want to.

Gripping the handrail, she made her way carefully down the icy steps, being cautious not to make any noise. She'd not like to be spotted now, since she'd decided to retreat. She once again took in the empty yard. People weren't beating down Violet's door to say goodbye today.

Returning to Logan Meadows, Beth ducked her face under her arm for protection from the stinging sleet and snow. When she straightened, she spotted a wagon at the bend of the road, moving toward her. Still too far away in the swirling white, she couldn't see the driver. Irritation at having been caught crackled inside. Couldn't be Marlene, unless she'd been offered somebody's rig. Who then? Jake? Mr. Logan? Dalton? The possibilities were endless.

No, the man's silhouette against the white wasn't anyone she recognized. Wary, she glanced behind at the inn and wondered if the wagon was headed there or continuing on the road to New Meringue. That'd be foolish in this weather.

"Whoa," the fella called in a deep voice when he was alongside. He pulled back on the long, leather lines and the wagon rocked to a halt.

He was a large man, bundled warmly, hat pulled down tight. A thick scarf wrapped around the lower half of his face protected his skin from the sleet and was tucked into his coat. She wished she'd had the foresight to have worn a scarf herself.

The horses, their manes and fetlocks covered in snow, puffed steam from their nostrils.

"Excuse me, ma'am. Should you be out in this weather?"

Nosy. She didn't answer.

He cleared his throat. "Would that be the Red Rooster Inn up ahead? I'm new to Logan Meadows and don't want to venture farther than I have to in this storm."

All but frozen through and through now, Beth could only think about the hot stove she'd left burning in the mercantile and how good the warmth would feel once she got home. With no time for chitchat, she drew up straight. She hitched her head at the inn. "That's what the sign says." Once finished, she gripped her chattering teeth so as not to make a fool of herself.

He gave a mirthless chuckle. "You're right. Seeing is a mite difficult in the sleet."

"Of course, I'm right. I'm *always* right." She wanted to be off, but the man stared so long she began to get twitchy.

"Beth? Is that *you*?"

At the sound of her name, she gaped at the man's half-covered face. As recognition dawned, blackness descended over the swirling white. She crumpled to the ground.

Chapter Forty-Two

Bedraggled after almost six hours of laundry, Courtney took her coat from the rack and slid her wobbly arms into the sleeves. The visitor had been Jake, checking on her and making sure Wil hadn't tried anything funny. She'd told him the truth. She hadn't seen Wil and had no plans to do so. What she hadn't said was she was sure he'd be seeing her, and sooner than later. A moment later Marlene arrived to relieve her.

"You look exhausted," Marlene said, taking in Courtney's disheveled appearance. "Remember, Tyler's in town with the wagon and plans to take you back to the ranch when he's finished. He said he'd meet you at the Silky Hen. Go eat a hearty meal. You've done enough work for five people."

"If I sit for more than one minute, I'll fall asleep," Courtney replied. "I don't remember a thing past white tablecloths, broadcloth work shirts, and filthy Levi jeans. Sitting will feel so good." Thoughts of a comfortable chair at the restaurant danced before her eyes.

With an understanding smile, Marlene laid an affectionate arm across her shoulders. "You're doing a fine job. Jessie, myself, and everyone are so thankful you've taken up the slack here at the Lings'. With Violet sick, we're short Jessie and Adaline. Poor thing, doesn't look like she has many more days on this earth. She was already

stick-thin, and with only eating a drop or two of soup now and then...
Jessie is beside herself."

Courtney considered her statement with sadness. "I'm so sorry
to hear that. She's the heart of Logan Meadows. I'll miss her scratchy
old voice—and so much more." She dashed away a tear. "I heard
from a customer the doctor is on the mend and making a rapid
recovery, as well as Hannah and the fella from New Meringue. I
guess Violet is just too old and frail."

Marlene nodded, her eyes suddenly watery, too. "More than that,
she's lost the will to live. Seems like that's more of the problem than
anything else. She's starving herself."

Mr. Ling came from the front of the building with another sack
of soiled laundry.

Lan, half his size, was at his heels, her small arms full as well as
she trotted behind him.

When he saw Marlene, he gave a polite nod but continued on.
Dark circles shadowed beneath his eyes, but he had a smile for the
women.

Marlene nodded back. "He's a good man," she whispered.
"Dedicated to his work and his family. Since I came to Logan
Meadows, he and Mrs. Ling have treated me very well. You'd think
me being a saloon girl in my past life, where my looks mattered, I'd
dislike working in a laundry house, but I don't. That's because
washing clothes is honest work. I'm able to hold my head high, not
hide away in the shadows. I fall into bed tired. And I actually sleep
through the night with a good conscience. When I gaze at the clean,
ironed, and folded garments ready to be delivered, I can see the fruits
of my labor. Makes me feel content. I'll never go back to drinking
and selling myself. That's a horrible life, one I wouldn't wish on any
girl."

Why on earth was Marlene telling her this? Had Jake's mother
somehow found out about her past? Had Jake shared her secret?

Courtney realized the fear of discovery weighed heavily on her shoulders. Her mouth went dry.

"Go on now, you're dead on your feet. Tyler will be along soon enough to pick you up. He knows where to find you."

She must face Tyler as well? This day couldn't get any worse.

Courtney nodded and proceeded to weave through the small building, skirting the hot kettles, irons, and other contraptions. She hadn't spoken with Tyler since their heated exchange at the Silky Hen three days ago. He wasn't aware she'd returned the money or that Chase had witnessed the action. Since then, she'd been spending most of her waking hours at the Lings', conveniently avoiding him all together.

Outside, she drew in a deep breath of frosty air, letting the change in temperature ground her senses. The cold air revived her heated skin. Two cowboys rode by, both dipping their chins in respect. She hastily crossed the street, taking in the view of the Christmas tree. Christmas would be here in the blink of an eye. The lights in shop windows glimmered and winked in the falling snow.

Hurrying through the hotel lobby, she entered the Silky Hen from the side door and took in the tables.

Frank, the only occupant at the time, looked up from his plate and smiled.

She smiled back, and then took a table in the corner, too tired to visit. After removing her coat and laying the garment across the back of her chair, she sank down.

Roberta, a white apron over her long blue dress, came through the swinging kitchen door and headed to her table. "Courtney, dear, you look exhausted. What can I get for you? I hope you're not working so hard at the Lings' you become ill, too. Be careful."

Everyone in this town knew everyone else's business. "Thank you, Mrs. Brown. I will."

"Good. Now what can I bring you?"

"A cup of hot cocoa, please." She glanced at the chalkboard where the specials were written. "And a plate of chicken and potatoes."

Roberta nodded and hurried away.

Frank stood, laid his napkin beside his plate, and came her way. "We've all heard what you and the other women are doing for Mr. and Mrs. Ling. I think your efforts are very commendable. If there's anything I can do to help, please let me know."

"Thank you, Mr. Lloyd. I'll do that."

"Don't be caught outside unawares. There's a storm brewing."

Courtney watched Mr. Lloyd gather his hat and coat and walk out the door.

Roberta brought her a large mug of hot cocoa.

The sweet beverage lifted her flagging spirits. Perhaps everything would somehow work out after all. They said miracles happened when you least expected them. Well, she could do for one right now.

When the café door opened, she expected to see Tyler. Instead, Wil walked in looking cold and hungry.

When he saw her alone in the empty room, he plastered an ugly smile on his lips. Without invitation, he proceeded to her table and pulled out a chair. He sat with a plop, his fists landing on the tabletop, making everything rattle and her cocoa spill over the rim.

"Time's past. I don't want the money no longer. I'll see you at the Christmas Eve party. I'm making my announcement then and there for the whole town to hear." His smile went from ear to ear. "No woman bests me and gets away with it! You're gonna curse the day we met."

She was too tired to fight. "I already do, Wil, and have for some time."

Roberta came out of the kitchen with Courtney's plate of chicken at the same time Tyler came through the café door. The unbuttoned sheepskin-lined coat Tyler often wore revealed a brown wool vest and brown bandanna around his neck. His leather chaps, protecting his denims, were wet and his Stetson dangled in his fingertips. No doubt he'd been working hard only minutes before. Looking like a thunderhead ready to burst, he stormed across the room, flipped his hat to a nearby tabletop without missing a beat, and grabbed Wil by his shoulder, yanking him from the chair.

The two men stood eye to eye.

"Stay *away* from Miss Costner!"

Wil sneered. "If you knew her true character, you might think different. But I'll save the telling until Christmas Eve. A little present for you all."

Courtney sucked in a breath. Facing Tyler's wrath, Wil wouldn't wait until the Christmas Eve party to spill the juicy truth he'd been itching to tell. Thankfully, the café was empty but for Roberta still standing at the kitchen door holding Courtney's plate of chicken.

"Blackmail doesn't sit well with me, Lemon, and especially not when your target is a young woman. I'm sick of your ugly face. Get out of town now, this minute. If not, I won't be responsible when I kill you. You hear me? This warning is the only one you'll get. I mean what I say."

"You're a dandy," Wil chortled. "I'm not afraid of you!"

Faster and more deadly than a rattlesnake, Tyler smashed Wil in the mouth.

Wil reeled across the room. His back hit a table, ending his momentum. Four clean coffee cups and a handful of utensils clattered to the floor. By the time Tyler stalked over, Wil was on his feet and had snatched a steak knife from the table. He slashed out.

The memory of the fight back in Newport, when Wil had attacked Jake with a knife, flashed in Courtney's mind. Already on her feet, she dashed to the wall for a cane she'd seen when she'd come in, forgotten by someone. Hoisting the weapon, she swung at Wil's head, striking him with a loud crack.

The knife sailed out of his hand and clattered under a chair across the room.

He whirled on her with flared nostrils. Hatred glittered in his eyes.

Tyler launched forward, wrapping Wil in his arms. The two fell with a thud.

Roberta grasped Courtney's arm. "Get out of here," she screamed. "Before you're hurt."

Courtney pulled away. "I can't leave Tyler. Please, go get help!"

Without being asked twice, Roberta dashed out the door.

The men rolled and punched in a tangle of rage.

Courtney shouted for them to stop, but they fought on like wild bulls. More tables were hit and upended.

With a burst of power, Tyler pummeled Wil's stomach and then his face.

Wil went limp on the floor.

Courtney gripped Tyler by the arm and tugged him out the door, determined to get the two men apart before they killed each other. Intermittent sleet and wind prickled her face. Tyler was bleeding from the corner of his left eyebrow and his bottom lip. His right knuckles were skinned. "Please get in the wagon," she begged, as she pushed him to climb up onto the passenger's seat. His feet stayed anchored to the ground. Any second, Wil might burst out the door.

Moving his jaw back and forth, he grimaced. "I'm not running from a fight. Wil Lemon doesn't scare me."

"Don't be stubborn!" she barked back. "Roberta went for Dalton. He'll jail Wil again for fighting. And you, too, just like he did Dwight. I don't want your misfortune on my head. Maybe Dalton'll cool down if you're nowhere to be found. Please, Tyler, let's go. Wil brings havoc wherever he goes. I *hate* him. I hate him with all my heart!" *And I don't want you locked up right next to him, knowing what he'd love to share.*

She realized Tyler hadn't responded and stood there, staring down into her face. The truth was out. Wil had done what he'd set out to do. Maybe not in so many words, but he didn't have to. He confirmed what Tyler had only before suspected.

Feeling bold, she glanced up into his bloodied face, resisting the urge to press her hand to his battered face in comfort.

His gaze locked on hers.

She couldn't tell what he thought—but she could imagine plenty. "I'm glad you finally know the truth," she said for his ears only. "Now I needn't pretend anymore."

He glanced past her shoulder at the wagon side.

She shook his arm, fearful Wil would regain consciousness and come out the door looking for more. "Let's go! The storm is building. We need to get back out to the ranch while we still can. Frank Lloyd said as much two minutes before you came into the café."

"Your food?"

"I've lost my appetite." She pushed his arm again.

This time, he climbed up but scooted into the driver's seat where she'd intended to be. He bent to the side and extended a hand.

Grasping her skirt with one hand and Tyler's hand with her other, she scrambled up with renewed energy. As the wagon crossed the bridge and turned up the road leading to the ranch, a blast of wind passed through her clothes chilling her skin. In their quick flight she'd left her coat in the café. She wrapped her arms around herself and stayed the impulse to shiver.

Tyler looked over and began to shrug out of his garment.

"Don't."

"Take it," he grumbled. "And hand me the blanket covering the supplies, if you would."

So formal. Of course, she didn't expect their friendship to remain the same. He knew about her tattered reputation. He'd judged her and found her lacking. That was easy enough to believe from the lack of attention he'd given her the last few days. No other outcome was possible.

Strands of her hair, loose from the work at Lings', whipped around her face as she threaded her arms into his coat. Heady warmth billowed from inside, and her heart beat faster. The scent—windy, wild, unpredictable. Tyler Weston was a good man. The way he spoke of his father and family was endearing. He did everything by the book. Honest. Noble at all times. Not a chance in heck existed he'd ever understand the mistakes she'd made in her past. Once she had the coat buttoned, she turned on the wobbly buckboard seat and reached into the back, grasping the blanket covering the sacks of grain and other supplies. She scooted closer and tucked the protection around Tyler's shoulders without saying a word and then placed the ends into his free hand. "Driving will be tricky."

"I can manage."

He wasn't much on talking, at least not now. What a change from the other time he had met her in the Silky Hen. They'd already turned the corner out of town and were passing Sheriff Preston's small yellow house on one side and Brenna and Gregory Hutton's house on the other.

The teacher was out on his front porch with a coffee cup in his hand. When he saw them, he waved and smiled broadly.

He expected her back at school when the Christmas break was over. Courtney forced herself to smile and waved back.

"Hurry on home, you two!" Mr. Hutton called cheerily. "Snow's in the air. Don't get caught! Tell Sarah to keep practicing her spelling words."

"I will, Mr. Hutton. We read every night."

He nodded. "That's wonderful. Thank you, Courtney. The children respond to you. I appreciate the help."

Mr. Hutton acted as if all was right with the world. If he only knew. Courtney had to turn halfway around and squint through the sleet to still see him. She waved. "Good day!" Thank heavens he hadn't noticed Tyler's bloodied face. The fewer people who knew of the incident, the better.

Once they were past the teacher's house, Tyler looked over, the once-bloody spots on his face darkening from the cold. "Will you tell me what happened? Or must I go on filling in the blanks myself?"

Chapter Forty-Three

Tyler didn't know if he should ask such personal information or if he had the right, but damn, he felt the need to know. And somehow, he felt the telling would be good for Courtney. He still had a hard time believing she wasn't the innocent child he'd thought her to be, but he'd had some time to ponder the last few days about her and the conversation about the stolen coins. He'd come to terms with the truth. In most cases, people weren't what they seemed. So she had a past. Secrets. Same as each and every living soul in this town. Him included, he admitted. Did her mistakes change who she was now? Wil Lemon had forced her. Stolen her virginity. That was a sad fact no woman wanted to tell. Since he'd uttered the words, Courtney had all but turned to stone. "Courtney?"

"You said you already knew. You guessed. Why must I say more?"

She didn't have to. But he hoped she would. Anything she said could help him understand a little better.

The road narrowed and went through a stand of swaying trees. They weren't so far from the ranch to be in danger, but with only this blanket, he was freezing and knew Courtney must feel the same. Sleet had changed to snow. He'd take the blowing snow over being blasted in the face by icy slush. His lip throbbed painfully, but the cut above his eye had gone numb. "You don't have to share, if you don't want. I just thought you'd like to get whatever you're hiding off your chest. There's no shame. You know you can press charges against him, don't you? What he did is a crime. People won't allow his kind of behavior—now or ever." He watched her closely as he spoke.

The team moved like molasses in the cold.

She turned away and gazed off the side of the road.

She was taking this hard, although Wil's attack must have happened long ago, when they were in Newport. Did time help this kind of assault? Soften them, as if they'd never happened? He didn't think so. Did Jake or Adaline know, so they could be a help to her? So many unanswered questions. "Courtney, please, say something. I want to help. You can't do this alone."

She turned back, pain clouding her eyes.

He pulled the team to a halt and scooted closer. The wind had eased, allowing the snowflakes to float slowly to the earth. She was rigid and cold. He lifted the blanket and wrapped the warmth around them both. "Tell me, Courtney. Don't be afraid. I won't think less of you. Wil overpowered you. I can tell you one thing, that skunk will pay dearly for hurting you—and then having the gall to follow you here. I promise you that."

"No, don't promise me anything," she whispered. "It wasn't like that..."

The quietly spoken words mingled with the gently falling snowflakes. White grew thicker along the horses' manes and backs. They really shouldn't dawdle. Getting back to the ranch should be a priority. He leaned forward, trying to see her face. In a moment of clarity, he realized she was more to him than just a friend. Just a girl he wanted to help. He'd protect her against any monster—*Wil Lemon*—with all his might. "What do you mean?"

"Wil didn't force me. I'm truly a fallen woman, Tyler. Someone you don't want to associate with or have in your life. Now that you know, please get the horses moving. Once I leave this wagon, you'll never have to deal with me again." A waver of sadness colored her voice.

Stunned, he stared straight ahead.

"I do want to tell you, though," she went on, "I returned the coins to their rightful spot the night of our last conversation, so you don't have to worry about my thievery any longer. Mr. Logan caught me. He knows only about the coins, nothing else." She breathed out deeply and then shivered.

"What happened?" Tyler forced the question through his lips. Frigid air seeped through the blanket and clothing, but he barely felt the cold. His mind was still circling her last revelation. "How'd he react?" he heard himself ask.

"He's forgiven me. But as soon as Christmas is past, I'm sure, he'll think better of the arrangements and suggest I find a new place to live. I certainly won't blame him in the least.

"Tyler, please, let's go! I'm cold, and so are you. I'm done talking. If we don't, we'll get stuck in this storm." She gestured to the countryside growing whiter with each passing moment. "The snow is building, making extra work for the horses. As soon as I can, I'm going home to Newport." She shivered and huddled in his coat. "I have friends there. I think Mrs. Bennet will give me Adaline's old job in the mercantile. I feel good about the decision. My mind's made up."

He wanted to respond. Keep the conversation light, help her in some way, but he'd been shocked into silence. He hadn't expected her response. And he also knew she was right about the snow and the urgency of returning to the ranch. He'd come to the incorrect conclusion Wil had attacked her, forced himself on her, and then afterwards, controlled her with threat of exposure. Tyler was sure the snake had pressured her and filled her with guilt. That account wasn't difficult to believe. The pain ripping his heart was almost unbearable. Even if she had been willing, Wil should have known better. Could Tyler kill a man outright? He certainly felt the need.

Chapter Forty-Four

When someone pounded on the inn's door so hard it sounded as if they'd kicked the barrier with their boot, Adaline practically dropped the cup raised to her lips. She cut her gaze to Dalton, who sat next to her. Dalton surged to his feet and strode to the door. Adaline followed.

Amid the flurry of snowflakes, a man stood in the open doorway, holding the limp form of a woman. They were both covered in snow.

Dalton yanked the door wider. "Come inside!"

Adaline ran to the couch and cleared away pillows, as well as a folded quilt. "Put her here."

Leaving a track of snow in his wake, the man did as he was instructed and laid the woman on the worn furniture and then propped a pillow behind her head. He gazed at her for several long moments.

Adaline gaped. "It's Beth! I didn't recognize her all bundled up and covered in snow." Adaline quickly brushed off most of the snow. She shook out the quilt and tucked it firmly around her. "What happened? Is she hurt?" Who was this man? Had he accosted her?

"My name's Thomas Hollyhock. The woman in the mercantile said my mother's taken sick." He studied Beth again. "I was coming this way and stopped to ask her if I was headed in the right direction.

When she recognized me, she swooned. I guess seeing me after all these years was too much."

The hint of sadness in his voice was impossible to miss. All of a sudden, Adaline remembered the unhappy tale about Violet's son and Beth Fairington. How he'd run out on their engagement. But he was *so much* older—which made sense now that she thought about that aspect, with Violet being the age she was. Age hadn't crossed her mind before, just the elements of the unfortunate story.

"She was only about thirty yards from the inn," he went on. "And headed for Logan Meadows. But you seem surprised to see her. She must have come from here, didn't she?"

He was tall, with wide shoulders and large hands. His face had wrinkles, but he looked kind and his voice was almost like warm whiskey. Without having reason to, Adaline instantly liked him.

Dalton shook his head. "Miss Fairington wasn't here today. She hasn't been out to the Red Rooster for days."

"I can't imagine why she'd venture all this way and not come inside," Adaline mumbled, shifting her attention between the newcomer and Beth. "Especially on a day like this."

Beth moaned and lifted a hand to her face, but still her eyes remained closed.

Mr. Hollyhock turned and looked down the hall. "As much as I'd like to stand here talking, I feel a need to see my ma. Too many years have passed."

"Tommy Hollyhock?"

Jessie had silently appeared from down the hallway and stood behind them.

A smile formed on Tommy's face. "Yes, ma'am. That's me. Do I know you?"

Her face lit up like the sun. "No, but I know you—from everything your mother has told me. I came to see who was pounding on the door. Thank God, you've come! Violet will be so surprised. She's always attested you'd return someday! And now you're here."

Tommy's smile faded. "How is she? May I see her?"

Beth had awakened and slowly sat up, an expression on her face unfamiliar to Adaline. She remained silent for the first time in her life.

"Of course you can see her." Jessie stepped closer. "You must see her! But be warned, she might not recognize you. She doesn't know where she is and speaks mostly in riddles. She's conscious minutes at a time before lapsing back into sleep. She's as weak as a sparrow, but the sight of you might be the medicine she needs. If we could get her to eat, I think she might recover. But she's refusing all food."

His gaze finally went to Beth. "I'm sorry I frightened you, Miss Fairington," he said very respectfully. "That wasn't my intention. Can we speak after I see my mother? Will you wait?"

Beth nodded.

Dalton glanced at the window. "No one's going anywhere until this snow lets up. Town's not far, but getting turned around with white vertigo is all too easy. I see you have horses and a wagon. I'll put them up in the shed on the back of the chicken coop, if you'd like, and toss them some hay. The rickety protection is better than nothing."

"I can't ask you to do that."

"You're not asking, I'm offering. Now, go on and see Violet. We're all mighty happy you've returned."

Tommy took a deep breath and smiled. "I'm much obliged."

Wrapped in a sea of peacefulness, Violet reposed without pain, floating on her mattress as if the bed were a double-soft pillow cloud resting in a lake of freshly churned butter. Was she dead? She wouldn't mind at all—and actually hoped she was. She'd be free of all the nosy townsfolk murmuring on the other side of the door. They were curious about her final moments on earth. Well, they could just go gawk at somebody else. She'd heard their whispers, but opening her eyes took too much effort. She'd just rest here all day without having to get up to feed her chickens, walk into town, make supper, or wash the linen. She felt a bit warm, but perhaps that was what heaven was all about with a harsh winter outside. The comfort of a lovely room to call all her own.

The annoying squeak of the door invaded her daydream, and she realized she was still on earth. Why hadn't she oiled that darn hinge months ago? Couldn't an old woman die in peace? She didn't want any more willow bark tea or dry toast. Her headache was gone. And, *please*, no more chicken soup! She would gain her wings sooner without. Violet felt a presence sit by her side but didn't have one ounce of energy to lift her eyelids.

Who was here? Jessie? Adaline? Violet's mind roused for one second wondering, and then she let the thought drift away.

Someone cleared their throat.

The sound was deep, not any of her three darling women. *A man?* Not caring, she drifted in and out of the ecstasy at hand.

"I'm sorry."

The gruffly spoken statement was soft and halting. Sorry? *Who* was sorry? Darn her curiosity, she could never ignore him now. Violet tried to lift one lid, but the effort proved too much. *Don't matter, really.* She had one foot in the grave and the other still planted here on earth. Dying didn't hurt at all.

"I've made some bad mistakes in my life but running away was the worst of all. I don't ask for your forgiveness, because I'm not worthy. Still, I'd like to say the words—and will say them—until my dying day."

Land sakes! What was this feller going on about? She didn't have the power to forgive anyone. The deep voice wasn't Jake, or Hunter, her newly adopted grandson. Wasn't any voice she recognized of the men around town. Angrily gripping her eyes more firmly together, she hoped the old coot, whoever he was, would get the hint and go away. Bother someone else. Let her die in peace.

"I've thought of you every day, hoping you were safe. Living a good life."

What in tarnation? The conversation was preposterous. The only way to get some quiet was to shoo him away. "I ain't no preacher ta forgive sins, *mister*." His sharp intake of breath fed her irritation. Using all her effort, she cracked her eyelids.

He sat hunched over, his head cradled in his large hands.

"Who are ya, anyway?"

He slowly straightened, tears shimmering in his eyes.

It was Chase Logan. Why in tarnation was he so upset? The two had had their disagreements when she'd questioned his motives about Jessie, and then threatened him at gunpoint to marry her, but those days were long past. They liked each other well enough now.

She narrowed her eyes, trying to focus. No, he wasn't Chase, unless his face had miraculously been toughened and aged overnight by—what? Harsh winds? Annoyed at the suddenly aged, presumptuous whippersnapper, she harrumphed. "Go disturb someone else's dying, would ya? Was almost over the edge. I don't know what this yammerin's about, but I can't hear the heavenly violins through the ruckus." She wanted to show him the door but was too weak. "Go have a good heart-ta-heart with Reverend Wilbrand. That's his job!"

"Ma, it's *me*—Tommy. Don't you recognize me? I'm sorry for staying away so long."

Tommy? My Tommy? She'd always marveled how much Chase Logan resembled her boy and told Chase and Jessie so more times than she could count. Was this really Tommy by her side, returned in the nick of time? Or had she lost her mind? Was she talking to an empty chair?

"Ma? Can you hear me?" He leaned closer, placing one warm, roughened hand along the curve of her cheek.

Then she recognized him. His eyes, his face, older, but still her dear, sweet boy. He'd come home, just as she'd always believed he would. A million words fluttered through her heart, but a stranglehold of love and emotion kept her speechless. Tears filled her eyes, and she finally nodded. "Tommy," she mumbled. "Tommy's come home."

Slipping off the chair, he dropped to his knees, leaning closer. Her hand nestled in his, next to his lips, as tears leaked from his eyes. "Yes, yes, Ma. Mrs. Logan says you'd recover if you'd only try and eat a little. Please eat for me, Ma. I don't want you to die, not now, not now that I finally came to my senses. Will you do that? Will you eat some broth if I go fetch you some?"

Could she? Give up on her desire to meet her maker and return to the living? Or was she too far gone? She'd been set to go, made her decision, and when the influenza didn't take her, she'd just stopped eating. But now, looking into the dear, wavering face before her eyes, she realized she couldn't. She didn't want to die. She wanted to live! And love! She had to learn about Tommy, where he'd been. What he'd been doing. How his life had played out. Maybe he had a family and was bringing her some grandbabies.

"Yessir." A tiny voice was all she could muster, but by the smile on his face, he'd heard her. "I'll eat whatever ya give me."

Chapter Forty-Five

A few moments after Tommy Hollyhock disappeared into his mother's bedroom, Beth took herself away to her old room, claiming she had a headache and needed to rest.

Jessie excused herself to the kitchen to make a new batch of chicken soup in hopes Violet's appetite would return.

That left him in the front room with Adaline, mostly just sitting by the fire and staring into their teacups. He chanced a glance in her direction, wondering what she was thinking. She held her cup with both hands, as if trying to warm her palms, or perhaps shield herself from him. Today, she'd seemed different. Like she'd come to some kind of revelation about him. He missed the stars he no longer saw in her eyes.

"How was Violet when you went to see her?" Adaline sipped her tea, her expression guarded.

"Much too weak. She's the spice of Logan Meadows. Keeps everyone on their toes. I remember a scolding she gave me and Albert for a little disagreement we had the last time I was in town. I actually think Albert blushed under her tongue-lashing."

"A tongue-lashing? What was it about?"

He'd walked right into that. Why did he bring up the fight under Shady Creek bridge? Hadn't his humiliation at the time been enough punishment for acting like a schoolboy? "Nothing important. I can't remember."

For one instant, her lips compressed as if she'd just tasted something rancid. He thought of the warmth in her voice when they'd been tucked away in the deserted pig shed, riding out the storm. No hint of that affection showed now.

"Not important? I can't imagine what you and Albert might have a disagreement about. Something had to draw Violet's attention—and scolding? You really can't remember? Sounds impossible."

Was she fishing? He'd long since turned over whatever affection he still held inside for Susanna to the Almighty. She was his past. Sometimes it still hurt, if he let himself dwell on what might have been. But since he'd lost her, he tried not to even do that. Best for everyone concerned. Fibbing by omission to Adaline didn't feel right but going into detail felt worse. "I shouldn't have brought it up."

She nodded and sipped from her cup.

Something had changed. Perhaps the situation was as he'd said, and her words of love had been the result of a surge of tension and fear the night little Ying Ling had been born. They could still be friends, possibly. They'd forget the fateful night and the words she'd uttered. He watched her lips on the edge of the cup, so chiseled and—he jerked his gaze to the lantern on the other side of the room, realizing he was imagining what a kiss would be like. Jake wouldn't cotton to a courtship. Dalton must remember himself whenever he weakened. She tipped her head, when only a week ago, she would have reached out and touched his arm. He liked the old Adaline better.

"What's wrong?" she asked. "Did you remember something you had to do?"

He got a grip of his emotions and took a sip from his cup, listening to Jessie rattling around in the kitchen. "Ahh, no. Just something Violet asked me to do, if I could."

"A case?"

He nodded, hating himself for avoiding the truth again.

"Anything I can help with?"

Her eyes brightened. Her interest pleased him immensely. "Maybe," he replied. Was he being selfish to accept her assistance, to aid them over this troubled spot in their friendship? She was as sharp as a whip. He'd welcome any input. "I don't think Violet would mind me telling you, since time is of the essence. She's asked me to uncover the do-gooder before she dies, so she can say thank you. I tried to dissuade her, but she's adamant. Do you think you might keep your eyes open? Let me know if you see anything suspicious. We won't tell anyone except Violet."

Adaline leaned in his direction, excitement dancing in her eyes. "Yes, I'd be delighted to help. And I won't tell a soul what you're doing. As a matter of fact, I heard Albert mention the day he and Susanna returned from New Meringue, a small welcome home sign was hanging on the doorknob of their house. They have no idea who's responsible but suspect the do-gooder as well."

Dalton tapped his chin with a forefinger. "If that's the case, the do-gooder can't be Susanna. She was gone and couldn't have accomplished the task." Setting his cup onto the hearth, he withdrew a list of names and a pencil from his pocket and drew a line through Jessie and Susanna. Adaline's fresh scent tickled his senses. For some reason, her lips kept drawing his attention.

"Jessie?" she asked.

"I spoke with her when I went in to see Violet. She denied being the person and promised me for Violet's sake she'd admit to the fact if she were. With everything going on in town concerning Wil Lemon and Christmas, I hadn't given Violet's request much thought, and then she took sick. I'd like to do this for her if I can, before she passes away."

Her lips quivered. "She might not pass, Dalton. Nothing is for sure."

That was true.

Adaline tipped her head as she leaned closer and read the list in his hand. When she looked up, their faces were barely an inch apart.

Again, he dropped his gaze to her lips. "Adaline," he whispered as he moved nearer, thinking he'd waited an eternity for this moment.

Adaline closed her eyes and their lips gently brushed.

"Soup's on and—"

They jerked apart.

Jessie disappeared back into the kitchen and the list of names fluttered to the floor.

Adaline's nearly empty cup spun sideways in his direction. She yelped.

He snatched it out of the air, her tea still safely inside. "Here you go," he barked, flustered and embarrassed. "Don't want this spilling on your skirt."

Adaline took the cup with shaky hands and stood, her bright face reminding him of the Christmas berries growing along the road. She stood and hurried to the kitchen herself.

He ambled over to a window and stared at the falling snow. As much as he hated to admit it, he'd fallen in love with Adaline— another woman he couldn't have.

Chapter Forty-Six

Beth huddled under the thick covers of her old bed, shaking uncontrollably. Her teeth clattered and an icy coldness had seeped all the way through to her bones, having nothing to do with her sodden dress lying crumpled in a heap on the floor or the thin layer of frost on the windowpane. She wiped the wetness from her cheeks and stared at a cobweb hanging in the corner of the ceiling.

Remaining out front by the fire—as Dalton and Adaline had encouraged her to do—hadn't been possible. Seeing Tommy rattled her soul. Why on earth had he returned? Memories from long ago rushed back full force.

At twelve, she held a childish infatuation for the handsome, thirty-nine-year-old man with the boyish smile and intoxicating chuckle and had visited the mercantile daily. Before school, after, and any time in-between. Tommy was a permanent fixture behind the counter, stacking shelves, or sweeping the floor. His wink and smile were sure to send a bevy of butterflies racing up and down her back and make her blush to her roots. He'd always chuckle and toss her a piece of hard candy from the jar.

The age difference between them never bothered Beth in the least. Thirty years separated her own parents, who'd had Beth late in life. Beth fancied Tommy distinguished and herself open-minded. The girls at school shied away, so she'd spent most of her time alone in her room, dreaming of the day she became Mrs. Tommy Hollyhock.

At fourteen, she suffered the death of her father. The small home they lived in was paid off, and he'd set away enough money for her and her mother to live on for years. Never very hardy, two years later her mother went to her grave from an unknown illness. But until then, she'd encouraged her daughter's feelings toward Tommy. She'd twist Beth's hair in rag curls each night, no matter how uncomfortable they were on the pillow, because the result of shiny brown ringlets swishing around her shoulders was sure to garner a compliment. *You look like a princess in a fairy tale with all those curls, Miss Fairington. You better be careful, or someday a handsome prince will scoop you up onto his white horse and spirit you away into the sunset.* Beth cherished each morsel of attention Tommy sent her way.

At eighteen and alone, she'd made her move, fearful another woman would come along and catch his eye. She applied for the part-time position Violet had advertised in the window—and got the job.

By then, Tommy was forty-five, a confirmed bachelor, with stories of taking off and seeing the world. More to life existed than his ma's small mercantile in Valley Springs, he'd say with a faraway gleam in his eyes.

The words always brought a haunted look to Violet and sent fear and pain slicing through Beth's heart. By then, he'd branched out and started a side business of his own. When he wasn't in the mercantile, he was doing odd jobs for anyone who'd pay. He roofed, built sheds or barns, painted, helped with plowing when planting season rolled around, and even branded cattle if a ranch in the area was short a hand. There wasn't anything he couldn't or wouldn't do.

Still, no matter how much Beth smiled, accidently-on-purpose touched his hand, or brought him baked cookies and left little notes, he thought her a girl, a child, and chucked her under her chin, to her frustration. More than a few times, she'd hurried home to an empty

house, ignoring concerned looks from passersby, to lock herself
away in her bedroom and cry her eyes out. Something had to be done.
Something drastic! If not, her beloved would pack his bag and leave
Valley Springs without a by-your-leave. The day after her nineteenth
birthday, she formulated a plan that was sure to succeed. And it had,
for a while.

Someone knocked on Beth's door.

Beth wiped her eyes and quietly blew her nose on the
handkerchief crumpled in her fist. "Go away. I'm resting."

The door slowly squeaked open, and Jessie peeked in. "I've
made some chicken soup that'll be finished soon. Can I set you a
place at the table? Lunchtime has come and gone. You must be
hungry."

"No, thank you, though. I ate before I came out, but I appreciate
the gesture."

As if she hadn't heard a word, Jessie stepped into the room and
softly closed the door, staying where she stood.

Jessie Strong Logan, one of the banes of Beth's life, showing
pity at her most vulnerable moment. Everyone in Valley Springs had
loved Jessie the instant Nathan Strong brought her home. She'd
stepped into town, and all the single men took notice. And who
wouldn't? Young, fresh-faced, and beautiful, with a blanket of long,
golden hair flowing down her back. Beth had been surprised she
hadn't come with angel wings. Didn't matter in the least that Jessie
was already married.

"Beth, your lips are blue. Please come out and warm yourself by
the fire. Or at least open your door so some of the heat can get inside.
This room is freezing." She came closer and edged her hip onto the
bed. "Mr. Hollyhock is still in with Violet, so you've nothing to
worry about."

Nothing to worry about? Just like Jessie to downplay the
situation. How would she feel if the joke was on her? When the town
got wind of this, Beth would be the laughingstock of Logan

Meadows, even more than she already was. Had Tommy returned to put the finishing touches on her never-healing broken heart?

"I'm not hungry, Jessie," Beth gritted out. "But thank you. You really don't need to worry. Go out where it's warmer." She'd like to give Jessie an earful, tell her to mind her own business, leave her in peace, but she just didn't have the energy anymore. Why bother? She was thirty-five, a spinster, and destined to live out her life in the back of Maude's store with the lumpy cot and broken mirror.

Jessie had two children, a loving, handsome husband, and a beautiful home.

All Beth had ever really wanted was Tommy. But he'd not wanted her in return. A wad of emotion pushed painfully up Beth's throat, threatening to strangle her. She gasped and turned away, embarrassed because she couldn't stem the hot tears threatening to fall.

Jessie surged forward and wrapped Beth in her arms. "Please don't cry. Things'll work out. Mr. Hollyhock asked you to stay. He probably wants to talk and tell you he's sorry for what happened."

No, he probably wanted to blame her for wrecking his life. As hard as she tried, she just couldn't keep her sobs inside. One was followed by two, then four. By the time she ran out of tears, she'd been in Jessie's arms for a good ten minutes. She prayed to God no one else had heard, especially Tommy.

They sat still for several moments longer, and then Jessie leaned back and gently brushed Beth's hair, soggy from the snow, out of her eyes.

Humiliated, Beth couldn't meet her gaze.

"I have no idea what Mr. Hollyhock is thinking, or what he'll say, but I hope you'll hear him out with an open heart. For your sake, as well as his. I know he hurt you in the worst way, and you have every reason to scorn him, but I hope you won't. He's been carrying the guilt of what he's done for a long time."

"Fifteen years," Beth whispered.

Jessie nodded. "That's punishment enough. And *you've* been carrying your own hurt. That must have been awfully heavy."

Using her hanky, Beth wiped the tears from her face and composed herself, feeling foolish to have fallen apart in such a manner. She should say something kind to Jessie, but her mind was still fogged with regrets and pain.

Jessie looked at the floor. "I'll take your dress out and hang it by the fire, but for now you can borrow one of mine. I've been staying here since Violet took sick and have the room down the hall."

"Oh no, I—"

"You can, and you will! The snowstorm has not lessened. I don't believe anyone will be going back to town today. It's a good thing the Red Rooster has plenty of rooms." She smiled and patted Beth's hand. "You came out to make peace with Violet and lost your nerve?"

Beth nodded. Why not admit to another foolish decision? It was only one in a million. Nothing mattered anymore. "After walking all the way from town, I hesitated, my resolve crumbling. I didn't want to get thrown out a second time. So I changed my mind at the door. Silly, I know…"

"Not silly. But I know she wouldn't have thrown you out. Even though she won't say as much, she misses you dearly and has been sad since you left. You're like the daughter she never had, Beth. You must know that by now, and all the years you've been together. Once, when she was delirious, she mumbled your name and said she was sorry. I'm happy you decided to come."

Boots clomped past her door.

Jessie's eyes widened. "That must be Mr. Hollyhock."

"I would think so." How old was Tommy now? To retain her sanity, she'd stopped keeping track years ago.

Jessie stood. "I'll go get a dress you can use and some fresh water to wash your face. Dinner will be ready as soon as I make a batch of biscuits to go along with the soup. Freshen up."

She never believed she'd be taking advice from Jessie Logan, but that was the case.

Jessie bundled up the dress crumpled on the floor and gave her a fleeting smile before she left the room.

Apparently, Jessie did have angel wings, just ones that couldn't be seen.

Chapter Forty-Seven

By the time the wagon reached the ranch, Courtney felt like a cube of ice. Snow swirled everywhere. The barn was buttoned up tight, and no ranch hands were around to be seen.

Tyler drove the wagon up to the ranch house. "Get inside and get warm," he shouted into the wind. "Could be a whiteout."

Courtney grasped his arm. "No. Drive to the barn, and I'll open the doors. The horses are weary."

"I've got it!"

Feeling hollow for all the shameful admissions, having the storm to argue about now was a relief. Gabe or Chase were caring for the children. They wouldn't miss her for a few more minutes. "Please, allow me to help, Tyler. I want to."

He shrugged, as if to say he couldn't stop her anyway. His lips were blue and his face wet. She suspected she didn't look much better. The biting cold was something she hadn't experienced in Newport. Storms happened on the Pacific coast but were nothing like a Wyoming whiteout.

"Fine then!" He slapped the long lines across the horses' backs, and the buckboard jerked forward. Tyler wrestled the horses around and headed toward the narrow road to the barn. "Sure you can get the doors? They're heavy." He stopped the wagon at the barn.

"Yes, I'm sure," she said. "I've been out here before." She climbed down as gracefully as she could with frozen fingers and feet and hobbled over to the tall doors. Heaving with all her might, she opened one side to the restless sound of the horses inside.

One horse nickered. Another kicked the side of his stall.

Working the other door, she backed away.

Then Tyler drove the wagon past and down the center passageway. He pulled up on the lines.

As she closed the barn doors, silence descended. The storm raged outside but being protected from the wind brought instant relief.

Tyler went straight to work, unhitching the snow-covered horses. The poor geldings waited patiently to be freed from their harness. Quickly stabled, Tyler climbed into the loft and tossed down a good amount of hay.

"They eat that much?" she asked, amazed.

"Today they deserve extra."

Shivering violently, she watched Tyler wipe the harnesses before hanging them in the tack room. "Will the horses be all right wet like that?"

He was on his way back. "They normally stay in the pasture. I'll put them out as soon as they eat."

He was a good man. He hadn't castigated her when he'd learned the true circumstances with Wil. She'd steeled herself for his reaction, which never really came. The barn around them was quiet, with just the sound of the sodden horses munching away. His battered face looked painful.

"Come on. You're cold, and your lips are bluer than a berry pie. If I didn't know better, I'd think you'd just eaten one. Let's get you inside."

His kindness touched her. For one moment, she didn't want to feel shame. She smiled back into his earnest eyes, which truly seemed concerned for her welfare. Wil had never been so solicitous in their courtship, if she could call what they'd been about by that term. As cold as she was, she didn't want to go just yet, didn't want to let go of the warm feelings tumbling around inside.

He stared, a small smile pulling the corners of his lips.

"Tyler, I like to—"

Somebody slid open one side of the barn doors and strode inside.

She and Tyler weren't standing that close, but still, she took a long step away.

"Ty!"

Jake, with snow-covered shoulders, closed the distance, his saddle horse trailing behind. They skirted the wagon and continued to where she and Tyler stood. "Thought I saw you arrive." His gaze took in Courtney's condition and the purpling of Tyler's face and frowned.

A spot of dried blood marked the corner of Tyler's left eyebrow. The cut in his lower lip crusted.

Tyler nodded. "Just came from town."

"Yeah, I followed your tracks. Good thing you didn't wait any longer to set off, or else you might've gotten stuck. Could have three feet by mornin'."

Her brother's gaze traced back and forth between her and Tyler. What was he thinking? *Something.* Jake didn't often string so many words at one time.

Tyler glanced out the door at the white wall of snow. "I think you're right." He rubbed a hand over his face and winced.

Jake gestured with his chin. "What happened to you?"

"You don't know? Since you've been in town, I was hoping you'd say Dalton or Thom jailed Wil for fighting. Courtney sent Roberta to fetch him. We tangled in the Silky Hen."

Jake dropped his gaze to the dirt at Courtney's feet.

Would she ever stop causing trouble for her family?

"News to me," Jake replied. "Dalton's at the Red Rooster, and I was with Thom at the livery, talking with Win. I guess Roberta never found anyone to deal with Wil."

Tyler swallowed a curse and glanced at her. "I wish you'd let me finish the job."

"Tyler!"

"Not kill him, Courtney, but see that he'd been properly locked up." His gaze again tracked to the open barn doors and the white wall of snow. "I don't like thinking he's out there somewhere, nursing a grudge," he looked at her, "over you or Jake. And now, with almost everyone else in town. He makes enemies faster than a rattlesnake strikes. I have a mind to ride back to Logan Meadows."

Courtney wanted to lay her hand on Tyler's arm. Maybe rekindle a little of the closeness she'd felt in the wagon, but she didn't dare. "You can't, Tyler. You were fighting, too. He'll say you threw the first punch. Leaving quickly was supposed to keep you out of trouble. Dalton jailed both Dwight and Wil when they fought, if you recall."

"Well, standing here chewing the situation won't get us anywhere." Jake glanced at his bay gelding. "I need to unsaddle, and Courtney needs to get inside."

Tyler nodded. "I'll walk her in and check things out. I don't put anything past Wil."

Courtney almost winced. *As you shouldn't.*

"He's right, Court," Jake said. "We all have to be careful. Seems Wil's gettin' bolder with each passing day. We can't take any chances." He gave her a dark stare. "And that means you as well. If you hear from him at all, you're to alert one of us, do you hear me?"

As much as she didn't like the authoritative sound of Jake's tone, she knew he was justified to speak to her in any way he wanted. He was the head of their family, and at the moment, their family was being threatened by a wild, unpredictable man—because of her. The Christmas Eve party was only seven days away, and then Wil would stand up in front of everyone and expose her shame. From then on, she'd be a different person.

Chapter Forty-Eight

Beth sat at the table across from Tommy, her stomach in knots. An hour before, because avoiding him forever would be impossible, she'd dressed in the garment Jessie had offered, washed up, brushed her hair, and then emerged from the room.

Tommy declared Violet had agreed to take some nourishment, causing Jessie to all but fly into her room with several biscuits and bowl of chicken soup, leaving Beth at the window watching the snow pile up outside. After what felt like a lifetime, and Violet had taken as much as she could at one time, the five of them—Dalton, Adaline, Tommy, Jessie, and Beth—had gathered around the table for prayer and then a simple supper.

When the meal was finished, Jessie went back to watch over Violet, Dalton sat with Adaline in front of the fire, speaking in soft tones, and Tommy asked her permission to have a private conversation at the table. If she had been able to think of an excuse to avoid this unpleasantness, she'd be the first to blurt out the suggestion. As it was, the quiet kitchen of the Red Rooster, dim from the waning light and the one lantern on the windowsill, was as good a place as any to face her demons.

He looked uncomfortable. He rubbed his hand over his mouth several times. A full chin of whiskers covered his still square jaw and not an ounce of fat had changed his powerful physique. She softly cleared her throat. A small smile curved his lips.

"So, you were coming from seeing my ma when I found you walking in the snow?"

What a strange way to begin a conversation fifteen years overdue. She nodded. "Not exactly. Speaking with Violet *had* been my intention, but I lost my nerve and turned around. Some days before we had a nasty argument and she threw me out of the inn. With the gravity of her health, necessity said we should make up. That exchange has yet to happen."

"I see."

He looked so old. Still handsome, still manly, but definitely much older than when she'd last seen him. His once-dark hair was almost all gray, and much too long for her liking. His forehead and around his eyes were plenty wrinkled, but his lips were still firm as they'd been back then. His large hands rested on the edge of the table, and he fingered a crumb on the blue-checkered tablecloth left over from the five biscuits he'd consumed.

"Perhaps tonight, if Violet feels able to listen, I'll finish what I started earlier today—apologize for the hurtful words I said."

How strange. His voice was so dear, the way he tipped his face down and looked up at her exactly the same as before. Who could explain life? Not her, never her.

"Miss Fairington, I want to apologize for any pain I caused you all those years ago." He dropped his gaze to the near-empty coffee cup engulfed in his palms.

She didn't know how to respond, so she just kept quiet. Fixing what once was and what might have been wasn't possible. All the flowery words in the world had no power to repair what she'd become. Before Tommy had broken her heart, she'd been a different person, happier despite her troubles, agreeable, if not lonely. Afterward, she'd let the hurt eat her alive.

"Beth?"

She looked up. Hearing her name on his lips brought a shudder of pleasure.

"Won't you say anything?"

"What can I say?" she whispered, after glancing at Dalton and Adaline watching the flames. "You want my forgiveness? I don't think that's mine to give."

He swiped a large hand over his face and then looked at her. "Then tell me about your life. What happened after I left Valley Springs?"

His gaze burned a hole into her soul. "You never wrote one letter to your mother … or to me. I'm not sure I should tell you anything."

"You have every reason to be angry, hell, to hate me. I just thought…"

"You thought wrong." A hurt she'd believed gone, buried deep in the most unattainable part of her heart, stirred to life. If she didn't say something, all the words inside her throat might strangle her. "Like you thought wrong when you ran out on me, saying I'd have a better life without you. Yes, you were wrong then, and you're wrong now thinking you can waltz back here fifteen years later and pretend nothing has changed. You're a fool, Tommy Hollyhock. I wish I'd recognized that truth years ago, before I spent my life dreaming about you." Her gaze narrowed. "Where have you been? What have you been doing?"

"You have a right to know. I told my ma, but I don't know how much she'll remember. I got most of the telling out first thing. I wandered, mostly. Never put down roots. Never married or had any children. Went from town to town, job to job, foolishly wasting away my life doing nothing at all."

"Being married to me was worse than wasting your life? How calmly you sit across the table and say that. Drifting was better than marrying me or being with the people who loved you? That's a fine statement!" How dare he pin his horrible actions on her, saying he wanted better for her? If he'd wanted out of their betrothal, he should have just said so. Told her face-to-face, not write a brief note and sneak away into the night. What a coward!

"That wasn't the way at all, Beth, and you know it! No matter how much sense I tried to talk into you, you weren't listening. You set your sights on me. You talked your way around all my concerns. When you couldn't sway me, you up and told everyone in the churchyard I'd asked for your hand. What was I supposed to do? Call you a liar?"

My shame. I was desperate, so frightened you'd marry someone else. "I was tired of waiting, Tommy. I knew your sense of honor wouldn't allow for our happiness. So I took matters into my own hands."

"I was a forty-six-year-*old* man, and you only nineteen! As the weddin' day approached, I just couldn't live up to my part."

She pointed in his face. "You loved me!"

"Maybe I did."

"No maybe about it! You did. You never told me in so many words, but in secret glances, a touch of your hand, and the sentimental stories you used to tell. You loved me for a long time—probably for as long as I had loved you. We could have had a good life. But you were weak. Too fearful to stand up for what you wanted! Too fearful of what people might say." The cuckoo clock behind her on the wall sounded. In the dim light, the bleakness of his expression almost made her soften.

"You always were smart, Beth. When I was with you, sitting on your porch drinking tea, or you having Sunday supper over at the store, yes, you're right, everything felt perfect," Tommy admitted. "But when I laid my head on the pillow each night, sleep wouldn't come. I was robbing the cradle in the worst way. You deserved better. Someone younger, a man who could give you the life you wanted. A man who wouldn't up and die of old age when your children were still cutting their teeth. I wasn't him. Look at me." He held both hands wide and stuck out his chest. "I'm an *old* man! Sixty-one years, to be exact. Look at you, still as beautiful as the day you turned sixteen."

Filled with indignation, Beth slammed a hand on the table, rattling the coffee cups and the few serving pieces that had yet to be cleared. "Don't sugarcoat what happened between us. I'm not pretty. I'm a spinster. A disgraced spinster. I'm sure your uncle in Valley Springs expounded on what I'd done. Sold my family home and ran off to Montana Territory—with a man!" *Roy Oscar Melden.* "We never married. When he'd had enough of me, and my money was gone, he snuck off in the middle of the night, too. So, you see, I'm used to being left behind, Tommy. I'm not crying over spilt milk any longer. You shouldn't feel any guilt where I'm concerned."

She chanced a glance into the living room, where Dalton and Adaline sat by the fire. They were too far away to hear the conversation, but the look on Adaline's face said everything.

Beth didn't care. What was one more humiliating hurt?

"Uncle Virgil did share your plight with me, because I asked him; I was concerned. And I was sorry to hear the telling. After you left Montana was when you came to Logan Meadows?"

Her rage cooling fast, she nodded. All she could do was stare at her cup as she traced the rim with her finger. "That's right. Violet was the only person in the world who might take me in. If she'd refused, my next step would've been the saloon." She glanced up and searched his face for several long minutes. "And here I've been ever since." *Thinking of you every day...*

Chapter Forty-Nine

For the thousandth time, Dalton berated himself for his lack of discretion. What in the heck had he been doing? If Jessie hadn't interrupted them, he would have kissed Adaline. He'd *wanted* to kiss her more than anything else he'd ever wanted in his life. One moment, they were looking at his list of possible suspects, and the next, he'd fallen deep into her eyes, drowning as sure as if he were back in the choppy waters of the Pacific. For one moment, his world had stopped, and all he'd been able to see, or think about, or desire, was Adaline and her butter-soft lips. Her eyes beckoned. The sweet scent of her skin tortured his senses. And then his lips had brushed hers.

He needed some distance before he did something more to regret—something that would hurt her in the long run. "Time to go," he said quietly. "I'd hoped the snow would let up some, but that's not the case. I best leave before night falls." He didn't want to go. He wanted to snuggle on the sofa with a blanket thrown over both of them.

She reached to touch his arm but pulled back. "You might get turned around. Albert's back in town. If something happens, he and Thom are there. Don't risk your life to prove yourself. Please, be reasonable."

A veneer of fear reflected in her eyes by the firelight. Her sweet words of concern both bolstered him and troubled him. He'd confused her. Almost kissed her. He had no one else to blame but himself. He'd selfishly acted like a fool. She was avoiding his gaze, as she'd been doing since his moment of weakness. "I'm from Colorado, Adaline. I know snow. I'll be fine."

"But I'll have no way to be sure you arrived safely. I'll worry."

"Can't be helped. Even though Hannah's feeling better, Thom's either at their home or the restaurant. He has little time to watch for trouble. Albert gave me this whole month to prove I can be a deputy. He's off duty and doesn't want to be bothered."

"You don't have to show you're fit for the job. Albert wouldn't have hired you otherwise."

He needed to prove to *himself* he could do this job. No one else had approached him for a case other than Violet. His future felt heavier than ever, especially with these feelings for Adaline.

"Well, if you're going back to town, are you letting Mr. Hollyhock and Beth know? They both wanted to go at one time."

"Better not yet. I'll travel faster by myself."

"So danger *does* exist!"

Placing his hands on her shoulders, he fingered some loose strands of hair behind her ear. "Life's full of risks, Adaline. Can't avoid 'em." The same was true for heartaches too, not just a winter storm.

"I wonder where Marlene is staying? She won't come home in this weather. And the hotel is so expensive." She tugged her bottom lip between her teeth.

"I'm sure someone will extend an invitation. Tabitha has an extra room, Brenna, even Susanna. No need to worry about her."

"What about Courtney, Daisy, and Jake? I wish I knew they were home and safe. I feel isolated out here."

"Are all these questions designed to keep me by the warm fire? Because if they are, they're working." She smiled her old smile, the one which always got him way down deep. He missed their bantering friendship, their easy way. Would they ever get back to that?

"Maybe they are. One less person to be concerned about." She took a small step away from the fire. "Christmas Eve is only seven days away. If we're all snowed in, we can't decorate the community hall properly, or go to church, or shop for food for a lovely Christmas feast."

"You're not the keeper of the world. And this is not the first storm in Wyoming."

In the kitchen, Tommy Hollyhock had scooted back his chair and stood.

Beth whisked herself away down the hall.

Knowing his departure was long overdue, Dalton stood and Adaline followed suit.

"Did I hear you're headed back to town, Deputy?" Tommy asked, shifting his weight from one leg to the other.

"I am. Will you be coming?"

Tommy shook his head. "That had been my first thought, but after seeing my mother's condition, I'd like to stay, if possible. My place, for however long, is at her side." He looked at Adaline. "I hope that won't be a problem."

"Not at all, Mr. Hollyhock."

Tommy glanced in the direction of Beth's footsteps. "I wish I could say Miss Fairington felt the same."

Dalton pressed his lips together as the crackling of the fire cut through the quiet. Tommy carried a heavy guilt over breaking Beth's heart. A fact Dalton should keep in mind. Love wasn't a game. Consequences could be long lasting.

"What about Beth?" Adaline moved closer to Dalton's side. "Will she want to leave?"

Tommy sighed heavily and then shook his head. "Best we leave her be for now. She's had plenty to deal with for one day."

Dalton nodded then took in Adaline's expression, wanting to remember how beautiful she looked in the firelight on a snowy day. He'd leave town before hurting her. Turning her into a scorned woman like Beth would be the absolute worst sin he could commit.

Chapter Fifty

In the kitchen of the Broken Horn, Courtney stirred a pan of gravy over the hot stove. The gooey substance swirling around her spoon reminded her of quicksand, which resembled her life. Blurting out the truth seemed the only way out of this trouble with Wil. Her confession was the only way to be free of him forever. Being snowed in for almost a week had given her solitude to think—and resolve.

With a sigh, she added a splash of flour water and then used her wooden spoon to poke at the lumpy mixture. This noon meal wouldn't be her finest fare, but Sarah and Shane wouldn't notice.

With a scuffling noise, Shane clomped into the room, dressed in the many layers she'd tugged over his head.

The toddler's striking blue eyes always amazed her. "Where's Sarah?" Courtney asked. "The biscuits are just out of the oven, and the gravy is ready. Are you hungry, Shane?"

The boy's gaze roamed the room, and his mouth pulled down.

He was still looking for his ma even after all these days. He'd taken to sleeping with Chase, even though he had a room of his own. His mischievous glint was nowhere to be seen. Feeling sad for him, Courtney picked him up even though he was heavy. "Don't worry, little cowboy. Your mama will be home today."

His eyes welled.

Probably not the right thing to mention just yet.

His bottom lip wobbled.

She needed to change the subject. Turning for a biscuit she'd just plated, movement outside the window caught her eye.

Tyler and Jake crossed the front yard on their way to the bunkhouse, deep in conversation. The two men pushed through the fallen snow, their faces red from the cold.

The only news she'd gathered from town was if Chase, Jake, Tyler, or one of the other men ventured there on horseback. She wondered who was helping Mr. Ling at the laundry. Also how Adaline and the rest of her friends had fared in the storm. But most of all, she wondered about Wil. Tomorrow was Christmas Eve. If the weather held, and no new snow fell, the Christmas Eve party would go on.

Breaking a biscuit in half, she handed a portion to Shane, still snuggled in her arms. "Sarah! Come eat before everything gets cold." She turned from the window after one more glimpse of Tyler.

Sarah hurried into the room, a doll gripped in her fist. "I'm a hungry bear!"

Her father's expression. Courtney hid a smile and set Shane in his high chair and then pushed him up to the table. Taking the clean diaper draped over the pine back, she pinned the material around his neck. "There, keep any spills to your bib, please."

A knock on the kitchen door sounded just as she finished serving their plates. *Jake or Tyler?* Chase never knocked.

Cold air gushed inside, along with a flurry of snow that had collected around the doorframe. Seeing Jake, she grabbed his arm and dragged him inside.

Tyler followed and closed the door.

"I'm just serving the meal. Have either of you eaten?" she asked, aware of Tyler's proximity. She thought about how close they'd huddled in the wagon, and how his words brought a flutter to her heart. "There's plenty."

Both men removed their hats.

Jake shook his head. "No, thanks. We're expected at the bunkhouse." He glanced at the table. "How do, Sarah? Shane? You having fun with Courtney?"

"Yes!" Sarah called as she waved a biscuit she'd dipped into her gravy over her head. "She likes to play dolls. Or cat and mouse. She even likes to snuggle."

Ignoring her burning cheeks, Courtney leaned closer. "Please don't mention Jessie's absence. The children are holding up the best they can, but any reference brings tears."

"Chase went to get her," Jake whispered back.

Courtney nodded, well aware Tyler was allowing her brother to do all the talking. That was fine with her. The cut by his eyebrow had dried into a small, dark scab. The abrasion on his lip was almost gone and probably not even noticeable to anyone except her. Guilt for being the reason he'd sustained such injuries in the first place pooled in her belly. She felt his gaze riveted to her face, and more warmth crawled up her cheeks. She didn't dare look at his knuckles.

"*Pleease*, eat with us," Sarah persisted.

Jake shook his head. "Can't, Sarah, darlin'. Although I'd love to. You know how cranky Tater Joe gets if we don't show up when he rattles that triangle. But I'll be back someday soon to see my best gal." He winked, drawing a giggle.

"Promise?"

"Promise." He clamped his hat to his chest and found Courtney's gaze. "Don't want to talk in front of little ears."

Whatever Jake came to say was important. Something about Wil? She stepped into the hallway, around the corner, and out of earshot. "What's this about?" He looked like he was wrestling with his thoughts.

"Well, truth be told, Wil hasn't been seen anywhere in town since he and Tyler fought in the Silky Hen." He glanced at Tyler.

Tyler nodded.

"Dalton, as well as Thom and Albert, have searched the town but can't find where he's holed up. Has 'em spooked. The room he'd taken before at the hotel's been empty. Being tomorrow is Christmas Eve, I just thought I might ask you."

"Ask me?" What on earth did he want her to say? She had no idea where Wil was. "Ask me what?" She looked between both their flint-hard stares, and realization dawned. She jerked straight. "You think I know where he is?"

Jake never wavered. "Maybe. Has he contacted you?"

"You think I'd protect him, Jake? And you, Tyler?" Hot indignation flashed through her body. Any warm feelings she'd felt for Tyler turned frosty cold. And what kind of brother would think such a thing? Heat scalded her face as a blinding hurt filled her. "I haven't seen Wil since the day of the fight." Refusing to say more, she defiantly clamped her mouth closed. *Reputations are lost in the blink of an eye, Courtney, and take years to rebuild.* Now she understood her father's words of warning. Would her family and— she chanced a glance at Tyler—friends, ever trust her again?

Both men stood there staring.

Jake had more to say, she could see the questions in his eyes, but he was leery. She took pity. "That's the truth, Jake. He hasn't tried to contact me, or I him. If he did, I'd send him away without a word and then tell you."

Tyler must have told Jake he knew the truth, or else Jake wouldn't have brought him along today.

In the kitchen, the children chatted and laughed as they ate their meals.

"I need to see to Sarah and Shane, unless you have more questions or suspicions. Feel free to ask away, if you do."

Jake glanced briefly at his fingernails and then back at her face. "Actually, one more. Are you going to the Christmas Eve party tomorrow night? Tyler told me about Wil's threat. Might be prudent if you stayed away."

She'd been pondering the same thought for the last few days. Time to make a firm decision. Wil wouldn't control her life for one more moment. "I'm going, all right. The women of Logan Meadows have provided me with a beautiful blue dress, and Jessie has a ribbon and pretty shawl to match. After all their generosity, how on earth can I now refuse to go? Wil is certain to be there and cause me heartache, but I must face him sooner or later—he's made that perfectly clear. I'll not allow him to ruin my life any more than he has already. My mind's made up, Jake, so you might as well save your breath."

Jake nodded, and Tyler seemed to be standing even taller. Their support of her decision bolstered her shaking insides. Saying and doing were two different animals, entirely.

"So be it," Jake said. "I'll be there with you—and Daisy, too."

"And Adaline," Tyler replied. "She'll be there. As well as myself."

Something akin to pride sparkled in Tyler's eyes. Her destiny was set. Come tomorrow night, all her fears would either be banished or confirmed. Which one would prevail?

Chapter Fifty-One

Dalton paced the length of the sheriff's office, wearing a path on the scuffed floorboards. He stopped at the window and gazed at the towering Christmas tree swaying slightly in the breeze. The Christmas Eve party would go on this year. The snowstorm had let up in time. Townsfolk were anxious. Perhaps the folks living the farthest out wouldn't attend, but residents in town had no intention of letting this year's Christmas pass them by.

He rubbed a hand over his tired face. Last night had been brutal. He hadn't slept a wink but had come to a conclusion. Today, he'd have a heart-to-heart with Jake. Dalton would spill his guts and see what his friend, and Adaline's brother, had to say. If Dalton didn't act on his feelings and lost Adaline to another, he'd never forgive himself. She'd already pulled away. Gone were the little touches, funny comments, and long looks filled with promise. Had his chance already passed him by?

The door opened.

Thom and Albert stepped inside.

"Any coffee brewed?" Albert asked.

How the tables had turned. "Fresh pot. Help yourself."

Thom held the door for Ivan, who followed.

The old dog looked stiff this frosty morning, his ambling gait jerky with each step he took. His thick gray-and-black coat glistened as if he'd just climbed thorough a snow-covered bush.

He stopped and glanced around, and then continued on toward his usual spot beside the stove where he'd take up residence and remain the entire day.

"You wanting your job back?" Dalton said from his position at the window. Surely, Albert must be getting bored spending all his time at home. Each time Dalton saw him, he was ready for the boot to drop.

With his coffee mug halfway to his lips, Albert smiled. He reached out to the stove with his gloved hand. "Why, you tired of being the deputy? Anytime you want to hand over your badge, I'll take it."

He'd walked right into that. "No, just asking. I sometimes think you might regret taking off so long."

"Regret? Hell, I'm enjoying myself. Just met Thom on the way here and thought I'd check on the office. You found Wil Lemon yet?"

No. And the fact was making Dalton testy. Since he'd gotten word of the most recent fight between Wil and Tyler, he'd been looking. Places where the cur could hide and not freeze to death didn't exist. Someone must be putting him up. "Nope. And that's what has me baffled." He looked at Donovan. "Come up with anything, Thom?"

Thom lowered his cup from taking a drink and shook his head. "Not a sign of him. I'm thinking he might have somehow made his way over to New Meringue. If not that, I'm stumped."

Dalton hefted a sigh at the same time Chase, Gabe, and Jake came through the door. At least he'd get a chance to speak with Jake this morning, as he'd promised himself he would last night. No more second guessing. He'd hear the words straight from the horse's mouth.

"What kind of meeting is this?" Chase asked on a smile. "Saw you three through the window as we rode in. Something happening?"

Albert straightened. "Not in so many words. Just still haven't located Wil Lemon. I know how much Jake wants us to keep an eye on him. We'd be happier if we knew where he was."

The three from the Broken Horn headed to the coffeepot.

"Hold up, boys," Dalton said. "I'll put on another pot. That one's about empty." He went to the stove, wrapped the small towel they used as a pot holder around the handle, and headed out the back door to toss the grounds. "Be back momentarily," he called over his shoulder.

Frigid air nipped his ears as his boots crunched on the frozen earth. Snatching off the top of the percolator, he swiftly withdrew the basket and tossed the grounds, followed by emptying the remaining dark sludge at the bottom onto the snow. In the process, sounds around town reached his ears. Hoof beats clomping across Shady Creek bridge. Win calling out a greeting to somebody. A rooster somewhere crowing in the distance.

Christmas Eve had arrived! He hadn't yet located Wil Lemon. He was no closer to knowing the identity of the do-gooder—something he'd promised Violet he'd do. He had no idea which business display he'd choose as the winner of the Christmas competition. *And I've not spoken to Jake about my feelings for Adaline.* At least he'd cross the last item off his list in the next hour.

By now, Dalton's teeth chattered loudly as cold seeped deep into his bones. He hurried to the water pump, rinsed out the pot, and filled the metal container to the brim. Back inside, the lull of the conversation stopped when he finished his duties of hospitality and set the pot back on the stove to boil. He glanced at Albert. "You need a larger pot!"

"Don't I know? I've been supplying coffee to this town for years. You have nothing to grumble about, Babcock. The chore is my main job!"

Dalton harrumphed, rubbing his hands up and down his cold arms. "Did you come up with anything while I was outside? We can't arrest a man if he hasn't done something to warrant the action. And fighting isn't much." He cut his gaze to Jake. This story had more details than he'd been told. Dalton wished Jake would come clean. *Trust him.* Even without an explanation, he could imagine what the problem might be and thought the others probably had as well.

"I wish you'd get back into bed, Ma." Tommy took the seat next to Violet in the front room.

Seven days ago, she'd been shocked speechless when her only son, a grown man—*an old fella,* more like it—had returned after being gone for fifteen years. Her heart was full to bursting. She'd never known life could feel so sweet. "I've been in bed far too long, son," she retorted. "Doc gave me the go-ahead ta get up and start livin'. Jessie left yesterday. This is Christmas Eve, and I won't be kept down a moment longer."

Beth clanged around the kitchen doing something. They'd had a brief encounter a few days ago. Beth had apologized for her hurtful words, and Violet had forgiven her. In return, she'd asked Beth for her pardon for tossing her out. The whole exchange took no more than one minute. They hadn't broached the subject since. And they hadn't spoken about her moving back into the Red Rooster either, and yet here Beth was, living in her old room. She'd not even gone back into town to collect her belongings.

Violet didn't mind. In fact, she was thrilled. Life was too short for grudges. Besides, she'd actually missed their spirited, back-and-forth jabs. But best of all, she enjoyed watching what was transpiring between Beth and Tommy. If the cold weather had Violet confined to the inn, she might as well have some entertainment. Young fools. Would they waste what remained of the time they had left?

"Who would like a slice of fresh gingerbread straight from the oven?" Beth called from the kitchen.

Her tone reminded Violet of a spring songbird. "Been smellin' something mighty good for the last twenty minutes. I never imagined ya was bakin' gingerbread. Been my favorite since I was a tiny tot." Violet glanced at her son and smiled sweetly. "Thank ya, Beth, dear."

"I didn't want the eggs to get old," Beth replied. "Thought I best use them up."

"I'll take some," Tommy replied. "Can I help you in there?"

"Oh, no. I'm almost finished now. Be patient."

Tommy glanced her way and she shrugged. "Hard to believe Adaline and Marlene have already set off for town. They could have at least waited until the temperature warmed."

"They're excited for tonight." Beth set a tray with gingerbread and a cup of tea on Violet's lap. A moment later, she handed Tommy his slice as well as a cup of coffee.

Her recent actions were the most thoughtful since she'd moved in two years ago. Did wonders never cease?

"With you and Tommy settled, I'll just go and make some beds. Having a neat room starts the day right."

The smile she gave looked genuine to Violet. Was this the *real* Beth or the other one, the one with the spiteful tongue? Violet truly didn't know. With Beth gone, the crackling of the fire filled the room.

"Ma, I have something I'd like to say."

Violet rolled the gingerbread around on her tongue, delighted to be eating once again. "Do ya now? We have a lot of livin' to catch up on. I'm all ears."

He stared into his coffee cup for a few moments and then up into her face. "I'm happy to be home, but I'm sorry I didn't bring any grandchildren. I remember how much babies mean to you. Whose baby was doing what was all you ever talked about—and having some grandbabies of your own. But the years flew by, and I never met anyone I wanted to marry." The flames in the hearth crackled brightly, spitting out a glowing ember onto the rug. He squashed it with his boot. "I'm sorry I let you down."

Violet's fork clattered to her plate. "Ya think I care one whit about that? Men! I'll never understand 'em. Nothin' matters except seeing ya sittin' here in front of the fire, speakin' with me, enjoyin' a warm piece of gingerbread. Thems more precious than gold. I have all the children and grandbabies I need! Jake's more or less been my son for eighteen years—and Gabe, too. Sarah and Shane Logan are my grandbabies, as well as Markus Donovan, Nate Preston, and darlin' little Maddie. Those tots keep me runnin' full steam ahead. And only a couple months ago, I adopted another grandson in Hunter Wade. He might be full-growed, but he needed me more than I needed him. I have grandbabies coming out my ears!" Emotion welled. With a shaky hand, she reached out and touched Tommy's strong fingers holding his coffee, marveling he was truly here. "But I only got me *one* son. With you home, I'm happier than I've got a right ta be. I don't need nothin' more outta this life than what I got now. You and me together is the best Christmas blessin' of my life."

That said, young man, I'm not giving up on blood grandbabies jist yet. Beth is still in her childbearing years, and ya'ren old, but ya'ren not dead. I've seen the looks flying when ya thought I was asleep. I'll jist bide my time and see what happens.

The smile she knew so well blossomed across her son's face.

"I'm relieved to hear that," Tommy uttered. "From now on, I'm taking over any and all chores here at the inn—that is, if you want me to. I know how you like to manage the goings on. Your task will be to direct me and welcome the guests." He glanced around. "You just let me know."

"I sure will." Her old bones had one more chore to get done—and that was to mend Tommy's mistake from all those years ago. He and Beth belonged together. Violet made a pledge to make happiness happen.

Chapter Fifty-Two

Excited for the evening to come, Adaline, dressed in a borrowed soft burgundy wool dress Brenna had altered, admired the community center, thinking she'd never seen such a festive room. Long garlands of pine draped the doorways, windows, fireplace, stairway, and the railway above. The sections were tied together with red ribbon and adorned with bows. Earthy pine scent permeated the air, as well as the sweet bouquet of warm apples and the tang of ginger and cinnamon. Paper snowflakes dangled from the beams that were within reach of the tallest ladder. Whenever anyone walked by, they gently swayed back and forth. Candles and lanterns winked, making the room appear as a fairy land. The fireplace crackled and popped with coziness.

Several long tables in the back of the room were heaped with platters of delectable dishes, all decorated with sprigs of holly and red berries. Sliced turkey, roast beef, ham, sweet potato pies sprinkled with nutmeg, bean casseroles, and baskets of rolls and biscuits sat in a row. Small bowls and crocks of jellies and jams gave the table color. Platters of sugar and molasses cookies were piled high. And gingerbread too, in every shape and size. Spice and apple cakes were drizzled generously with white sugar icing. Fruitcakes, never one of Adaline's favorites, were colorful with raisins, nuts, and berries. Pies, of course, crowded the table: pumpkin, dried apple, and mincemeat. Berry too... Not to leave out the fudge—mounds and mounds of the confection just waiting to be consumed.

Adaline's heart warmed remembering the Christmas brandy cake Violet had insisted on making herself to send with her and Marlene this morning. The concoction contained four *extra* tablespoons of brandy and an eye-popping amount of additional cinnamon, which, she claimed, made her recipe special and more delicious than any other. She'd had each one of them, including her son, stir the batter once and make a wish. Adaline hadn't had to think long on hers.

At the punch table, hot mulled wine and cinnamon-speckled eggnog filled the jugs.

The table on the band stage was slowly collecting wrapped presents to give to the needy children of Logan Meadows. The night promised to be magical.

Earlier today, Adaline had walked into town with Marlene, carrying their dresses and other party essentials, being cautious not to slip on the snow-packed road. The seven-day-old snowfall had melted and refrozen several times, making the going slow and dangerous. But the trip had been worth every judiciously placed step. From there, she'd spent the day with a good number of the townsfolk, making sure the community center was decorated to the hilt and a sight to behold. Finished with those tasks, she and Marlene had accepted Tabitha's kind invitation to refresh themselves and dress at Storybook Lodge just down the street.

Thirty minutes ago, Win and his buckboard had stopped by to see if they'd like a lift. He'd gone around town picking up people who fancied a ride to the shindig. The convenience was greatly appreciated and made bringing the goodies of food and gifts to give away so much easier.

Gabe and Julia strolled across the room hand in hand, admiring the decorations. Julia was as beautiful as ever in a green velvet dress, he in his Sunday best, if Adaline had to guess. They'd both helped with the earlier preparations, and like her, had gone home as ugly ducklings and changed, only to return as beautiful swans. With Gabe's chestnut hair and Julia's strawberry-blond tresses, the picture they created was quite striking. Content to keep to themselves on this very special evening, they wandered to the fireplace. He whispered something into her ear making her giggle.

"Aren't they cute?"

Adaline whirled, surprised someone had come up behind her without making a noise. Tabitha's satisfied grin made her laugh.

"They're two of the nicest people in Logan Meadows," Tabitha went on. "I wonder when we can expect wedding bells. Surely, not much longer."

The main door opened again, and more excited people entered. Their eyes widened for a moment when they stopped to admire the beauty of the room and then proceeded to place their foods and gifts in the appropriate place. From there, they removed their outer garments, gloves, and hats, taking them to the small coatroom.

Adaline smiled and nodded. "I don't know Gabe and Julia well enough to speak about a wedding, but they look like a perfect couple to me. I think Gabe is incredibly nice, and Julia, too." The thought of a wedding between the young couple brought a pang of sadness to Adaline's heart. Would she ever get over Dalton and find a new love? Even if she could, she didn't want to. Her heart wanted Dalton and no other. So she was bound to be a spinster.

Why had Dalton almost kissed her? Since then, she'd fallen asleep each night and awoken with the same question on her mind. She didn't understand him in the least.

"They've been moving toward marriage since the day she survived the train wreck. Only have eyes for each other. A love like that is what stories are made of."

"What kind of love?" Hunter asked, appearing behind his wife. "Are you talking about us?"

Hunter Wade was dashing in his dark gray coat and string tie. His rugged handsomeness complemented Tabitha's soft beauty.

Tabitha winked at Adaline and then smiled up into her husband's eyes. "I was speaking about Gabe and Julia. But true, the statement also fits our love, Hunter. Once in a lifetime and never ending."

Oh my. If gazes could speak, Adaline thought this newly wedded couple just might go up in flames. His face actually turned red.

"Have you seen Chase or Dalton yet?" Hunter looked around.

"No." Adaline had been watching for Dalton as well. Would he ask her to dance, or would he keep a distance? When she thought of him, and imagined his eyes gazing into hers, her stomach exploded into a throng of butterflies racing the wind.

Tabitha shook her head. "Neither one."

More people poured in, filling the lodge with talk and laughter.

Where was Courtney? She'd hoped to have a private moment to talk before the snowstorm, and then after that, everything came to a standstill. Mrs. Hollyhock wouldn't be attending tonight or Tommy. Would Beth appear? This morning, she'd said she wanted to stay home with Violet in case she needed something. How times had changed.

Thom, Hannah, and Markus arrived with Albert, Susanna, and Nate. The little boys' faces were alight with excitement. They raced to the gift table and made room for their wrapped boxes.

Susanna looked beautiful, and Adaline tried not to be envious. No wonder Dalton was in love with her. The young woman was as lovely inside as she was on the outside. Christmas Eve was not a time for jealousy but a night for love, peace, and goodwill.

Still no Dalton.

"Hannah looks so much better. I'm so relieved. She was quite sick. I love her dress. My cousin has such a flair for fashion."

Adaline didn't know what Tabitha was talking about. Rarely did anyone ever outshine the bookshop owner.

"I wonder where your Aunt Roberta is?" Hunter asked, still standing close. "I would have thought they'd all come together."

"Your Aunt Roberta, too," Tabitha said, a slight giggle to her tone. "She'll be along with Mother. The two are probably primping. This party is the most anticipated event of the year. I'm sure they want to make an entrance once everyone else is here."

"I'm sure you're right," Hunter affirmed. "Think I'll go inspect the food table and leave you two ladies to your girl talk." He ambled away.

Still no Dalton. She looked in every corner and even upstairs. Where was he? Had he decided not to come? Did he think he had to stay in the sheriff's office and watch the town? Her heart sank. Without him, the party wouldn't be fun in the slightest. The room was so full, seeing who entered was nearly impossible.

"Are you waiting for someone special, Adaline?" Tabitha asked.

Was she? She didn't want to fib, but what else could she do? Waiting for Dalton was a lost cause. Not only did he think of her as just a girl, but he still had feelings for Susanna. Maybe he'd never get over her. "Not really, just enjoying the moment. And I am waiting for Courtney. Because of the snow, I haven't seen her for days. I'm not happy we're living apart. I know it's temporary until we're truly settled, but I worry about her. She hasn't made an easy transition to Logan Meadows." Tabitha's concerned gaze warmed her. "She's the only little sister I have, and I don't want to see her unhappy."

Tabitha ran a hand down Adaline's arm. "I understand your concern. Maybe we can dream up some ideas to help her settle in."

A burst of laughter sounded at the entrance. Chase and the gang from the Broken Horn moved through the crowd, their faces red from the cold. Jake and Daisy followed while Tyler stayed close to Courtney's side. Adaline liked Tyler. She was glad he'd taken an interest in Courtney and gave her someone besides family to confide in.

When she saw Dalton above the others, Adaline's heart lurched into her throat. He was with Frank Lloyd, and the two were laughing about something.

When Dalton noticed Albert and Susanna at the refreshment table, he hurried their way.

They made room for him and struck up a conversation.

Tabitha smiled. "So. The secret love is Dalton Babcock. I've wondered about the two of you since you arrived in town." She looked over at Dalton and his group and then back at Adaline. "Is he aware of your feelings?"

What could saying so hurt? Adaline was tired of keeping everything tucked away inside. Like Courtney, she needed a friend, too.

"Adaline?"

"He thinks me just a girl." That's all she would say. Mentioning Susanna did no one any good. She'd not make her friend the scapegoat.

Tabitha took Adaline's hands and tipped her head. "You sure about that? I distinctly got another impression."

Was she wearing her heart on her sleeve for all to notice? Her face warmed. "Positive."

"Love is fickle, dear one. Don't count yourself out until you want to be out. Look at me and Hunter. I'd never have thought we'd end up together—and here we are. Husband and wife and as happy as two little clams in the same shell."

A spark of hope seared Adaline's heart. The confident smile on Tabitha's lips gave her courage. Did the bookshop owner know what she was talking about? Adaline wanted to believe she did, to have hope, but doing so was dangerous, too.

Chapter Fifty-Three

Dalton could hardly contain his excitement. Above and beyond his call to keep an eye out for Wil Lemon, especially tonight at the party, he'd finally have Jake where he wanted him. Jake had left the sheriff's office by the time Dalton returned from filling the coffeepot. Speaking with him tonight would be Dalton's first course of action. As Dalton entered the hall, he'd caught sight of Adaline, looking more beautiful than ever, across the room with Tabitha. Tonight was their night—but only after he spoke with Jake. Jake just might dash all hope, and Dalton better keep any thoughts of Adaline in check before he got ahead of himself. The only reason Dalton wasn't imprisoned right now, but was here tonight to celebrate Christmas, was because Jake had been honorable, brave, and clever. Jake had risked his own neck in Newport to save his.

I owe Jake everything! But I'll fight for my love. I'll make Jake see I'm the one to make his sister happy.

Now was Dalton's chance.

Jake and Daisy made their way across the room, hand in hand.

"Jake," Dalton called, following quickly and halving the distance between them.

The couple stopped and turned. Daisy reached up on tiptoe and kissed Jake on the cheek before hurrying away.

"Dalton?"

"I hope I didn't scare Daisy away." He watched her go, actually relieved he wouldn't create curiosity when asking to speak with Jake in private.

"No, she's anxious to see what everyone is wearing, how they've styled their hair, and so on and so forth. At social events, I can't keep her around for long."

Dalton glanced around quickly and leaned closer. "I need a moment of your time before the shindig really gets underway. Can we speak in private?"

His brows drew together. "Fine. What about?"

"Not here." Dalton hitched his head toward the stairway leading to the second-story landing. "Follow me."

A hive of bees erupted inside of Dalton, knowing this was the moment. He wouldn't back out now. The view of the community center from up there was splendid. He could observe the whole room, as well as Adaline and Tabitha standing below.

The two women leaned close together, talking.

He wondered about the topic of their conversation. The feel of her lips had been branded on his mind since his visit to the Red Rooster the day Tommy Hollyhock had returned. As brief as the kiss had been, he couldn't get the moment off his mind. This talk with Jake was long overdue.

"This about Wil? Has the skunk been found?"

"No. But I have no doubt he's still around. I'm keeping close watch. As are others."

"If not Wil, what's on your mind? I'm anxious to get back to Daisy. Some other cowboy might catch her eye."

The last was said in jest, and they both smiled.

Dalton's mouth went dry. "I wanted to speak to you about Adaline."

Jake dropped his gaze to his sister downstairs, then lifted it at Dalton. "Adaline? What about Adaline?"

This was his moment of truth. Dalton had rehearsed in his mind a hundred times the words he wanted to say, now he just had to spit them out. Chickening out at this point was not an option. "I'm in love with her." He waited for Jake's reaction. A silly grin crept across Jake's face.

"I've known that for some time. So?"

Dalton dropped his gaze to the floor. What did he mean? Jake knew he had feelings for his sister but hadn't said anything to discourage him because of the age difference? At this point, just about everyone in Logan Meadows had either heard about or met Violet's son, Tommy. The age difference between him and Beth was substantial. Dalton would mention them if the conversation didn't go his way.

A burst of laughter from below drew their attention to a group of women where Susanna and Hannah, as well as Roberta, Brenna, Courtney, and Nell had joined Adaline and Tabitha.

They were chattering faster than a nest of squirrels working on a walnut tree. Adaline must have felt his gaze and glanced up.

He gave a slight nod and smiled, although he felt as if an apple had suddenly wedged inside his throat. "I'm not sure what to make of your response, Jake," he finally got out. "You've told me what you think of Wil Lemon and Courtney. The age difference between me and Adaline is greater than theirs. I've fought the feeling as long as I can—or plan to. I need to know how you'd feel about me courting her."

Jake held out his hands, palms up. "Why? You don't need my permission."

"You risked your life to save mine. And with your father gone, you're the head of the household."

Jake scoffed. "Are you comparing yourself to Wil Lemon? With Wil, the age difference bothered my pa because of his dishonest character. A fellow like him is out to get what he can, no matter who he ruins. Rumors circulated he pushed a young woman over a cliff in Newport, but her parents have no proof, and Wil's comrades gave him an alibi. She was nice and respectable, like Courtney. As long as Wil gets what he wants, nothin' else matters." A slow smile broke across Jake's face. "Dalton, you must know you're *nothing* like Wil. I'd be proud to call you brother. That is, if my sister will have you. Are the two of you moving that way?"

Were they? "You might say that. Or, at least, I hope we are."

Jake slapped him on the shoulder and then pulled him into a bear hug. "Well, man, get busy. Nothin' I'd like better than to hear you two are betrothed."

Dalton swallowed. "There's *another* problem. I'm not gainfully employed. I do have an offer back in San Francisco from the Fords. I'd take Adaline with me."

Jake's smile fell away. "San Francisco? No, I wouldn't like her going at all. Not after just finding her. My father wanted us to be a family here in Logan Meadows. Together. San Francisco's a long way away."

Dalton hefted a sigh. "I know, I know. I thought as much."

Jake pulled back, his eyes wide. "You giving up so easily?"

"No. But I don't want to break Adaline's heart, either. She won't want to leave you and Courtney. She loves her family. And I can't marry her and stay here if I don't have a way to support her. She deserves to have the best. As you know, my employment ends in about twenty days. And then I'm once again living from day to day."

Jake rubbed his chin for a long second. "Maybe I spoke too quickly. I guess Adaline's happiness is more important than my own. I know I'd want to go wherever Daisy went, wouldn't matter to me the location. I'm devoted to the folks here in town; the Logans gave me everything, but Daisy is my destiny. If Adaline is willing to move, who am I to stop her? To stand in the way of her happiness? I think such a decision should be up to her and you."

Hope sprouted in Dalton's chest. Maybe their love had a chance. And then again, she had been acting quite differently for a number of days. Perhaps his heart was about to be broken, not hers. Only one way to find out.

Gabe tuned up his guitar and Seth his fiddle.

People moved down the long tables laden with food, filling their plates.

Dalton assumed the dancing would commence and then, at some point, he'd be asked to announce who won the Christmas contest. He'd better get downstairs, test the waters with Adaline, and keep an eye on Courtney. He didn't want anyone else dancing with Adaline even once. He wanted her all to himself!

Chapter Fifty-Four

Courtney surveyed the room as she nibbled the slice of spiced pumpkin bread she held to keep her hands steady. Was there any chance under heaven and earth Wil would actually stay away? Had he taken her words to heart and decided to let bygones be bygones? Knowing him the way she did, even if he had forgiven their past and had no intention of exposing her, he'd not likely miss out on a chance to ruin her in front of everyone—or a free meal.

By now, most everyone had eaten, and the time had come to delve into the delectable desserts. The sweets table was full to overflowing with choices, but Courtney's nerves made even finishing the small morsel in her hand difficult. She set what was left on an abandoned plate.

Chocolate and white powder ringed Markus Donovan's and Nate Preston's mouths as they darted off.

Jovial laughter and talking floated on the air.

Win, dressed in his Sunday best, had joined Seth and Gabe on the stage with a mandolin. Until this moment, she hadn't known he played. Eddie Brinkley ambled up with another violin. As they warmed up, sweet music filled the room.

So many aspects of Logan Meadows to discover. The thought of leaving now pulled gently at her heartstrings, and a sad aching pulsated inside. This town could have been home. Where she lived, loved, married, and died. If she were honest with herself, more likely than not, this would be her last night as a respected citizen.

"Here you are." Adaline stepped out of the crowd. "I've been looking for you everywhere. Are you feeling all right, Courtney?" She briefly glanced around. "Why are you here all alone?"

Adaline looked beautiful. Little golden ringlets framed her face, and the dress she'd been given for tonight fit perfectly. She'd do well in Logan Meadows and was doing so already. Courtney's heart stirred with sadness. She knew what she had to do. "I've been waiting for you."

Adaline's head tipped. "Well, good. I've wanted a word with you all week. How are you? I'm worried about you. I miss seeing you every day."

All these other questions could wait. Courtney didn't know when Wil would pop out of the woodwork with his exciting announcement. At least Courtney could soften the blow for Adaline by telling her now. "I have something I need to tell you, Adaline. And I want you to hear the words from me." She searched her sister's worried face.

"Yes? Go on."

This was the most difficult moment of her life.

"Courtney?"

"Wil's coming here tonight. He'll have some things to say about me." Her throat tightened. "I can't begin to tell you how sorry I am. For all the trouble and heartache I've caused our family. The worry Papa suffered because of me before he died. I was a horrible daughter … and sister."

Shock registered on Adaline's face. "Stop speaking so! I won't hear another word. The past is the past, where the past will stay. We must look forward only. I won't have you speaking so harshly about yourself."

People had moved farther away from where the two stood. This was her chance. "Please listen, Adaline. I don't have much time.

Wil's going to expose me. Share with everyone the things we did together back in Newport. I tried to stop him every way I knew how. Nothing worked, not even begging. He demanded I steal from the Logans to pay him a hundred dollars for shaming him. If I complied, he promised he'd stay quiet. I just couldn't.''

Adaline's face blanched. She reached out.

But Courtney stepped back and wrapped her arms around her middle. "Please, let me finish while I'm still brave enough to speak. I'm not an innocent any longer. You were correct about me and him. Right all along. He never forced me. I could have walked away any time I wanted. But I didn't want to. I wanted to be with him. Now, I feel differently and am so sorry for my actions.''

Adaline began to shiver. Even in the dim, romantic light of the candles and lanterns, the tears filling her eyes were visible. "What do you mean? He's coming here tonight ... to the party?''

"That's my punishment for running out on him, and then making him a laughingstock. I expect him, but he hasn't yet shown up.''

"Let's leave! I'll go with you!'' She caught her sister's arm and tried to pull her away.

"That won't matter, Adaline. He'll have his say, whether I'm here or not. My reputation will be ruined.''

"Does Jake know?''

Courtney dropped her gaze. Adaline would be angry she'd been kept out of her confidences, but she couldn't help that now. "He does. He caught me and Wil in a compromising situation after Father died. I was so ashamed. They fought, and Wil tried to kill Jake and would have if Jake hadn't gotten the upper hand. I finally came to my senses and saw what kind of a man Wil Lemon actually was. He'd have killed a man for protecting his sister.''

"That's the night you finally agreed to leave Newport with us and travel to Logan Meadows?''

Courtney nodded, surprised her sister hadn't already blown up. Adaline just looked sad. Courtney was sorry to be the one to extinguish the beauty shining in her eyes. "Yes. I'll never forget the sight of Wil slashing at Jake with his knife. The look in his eyes froze my blood. Jake promised not to tell a soul, not even you or Daisy. But every moment thereafter, I was terrified I might be carrying Wil's child. Then, the day of Jake and Daisy's wedding, my prayers were answered."

Adaline stared at her face, surely stunned speechless.

"My secret would have been safe if Wil hadn't come to Logan Meadows. I wanted to tell you tonight. To prepare you. So you wouldn't be shocked to death with everyone else. I'm so sorry I didn't listen to you, Adaline." Guilt pushed down on her shoulders and her heart ached. "I was foolish and stupid—and mean. I'll never forgive myself."

Adaline reached out and gently brushed away the scalding tear escaping Courtney's eye. "Everyone makes mistakes, little sister. Not a person in this room doesn't have regrets. You must forgive yourself. We're all only human. We do the best we can."

Adaline's eyes were actually smiling. Courtney felt loved, even now, after her shocking confession. She stepped into Adaline's arms, and the two embraced, letting everyone and everything else fall away.

Moments later, Adaline stepped back, her eyes watery. "Maybe he won't come."

"He'll come. He's just making me sweat." She squared her shoulders. "And actually, since I've told you, I don't mind. I feel stronger every minute he stays away."

The band started up and two by two, couples populated the dance floor. Over Adaline's shoulder, Courtney saw Dalton heading their way. Tall, with wide, straight shoulders, combed-back hair, and a sparkle in his eye, he looked devilishly handsome tonight. Jake had told him some about Wil, but not the whole story—never the whole story. Now she wished he had. His knowing would be one less look of condemnation and betrayal she'd have to endure when the time arrived.

Where was Wil? Any moment, he would appear out of thin air and ruin her life forever. She wished he'd just get the horrible task over with.

Chapter Fifty-Five

"I wish ya two youn'uns would go to the Christmas shindig afore the party's over," Violet complained as she sat next to the fire, a quilt over her lap and a cup of tea on the nearby table. "Ya make me fidgety thinkin' of all the fun you're missin' because of little ol' me."

She admired the small fir tree Tommy had brought in just before nightfall. He and Beth had strung a few strands of popcorn, dried raisins, and red berries from outside. The strands draped haphazardly from branch to branch, looking prettier than anything she'd ever seen.

Tannenbaum—the only German word Violet knew, taught to her by her dear pappy when she was no more than a tadpole. His memory still brought a wedge of sadness to her heart. Seemed like yesterday—or a million years—since those days. "Go on and get gussied up! Ya'll be sorry tomorrow if ya don't."

"I'm not going anywhere, Ma." Tommy closed the book in his lap and set the volume beside him. "I'm content to sit here for a year or two before I move for anything. God answered my prayers keeping you alive until my return. There's no other place I'd rather be."

So much about her son was familiar, and at times, so much was new and strange. He'd aged quite a bit since he'd taken leave of them those years ago, but she had to admit he still cut a fine figure of a man—with many fruitful years left to live. No stooped shoulders on him. Or shaky hands. They were still steady and his shoulders as wide and straight as they'd ever been. Pride filled her feeble chest with love. Oh, how she adored him. Just the sound of his voice brought a song to her heart.

And she wasn't the only one who'd noticed Tommy's fine attributes. Beth, as much as she liked to act wronged and righteous, was just so amusing. Violet would never let on she knew, but the girl was as smitten with him now as she'd been when she was a girl. Some loves were meant to be—as this one was. Violet was thankful the two would get a second chance to get their story right. As well, the heavy burden of guilt Violet felt from her son's actions was lifted from her frail shoulders. Since the day Tommy ran off, breaking Beth's heart, she'd carried the culpability even though she hadn't been the one at fault. As long as Beth didn't hang on to her well-justified pride, Violet felt down deep in her bones they would find their way back to each other. They could have many wonderful years together.

Beth came into the room, her hair recently combed and styled in a nice, neat bun at the nape of her slim neck. Violet could tell she was ill at ease, still wearing borrowed clothes. Maybe she believed once she left for her belongings, she wasn't welcome to return.

"Beth, honey, are you still wearin' Jessie's borrowed dress? Tommy'll fetch yer other belongings back if ya ask him. Ain't been the same around here since ya moved out."

Beth, who was drying a mixing bowl, frowned.

She'd done more work around the inn in the last few days than the two years since she'd arrived. No bother. The closer to Tommy the better, Violet figured, to get the courtship moving properly. Violet was working on borrowed time.

"I won't ask such a task, Violet. The weather's still so cold. Win can help me after Christmas, when the temperature warms up a little."

"Oh, phooey! Not so cold others haven't ventured ta town. Still got yer key to the mercantile?"

"Of course."

"Then why don't the two of ya take a moonlight walk and fetch back a few of yer belongings, garments, and doohickeys? Ya won't freeze ta death iffin ya walk fast. I want a little peace and quiet. Ya've been bangin' in the kitchen for hours trying ta raise the dead." She shook her head, keeping her gaze far away from Tommy.

"I'll be happy to help, Beth," he offered. "If you'd like to get some of your possessions now, to make your stay easier, I'm glad to oblige."

Beth's face grew as red as mulled wine.

The deepness of his voice touched Violet. She wanted to chortle but knew such an outburst just might wreck everything.

Beth tapped her lips. "Well, maybe we—"

"'Course ya can! Now, bundle up. Take two lanterns so ya don't lose yer way."

Beth snapped straight. "I've traveled this way a hundred times in the dark, Violet, no need to be so boss—" She clamped her mouth closed.

As if she hadn't heard a thing, Violet averted her eyes to heaven. Breaking her daughter-in-law-to-be of all her bad habits would be a delight.

Chapter Fifty-Six

Dalton waltzed Adaline around the dance floor holding her at a respectable distance. She felt perfect in his arms, like he'd imagined she would. She was so beautiful, not staring was difficult. Still, uneasiness stirred inside. She was preoccupied. Sidetracked, perhaps even *uninterested*. Maybe he'd been wrong about her feelings. Or had he waited too long to make his move?

When Adaline had apologized for her words of love the night baby Ying was born, agreeing with him the tense situation at hand had made her speak out, he hadn't taken her at her word. He sneaked a glance at her scanning the watching crowd, and unease pushed at his chest. After his conversation with Jake earlier this evening and receiving his friend's wholehearted blessing to court his sister, Dalton hadn't wasted any time finding her and asking her to dance.

But she'd declined with a ridiculous excuse about remaining by Courtney's side; something about watching the gift table to be sure no child peeked inside the presents. Then later, he'd practically had to pry her away from Courtney. Since then she'd been quiet, distracted, and hadn't shared her special smile with him even once.

The music slowed and ended.

"Thank you, Adaline." How mundane, but he couldn't think of one romantic word to say. His heart was in his boots. How had he gotten everything so wrong? She hadn't even heard him.

She jerked her gaze back to his face. "I'm sorry, Dalton, did you say something?"

Did you say something? Had she met someone new? Were there any recent arrivals in Logan Meadows? Nothing tonight felt right. "Yes, I thanked you for the dance. And all the dances we've shared. Are you tired? Would you like to sit down?" *Or dance this one with someone else?* He sounded like a whipped dog.

She smiled, but the expression didn't reach her eyes.

She was being kind to him. Letting him down easy.

"You're welcome. And no, I'm not tired. If you want to keep dancing, I'm game."

The musicians had started again, this time without Gabe, who was dancing with Julia.

Her tone held no conviction. He didn't want to force her against her will. "That's all right. I'll be polite and give the other fellas a chance to ask you themselves. Keeping the prettiest girl all to myself isn't very gallant."

Adaline was looking up at the balcony.

She hadn't heard a word he'd said. With a hand to her back, he escorted her over to some chairs where a few others sat. "I'll go fetch you a cup of punch and be right back." He didn't wait for her reply because he felt one wouldn't come.

Dalton moved toward the punch table in a fog. Couples danced around the room, enjoying themselves. Excited children darted between the shadows. Everyone was having a good time except him—and presumably Adaline.

Courtney stood by the dessert table where she'd been most of the night since the dancing had started.

He'd made a conscious effort to stay aware of where she went—with an eye out for Wil. At the moment, Mr. Hutton, the teacher, and Brenna, his wife, were with her. Tyler sat in a chair by the fire, brooding over something. Dalton was surprised. He'd have thought Tyler would be dancing with some of the pretty girls. Dances didn't come often. Could Tyler be the one Adaline was pining for? The two were much closer in age than Dalton was with her. Feeling more miserable by the second, Dalton ladled out two glasses of punch, wishing for something stronger—like a straight shot of whiskey.

"Dalton!"

Frank Lloyd headed his way in his dapper slacks, wool coat, and a black string tie circling his starched white collar. He was the picture of prosperity.

"Time's come to announce the winner of the Christmas competition. The evening is getting late, and soon folks will want to head over to the church for the Christmas Eve service."

Dalton felt the steely gaze of others closely watching to see if Frank was making one last effort to sway his vote. What could he say? He hadn't really made a decision yet. Some judge he'd turned out to be. "Sure, Frank. Where do you want me to do this?"

"On the stage. Musicians are on a break, and Winthrop is ready in the Santa suit to hand out gifts as soon as you've finished." He smiled and grasped Dalton's shoulder in a friendly gesture.

"Let me take Adaline her punch and then I'll get right to it." In the face of Adaline's indifference, his Christmas spirit had disappeared. He found her in a small group of women, Courtney so close to her side he wondered if something was wrong. "Adaline."

Surprised, she turned, and then smiled when she saw who stood behind her. She tipped her head in question.

"Your punch." He held out the glass, feeling like a squashed ant. She hadn't even remembered he'd gone to get her something to drink.

"Thank you." She glanced at the cup and then up into his face. "I guess I *am* a bit parched."

Nothing was left to say. At least, he couldn't think of anything. "You have fun. I'm off to announce the winner."

"So, you've decided?"

Not really, but what does that matter? "Of course, I have. What kind of judge leaves the decision to the last second?" He nodded and turned to go but was stopped by a touch on his arm.

"Thank you again for the dances, Dalton. I enjoyed them."

Her tone sounded authentic, and maybe a spark of warmth shone in her gaze. Or then again, maybe his hope was working overtime. "You're welcome, Adaline. Merry Christmas."

Folks nodded his way as he stepped onto the stage. He forced a smile and glanced around. All the eager faces. Goodhearted people who'd waited all year for this one moment. He'd dash the spirits of a handful for the jubilation of one. Didn't feel right, but he should have thought of that outcome before accepting the position.

Maude Miller edged through the crowd, coming closer to the stage, most certainly so she could hear. Mr. and Mrs. Harrell stood close to Frank, the three of them chatting amiably, but with an eye on Dalton. Lettie, from the bakery, looked so different in her Christmas clothes he hardly recognized her. He couldn't ever recall seeing her anywhere but behind her counter with a dash of flour across her forehead. Abner Wesserman, of the telegraph office, had actually brought the elf from his display and carried the cornstalk gnome in his arms like a doll.

So many people counting on his words. The feeling was daunting.

Mr. Hatfield, the depot manager, waited on the periphery of the multitude.

Close by stood Kendall Martin and Hunter Wade, both with arms crossed over their chests and narrowed eyes, as if they knew already Dalton wouldn't award a family-friendly prize to an adult-driven enterprise such as a saloon—and they'd be right.

He cleared his throat. Seemed Wil Lemon had thought better of making some sort of stupid play for Courtney tonight and was still hiding out, or perhaps he'd gone.

"Quit stalling, Deputy Babcock!"

The comment was called out in good humor by none other than Albert. Enough light still remained in the shadowy room to see the sheriff was goading him good-naturedly. "Good evening, ladies and gentlemen of Logan Meadows," Dalton greeted. "The time has arrived to announce the winner of this year's Christmas competition. Let me say one more time, I'm touched by your acceptance of me. I've felt a valued member of this community since arriving those months ago on the ill-fated train crash at Three Pines Turn. And so…"

"Quit stalling!"

Yes, he was rambling. He held up a hand. "We'll get there. But first, let me say, everyone's displays were unique in their own way and exuded the Christmas spirit. Maude's Mercantile's, the El Dorado Hotel's, and the Silky Hen's displays are something to rival a shop in Miles City, Cheyenne, Denver, or another large metropolitan area. Good job, all three of you." That seemed enough praise to have Maude, the manager of the El Dorado, and Hannah and Thom preening and puffing their chests. "Hunter and Kendall, you know I love the saloon as much as any man, but I can only take so much female attention."

The men laughed, and more than a few women peaked a brow.

"But thank you all the same for the free coffee."

Adaline's startled gaze gave Dalton a moment of hope. *Choose the display that means something to you. One that touches your heart.* Adaline's words filtered through his mind, and a peace descended on his shoulders.

"Lettie and Abner, job well done. I liked both of yours as well as the school's." He swallowed. Two left which had moved him. He glanced at an expectant Frank Lloyd and equally eager Mr. Hatfield. The moment had come, and he couldn't delay any longer. "The last two displays almost tied, but I know only one can win. I can't tell you how much I've enjoyed studying Frank's small replica of Logan Meadows. For a multitude of reasons, of course, the buildings are very finely made, colorful, and quaint, but the feeling the image evokes is what's the most endearing. Because of how much everyone in town have come to mean to me."

Everyone was listening intently.

Dalton wondered if they could hear the beating of his heart. "I think Frank should leave his display up all year long."

"That said, I award this year's Christmas competition first prize to Mr. Hatfield and his display of the miniature train circling the Christmas tree. Without the Union Pacific wreck at Three Pines Turn, chances are I'd never have met *any* of you. We would have stopped at the depot, taken on water, and continued on our way as planned. As horrible as the crash was, it changed many lives, mine included." He searched out Adaline, who seemed to hang on each and every word out of his mouth. "I hope to make Logan Meadows my home. But only time will tell if that dream becomes a reality. Congratulations, Mr. Hatfield!"

Thunderous applause echoed around the room. None of the losers looked any less excited than Mr. Hatfield himself. Truly, the spirit of Christmas was well and alive in Logan Meadows.

Albert stepped forward, pushing his hands at the crowd for silence. "Thank you to Deputy Babcock for his thoughtful consideration in this year's competition." He gave Dalton an approving nod. "Santa will hand out these gifts before we have the final waltz of the night so those interested will have time to head over to the church service."

With the huge weight gone from his shoulders, Dalton breathed out and stepped off the stage. Folks reached out and shook his hand. Many complimented him on his fine speech and eloquent manner. All he'd done was speak the truth.

With shouts of joy, the children rushed forward, and Winthrop did his best not to get trampled as he dished out the goods.

Chapter Fifty-Seven

Courtney finally allowed herself to breathe a tad bit easier. Wil hadn't showed. Hadn't been seen for a week, since the day he and Tyler had fought in the Silky Hen. The possibility was good he'd left town. Jake and the others had hunted but turned up emptyhanded. Where was he? What was he thinking? Maybe, in the spirit of Christmas, he'd decided to leave her alone. Was there a possibility she wouldn't shame her family after all?

With the children's gifts passed out, Gabe and the other musicians mounted the stage. One final waltz and they'd all head over to the quaint little church on the hill.

The shrill sound of a hard object tapping on glass made everyone stop and look toward the balcony.

Wil! Staring down at her. He was ragged and wet, dirt and grime covering his clothing. He looked as if he'd been living in a ditch for the last week. A scraggly black beard covered his jaw but did little to hide the animosity gleaming from his eyes. Revenge had changed him into an animal.

"Good evening, ladies and gentlemen," he slurred. "All good things must come to an end, as they say—although I never understood who '*they*' are." He laughed mirthlessly at his own joke.

Dalton and Tyler, both close to the stairway, bolted up but when Wil swung around and pointed his gun at their chests they halted halfway. He swayed, unsteady on his feet.

Fear spiked through Courtney for the safety of her friends and children in the room.

A few feet away, Jake bit out a curse, his anger palpable.

"No need for bloodshed on Christmas Eve. Get back where you belong," Wil commanded.

Both men stayed exactly where they'd stopped.

Wil's eyes narrowed.

Courtney had no doubt he'd shoot them in cold blood. "Please, Dalton and Tyler, give Wil some room," she called, finding her voice. In a daze, she stepped onto the dance floor with everyone's gaze watching in fear.

Adaline pushed her way through the people and rushed to Courtney's side. She grasped her arm and tried to pull her away.

Courtney smiled into her sister's eyes. "I'm sorry, Adaline. If I don't have my say, I'll never be free." She looked up at Wil and then into the faces of everyone watching.

"You come to your senses, darlin'?" Wil stage whispered, loud enough for everyone to hear. "You missing me as much as I'm missing you?" He lifted a flask and took a long pull.

She'd need to hurry before Wil beat her to the punch. Straightening her back, she fortified her courage. "Wil Lemon was my beau when I lived in Newport. Since he came to Logan Meadows, he's been blackmailing me. Threatening to expose our private relationship."

Nervous whispers drifted around the room.

"Court! Don't you steal my thunder!" He flung the flask aside and grasped the handrail. The barrel of his gun waved unsteadily around the room.

His love of drawing out a tense moment, combined with too much whiskey, would be his downfall. "My father, God rest his soul," Courtney hurried on, "warned me many times about Wil. As did my sister—and brother, Jake, once he arrived in Newport. I wouldn't listen. I laughed in their faces. When Wil showed up in Logan Meadows with threats, my fear of being exposed as the fallen girl made me steal from the Logans to pay him off. I'm very ashamed of that. Not a kind way to repay the people who treated me like family. As I've waited for Wil to expose me, I realized the fear of the truth coming out was worse than what your rejection will be. By my confession tonight, Wil's power over me is gone."

Wil gaped from above, speechless.

"I understand, after tonight, you'll see me differently. I'll be an exile. I only pray you won't let my bad behavior hurt my brother and sister. Unlike me, they're good in every way. Please don't allow what I've said tonight change the way you think or feel about them."

Adaline wiped at tears.

Jake, Daisy, and all her friends—if they were still her friends—looked astounded. Had she said everything? Was there more? She'd best get out every detail now because she never wanted to revisit this again.

"I've said all I'm going to say." She shrugged. Her future was uncertain. "And I actually feel better. This is Christmas Eve, a night of miracles." Glancing up, she slowly shook her head. "Goodbye, Wil. You have no more power over me."

Murmuring around her erupted.

She dropped her head, heat infusing her face, and headed for the coatroom. All she wanted was to find the door. She'd pack her carpetbag immediately and leave Logan Meadows in the morning forever. She didn't know how she'd accomplish the deed as of yet, but she would. She'd already done the most difficult thing she could ever imagine.

"Wait!"

Tyler.

She didn't want to stop.

He caught her arm and turned her to face him. "Don't run off." His gaze searched hers.

His hair had been trimmed, and he smelled good, like pine trees and a tiny splash of men's cologne. So much of what they'd talked about washed through her. If nothing else, he was a very good friend.

"That was brave," he whispered. "I don't know if I could have been so bold. I admire your honesty very much."

Horrified, she felt a prickle of heat behind her eyes. If Tyler didn't let her leave this instant, she'd cry in front of everyone. The enormity of the situation sat on her chest like a mountain.

Music lilted. Over Tyler's shoulder, she could see Dalton marching Wil down the stairs. Albert, Thom, and Chase encouraged people to stop talking and join in on the last waltz. The party would soon be over. Adaline stood with Jake and Daisy, watching her and Tyler.

Her lips wobbled, and she cut her gaze to the button on his shirt.

With a gentle touch, Tyler lifted her chin. "Dance with me?"

She swallowed. Didn't he know she couldn't show her face? She wanted out. Away from prying eyes. "I can't."

"You can."

His words were warm, sweet—offering a ray of hope.

"Please, don't deprive me a dance with the prettiest, most special girl here."

Her throat clogged on an ocean of tears. She couldn't breathe. Couldn't move. Couldn't think. All around her, the music played and others floated by as if nothing monumental had taken place. She'd held this secret inside for so long she'd become one with the hurt, so she didn't know where her shame ended and she began.

Tyler took her hand into his warm one and led her to the middle of the dancers, but she was careful not to meet anyone's gaze. To her horror, one by one, the couples stopped and pulled away. They fell back to the ring of others watching. Just as she'd believed they would when the truth about her was revealed. They didn't want to be close.

To be corrupted by her depravity. Unable to stand the scrutiny, she closed her eyes. She concentrated on Tyler's steps as they moved around the floor. She wished she could hide her face against his neck but didn't dare for the scandal the display of affection would create.

"It's all right," Tyler whispered. He held one hand on her waist and the other her hand. "Open your eyes."

The warmth of his breath tickled her ear. She dared a glance. As she'd thought, the dance floor was theirs alone and all of Logan Meadows ringed them. But their expressions weren't angry. She was shocked to see compassion and understanding. Had no one judged her harshly?

Then, someone in back began to clap. More joined in.

Without missing a step, Tyler removed his hand from her waist, pulled a handkerchief from his pocket and wiped the tears from her cheeks.

A moment later, Jake and Daisy joined them in the waltz, as did Chase and Jessie, Brenna and Mr. Hutton, Win and Lettie, Frank and his sister, Roberta. Soon, the whole of the town didn't mind dancing on the same floor as a fallen woman.

Chapter Fifty-Eight

The night was cold and clear. Beth couldn't remember one so beautiful. She tried not to think of the frigid air kissing her face, and concentrate on the thick, warm coats she'd layered on before starting out. A slight breeze moved the upper branches of the tall pines causing the vestiges of snow to rain down from above. The snow from a few days ago was all but gone. She also tried not to consider Tommy Hollyhock walking at her side. He'd always been a quiet man, unless he had a funny story to tell. Now was no exception. The magnitude of the brilliant stars above had her almost speechless herself.

"You warm enough?" His deep voice came out of the darkness.

She glanced to his face in time to see the puffs of white his warm breath created in the air. "Can't say I'm not cold but getting out into the night air has cleared my head. This is Christmas Eve. We almost let the holy night pass us by."

He chuckled. "You're not afraid of wolves and bears?"

"Once a woman reaches my age, Tommy, only another wrinkle or gray hair gives her pause. I'm no exception. I won't let something as insignificant as a wild animal scare me away from a Christmas Eve walk to town."

"Your age?" he said incredulously. "You're barely over thirty."

"I'm halfway to forty."

He glanced down at her and smiled.

Then he did the strangest thing, taking her hand in his as if all the years of heartache between them hadn't happened at all. When they rounded the corner and started the walk toward the hotel, she noticed others crossing the street from the community center toward the hill where the church stood atop, a soft glow shining from the windows. Reverend Wilbrand must already be there, lighting the candles and feeding the iron stove.

Some of the townsfolk carried lanterns and others traveled in large groups.

Sadness for missing the Christmas shindig tried to compete with her joy at being with Tommy, her hand in his, but was shut out. This magical night would live in her heart forever.

"What's this?" he asked when he spotted the others.

"The party has ended, and most of Logan Meadows are headed to the Christmas Eve service in the church."

He made a sound deep in his throat. "Are you still a church-going woman, Beth?"

"I am, Tommy. I never miss a Sunday."

"What do you say we put off getting your belongings for another hour? I think I'd like to sit next to you in a pew and sing some Christmas carols." He gently squeezed her hand.

She felt nineteen again—young and in love. Had they been given a second chance? Christmas Eve made her believe they had.

Dalton emerged from the sheriff's office and glanced up and down the empty street. All was still on this chilly Christmas Eve. The soft strains of a Christmas carol floated down the hill.

By law, Dalton could have jailed Wil Lemon for the fight he and Tyler had in the café but thought better of the action, deciding the filth being gone from town would suit Courtney, and everyone else, much better. In no uncertain terms, Dalton had demanded he clear out tonight and never show his face in Logan Meadows again. They might not lock him up and throw away the key for being a cad, but when the men of this town gave him a taste of his own medicine, he'd wish for jail time.

Being upstaged by Courtney had shocked him into a silent, despondent shell. The fact Adaline's little sister had been brave enough to take back the power of her life filled Dalton with pride. A rush of warmth filled his chest. That girl had grit—*just like her sister*—and brother! Logan Meadows was a better place because of the Costner siblings.

Taking a few steps into the street, Dalton stopped. He glanced at the crystal-clear sky filled with glittering stars. The hush felt holy—as if he were the only person alive on the earth. What did his life have in store? He'd told the townspeople Logan Meadows was his new home, but could he stay if Adaline didn't love him? Could he see her every day? Converse about everyday events, if they were destined to only be friends? Watch her fall in love with some other man? The thought was a sentence worse than death. Her disinterest tonight had been a pain he didn't think he could endure for long.

What was the answer? What should he do? The fact Jake, from Logan Meadows, had rescued him from the prison camp had been another indication this town was where he was destined to sink his roots. It gave him permission not to return to Breckenridge, to his mother and father, and see to his own happiness. But now? After tonight? And no employment opportunities on the horizon here, either. Were the heavens telling him something?

A gentle wind moved the branches of the tall Christmas tree, as well as sending a brisk chill up Dalton's back. He had two choices tonight. Return to his cold, lonely apartment above the sheriff's office, retrieve his book, and then take up his cot by the woodstove downstairs with Ivan, or head up the hill to where everyone else was joyously ringing in Christmas morning. By now, the church was sure to be filled, but he could stand in the back. He glanced over his shoulder at the sheriff's office and then up to the church. The answer seemed easy.

Chapter Fifty-Nine

Squeezed in between Courtney and Daisy in a long church pew, Adaline tamped down the deep sorrow she felt for her sister. Why hadn't Courtney confided in her during all these weeks? The thought broke her heart, and she vowed never to let such a distance between them ever grow so wide again.

She was thankful Tyler had stepped in to ask her little sister to dance, as well as make known his affection for her, walking her to church and taking a place by her side. He was a fine young man. She could see them forging a future together. And what about the good folks who'd rallied around Courtney in the community center? The picture of them dancing around Courtney and Tyler had moved Adaline to tears. Still, others who were not so goodhearted, who would judge Courtney harshly could be a possibility. She'd have a bumpy road ahead.

Courtney leaned in. "You're not singing?"

This sister was the dear Court she knew. The one with a tender heart, always watching out for others' feelings—not the person she'd become their last year in Newport after meeting Wil Lemon. "I'm just thinking," Adaline replied into Courtney's ear.

"Please, don't worry. I know my future won't be easy, but I'm happy. I feel lighter, like I could do anything tonight. My life will get better—with time."

Courtney was wise beyond her years.

At their whispers, Tyler leaned forward and looked at them, questions in his eyes. His hand hadn't left Courtney's since asking her to dance. Adaline gave him a reassuring smile.

He nodded and sat back.

What had gotten into Dalton tonight? He'd been so attentive to her every need. Was he feeling guilty over their brief kiss at the Red Rooster? Dancing in his arms had been magical, and if she hadn't been so blindsided by what Courtney had just revealed, Adaline would have been walking—*or dancing*—on air.

She glanced around the small church at the couples who had found their way to each other. Chase and Jessie, Hannah and Thom, Brenna and Gregory, Jake and Daisy, Charlie and Nell, Seth and Ivy, Hunter and Tabitha, and soon to be Gabe and Julia—the list could go on and on.

She drifted her gaze to Albert and Susanna—Dalton's *true* love. Nate was slumped on Susanna's arm, the child tired out by all the excitement. Every single couple had trials and tribulations on their way to this incredible happiness they all seemed to enjoy. She wanted the same.

The hair on the back of her neck prickled. Glancing around, she found Beth looking at her—wearing a small, apologetic smile. Even Beth and Tommy Hollyhock had found their way back to each other after fifteen years. They sat side by side, happily scrunched together.

Christmas magic was happening everywhere.

The congregation had just finished the last hymn of "Angels We Have Heard on High," sending a wave of goose bumps over Adaline's body. How she loved Christmas. She'd been blessed beyond measure to find she and Courtney had a loving brother in Jake and a new sister in Daisy. Their hometown of Logan Meadows was the perfect spot for them. Somehow, she'd find her own happiness. Somewhere, sometime.

"Merry Christmas, everyone!" Reverend Wilbrand called out from the sanctuary. "May the peace and joy of Christmas descend upon you and remain forever. Now, bundle these sleepy children off to bed and enjoy a few moments of quiet before tomorrow arrives."

Leaning on the back wall, Dalton waited as the reverend's flock filed out. No one had removed their outer layers, so they were ready for the cold blast of air when Win opened the door.

"Everything go all right?" Albert asked when he and Susanna reached him. Albert cradled Nate in his arms.

Dalton nodded. "It did. Wil Lemon has seen the last of Logan Meadows."

Albert clapped Dalton's shoulder. "Good job."

"You missed the excitement, Dalton," Susanna said, almost past and into the dark night. "Gabe proposed to Julia in the front of the church just before the service started. Come January, another wedding will take place."

Dalton smiled but didn't feel the joy. He wanted to make Adaline his wife, but such a miracle wasn't written in his stars. "Happy for them. I'll tell 'em so when they come out."

Others passed by, giving him a nod, handshake, or holiday greeting. Everyone had accepted him as deputy, and even Thom was holding back, letting him enjoy the stint in the office. Ahhh, life was good…

He caught sight of Adaline toward the front of the church as she turned and started his way. Of course, he'd found her earlier between Daisy and Courtney, and most of the service passed with him lost in thought. Her cheeks were rosy from the cold beneath her striking blue eyes. She was young, but she possessed a maturity about her, too. He needed her, he wanted her. He'd spend the rest of his life making her happy—if only she'd give him the chance.

"Here you are, Dalton," Jake said on a laugh. He guided Daisy to the side of the vestibule, and the others followed. "I was wondering if you'd join us. Sorry, there were no seats to be saved."

Dalton was aware of Adaline's gaze roaming his face. He didn't dare glance at her for fear he'd scare her away. He felt her skittishness—something had changed. Had she been thinking of him as much as he'd been thinking about her? The last thing he wanted was for Adaline to run off without getting to speak with her and wish her a merry Christmas. Had she arranged a ride home?

"I was more than comfortable standing back here," said Dalton. "I had a good view." He and Tyler exchanged a brief greeting and others filed out. "Adaline, may I speak with you?" People wouldn't stay out long in this cold. He didn't have a second to waste.

Jake glanced back. "Talk fast, Dalton. We're driving Adaline and Marlene home to the Red Rooster. At the moment, Marlene is escorting Maude to the mercantile, and we're stopping by there to pick her up. Courtney and Tyler will ride with Chase and Jessie."

Alone, a few feet away from the doorway, Dalton and Adaline stood face-to-face. He could see having an important conversation now wasn't going to work at all. She was too cold, shivering in her coat. Her breath came out in little puffs of white. This moment was much too important to rush.

Jake and Daisy sat huddled in a buggy they'd driven up from the community center as they waited for Adaline to join them.

"Merry Christmas, Adaline," he said, warming up his voice. He had requested these few moments alone with her. He had to say something.

She gave a tentative smile, looking more beautiful than an angel. "Merry Christmas, Dalton."

He reached out and gently lifted her gloved hand, encasing it between his own. "I enjoyed dancing with you tonight." And he had, even with her ambivalence. He'd take any crumb of affection she had to give.

"I did as well," she whispered, her gaze darting to a few families still chancing the cold.

Other than them, the yard had cleared out fast. His heart leapt at the admission. "You did? I wasn't sure."

"I'm so sorry. Courtney had just told me about"—she glanced away and then back at him—"about her past. I hadn't known until tonight."

Unfettered joy burst within Dalton. Another explanation for her distraction existed. He still had a chance. Resisting the urge to hoist her into his arms and twirl her around, all the while kissing her soundly on her beautifully sculpted lips, he just smiled between his shivers. He'd not scare her off now. Too much remained to be said.

"Dalton!" Jake barked out. "Your time's up! Daisy is freezing, and so am I!"

"May I call on you tomorrow?"

She beamed. "Would you like to come for Christmas supper? We have a goose we're roasting. Jake and Daisy are coming, too, after spending Christmas morning with the Logans, and bringing Courtney."

He'd never last that long. He wanted to go home with her now. "I would. But would I inconvenience anyone if I come out a few hours earlier? Say about ten in the morning?" Nobody slept late on Christmas.

Jake turned the buggy and came in their direction. "Dalton!"

Adaline's laughter sounded musical.

"Sure, you can! Everyone will be happy to see you."

He felt twenty feet tall as he handed his love into the buggy. "I'll see you at ten—and not a minute after." Jake's amused chuckle didn't even bother him. Nothing would bother him ever again. Hope lived and he planned to act on the gift he'd been given by the Almighty.

Chapter Sixty

"Merry Christmas, Dalton!" Albert strode into the sheriff's office Christmas morning, a small wrapped package in his hands. He set the gift on the edge of the desk where Dalton sat and made his way to the coffeepot.

"Thanks, Albert." He glanced at the clock. Not yet nine. Early for a family man to be out and about on a special day like this. Didn't he have father-son activities to do? "Merry Christmas to you, too. I'm surprised to see you here today. Any special reason?"

When he gulped down his first swallow, Albert winced. "Extra hot this morning."

Dalton nodded. Albert would get around to his reasons when he felt good and ready.

"Susanna sent me with that little gift. It's huckleberry jam, just so you know."

Was there an edge of jealousy in his tone? Dalton picked up the gift, gauging the weight in his palm. "That was awfully kind. Please thank her for me."

Albert took a good, long gaze, narrowing his eyes. "You can thank her yourself. She sent me to invite you to Christmas dinner. Says you don't have anywhere to go."

Sure, Albert, make the gesture sound like a pity invitation. "Well, I'll be. That was thoughtful. But actually, I do have an invite already, although I'll miss her good cooking. All those years she's worked at the Silky Hen has been beneficial. I can just imagine what her Christmas dinner spread will look like."

Albert harrumphed. "An invitation? Where to?"

"The Red Rooster."

"So, you and Adaline are finally owning up to your feelings?"

Did everybody see what they couldn't? "Maybe."

Albert strode to the window. At a scratching sound which usually meant Ivan wanted in, Albert opened the door.

The dog trotted to the stove without even acknowledging either of them.

Dalton chuckled. "Thinks he owns the place. Is Thom on the way?"

Albert looked out, glanced up and down the street, and pulled his head back inside. He shut the door tight. "Don't see him."

Ivan circled several times on the worn rug in front of the woodstove and then dropped to the floor with a kerplunk.

Albert seemed agitated. Dalton couldn't imagine why.

"You popping the question to Adaline?"

A mite irritated, Dalton stood. "What's with you and all the personal questions this morning? This is Christmas. Can't you bury the hatchet? Susanna picked *you*—remember? Her inviting me to supper has no bearing on that."

Albert took a deep breath. "Yeah, I can—and have. You weren't at the church last night when Thom and Hannah announced she's expecting."

Dalton snapped straight. "What? You're right! I didn't hear that news. More congratulations are in order. I heard about Gabe's proposal. Thom must be walking on air." Albert must want to say more, Dalton was sure. "And?"

"With Roberta going back East with her sister, Marigold, when she leaves, and Hannah in the family way and queasy with morning sickness, Thom thinks he needs to take over at the Silky Hen right away."

A million questions crashed through Dalton's mind, pushing out the surge of elation about Thom and Hannah. "How long will Roberta be gone?"

"Undetermined. But even when she comes back, with a baby, Hannah will be out for some time. Susanna and Daisy can't handle the Silky Hen themselves."

By his look, Albert wasn't finished. "And…?"

"Susanna and I have reason to believe she might be in the family way as well—but we're not ready to spill those beans just yet, so keep the possibility under your hat. Her absence will create another void at the Silky Hen."

Dalton surged forward in happiness. He grasped Albert's hand and pumped it vigorously. "Congratulations! You're going to be a father—again! I'm happy for you both." And he was … very. And delighted for Susanna. She'd make a wonderful mother, as she'd already proven with her care of Nate.

A silly grin appeared on Albert's face. "Thanks, Dalton. In all honesty, I'm tickled pink. I wasn't around for Nate's birth or early years and only learned of his existence a few months back. This is a true blessing."

This turn of events was too good to be true. What a Christmas gift! "What will you do for a deputy, then?" Dalton held his breath. There could be only one reason Albert was sharing such private information on Christmas morning.

"Offering you the job, if you want it."

Just like Albert to play down the situation. But that wouldn't sway Dalton. He'd learned to navigate around Albert. Everyone in town would agree Dalton was the best candidate for a permanent position. "I accept!"

"Don't you want to know the details?"

"Sure, I do. But I also want you to know unequivocally I'm accepting the job. You've just hired your new *full-time* deputy! When will the position start?"

"How about right now?"

Chapter Sixty-One

Delirious with happiness, Adaline floated around the Red Rooster, preparing the supper table for the feast which would take place later in the day, as well as the arrival of Dalton—*any time*. The sincerity of his voice last night, as well as the expression in his eyes, had kept her awake long after she'd placed her small gifts under the tiny Christmas tree. Something had drastically changed between her and Dalton, and the possibilities had her hopeful. The memory of dancing in his arms had waltzed around in her heart long past midnight. But still, she'd jumped enthusiastically from her bed at the first glimmer of daylight. Lack of sleep wouldn't slow her steps today. Her heart had wings, and she felt ready to fly.

Adaline wore the pretty new shawl Violet had given her for Christmas. The fact Violet had crocheted the delicate rust-and-yellow garment weeks before she'd taken ill touched Adaline deeply. Adaline had given her a small cameo pin she'd purchased from Mrs. Harrell at the haberdashery at a discounted price.

At the sight, Violet's eyes had gone wide, and she'd asked Adaline to pin the jewelry to her nightgown right away, because her hands had been too shaky for the task. Adaline hadn't had a gift for Beth or Mr. Hollyhock because she hadn't known soon enough the two would be with them on Christmas morning. She had given Marlene a poem she'd written about snowflakes in the wind.

Marlene had given Adaline a pair of warm socks she'd knitted. The gift giving had been fun with Beth and Mr. Hollyhock watching.

He'd given his mother a thick parcel to look through later. "All the letters I wrote but never sent," he said, looking sheepish. "They're yours."

Violet sat by the fire, dozing, where she'd been for the past half hour.

Beth and Marlene were busy in the kitchen, whipping up cinnamon pound cake for dessert, and some other delectable dishes to complement the large goose already in the oven.

Mr. Hollyhock had taken himself out back for a smoke and planned to split more logs as long as he was already bundled up.

She had felt a little uncomfortable mentioning she'd invited Dalton without first asking permission.

Violet assured her everyone was welcome, especially the handsome deputy. The more the merrier.

The sound of jingle bells made Adaline run to the window.

"Dalton?" Beth asked from the sink where she was peeling carrots.

Marlene laughed softly. "Or Santa Claus? I don't think anyone else is set to arrive to the pretty jingle of bells. That sounds nice." She winked when Adaline briefly glanced her way. "If it's not Dalton, our Adaline will die with disappointment. The time is two minutes until ten. Your young man knows how to tell time—a fine quality to have."

Adaline scarcely heard the teasing. "Yes." She could barely say the word between her shaky voice and thundering heart. "It's Dalton in an open buggy. And along with the bells, he's put a wreath with a big red bow around the horse's neck. How sweet."

Adaline wished she could see Dalton's eyes, but he had his hat pulled low and collar turned up against the cold. A black scarf wrapped his neck, the ends tucked in tight. Large puffs of white came out of his mouth. His lips moved as if he were talking to the horse, or maybe himself. He'd never looked so handsome.

Setting the brake, he stood, climbed out of the buggy, and taking one line, draped the leather around the hitching rail. Next, he unbuckled his holster and placed his gun under the seat on his side. Reaching down again, he withdrew a blanket, shook it out, and draped the horse. Finished, he gathered two presents and started for the door.

Corralling her excitement, she skipped to the door to meet him. Was her dream about to come true? She opened the door before he had a chance to knock.

He smiled.

She returned the gesture.

"Mornin', Adaline," he drawled out slowly, merriment sparkling in his eyes. Two prettily wrapped packages rested in his arms. One medium-sized, the other tiny. "Merry Christmas."

Watching him remove his hat, she wanted to vault into his arms. "Good morning, Dalton. Merry Christmas to you as well. Won't you come in?" She stepped back, opening the door wider to a rush of frigid air. "A wonder you didn't freeze to death on your way over." Silly thing to say, but her mind felt frozen at the sight of his face, how he looked into her eyes. The feelings he stirred deep in her soul.

He stepped inside and glanced around. "Actually, I nearly did— and would have, if the Red Rooster were any farther away." He nodded to Violet, who was now awake and watching them closely. "Merry Christmas, Violet." He glanced at Marlene and Beth, who stood at the doorway to the kitchen. "Ladies. Smells awfully good in here. My mouth is watering already. Thank you for the invitation."

At Dalton's dashing smile, both Marlene and Beth blushed.

With trembling hands, Adaline took his hat and hung the Stetson on the hat rack.

Violet peaked a scanty brow. "Come in here and give my cheek a kiss, young man. Ya should know better than to make me wait."

With a chuckle, and still wearing his coat, he crossed the round, braided, multicolored rug and bent low, kissing Violet's chalky cheek. He held out the tiny package.

Disappointment plummeted inside Adaline. She'd let her fantasies run wild...

"For me?" Violet asked, her hand covering her lips.

"That's what the envelope says. I found the package on the sheriff's desk this morning. Don't know how they knew my plans to stop out here. And I'm still wondering how I didn't hear whoever snuck the package inside with me sleeping only a few feet away. I feel rather sheepish about that." He turned to Adaline, who had followed him to Violet's side by the fireplace. "And this one is for you, Adaline."

Already over her flash of disappointment, excitement bubbled up at the medium-sized green box adorned with a red ribbon. What was inside? How had he afforded to buy anything? She knew he was strapped for funds. "Thank you, Dalton. I'm sorry I don't have anything for you." She had so little money, and with the uncertainty between them, she'd thought giving him a gift would be presumptuous. Now, she wished she'd at least written him a poem.

"Your smile is enough gift for me."

Mr. Hollyhock came through the front door with an armload of wood. He smiled at Dalton. "Merry Christmas, Deputy. Would you like me to put your horse out of the cold?"

"Thanks, but I was hoping Adaline might get away for an hour or two. The day's still early. Maybe go by the Broken Horn. Give the children a ride with the jingle bells. She could see Courtney and most likely Jake and Daisy."

A buggy ride with Dalton! How romantic! She glanced over her shoulder at Marlene. "Do I have time? I don't want to leave all the work for you two."

Marlene smiled, her eyes wide.

Beth waved her hand in a shooing motion. "Most all the work is done, Adaline. From now until supper, we'll just be sitting around the fire, telling stories. I think everyone would agree you have plenty of time for a visit."

"That's so," Marlene added. "Be sure to give my son, and everyone else, our love. And tell them not to be late for supper. The goose will be ready at three o'clock sharp."

"I guess that's a yes," Dalton said, his bright smile reappearing.

Did he have something important he wanted to ask her? She couldn't help but hope. "Fine, then just let me go get my coat and gloves."

"First, you must open your present." He glanced at Violet. "And so does Violet. I'm curious about what's inside."

Disappointment again. If Adaline's gift was personal, he'd have saved the giving until they were alone.

Dalton nudged the tiny gift on Mrs. Hollyhock's lap. "Violet, you first."

With unsteady hands, Violet carefully opened the envelope and slipped out a single white sheet of stationery. She pushed her silver-rimmed glasses closer to her eyes, perusing the page. "Well, I'll be," she whispered with wobbling lips and then slowly opened the small box. Inside was a square of pink fabric with a needlepointed heart. She held her treasure for all to see.

Dalton shifted his weight. "Who's it from? What's the note say?"

Lifting the missive again, she read aloud, "Merry Christmas, dear Violet. May yer hot chocolate be as warm and sweet as the expression in yer eyes. I'm happy you've recovered. Merry Christmas, dear friend. Love, the do-gooder." A moment passed, and then Violet drilled Dalton with her no-nonsense stare. "Ya failed me, my boy."

Dalton actually slumped. "I did, Violet, and I'm sorry. But the do-gooder doesn't want to be identified."

Violet winked. "I'm joshin' ya. Ya need ta learn some humor, Deputy."

Looking relieved, Dalton turned to Adaline. "Your turn."

She sat on the sofa and slowly unwrapped the gift, being careful not to tear the pretty paper even the tiniest bit. Inside was a beautiful, warm scarf she'd admired at the haberdashery.

"Mrs. Harrell said you liked this one. You can wear it today, if you want."

His face had taken on an uncharacteristically rosy hue, and she smiled. "Thank you, Dalton. I'm surprised she remembered."

"She opened the store just for me this morning."

He'd gone to so much trouble—but why? She didn't know how to respond in front of everyone watching. "It's beautiful. I'll be honored to wear your gift today." Standing, excitement propelled her to her room. Things weren't always what they seemed, she counseled her heart. He may be reaching out, but the sentiment could still just be friendship. She shouldn't let her hopes get too high. *Friendship is better than nothing.*

With the sensible self-talk out of the way, Adaline quickly ran a trembling hand over her hair, pinched both her cheeks, turning her face in the reflection of the mirror. Friendship, bah—love was in the air. She could feel it. This would be a Christmas to remember.

Chapter Sixty-Two

The livery horse trotted along at a nice clip, acting happy to be headed back toward town. The gelding wouldn't be as pleased when Dalton pushed him past the livery, across the bridge, and up the road to the Broken Horn. Adaline's presence beside him was like a burst of sunshine. She made every inch of nerves sing with anticipation. Where was a good spot to stop? Before town? After? He could hardly think of anything except the tiny box burning a hole in his coat pocket. This time, he was sure of Adaline. She'd say yes to his proposal. Who knew? Maybe they'd be man and wife by next week. He surely wouldn't object. "You warm enough over there?" he asked, looking her way.

Sitting as straight as an arrow, she smiled brightly as she took in the sights. "I am. I love the wreath around Slow Poke's neck, but I love the jingling bells even more. The festive sound makes me feel like I'm riding in Santa's sleigh."

Wiggling his eyebrows made her laugh. "Maybe you are. We might be in for a little magic. One never knows." Dalton dragged his gaze from Adaline's lips, which were distracting his thoughts. "Whoa," he called to Slow Poke, pulling back gently on the lines.

The gelding slowed to a walk and finally stopped under the tunnel of trees a few yards before the turn leading into town. Dalton steadied his breathing and tried to calm his heart. This was the most important moment of his life.

"Why are we stopping?" Adaline asked, glancing about.

Her voice held a tremble of anticipation, making him think she knew good and well what was on his mind. "Just wanted to take a moment and look at you. Doing so is difficult with everyone watching—or in a moving buggy. I hope you don't mind." He turned to face her, and the buggy seat squeaked loudly. The swish of the horse's tail was the only other sound on this bright Christmas morning. Most of the snow had melted except for large patches lingering under the trees.

Adaline lowered her lashes. "I know what you mean. And I feel the same."

With a finger, Dalton gently tipped up her chin. The December cold closed in around them. A slight breeze ruffled her hair as he stared into her eyes. A growing need coaxed him forward. He'd never seen anything more beautiful in his life. "May I kiss you, Adaline? I've wanted to for a long time."

Bundled, and wearing the new scarf he'd given her, she shyly nodded.

Taking her into his arms, Dalton pressed his cold lips to hers, marveling at their softness. In an instant, he was gone, falling, tumbling, rejoicing in his true love and wife-to-be, or so he hoped. Drunk with love, he drew her closer still, wondering how he'd ever lived even one second without her in his arms. In response to his thoughts, her arms entwined his neck, pulling him farther into the embrace.

"Oh, Dalton…," she whispered, her breath coming fast.

After several long, passionate seconds, he pulled back and gazed into her eyes. "The feel of your lips, silky and *soft*, are so dear to me, even in *frost*."

Her eyelashes fluttered encouragingly, and then she giggled. White puffs of her breath kissed his face.

"Like a rich wine, your beauty goes straight to my *heart*, your love needed more than a rich piece of *art,*" he whispered, knowing his rhyme left much to be desired, but the feelings Adaline, the wintery backdrop, and the fullness of his heart created were too much to keep inside a moment longer. He leaned forward and kissed her again, soft and sweet. He felt her smile upon his lips. "No poet am I, as you now *know*, just a common man, trying his love to *show*."

Her gaze darkened, and their kisses intensified, quieted, and then lingered, as if the feeling between them had a life of its own, unwilling now to be put aside ever again.

With her gloved hands she rubbed his coat-covered chest.

Surprised with her boldness, he pulled her closer.

"*Your* lips are warm, Dalton," she began slowly. "Melted chocolate on a *spoon*. If you're not careful, I feel I might *swoon*." She nuzzled his neck.

As important as this moment was to them both, he had to chuckle. Their poetry was terrible. "*Your* sweet lips warmed mine. Made them that *way*. Come closer still," he wiggled his eyebrows again, "don't run *away*."

The quiet winter day closed in around their playful desire. Was proposing to a woman after less than a handful of kisses unwise? If so, he didn't care. He couldn't go a day longer without knowing how she felt about him. About them. And their future.

"Are you cold? Shall we drive on?"

Her eyes smiled. "Not just yet."

Without asking this time, he kissed her again and was rewarded with a soft mew of desire from her throat. He didn't have to guess; she enjoyed his kisses as much as he did hers. But he couldn't ignore the shivers racking her body. He needed to take care of business and get to the Broken Horn. He shouldn't keep her out longer than necessary.

Pulling back to her sound of disappointment, he pressed his lips to her forehead and let them linger as his breathing slowed. With as much aplomb as he could muster, he pulled another small box out of his pocket.

Her eyes went wide.

"I love you, Adaline. I don't want to live my life another day without you." He removed the lid to a small gold band with a tiny red stone. "Would you do me the honor of marrying me and becoming my wife?"

She pushed back so she could look into his face.

The beautiful smile she wore gave him hope. Her eyes searched his for so long he began to wonder.

"Oh, Dalton, yes! I love you so much. I'll make you the happiest man on earth, I promise. I've loved you for so long, hoping and praying. And now…" She flew into his arms, urgently kissing his face, his eyes, his nose, his forehead—finally, his lips. "I'm so happy I think I might cry. Dalton, my Dalton, my only true love."

She sat back, her gloved hands, pressed together, rested on her chest as if in prayer. Excitement beamed from her eyes. "But, why now? What prompted your change of heart? You've been holding me at arm's length for so long. I had all but given up hope because Susanna is your true love…"

Embarrassed now, because the reason sounded silly even to his ears, he hated to say. But he'd not have any falsehoods between them … not now, not ever. "I didn't think Jake would approve, being he was so set against Wil because of the age difference between him and your sister. But I finally made up my mind I'd not lose you because of anyone. When we talked, he set me straight."

"Last night?"

He nodded.

"And Susanna?"

"Susanna, well… She is my past. By the time I'd found her again here in Logan Meadows, she was in love with Albert. Besides, I don't think she held anything more than affection for me. I'd known her when I was young and we lived in Breckenridge. I thought fate had brought us together again when we were reunited, but now I believe fate took me to Newport so I could meet you, and then be with you here in Logan Meadows, when the time was right."

"You're sure?"

He nodded. "I promise. No one has my heart except Adaline Costner, soon to be Adaline Babcock. Your *eyes* are like the—"

With a giggle, Adaline pressed her fingers to his lips. "I believe you, I believe you. But what a roundabout way fate brought us together. I'm sorry you had to suffer. Being shanghaied, imprisoned, and drugged. You almost died." She softly stroked his cheek.

Her eyes glimmered like diamonds. "And I'd do everything all over again for your love." He lifted the ring out of the box.

Removing her glove, she let Dalton slip the delicate ring on her finger. She gazed at the tiny ruby for several long seconds and then looked up into his face. "But how? I know you're short on funds, Dalton. I don't need a ring to prove your love. This must have cost a fortune. The money will be better—"

Never taking his gaze from hers, he lifted her hand and kissed her fingers. "Shush, now. A symbol of my never-ending love is the best use of all. This morning, I learned Hannah is expecting. Thom will be needed in the café. I've been offered his position. A permanent deputy here in Logan Meadows."

Her eyes grew round. "Dalton! That's wonderful! I know how much you had hoped."

"So, as soon as Albert left, I went straight to the haberdashery and knocked, refusing to leave until Mrs. Harrell opened up. I bought your scarf," he said, fingering the gift, "and also the ring. She gave them to me on credit." Face radiant with joy, Adaline admired the ring, one hand cupped in the other, creating a picture he'd never forget. He was so lost in Adaline, the sound of a gun being cocked took several seconds to drill through his love-fogged brain. With a feeling of doom, he slowly turned.

Adaline gasped and grabbed his arm.

Wil Lemon, more disheveled than he'd been the previous night, stood several feet in front of Slow Poke, the man's booted feet planted wide in the middle of the road.

A ray of sun came out and made the barrel of the gun, pointed directly at Dalton's chest, glimmer with evil intent. What a fool! Dalton's Colt was stored safely under the buggy seat where the weapon wouldn't help him a whit. A man didn't wear his sidearm to go courting on Christmas Day. If he didn't think fast, the look in Wil's eyes said nothing short of seeing him and Adaline dead would do.

"Well, well, well—what do we have here?" Wil's mouth pulled down in an ugly sneer. "Two little lovebirds, sittin' in a tree…"

Hot fury ricocheted through Dalton. He wouldn't let Wil kill Adaline! "You're a fool, Lemon!" he bit out, mentally calculating the distance between them. Maybe he could push Adaline onto the floorboard before the man pulled the trigger. "I gave you a chance to drag your mangy hide out of town, and you didn't listen."

"I'm a fool?" He barked out a laugh. "Your *first* mistake was letting me go! The thought of teaching you your *last* mistake was just too tempting." He moved the gun toward Adaline. "And her, too. If I can't punish Courtney, her sister is the next best thing."

"Don't do this, Wil, please," Adaline begged, her heart racing in her throat. The thought of losing Dalton had her breath coming fast. Wil looked like he hadn't slept in days. His open coat showed a filthy shirt, and his pants were marred with caked-on dirt. "Courtney never meant to hurt you. She always stood up for you. We forced her to leave Newport. Kidnapped her away. And now all she wants is to begin a new life here. You can't blame her for that. Just go home and leave us alone. I'm sure the ranch you work for wonders about your absence."

Wil scowled. "You don't know nothin'. They fired me. I got nowhere else to go."

"Plenty of other towns have jobs besides Logan Meadows," Dalton said, scooting toward the edge of the seat. "Take your pick and start a new life."

Moving slower than a slug, he edged one leg out of the buggy. Adaline feared he was about to do something heroic and get killed in the process.

Once on the ground, Dalton slowly unbuttoned and opened his coat. "I'm unarmed, Lemon. You haven't committed any real crimes yet. If you kill us in cold blood, you'll have every lawman in the territory on your tail until you're caught and hanged. Is that the kind of life you want?"

"Shut up and stay where you are! I'm gunna enjoy killin' you, Babcock. Adaline, too; more than I thought I would."

Tension and fear twisted Adaline's heart. She could feel something horrible was about to happen. Would Dalton rush a man with a gun pointed at his chest to protect her? He might be fast, but he couldn't beat a bullet. Her nerves twined tighter and tighter.

Movement at the edge of the trees made her turn her head. Seeing a bloodied Mr. Ling, she sucked in a breath.

Wil turned.

Using the split-second distraction, Adaline dropped to her knees, grasped the handle of Dalton's heavy gun, and surged to her feet. The substantial weapon was difficult to hold straight even with two hands. The barrel wobbled as she pointed it at Wil's chest. "Drop your gun!" she shouted. She didn't dare take her eyes off Wil to look at Dalton, but she could hear his heavy breathing on the other side of the buggy. "You heard me! Drop it or I'll shoot!"

Wil began to laugh. "When pigs fly!" His gun was now pointed at her.

"Don't test me!"

"Adaline…"

That was Dalton, the unconcealed fear in his voice blatant. Her arm muscles screamed with pain as red-hot fire flashed through her body. Sweat broke out on her forehead. She wouldn't be able to hold this gun much longer. And when she lowered it, this madman would kill her and then Dalton. Probably poor Mr. Ling as well.

Mustering every ounce of strength, she held the gun level. "I'm counting to two, Wil Lemon, and then I'm blasting you to kingdom come! Mark my words! One—"

Dalton surged forward and Wil swung his gun at her beloved.

Following Wil's movement with the barrel of her gun, she closed her eyes and squeezed the trigger. The force of the blast knocked her backward over the seat and she landed with a thud on the ground, every ounce of air expelled from her lungs.

Frightened, the horse bolted forward. Within seconds the conveyance was out of sight.

Struggling for breath, it felt like an eternity before Dalton was at her side.

"Adaline!"

Her mouth opened and closed several times before she was finally able to speak. "I'm okay." She searched him the best she could from her position in the mud.

"I'm fine, darlin', thanks to your fancy shooting. Your shot actually blasted the gun from Wil's hands before he could pull his trigger." He winked as he lifted her into his arms and then steadied her on her feet. "And then Slow Poke ran him over with the buggy. Snapped his neck. He's dead."

Mr. Ling appeared beside them. A large bruise was on his temple, as well as dried blood.

"He hide in my supply shed, rob us with gun. Scare family, scare Lan. He hit me on the head, believe me dead." He pointed to Wil's pocket.

Dalton pulled out a small bag of money, the stolen earnings from the laundry house and handed it to Mr. Ling.

"He think I not follow."

All three gazed at the crumpled, bloody form of Wil Lemon.

"He think wrong."

Dalton nodded. "We're much obliged you showed up when you did, Mr. Ling. He was about to kill us. You gave Adaline the much-needed diversion to retrieve my gun." He smiled down into Adaline's face and then kissed her. "After seeing her in action though, I'm wondering if Albert gave the deputy position to the right person."

Chapter Sixty-Three

About Five Months Later

Lugging a stack of blankets, as well as a hamper filled with picnic food, Adaline threaded through the sea of brightly colored quilts and blankets dotting the grass of the festival grounds, making her way toward the band stage. Already teeming with people, the area was decorated nicely for the May Day celebration. A dance floor had been built. The maypole, a favorite of the children, stood tall with an array of colorful fabric streamers still twisted around the shaft. A town-sponsored lemonade stand was doing a splendid pre-party business with a line wrapping around the back of the booth and stretching out toward town, as thirsty townsfolk waited to wet their whistles. The feeling in the air had never been better.

Finding a spot to accommodate all three of her blankets, as well as more room for others who wanted to join their party, Adaline fluffed her large coverlets as sunshine warmed her shoulders. She pulled each corner until they were perfectly flat and made sure the edges were flawlessly aligned. The day couldn't be more perfect. Glancing up, she watched a flock of sparrows playing in the clouds.

Excitement coursed through her veins. In four months, and just six days after her eighteenth birthday, she'd become Mrs. Dalton Babcock. Her in-laws would be here, as well as Dalton's younger sister, Eloisa, an uncle, and two cousins. Her small family of three was soon to explode, and she couldn't be happier.

Kneeling, she opened the lid to her covered picnic basket and removed a stack of napkins. She withdrew the still-warm fried chicken she'd made early this morning, a large bowl of potato salad from Marlene, and a lovely apple pie baked by Violet. Courtney and Daisy were bringing the rest.

"Hello, Adaline," Maude Miller called from a few blankets over. The mercantile owner relaxed on her quilt, a large bonnet shading her face. "Is the *Gazette* out? Do you have a copy? I'd like to see how my advertisement looks."

"Not yet, Maude, but I hope to have them soon. Dalton is bringing them shortly. I had to come early and get this spot so we didn't end up too far away from the dance floor, or else I'd have brought them myself. I'm very excited!"

"As you should be, young lady. This is an exhilarating day for Logan Meadows and the *Logan Meadows Gazette*. You save me a copy, you hear? As you know, I've already paid for a subscription."

"I'll be sure to, Maude. And thank you!"

Maude wagged a finger. "And don't forget to bring a stack to put out on my counter. I've cleared a spot right in front. Everyone in Logan Meadows is eager. I'm sure you'll need to print more right away."

Butterflies tumbled inside. Adaline hadn't worked but a couple of weeks in the haberdashery when she knew being a clerk was not her future. She'd always been a good reader, and English was her best and favorite subject. She'd never considered starting a newspaper until, one day in late January, she overheard Mr. Lloyd speaking over his supper in the café about a secondhand printing press he'd heard about that was selling for a good price.

The idea germinated. Sprouted like a tiny acorn and soon burst into a giant oak. If she were brave enough to follow her heart, willing to work harder than she'd ever done before, she'd walk in her father's footsteps. James Costner, a typesetter for most of his life, had never advanced to the reporter position he'd dreamt of. If her vision materialized, she'd be publisher, reporter, editor, sales, and office clerk. At first, Dalton had been uncertain, but she'd convinced him the idea had merit. Such a career would afford her flexibility many occupations would not. She could easily work from home when they were blessed with children. Until then, she would grow the business into something meaningful. And she had begun already, with a few advertisements from several of the businesses on Main Street.

She'd hammered out the details with Mr. Lloyd, and he helped her purchase the printing press with a line of credit. That was around the same time Jake accepted the reward Mr. Ford had left for him in the bank, but only if Adaline and Courtney agreed to a three-way split. Courtney had thrown her share in with Adaline and would take a much-larger role in the operation of the weekly once her final term of school was finished next month. The *Logan Meadows Gazette* was set up in an empty back office in the bank. Each day Adaline went to work, she enjoyed the bank's lovely décor. The situation was perfect.

"Adaline!"

Turning, she saw Hannah as she made her way with a large hamper on her arm. Even with her ever-growing belly, she was still as graceful as she'd ever been.

Markus hurried along beside her.

Adaline ran to meet them. "Let me take your basket, Hannah. You shouldn't overexert yourself."

Hannah swiveled out of her reach. "I'm fine. Thom's mollycoddling is driving me crazy. Says I'm not allowed in the Silky Hen for any reason. That's utter nonsense." She glanced down at Markus and smiled. "Markus is taking fine care of me, too." The warmth of the day and her excursion had turned Hannah's cheeks rosy and moist. "Oh!" She laughed and ran a hand over her protruding belly. "That was a strong one."

"Must be a boy, Ma," Markus said. "Want's ta come out and play."

"Girls can be strong, too." Adaline winked at Hannah. Her friend had confided she'd love a little girl this time around.

"You hoo!"

Susanna and Albert approached, their arms filled with an array of baskets, quilts, and bonnets. When they reached Adaline's blankets, Albert assisted Hannah to the ground and then turned to Susanna.

"I'm not that far along yet, dear husband," she said with a smile, carefully lowering herself to the ground. "I can still manage on my own."

Adaline sank to her knees beside her friends.

Hannah chuckled. "You just wait, Susanna. I'm not too proud to lean on Albert's arm when Thom isn't around. My back hurt something terrible this morning, I could hardly roll out of bed." She stretched with a hand to her back and let out an *ahhh*. "Where's your sister?"

"Courtney'll be along shortly. I believe she and Tyler are riding over with Jake, Daisy, Gabe, and Julia. I'm sure they're taking the long way around and enjoying the buggy ride. The weather doesn't get much prettier than this."

Not everyone forgave her sister on Christmas Eve. The gossips kept nattering but eventually, when nothing else happened, and they received a cold shoulder from Courtney's friends whenever the subject was intoned, they lost interest. Ultimately, her disgrace lost its sting and life went on. Courtney was now happier than Adaline had ever seen her. Her younger sister was energetic and full of life—as well as besotted with her dear friend and sweetheart, Tyler Weston.

Markus dashed off toward a group of youngsters.

"Stay out of trouble, young man," Hannah called to his retreating backside. Her eyes sparkled as she glanced around. "Where's the paper? I can hardly wait!"

"Dalton's bringing it, or I should say, several. Enough to go around, anyway. I'm so nervous I could toss up my breakfast."

Hannah's eyes widened, and then she laughed. "You better not say that or people will start to talk."

Adaline slapped a hand over her mouth.

Albert took in the three women bubbling with excitement, and a silly grin appeared on his lips. "I think I'll just take myself off and go find Dalton. He might need my help. You ladies enjoy..." He turned on his heel and hurried away.

All three broke into laughter.

"I hear your mother, aunt, and Dichelle left yesterday, Hannah," Adaline said. "Roberta must be thrilled to be going to New York."

Hannah nodded. "She is. But she's more excited about this baby. She's cutting the trip short to be home in plenty of time for the birth." She caressed her protruding belly. "Dichelle is the most enthusiastic, I think, flitting around the house like a butterfly. Singing in New York has been her lifelong dream. Only time will tell if her singing career takes off on wings. I sure hope it does. Now," she went on after a breath, "have you and Albert come up with any baby names?"

In the chatter about names, birthdates, and remedies for colicky infants, Adaline or the others didn't hear Mrs. Hollyhock approach.

"Here ya be, ya young chitter-chatterers. Thought I'd never find ya."

"Violet!" Adaline jumped up from where she knelt, heads together with Susanna and Hannah, and took Violet's arm. She glanced about. "Where's Beth? I thought you were coming together."

"That daughter-in-law of mine was busy icing a devil's food cake," she replied sternly, but her eyes snapped with happiness. "She was eatin' more than icin'. Babe's given her a sweet tooth."

Three heads snapped her way. "Did you say babe?" the women chorused as one.

Violet actually laughed. She looked young and beautiful. Her eyes were brighter than the shining sun above. Adaline was thankful her friend had lived to see this day.

"Darn tootin' I said babe! Beth and Tommy don't know it yet though, but I've seen the signs for a good week. I'll have me a grandbaby to spoil by next Christmas mornin'."

Beth? Expecting? Adaline was stunned.

"How exciting," Susanna gushed, rubbing her own huge belly.

Hannah's mouth stood open like a barn door.

Adaline pulled Violet into a tight hug. "I'm so happy for you, my dear old friend! You've been blessed beyond measure."

"I certainly have." She gestured to the two pregnant women gazing up at her. "These littles will be my grandbabies, as well—and all the children of Logan Meadows. My heart has an ocean of love to give." Violet leaned back, and her voice rose several decibels so the people a few blankets away glanced their way. "That fine boy of mine had no trouble gettin' down to business, so to speak—and right quick! I couldn't be happier. Those two are makin' up for lost time."

It was true, Tommy and Beth had married shortly after the new year in a private ceremony in the church. Since then, they'd taken over all the work of the Red Rooster. Gave the place a thorough spring cleaning in March and were thinking about possibly advertising to other towns to bring in more clientele. They had big dreams. That left Violet to her chickens, her knitting, doctoring, gossiping, and helping Adaline at the paper, at Violet's request.

In a moment of uncertainty, Adaline hoped the short article Violet had authored would be a hit and not a miss. If the piece was well received, they'd collaborate on more.

Adaline crossed her fingers behind her back when she spotted Dalton hurrying her way with a stack of the very first *Logan Meadows Gazette* cradled safely in his arms. Her dream of being a professional writer had materialized, but only after countless hours of blood, sweat, and tears. This was the best day of her life, except for her upcoming nuptials, of course. She prayed *"her baby"* would be well received.

Chapter Sixty-Four

Within moments of Dalton's arrival, he was swamped by well-wishers and curiosity seekers wanting to get their hands on a copy of the paper.

Hannah and Susanna huddled together almost fearfully to avoid the pushing.

"Everybody take three steps back," Dalton bellowed. "And be careful where you put your feet. You don't want to hurt anyone."

Mumbling went around the crowd, but they did as instructed.

Dalton wished he and Adaline were alone, so Adaline could peruse the paper at her leisure without everyone breathing down her neck. She'd worked diligently since January. This last week, she'd worked into the wee morning hours to make sure every article, advertisement, and column was perfect. He'd stayed by her side, doing whatever he could to help—and then made sure she got home safely to the Red Rooster. When he'd proposed, Dalton had had no idea she was so smart. Or that so much thought and planning went into writing. He'd already learned a multitude of rules—or at least, heard about them. He hadn't believed his admiration or love for her could be any more than it already was, but he'd been wrong. He handed the top copy to Adaline. "Give her a chance, folks. The editor gets first dibs."

Everyone stood with a nickel in hand.

He'd be sure to collect. This endeavor had cost Adaline a pretty penny. No one on his watch would read for free. After a few moments of back-and-forth paper shuffling and a hawk-like vision roaming the pages, she nodded, and a beautiful smile appeared.

"Go ahead, Dalton," she said in a breathy voice. "Happy birthday to the *Logan Meadows Gazette*."

Within a matter of minutes, the paper was passed into the hands of Gregory and Brenna Hutton, Frank Lloyd, Chase and Jessie, and many others.

"Sorry, folks." He handed out the last one. "I'll print more for the rest of you just as soon as I have a chance to visit a bit with the publisher." He leaned over and kissed Adaline on the top of her head. "You'll see me on the dance floor when I have 'em ready to sell."

With some grumbles, the rest wandered away but still left a crowd of their friends. Everyone was quietly reading, chuckling, or looking in wonder.

Frank puffed out his chest. "What do you think of my article, MONEY MATTERS?" he asked the silently reading crowd. "Saving and planning for your future might be easier than you think. I'll have something new to say the first issue of the month. If you have any requests, just let me know."

"Won't do me much good," Violet chortled, "because I ain't got much money. What I do have, I keep under my bed."

"Violet!" Albert, who had arrived with Dalton, admonished. "You shouldn't be doing that! It's not safe. And if you do, keep the fact to yourself."

"No one with a lick of sense is gonna rob me of ten dollars, Sheriff. I sustain myself most by bartering my eggs, cockerels, homeopathic remedies and tinctures. The inn is Tommy's and Beth's now." Her face softened. "I don't gotta worry about nothin' no more."

"Tabitha," Win called out from the back of the multitude. "This book sounds real good. I'd like to check it out, if it's still available."

Tabitha, who leaned on Hunter's chest as the two read together, lowered the paper from in front of her face. "Certainly, Win. You're the first person to request the title, so I'll hold it for you. I wanted to highlight a book appealing to both men and women for my READ OF THE WEEK column." The ring of pride in her voice was apparent. "*The Prince and the Pauper* fits the bill well. It's a wonderful adventure." She looked around at the women. "But don't worry, ladies. Next week, I'll choose a more romantic story I think you'll all appreciate."

"What's the title?" Mr. Merryweather called out, and then blushed straight to his hairline.

Tabitha shook her finger at him. "You'll have to wait and see, Mr. Merryweather. But it's not one you've already checked out, to date." Her smile grew. "You're a very fast reader."

A ripple of laughter filled the air. Merryweather didn't look half bad in the new glasses he'd finally received from his optometrist back in San Francisco. Dalton wondered if the man had set his sights on someone in town.

Adaline had written three good-sized articles, judged by word count, Dalton had learned. One, the White and Chinese tensions which were still boiling over in Rock Springs. She'd gathered most of her information by speaking with a deputy from Rock Springs who rode through town, and then by sending a couple of telegrams. Another article on wedding customs, a topic close to her heart these days, she had researched in Tabitha's bookshop, Storybook Lodge. The shop was a goldmine of information. When Adaline wasn't home, or at work in the *Gazette*'s office she rented in the bank, she was in the big chair on the other side of Tabitha's large picture window, her nose stuck in a book, pad and pencil close by.

He was plenty proud of his wife-to-be. She'd blossomed into something quite remarkable. The third article was a report on last month's town council meeting, letting everyone, not just a handful of folks, know what was in store for their hometown. It was the shortest of the three, a brief seventy-five words.

Seventy-five, brief! He needed to step up his game. He could barely get through a deputy's report.

"Looky here," Violet called in a voice filled with wonder. "A message from the do-gooder." She cut her gaze to Adaline, who put out her hands.

"I have no idea who the author is, Violet. The note was left on my desk along with a basket of fudge. Frank, even though he's usually always in the bank to see the comings and goings, swears he has no idea who brought it in. The note, addressed to me, asked about the possibility of running the small notice. After all the charity the kind-hearted person has done for our town, how could I refuse? I was more than happy to oblige, since we all *love* the do-gooder."

Adaline cleared her voice to read, "Dearest friends of Logan Meadows, it has come to my attention a dear certain someone has been seeking my identity. She avows she'd like to thank me in person for my small actions of goodwill. But I want you all to know, I need no thanks. Just being a member of this community, this delightful little town, where friends are family, and everyone watches out for each other's well-being, is thank you enough. And, as everyone would agree, Violet Hollyhock is the icing on the cake. Please don't try to unmask me any longer. Doing little acts of kindness makes me happier than anything else in the whole wide world... well, almost. Wishing you all a very happy May Day celebration. Congratulations on the inaugural edition of the *Logan Meadows Gazette*! Love, the do-gooder."

A pleased sound of *aww* rippled around the gathering.

"Well, I'll be." Violet wiped tears from her eyes with a wrinkled hand. She gazed around speculatively at all the others doing the same. "Might be the do-gooder is here amongst us right now. My heart's so full I wish I could hug 'em."

"Howdy, everyone." Tommy arrived to the group with Beth. Beth held a large chocolate cake and Tommy a picnic basket. "This must be the new paper everyone's been waiting for. Congratulations on your momentous achievement, Miss Costner," he said to Adaline and tipped his head at Dalton.

"Thank you, Mr. Hollyhock," Adaline responded, her cheeks turning a deeper pink. "Since you and Beth have arrived, I think the time's come your mother read her human-interest advice piece." She glanced at Violet. "She's worked diligently to make the article interesting, as well as informative. Will you please do the honors, Violet?"

"Sure will, boss." Violet pushed her glasses farther up her nose and brought the paper close to her face. "As spring has sprung on us, dear people, I'd like to remind everyone to drink a little dandelion, goldenseal, or ginseng tea each morning and before retiring for the night. Not all at once, mind ya, but one at a time. They're good for digestive ailments and to prevent infections in organs such as the one which discharges yer urine—that's a fancy word for pee. In the same vein, and for a glowing look of health, eat garlic at every meal. Smelly bedsheets are a small price ta pay for ample vim and vigor."

Laughter rippled, and Dalton felt Adaline relax beside him. She'd been anxious about this.

"Now, for the expectant mothers out there," Violet lowered her paper and looked around, "and I'm not jist speakin' to Susanna and Hannah here." She smiled at Beth, who blanched white, and then craned her neck until she made eye contact with Jessie, Brenna, and Daisy, who'd arrived with the younger group moments before. "Ginger is the best cure-all for mornin' sickness, as some of ya know, but for severe cases, use wild yam root tea or a tincture of the same in water. Now, iffin ya get ta feeling weepy, as can happen for no apparent reason, place some flowers in a bowl of fresh spring water and set them in the sun for several hours. Monkeyflowers, the little yellow flower ya'll find growing around rocks, is best if ya can find 'em. If not, hunt for the tiny wild carnations growing plentifully in the meadow on the road out to the Broken Horn. After time in the sunlight, add several healthy drops of brandy to preserve the mixture—and then sniff, sniff, sniff. The happy mixture hasn't failed my expectant mothers yet."

Everyone was spellbound.

Violet put down the paper. "I see the questions in yer eyes, good people. I'm usually pretty close-mouthed about my cures and such because doctoring was one of the ways I earned my living. But, truth be told, I won't be around forever. And the doctor only knows so much." She looked around until she spotted Dr. Thorn. "I mean no offense. I've decided I need ta write down as much as I can before the Good Lord calls me home."

Dr. Thorn held out his hand toward her. "No offense taken, Violet. I thank God you were around to deliver the Lings' little one when I was sick. You're a very good doctor, and that's no lie."

She breathed deeply as a serene look passed over her eyes. "Thankee. Now, listen up, everyone, I'm almost finished." She cleared her throat. "I've learned over my many years, kindness works as good as any medicine for curing many ailments. A sweet word here or a gentle touch there can mend a hurting heart or bruised soul. We mustn't forget about the power behind a smile or glitter in the eye. Be the good ya'd like to find yerself. Treat others with respect, gentleness, and love. Such a remedy will cure any ailment on earth."

Not an eye in the group remained dry. Dalton himself swiped away several drops of moisture. Adaline had kept Violet's piece a secret, even from him. If today's reaction to her writing was any indicator, there'd be more articles to come.

Chapter Sixty-Five

Wrapped in a light shawl, with a sleeping Shane Logan snug on her lap, Violet sat in a comfortable chair her son had provided as she watched the dance floor some thirty feet away. Beside her, Sarah Logan slept peacefully on a quilt, probably dreaming of all the fun she'd had dancing around the maypole like a gangly fawn with all her friends.

A contented sigh slipped from Violet's lips as she gazed at the dark sky. Tonight, the stars were the brightest she'd ever seen. She should have added to her health column the effect a tuckered-out little tyke could have on one's soul, for she felt younger than she had in thirty years. Life was good.

Shane shifted in her arms.

As she watched the young couples glide by, two by two, nestled in each other's arms, a pang squeezed her heart. Neither good nor bad, just one of yearning for things long past. Chase and Jessie, Thom and Hannah, Charlie and Nell, Seth and Ivy, Albert and Susanna, Dalton and Adaline, Jake and Daisy, Gabe and Julia, Hunter and Tabitha, Tyler and Courtney, Mr. and Mrs. Harrell, and, of course, Tommy and Beth. They were all so beautiful, the sight stole her breath.

Others were present, too, like Jay Merryweather and Marlene. The dandy turned short-order cook for the Silky Hen, had surprised her almost speechless when he'd ambled over to where she sat with Marlene and asked Jake's mother for a dance. That had been six dances ago, because Violet had been counting. The two looked a little strange, with her being quite a bit older, and a tad taller, but nobody cared. The smiles on their faces said everything. Win was dancing with Lettie and now with some thought to the idea, Violet realized she saw the two together quite often. Tater Joe swished by gracefully with Maude, a woman twice his age, in his arms. May Day made for strange dance partners, for sure.

Mr. Lloyd, dressed in his fine clothes and looking regal, stood at the edge of the dance floor, watching, smiling, and sipping his punch.

She wondered if the drink was spiked. She actually wondered about him alone. Whether he'd ever find someone to love. Fact was, he didn't seem all-fired interested in doing so.

Mrs. Brinkley's oldest grandson was playing the fiddle, and Abner Wesserman, the guitar, which gave Seth and Gabe a richly deserved break so they could have the night off.

Earlier, after everyone had dispersed to their own blankets to eat their supper, the couples she'd suspected to be in the family way had snuck over one by one to confirm her suspicions—and even some she hadn't suspected. Nell and Charlie were to be new parents as well, giving them another child to love along with Maddie! Oh, how good was the Lord! Logan Meadows was having a population explosion right before her old eyes, and Violet planned to be around to hold all the babes, rock all the babes, and sing as many lullabies as she wanted. Besides, she wouldn't dare think about missing Dalton and Adaline's wedding this September.

The song ended, and Tommy and Beth headed her way, hand in hand, and never happier.

"How're you feeling, Violet?" Beth asked. "Tired?"

A pretty blue frock showcased her daughter-in-law's thin, but graceful, frame. When had she gone through such a transformation? The few pounds she'd only recently gained because of the pregnancy were detectible mostly in her face, softening the lines and gentling her features. She was actually beautiful now, since she smiled most all the day. "No, dear girl, I'm enjoying watchin' everyone dance by as they make turtledove eyes at each other." She gave Shane a squeeze. "Especially you and Tommy."

Beth smiled shyly and then glanced up at Tommy, who returned the expression.

"I'd like ta hang on to this night for as long as I can, iffin you don't mind."

Beth gave a soft laugh and rubbed Tommy's arm. "Not at all. If you change your mind, we can easily run you home with the new Red Rooster Inn Taxi."

She and Tommy had painted his wagon red, and installed three seats in the bed. The name was painted on the side in white.

Tommy put his arm around Beth's shoulder and kissed her temple. "We enjoy watching you watching us," he said. "It's a sight I've longed to see for years. God bless you for never giving up on me. I believe your prayers have brought me home."

The contentment on his face would keep Violet happy for the rest of her days—and beyond.

Read on for an excerpt of Montana Dawn!

Book one of the award-winning, ten-book McCutcheon Family series…

Other Books by Caroline Fyffe

Prairie Hearts Series

Where the Wind Blows

Before the Larkspur Blooms

West Winds of Wyoming

Under a Falling Star

Whispers on the Wind

Where Wind Meets Wave

Winter Winds of Wyoming

~~~*~~~

Colorado Hearts Series

Heart of Eden

True Heart's Desire

Heart of Mine

An American Duchess

~~~*~~~

McCutcheon Family Series

Montana Dawn

Texas Twilight

Mail-Order Brides of the West: Evie

Caroline Fyffe

Mail-Order Brides of the West: Heather

Moon Over Montana

Mail-Order Brides of the West: Kathryn

Montana Snowfall

Texas Lonesome

Montana Courage

Montana Promise

~~~*~~~

Stand Alone Western Historical

Sourdough Creek

~~~*~~~

Stand Alone Contemporary Women's Fiction

Three And A Half Minutes

~~~*~~~

All titles in AUDIO!

Take your reading experience to the next level!

Caroline's Books @ Audible.com

Caroline Fyffe Readers Group—We're waiting for YOU!

Don't miss a single title!

Sign up for Caroline's Newsletter

www.carolinefyffe.com

Excerpt of Montana Dawn

Book one of the award-winning, ten-book McCutcheon Family series…

Chapter One

Montana Territory, August 1883

An eerie keening echoed through the trees. Luke McCutcheon straightened in the saddle, and his filly's ears flicked forward, then back. "Easy, girl. Don't dump me now." Not with ten miles to go, he thought as he felt the green-broke filly hesitate. Lightly reining her to the solid side of the slippery embankment, he pressed her forward. Still, she balked at a mud-covered tree stump, snorting and humping her back.

Rain came down in sheets now, drenching them both. Squinting through the darkness, Luke scanned the clearing for any sign of the others he'd split from some three hours before.

A bolt of lightning flashed across the sky, followed by an explosive boom. Chiquita whirled a complete circle and crow-hopped several strides, sending an icy rivulet gushing from the brim of Luke's hat.

"Hell." Luke squeezed with his legs, pushing her onto the bit. "Flighty filly," he said under his breath. "You'd be a great one if you'd ever settle down."

Cresting the rise, Luke searched the horizon through the downpour. Nothing. Nobody in sight. "Long gone." Frustrated, he slapped his gloved hand against his thigh and spun Chiquita in the opposite direction. He'd head back to camp and try again at daybreak.

Suddenly the uncanny cry came again, peculiar in its tone and just as troubling as the first time he'd heard it. "What...?" He'd never heard anything like it in his twenty-six years. He reined up for a moment, listening.

A minute slipped by, and then two. Still nothing but the unrelenting storm. A wounded animal? No. That queer sound was totally unfamiliar. He headed in its direction to investigate.

His efforts proved useless, and after several minutes he stopped. As if called, a streak of lightning lit up the landscape, revealing a dilapidated wagon half-hidden in the brush. It listed to one side, the wheels buried up to the axles. As quick as the light came, it vanished, leaving him in darkness.

He dismounted, cursing the jingle of his spurs. His gloved hand dropped to his sidearm and slid the gun from its holster. Another ghostly cry emanated from the wagon, raising the hair on his neck. Silently, he made his way over the uneven ground. With his back to the wagon's side he reached around with his free hand and cautiously pulled back the canvas cover.

"Hello?"

Only the wind answered, whipping a smattering of rain against his face. Not daring to take his eyes from the dark opening, he steeled himself against the chilly water dripping down his neck. He flexed his shoulders, willed himself to relax. Then a sound, like the rustling of a mouse, caught his attention. He held his breath.

"Coming in," Luke warned. He trusted his instincts, and it didn't feel like someone had a gun pointed at him. Cautious, however, his boot on the wheel axle, he lifted himself slowly through the opening. He paused, letting his eyes adjust to the dark interior.

The aroma of musty canvas engulfed him. And the smell of something else. Fear? Bending low he inched slowly through the cramped interior. He winced: a sharp edge. Fire and ice coursed up his leg. He stopped. Something was in the corner.

With his teeth, he pulled his glove from his hand and reached into his inside pocket for a match. He struck it and held it high. It winked brightly for only a moment and was extinguished by a gust of wind. But not before he saw a woman crouched down, her eyes the size of twin harvest moons.

"You're hurt?"

A soft panting was her reply.

"Your lantern. Where is it?" He felt around the rafters. Finding a lamp, he lit it and turned down the wick until a soft light glowed around the cramped area.

He knelt beside the woman. Beads of sweat trickled off her brow and her breath came fast. Eyes wide with fright were riveted on the gun he held. Then he noticed a stick clenched between her teeth. His gaze flew downward. Her knees were drawn up and a blanket covered the lower half of her body. But there was no mistaking what was underneath.

Luke leaned toward her, intending to take the stick from her mouth when excruciating pain exploded in his head and shot down his neck. "What the…?" He turned. Stars danced before his eyes and he fell to the wagon floor. His gun slid from his grasp.

A groan was all Faith could manage before she was overcome by an all-consuming urge to bite down on the stick with all her might. She wanted, needed, to keep her eyes open and on the stranger, the large man who'd climbed into her wagon, sending her heart skittering up her throat. But it was no use. Another contraction began, and it was next to impossible to keep her eyes open; the icy fire gripped her stomach with a grasp as strong as the devil's.

Mentally counting, she wrestled against her impulse to tighten up as burning beads of sweat dripped into her eyes. Eight… nine… ten. Ten seconds of sheer torture. Then the hurt eased, and Faith lay on her pallet, spent. The stick dropped from her teeth.

Summoning what strength she had, she pushed up on her elbow. "Why'd you hit him, Colton?" she asked the wide-eyed boy, a frying pan dangling in his hands. "I hate to think how mad he'll be when he wakes up." Dread rippled within her as she studied the cowboy lying within an arm's reach.

"Thought he was gonna hurt ya, Ma."

Faith drew in a shaky breath. "Quick, give me the gun."

Colton carefully picked up the revolver. Faith took it, feeling its steely cold weight in her hands.

The man moved slightly and his lashes quivered on his darkly whiskered cheek. His face, hard with angles and chapped from the cold, lay flat against the wagon bed. He moaned as his face screwed up in a grimace, which sent Faith's heart careening. The rest of him looked mighty big under his rain slicker and leather chaps.

Overwhelming despair descended. Just today she'd dared to dream that she and Colton had escaped her brother-in-law Ward, and that he'd given up his hunt for them. Horses couldn't drag her back to Nebraska to marry him and subject her children to the cruelty of that family. Their despicable plot framing her for Samuel's accidental fall was evil. Truth didn't matter, though, when they had the law, or lack of it, on their side. She felt like crying every time she thought about it. The Browns wanted her farm in Kearney and would stop at nothing, it seemed, to get it. So far this journey had been extremely difficult—long days and nights full of danger and fear—and one she wasn't ready to see end futilely.

And now this. In her mind she weighed their chances against the man before her. When her gaze moved back up to his face, her heart stopped.

Chapter Two

The stranger watched her through narrowed eyes. He struggled to a sitting position and stared at the gun she had pointed at his chest. "Give it…to me."

His tone was colder than the weapon she held. Faith shook her head.

He turned and frowned at Colton, whose hair was rumpled, eyes hot and angry. "You're dangerous with that thing," he accused, and reached for the offending object. The small boy reared back, the heavy iron skillet raised high in the air. "Just settle down, kid. I'm one of the good guys."

"Colton, go back to your bed," Faith ordered. The firm grip of a contraction began and would soon move painfully to her back. The boy did as he was told, crawling behind some crates in the opposite corner. "Don't"—Faith panted a few times, the gun wobbling in her hands—"come out till I call."

"Yes, Ma. I just didn't want that sidewinder to hurt ya none."

Even in the darkened interior Faith couldn't miss the stranger's amused expression.

"Sidewinder? The name's Luke. Luke McCutcheon."

"Well, mister, as soon as my ma is finished birthin' my brother, we'll be on our way. Won't we, Ma?"

Faith didn't answer. It was all she could do to hold the gun.

Mr. McCutcheon's face softened, and his gaze touched hers. He reached out and gently took the heavy weapon from her hands. Her fear ebbed slightly. Deep inside she felt this wasn't the kind of man a woman had to fear. Not like Samuel.

He holstered the firearm and stood, a little unsteady. "I'll get help. Someone who's done this before. Our camp cook is always boasting on all his accomplishments. I'm sure delivering a baby is one of 'em. I'll be back as soon as I can."

But, he hesitated. Looked to the wagon opening and back at her, clearly uncertain. Fingered the rim of his hat. "It's best. If you have trouble, Lucky is the man to help."

"Don't go." Even though she didn't know him, his presence was comforting. Something inside her chest—something she hadn't felt in a very long time—ached. She wanted to trust him.

Without warning, hot liquid gushed between her legs. Faith gasped in surprise, cradling her belly for support. Mortified, she pressed some folded towels under the blanket to her body. An unmerciful urge to cry surfaced. She turned her face into the darkness and let the tears fall.

"No, no, don't cry. It's natural. No need to worry." He slowly backed away. "I'm going now. But I'll be back. I promise."

Luke pulled off his hat and let the rain buffet his face. It felt good, cold and clean. He knew weather. He knew rain. He didn't know the mystery of a woman's body in childbirth. Before he could change his mind, he strode over to where Chiquita stood. The filly stuck out her muzzle and nudged him.

"All right. We're going." He looked back at the wagon. Everything was quiet within. Sliding his foot into the stirrup, he swung into the saddle.

He'd faced danger and even death many times. Hell, he'd once killed a cougar with only a knife. He considered himself a brave man. But right now, he was scared to death. Scared by a small woman and a baby.

"Damnation!" He couldn't just ride off and leave her alone. What if it were his little sister out here? He'd sure want someone to help her.

Riding back to the wagon, he dismounted and tied Chiquita to the rear wagon wheel and climbed back inside. "We'll get through this together," he announced. "I've delivered my share of calves. It can't be much different."

Without much trouble he found a cloth and held it out in the rain. He stroked the young woman's forehead and cheeks with the cool cotton rag, wiping away drops of beaded moisture and tears. Her face contorted and her shaky hand snaked from under the cover and rubbed her large belly.

"Please," the woman said. "Can you help me sit up?"

Her plea was a velvety whisper as she watched him closely with distrustful eyes. What was she thinking? Her gaze followed his hand as he reached out to help her. So wary. So *alone*.

Gently, he eased her up, bracing her back against a trunk. "Better?"

She nodded.

Luke went for the canteen on his saddle. Hunching his shoulders against the wind, he inhaled the sweetness of wet earth. It grounded him. He desperately needed that now with the woman in the wagon doing crazy things to his insides. He wanted to help her. To take the pain away. He wanted to be what she needed, though that made no logical sense whatsoever.

Inside, he held the canteen to her dry lips. A blast of wind rocked the wagon, swaying it precariously to one side. She grasped his arm, clinging to him with strength at odds with her size. "Whoa, easy now. Just the wind. This wagon's not going anywhere." Her expression, tight and apologetic, tore at his gut.

Moments ticked by. She rested. What should he do in preparation—boil some water? Not in this storm. He fidgeted with the horsehair clip he kept in his pocket, turning it over in his fingers.

She was watching him again with those big coffee-colored eyes. Her hair, mussed and tangled, lay heavily across her small shoulders, a combination of rich chocolate and flaxen highlights. Mahogany. The exact color of the rocker his ma had in the kitchen at home.

"What's your name?"

"Faith."

"Is someone out there looking for you, Faith? A husband?"

She shook her head and began to pant.

Anxiety burned hot in his belly as he watched her struggle. Taking her hand he fitted it tightly in his. "Go on. Squeeze. It might help."

She did. Luke was astonished again by her strength. Her forehead crinkled and her mouth pursed. Sweat trickled down both temples. Nostrils flared. A series of expressions slid across her face as fast as clouds move in a storm. Then she quieted and her grip eased up, but she didn't let go. Her eyes drifted closed. Minutes crawled by. His thumb stroked softly across her fingers, which were delicate in size, but roughened from hard work....

One hour of torture crept by, then another. Would Roady come looking for him when he didn't make it back to camp? Even if he did, Luke had ridden farther north than he normally would have. He had a slim-to-nothin' chance of getting any help here.

It was dawn, and Luke wondered how she kept on. Her grasp had long since lost its strength. When he'd laid her back onto her pallet she was no stronger than a kitten; he was more or less holding on to her.

She gave a gentle tug. "I think it's coming."

Chapter Three

At her words, Luke took courage. He scooted to her feet, lifting the blanket that covered her body. She was bloody, but if things went right, it wouldn't be too long before this baby was born. He wasn't weary anymore but filled with excitement.

"You're doing fine." He smiled into the expectant mother's exhausted face and brushed some strands of hair off her forehead. "Next time, you should push a little. Think you can?"

With bleary eyes, she nodded and soon began to whimper and pant.

Luke grasped her hand. "Start bearing down slowly at first, slowly, slowly, good girl, good, good, now...*push*." Faith grunted and strained. Her face went from crimson to stark white. "That's it, easy, easy, that's it, good. Keep pushing."

After the contraction eased, she relaxed and her eyes slowly drifted closed. She looked...dead. Luke banished the horrible thought from his mind. Within moments she was up and panting again.

"Already?" Luke checked her again. The baby hadn't proceeded any farther.

"Something's wrong," Faith said. Fear, stark and vivid, glittered in her eyes.

"No, you're doing fine. He's just taking his own sweet time."

She was limp. Like a rag doll. If she didn't deliver this baby soon, she'd surely run out of steam. And blood. It looked as if she'd lost a bucketful. With barely any force, she pushed again. Nothing. Was the baby turned? He'd seen it in livestock.

A shallow contraction. Then another. Faith was growing weaker by the second; her face was whiter than the first snowfall of winter. Now would be a good time to pray. Luke searched his recollection for any of the prayers his ma had insisted he learn as a boy. Frustrated, he realized he'd have to improvise.

Lord, I know you're not used to hearing from me very often, but this girl needs your help, and she needs it now. I don't really know what to do. Any assistance you could send our way would be appreciated. He thought for a moment to see if there was anything he'd left out. *Amen.*

Almost before he could see what was happening, and with no sound at all, Faith gave a weak push and the baby was delivered. Caught off guard, Luke barely had time to catch the infant. Its skin was slick and slippery, its eyes opened wide as if surprised at the new surroundings. Luke grinned up at Faith, unable to hide his excitement.

"A filly," he said. "As pretty as, as…as anything I've ever seen. She's beautiful."

"A girl?" Creases lined Faith's tired brow. She looked at the tiny baby he held in his hands. "I never dreamed…"

The baby began to shiver and cry as Luke tied off the umbilical cord with some twine he'd found in a box, and then, before he could think about what he was about to do, he made a fast cut. He gently handed the baby to her mother.

"Do you have something to wrap her in? Won't take but a moment for her to catch a chill."

Faith glanced around the wagon. "Yes, but it's all packed away. I wasn't expecting this so soon." Her eyes drifted down. "It all came on so quickly."

Without thought, Luke swiftly unbuttoned his shirt and pulled it off. He yanked his thick undershirt over his head and handed it to Faith. "Here. Wrap her in this." He threaded his arms back into his shirt as she swaddled the baby and snuggled her close. The infant whimpered softly and began rooting around, looking for her first meal.

The next contraction delivered the afterbirth, and Luke set it aside in a towel to be buried later. When he was sure he'd done all that he could for the pair, he donned his coat and went out to check on his horse, giving Faith some privacy. Chiquita stood tied to the wagon, tail tucked, head low. She looked his way when he ran his hand along her sodden neck, and then scratched her withers. Her head tipped in pleasure, bringing a smile to his lips.

What should he do now for Faith? He didn't have any supplies with him. After that expenditure of energy, she must be famished. Somehow the boy had slept through the whole thing, but surely he'd be up now that the sun was peeking over the treetops. Luke leaned his weight onto Chiquita and rubbed his hand down his face. This had been the most gut-twisting experience he'd ever been through. Thank God it was over.

The rain had stopped sometime around dawn. Luke rounded up some wood, and after several tries he had a fire burning. First he'd warm some water for her to wash with; then he'd see what she had in the way of food fixin's he could whip up. Right now a cup of strong black coffee would be better than his ma's warm apple pie with a double dollop of sweet ice cream.

"Still here?" The kid who'd hit him with the frying pan climbed from the back of the wagon.

Irritated from lack of sleep and the boy's highfalutin tone, Luke bristled. "Yeah, I'm still here."

"We can manage now."

The cocky little…Luke reined in his temper. A boy barely out of short pants shouldn't be able to get his goat. "Sure you can. Still, I'm going to fix something to eat for your ma and then talk to her. I'll be out of your hair soon."

"Good." The boy trotted around the far side of the wagon, his messy brown hair bouncing up and down as he went. Luke heard him relieving himself against a rock. When he returned, he eyed Luke suspiciously.

"You aren't too trusting, are you?" Luke said.

"Got no reason to be."

"I stayed all night, helped your ma deliver, never gave you any reason to mistrust me. Did I? Not even when you bashed me on the head."

"That don't mean you ain't waiting for the right chance."

Luke slowly shook his head. The boy was serious. He was also protecting his mother, a heavy burden for such small shoulders. "I'm not waiting for the right chance. I won't hurt you or your ma." Colton's intense stare never wavered, so Luke changed the subject. "What do you think of the baby?"

"They were asleep, so I didn't get a good look at him yet. But I can't hardly wait to take him froggin'."

"You mean *her*. Take *her* froggin'."

"Her? You mean he's a girl?" Colton screwed up his face in disgust, and it reddened with annoyance. "Ma said it'd be a boy for sure. No, sir, you must be wrong."

"Sorry, Colton." It was hard to hide his delight at having disappointed the kid. "One thing I'm sure about, that's one itsy-bitsy female in that wagon with your ma."

Colton cursed. He kicked the ground so hard a wet clump of mud flew in Luke's direction. It missed him by inches.

Although surprised that someone so young would use such language and display such anger, Luke hid his astonishment. If he'd talked or acted like that when he was a boy, his skin would have been tanned off his backside right quick. "Your pa let you talk like that?"

"Sure, why not?"

"Because it's not polite. Decent folk don't take kindly to it. I can't believe your ma doesn't care if you sound like a donkey."

"Well, maybe she does, but she can't hear me now."

"I hear you, Colton John," Faith called from within. "If I had any strength, I'd jump up and wash your mouth out with soap. Now, say you're sorry." The baby started crying, and Luke heard Faith trying to comfort her.

The boy glared at Luke, not intimidated at all by his size or age.

Luke grinned anyway. "Say you're sorry."

The boy's face turned bright red. "Sorry," he spat out.

"Apology accepted."

Faith's voice interrupted the scene. "Come in and meet your sister," she called to Colton.

"I don't want to meet no sissy girl." His expression still obstinate, the boy fiddled nervously with a slingshot he'd pulled from his pocket.

It was Luke's turn to glare. He was almost overcome by an all-powerful urge to throttle the mouthy child. Pointing, he silently mouthed the word, "Go."

Colton held his ground.

Stretching to his full height, Luke took one step toward the boy. Colton hurried to the wagon and climbed inside.

About The Author

Caroline Fyffe was born in Waco, Texas, the first of many towns she would call home during her father's career with the US Air Force. A horse aficionado from an early age, she earned a Bachelor of Arts in communications from California State University-Chico before launching what would become a twenty-year career as an equine photographer. She began writing fiction to pass the time during long days in the show arena, channeling her love of horses and the Old West into a series of Western historicals. Her debut novel, *Where the Wind Blows*, won the Romance Writers of America's prestigious Golden Heart Award as well as the Wisconsin RWA's Write Touch Readers' Award. She and her husband have two grown sons and live in the Pacific Northwest.

Want news on releases, giveaways, and bonus reads? Sign up for
Caroline's newsletter at: www.carolinefyffe.com

See her Equine Photography: www.carolinefyffephoto.com

LIKE her FaceBook Author Page:
Facebook.com/CarolineFyffe

Twitter: @carolinefyffe

Write to her at: caroline@carolinefyffe.com